Alone

(Book 8 in the *Chop, Chop* Series)

by

L.N. Cronk

ISBN Number: 978-0-9820027-9-7

Published by Rivulet Publishing
West Jefferson, NC, 28694, U.S.A.

In memory of Daniel Myslivecek . . .
and in honor of his family: Dean, Tammie, Alyssa, Abigail, and David.

If someone is inspired by what you went through, that is something . . .

But if someone spends eternity with Christ because of what you went through . . . that is everything.

To learn more about Daniel, please visit www.Daniels5k.com

*Love the Lord your God with all your heart and with
all your soul and with all your mind.
This is the first and greatest commandment.
Matthew 22:37-38*

~ ~ ~

You don't know about me without you have read a book by the name of The Adventures of Tom Sawyer; *but that ain't no matter. That book was made by Mr. Mark Twain, and he told the truth, mainly.*

Of course that's how Huckleberry Finn starts out. Maybe I should do the same thing here: *You don't know about me without you have read a book by the name of* Chop, Chop; *but that ain't no matter. That book was made by Mr. David Holland, and he told the truth, mainly.*

The point is that you really shouldn't even be reading this unless you've already heard David's side of things, and my little brother's, too, for that matter, because I'm not going to spend a lot of time on stuff that you've already heard – like about how we found out that my middle brother Chase had Huntington's disease and how we figure he got it from my dad, which is probably why my dad killed himself.

But just because I'm not going to spend a lot of time on things like that doesn't mean that they're not important to me.
They are.
It's just that I'm not here to tell you about the things you already know . . .

I'm here to fill in the blanks.

1

~ ~ ~

IT WAS THE summer before our junior year in high school and I was lying on my stomach in a lounge chair by the pool.

"Hi, Tanner."

I sat up on my elbows and stared up at Laci. She looked at me forlornly.

"What's the matter, Lace?" I asked, grinning at her. "Did your best friends go away and leave you all alone?"

She stuck her bottom lip out and nodded at me pitifully.

There were seven of us who hung out together, but only Laci and I were in Cavendish right now. Mike was at Governor's School and Natalie and Ashlyn were at a retreat with their church, which Laci hadn't gone to because she'd just started her new job at the mall and couldn't miss work. David and Greg, with whom Laci was particularly thick as thieves, were both in Florida, visiting Greg's grandmother. For seven days, it was just going to be me and Laci, alone.

"Me too," I said, patting the chair next to me. "Come on ... have a seat. We'll talk about how good looking our kids are gonna be one day."

"This must be like a dream come true for you, Tanner," she smiled, sitting down, "having me all to yourself for a *whole week*!"

"Yes," I agreed. "I have very big plans for you."

"I'll bet," she laughed, as her phone rang. She glanced at it before answering. "Sorry. It's Greg."

Of course.

"Hey ... yeah ... sitting at the pool with Tanner ... Uh-huh ... Nothing. He's just trying to seduce me again."

She smiled at me and winked.

"Don't worry," she assured Greg. "I'm staying strong."

They talked a while longer and then she hung up and turned to me. "Apparently David thinks the ocean is very *cool*."

I rolled my eyes and shook my head.

2

"So what are we gonna do all week?" she asked. "What are your 'big plans' for me?"

"You think I'm kidding, don't you?" I asked.

She grinned at me.

"I'm serious, Lace," I told her. "By the end of the week you're going to be completely in love with me. You'll see."

She laughed at me and I smiled back at her . . .

Both of us knew I was only kidding.

My girlfriend, Alden, worked at the movie theater near the mall and she had Wednesday and Friday off, but – other than that – Laci and I figured that we'd be able to do something together pretty much every day of the week. By the time we left the pool, we had decided that we'd go to the movies that evening. Alden didn't get off until after ten anyway, and since she usually worked the ticket booth, she'd be able to give us an employee discount.

I picked Laci up early enough so that we could go out to dinner first.

"Where to?" I asked her after we'd started driving down the road away from her house.

"You're the one with *big plans*," she said. "You tell me."

"Ah, but part of my big plan is to take you wherever you want to go . . . so what'll it be?"

"Anywhere but *Hunter's*," she sighed. "I am so sick of that place."

"Well then why don't you tell David that you're going somewhere else and if he doesn't like it then he can eat at *Hunter's* all by himself?"

"Because then he mopes."

"David?" I asked sarcastically. "No."

"Hard to imagine, isn't it?"

"How about *Casa Delgado*?" I suggested.

Laci was planning on spending her life down in Mexico, helping people. I figured a trip to a Mexican restaurant would be right up her alley.

"That sounds great!" she smiled.

We pulled into the parking lot ten minutes later and I cut the engine, hopped out, and started walking toward the restaurant. After a moment, I realized that Laci wasn't with me. I looked back. She was still sitting in the truck.

I walked back and opened my door.

"Is there a problem?" I asked.

"You're supposed to come around and open my door for me."

"You're kidding."

"No," she said, shaking her head.

"You really expect me to walk *all the way* around the truck and open the door for you?"

"A *gentleman* would."

"Isn't that sexist?" I asked her.

"Do I come across to you as a feminist?"

I rolled my eyes at her.

"*David* opens the door for me," she said, starting to tick names off on her fingers, "*Greg* opens the door for me—"

"David and Greg are wusses," I pointed out.

"Your chances of my falling in love with you this week will be greatly improved if you open the door for me."

"Oh! Well, then," I said. "I'll be right there."

She grinned at me as I closed my door again and trotted around the front of the truck.

"Here you go, madam," I said, opening the door and ushering her out with an exaggerated sweep of my arm.

"Take my hand," she insisted, holding it out to me like a queen.

"You're really pushing it, missy," I said, taking her hand and helping her down. She laughed.

"Please tell me that you get the door for your girlfriends," she said as we walked toward the restaurant.

"Of course I do."

"You don't, do you?" she asked.

"Nope."

"I've really got my work cut out for me," she said, shaking her head.

"I'm well worth the effort," I assured her.

Laci was scheduled to work at three the next afternoon, so we decided that we'd go fishing early in the morning, have a quick picnic brunch, and then get back to town in time for her to get showered up before going to work. Alden had the whole evening off completely, so that was going to work out well.

We hadn't been out on the lake very long at all the next morning, when Laci announced that she had to go to the bathroom.

"Whatdya telling me for?" I asked.

She raised an eyebrow at me.

"Just hang it right over the edge there," I said, pointing to the front of the boat with the tip of my rod. "I won't look."

She put her hands on her hips.

"You should have gone before we left," I told her.

"To the *shore*, Tanner," she demanded, pointing to a nearby island with one hand, her other hand still on her hip.

I shook my head and gave her an exaggerated sigh.

"You're a lot of work, you know that?" I asked, reeling in my line.

"I'm well worth the effort," she smiled and I started the motor.

I pulled the boat into a sandy cove and Laci jumped out with the tow rope in her hand, pulling us up onto the shore.

"You want me to put that new plug on?" I asked as she looped the rope onto a large piece of driftwood.

"Sure," she said. "Thanks. I'll be right back."

"You've got two minutes," I said. "After that you're swimming home."

She smirked at me and turned, disappearing into the woods.

After she was gone I rifled through my tackle box and found the lure I'd been telling her about. I tied it to Laci's line and, after I'd finished, I cast it along the shore near the entrance of the cove. I was reeling it in when I thought I heard a noise.

I stopped reeling and listened. I didn't hear anything else, but something made me set her rod down and hop out onto the shore.

I walked to the edge of the woods, keeping my eyes down on the sandy ground. I kept listening, but I still didn't hear anything else.

"Lace?" I called out.

Nothing. I took a couple of steps into the trees.

"Laci?" I called again, louder this time.

"Tanner!" She sounded . . . *scared.*

"Are you okay?" I shouted, stepping toward her voice.

I heard her call my name again and I bolted into the woods.

I didn't have to go far before I found her, sprawled on the ground. She raised a shaky hand and pointed, just as a sound made me turn my head in the same direction.

I saw a man pushing through the underbrush toward the shore. Instinctively I took off, following after him, but by the time I'd made it through the briars, he'd reached the shore and was running down the beach. He glanced back, saw me, and sprinted away even faster. I stopped running when he reached a small boat, jumped in and pushed off from the shore. He quickly started the motor and sped away, so I turned around and retraced my steps.

I headed back inland to find Laci struggling with the zipper on her shorts.

"*What happened?*"

"Nothing," she insisted in a quavering voice, shaking her head. She tried to do up the button on her pants, but her hands were trembling too badly.

"What did he do to you?" I asked, very alarmed.

"Nothing," she said again.

"Then why are your pants undone?"

"I was going to the *bathroom*," she reminded me, still fighting with the button.

I felt myself calm down a bit.

"Here," I said, stepping toward her. "Let me help you."

"I can get it," she insisted, but the shaking of her hands seemed to be getting worse, not better. Finally she gave up and looked at me helplessly. "Maybe I can't."

I took another step forward, held the waist of her shorts together, and pushed the button through the buttonhole.

"Are you okay?" I asked, putting my hand on her arm and looking into her eyes.

She nodded.

"What happened?" I asked again.

"Can we get out of here first?"

"Sure," I said, putting my arm around her shoulder. "Come on."

We walked to the shore and sat down on the driftwood that she'd tied the boat to. She glanced nervously behind us, still trembling.

"He's gone," I assured her, rubbing her back. "Now *what happened?*"

"He just . . . he just came out of nowhere and started coming at me and I fell and I hurt my hand and I was trying to get away from him and then I heard you call me and then *he* heard you call me and then he took off."

6

"He never touched you?"

"No," she said.

"Let me see your hand."

She held it out to me, palm up. A piece of wood, about the diameter of a pencil, was sticking out of her hand, blood dripping from the wound.

"Oh, man, Laci. We need to get you to a doctor."

"No, no, no," she said. "Just pull it out for me."

"NO!" I said. "Haven't you ever had a first aid class? You're never supposed to remove an impaled object . . ."

"It's not plugging a major artery or anything," she assured me. "Just pull it out."

She pressed the thumb of her other hand near the wound and thrust both hands toward me, turning her head away.

"I don't think this is a good idea . . ."

"Pull it out."

"Okay," I said, looking at it hesitantly, "but just for the record, I want you to remember that I thought this was a bad idea."

"Would you just *get it out of there*, please?" she asked, looking back at me.

"Well, let me go get some tweezers or something out of my tackle box . . ."

"Oh my *gosh!*" she said. "And you think David and Greg are wusses! Either one of them would have just pulled it out by now!"

"That's because they don't care about you as much as I do," I said, standing up and grabbing my tackle box from the boat. I lifted boat seats until I found a first aid kit. She shook her head in disbelief.

"Just be glad you're not with Mike," I said. "He'd be sterilizing an operating table by now and wanting to put in sutures and everything."

Laci managed a laugh. I reached into my tackle box and pulled out a pair of forceps that I used for getting hooks out of fish.

"Those look *real* sanitary," Laci said, eying some dried fish blood.

I wiped them off on my shirt.

"Oh, that's much better," she said dryly.

"Look," I said. "*I'm* the one that wants you to go to the doctor . . ."

"Pull," she ordered, pressing her thumb behind the stick again and turning her head away once more.

I gently grabbed the wood with the forceps and pulled it out slowly. She didn't flinch.

"It's out," I told her, "but there's dirt and crap down in there."

"Do you think it went very deep?" she asked, looking.

"Maybe a quarter of an inch or so," I said. She nodded, walked over to the water's edge, and plunged her hand into the water to swish it around.

"Oh, that's *real* sanitary," I said, mimicking her earlier remark. I opened the first aid kit and found a wad of gauze and a packet of triple antibiotic ointment. "Come here."

She walked back, sat down next to me, and held out her wet hand. I wiped it dry with the edge of my shirt and then squirted some antibiotic down into the wound. I wadded up some clean gauze and laid it on top of it.

"Hold this here," I said. She put her good hand over the gauze while I rifled through the first aid kit again.

"There's no tape," I finally said, looking up at her.

"Can't you just wrap some more of that gauze all the way around my hand and tie it?"

"I don't think it'll stay very good," I said. "Hang on."

I went back to the boat and started lifting seats again.

"You've gotta be kidding," she said when I returned.

"Duct tape fixes everything!"

She sighed and let me wrap her hand up.

"I think that actually looks pretty good," I told her when I was finished. "Mike would be proud. How's it feel?"

"Good," she said, but her voice was unsteady.

"You okay?"

She nodded, but I noticed tears welling up in her eyes.

"What's wrong then?" I asked, putting my arm around her shoulder again.

She hesitated for a moment, but finally spoke.

"Why did I act like that?" she asked, her voice breaking this time.

"Like what?"

"Like this!" she cried, holding her good hand out in front of her and exaggerating the way it had been shaking earlier. "I had absolutely no control of myself! I couldn't even do up my pants!"

"You were scared," I said, squeezing her shoulder. "It was just a visceral response."

"Visceral?" she asked. "What's that?"

"Visceral's like . . ." I thought for a moment, "it's like something you don't have any control over. It's like basic instincts that catch you off guard and override everything else."

"But I can't act like that, Tanner," she said, pulling away a bit to look at me. "I'm going to spend my life working around all sorts of people who might scare me. I can't turn into a helpless puddle of mush every time something scares me a little bit."

"This is completely different than what it's going to be like in Mexico."

"You don't know what it's like," she protested. "There were all sorts of scary things down there!"

"Did you turn into a puddle of mush?"

"Well, no," she admitted.

"Because it didn't catch you off guard . . . you were prepared for it," I pointed out. "And you'll be prepared when you're working there, too."

She looked at me with uncertainty.

"Even *more* prepared," I went on, "because you'll have been to college by then and you'll have been trained how to handle all sorts of different situations. You'll be totally ready for it."

She bit her lip and seemed to be trying to process what I was saying. She nodded slowly and I could tell that she felt better.

"You'll be fine," I promised, squeezing her shoulder again.

She wrapped her arms around me and squeezed back, holding me for a long moment and pressing her face against my neck. I could feel her breath, warm against my neck, and I could smell the scent of her hair. *Vanilla.* I was surprised to notice how soft her skin felt.

"Thank you, Tanner," she finally said, pulling slightly away from me.

"You're welcome."

She gave me a kiss on the cheek and a final squeeze. "I feel a lot better."

"Good," I nodded.

She pulled away completely and I immediately missed the feel of her body against mine.

My cheek burned where her lips had been . . .

That night, Alden and I went out to eat Italian. After our meal arrived, I found myself slowly twirling my fork, watching my fettuccini noodles as they moved along the plate.

9

"Tanner?"

"Hmmm?" I asked, looking up from my Alfredo.

"I said, 'Is there something wrong with your food?'"

"Oh. No," I answered, shaking my head. "It's fine."

I took a bite to prove to her just how fine it was.

"You don't seem to be eating very much of it," she observed.

"I was just thinking about something," I admitted.

"What?"

Laci.

I don't know why, but I'd been thinking about her all day. I hadn't been able to *stop* thinking about her ever since she'd wrapped her arms around me . . . breathed against my neck . . . smelled like vanilla . . . kissed my cheek . . .

It was common for Laci to give me a hug or a kiss on the cheek – all of the girls were touchy-feely toward us guys like that. But what I was feeling now wasn't common at all . . .

I had tried to stop thinking about her (just like I'd tried to stop sneaking glances at her while we'd continued fishing and while I'd driven her home). I hadn't been able to though . . . not since I'd felt the warmth where her lips had kissed me and missed the feel of her soft skin against mine. When I'd finally realized that I wasn't going to be able to stop thinking about her, I had tried instead to figure out *why* I was thinking about her.

But I was just as unsuccessful at that . . . because the feelings I was having for Laci, made absolutely no sense.

Laci was – had *always* been – like a sister to me. We'd known each other ever since we were little kids because we lived on the same block – her backyard was diagonal to mine. Our dads were good friends, too, and the two of them went hunting and fishing together a lot.

I was the oldest of three boys and – until Chase and Jordan got old enough – I was the only one who got to go with my dad whenever he went somewhere. Laci (an only child who'd never had a problem playing the tomboy), accompanied her dad on hunting and fishing trips just as often as I accompanied mine.

I couldn't count the number of nights the two of us had spent together, curled up in our sleeping bags on her dad's houseboat on the

Mississippi, or in a tent at some hunting camp, listening to our dads drinking beer and talking long into the night. We'd fallen asleep against each other on long truck rides home and sat beside each other late into many evenings, watching campfires as they slowly died away.

Our birthdays were only two days apart (hers on June first, and mine on June third), and on more than one occasion, our moms had pooled their resources together to throw us a combined birthday party on the second. I remembered one in particular with a bouncy house and another with a lame pony that refused to walk whenever anyone was on its back, (but who had chewed the laces off one of Mike's sneakers and made him cry).

My last name was Clemmons, and Laci's last name was Cline. There had only been one time – when Jonathan Cleveland had moved to town and stayed for about three months – that the two of us hadn't sat next to each other in homeroom.

Like I said, Laci had always been like a sister to me.

So, how was it that now – after all these years – I suddenly couldn't stop thinking about Laci in a very *un*sisterly way? Or, maybe the question should have been, how had I never had these feelings for her before now?

I didn't have an answer to either one of these questions – all I knew was that I couldn't stop thinking about her. I'd tried to, but I couldn't. It was something that totally caught me off guard and something that I didn't have any control over.

It was . . . *visceral.*

"What?" I heard Alden ask again.

"Huh?"

"*What* are you thinking about?"

"Oh," I said. "Mike. I was just wondering if he's having a good time at Governor's School."

"I'm sure he is," she smiled, and I nodded.

~ ~ ~

I MADE IT through dinner, but told Alden I was too tired for anything else after that. I drove her home, kissed her goodnight, and then went home and stretched out on my bed, hoping that while I was sleeping, all the crazy thoughts I was having about Laci would go away.

They didn't.

Alden had the entire day off the next day, so I had to spend it with her. I was – in a word – miserable. Everything she did annoyed me, or at the very least, reminded me that she wasn't Laci. We were supposed to go out to eat together again that night, but I told her I had a headache and I took her home early.

The next morning, I rang her doorbell at eight-thirty, knowing that her parents had already gone to work. Alden was scheduled to go in to work to open the theater at ten, and she answered the door with one towel around her body and another on her head.

"Hi," she smiled.

"Can we talk?" I asked, not smiling back.

She looked a bit startled, but held the door open for me and I stepped into the foyer.

"I think we should break up," I said as soon as she'd closed the door.

Alden and I had been dating for over three months ... sleeping together for two. It wasn't like there was going to be an easy way to do this.

"What?" she cried, definitely startled now. "*Why?*"

"I just don't think this is working anymore."

"Not working anymore," she repeated after me slowly, tightening her grip on her towel.

I stared at her, wondering what to expect. Was she going to cry and beg me not to leave her? Would she get mad and cuss me out, throwing things at me as I ducked out the door? The fact that I really had no idea what to expect probably tells you something about our relationship.

I continued to stare at her, waiting for her reaction.

"I'm sorry," I said when she didn't say anything.

"Sorry," she nodded. "Well that does me a lot of good, doesn't it?"

"It's not you," I added. "I don't want you to think you did anything wrong . . ."

"Oh, I *know* I didn't do anything wrong," she said, raising an eyebrow at me.

"I'm sorry," I said again quietly.

"Whatever, Tanner," she said, sounding thoroughly disgusted with me. She pulled the front door back open. "Get out. I've gotta get ready for work."

I stepped out onto the front porch and she closed the door without so much as a *'Let's still be friends'*.

I closed my eyes and took a deep breath.

I let it out slowly and opened my eyes. Then I headed to my truck, pulling out my phone as I went.

One really weird thing about Laci was that she didn't like to text. I mean, what teenage girl doesn't like to text?

Don't get me wrong, she had a cell phone and everything and would *read* texts if you sent her one, but then she'd *call* you back and talk to you. After a while, everyone just kind of gave up and called her when they wanted something, since they knew they were going to wind up talking to her anyway.

"Hey," she answered her phone.

"You aren't working tonight, are you?" I asked.

"Nope," she replied. "I've got the whole day off!"

"Wanna go out to Dante's after we're done fishing?"

"I thought Alden got off work at five."

"We broke up."

"Oh," was all she said. Me breaking up with someone wasn't exactly earthshattering news.

"So do you wanna go?" I asked.

"Sure," she said. "But Dante's is pretty nice. Don't you think we should bring some stuff to change into?"

"Definitely," I said. "We can clean up at the bathhouse before we go."

"Okay," she agreed. "Sounds great. Still picking me up in an hour?"

"Definitely," I said again.

"See you then."

By the time we got out onto the lake, it was after eleven and both of us were hungry.

"This is *so* good," Laci enthused, taking another bite of fried chicken. "Did your mom make this?"

"Do you even *know* my mom?" I asked.

She laughed.

"How'd you learn to do this then?"

"Same way I learned to make everything else I cook," I shrugged. "Internet. If it wasn't for the Internet, my brothers and I would've starved to death by now."

"Your mom's not *that* bad," she said, but when I raised my eyebrow at her, she laughed again and said, "Okay, maybe she is."

Laci had brought the potato salad and biscuits and we continued to eat along for a few minutes. When we were finished, I pulled out a container of chocolate chip cookies.

"These are awesome," Laci said, after she had taken a bite. "The only thing that would have made them better is if you hadn't baked them . . . that, and a big glass of milk."

"Next time I'll be sure to bring the salmonella," I promised, and she laughed one more time.

We fished all afternoon, and I was happier than I'd ever been in my entire life. It was the first of many times in my life that I would realize, that even if there was nothing more than a friendship between the two of us, nothing was better than spending time with Laci.

Of course I desperately wanted for there to be more between us than just a friendship, and by the time we cleaned up at the bathhouse and changed into nicer clothes, I was searching for a way to make that happen.

Dante's was an upscale restaurant that was on the southern end of the lake. You could access it by car or boat, but we drove so that we wouldn't have to mess with the boat while we were wearing our nice clothes. I had called to make reservations that morning, but found out that they didn't accept any less than twenty-four hours ahead of time, so when we arrived, we put our names on the waiting list, and walked around outside to wait.

Ambiance was one of the big things Dante's had going for it. In addition to dining tables outside, there were lots of places to sit and look out over the lake as well. Hedges lined a path through an Italian garden and we admired the grotto and fountains that we found as we walked down toward the dock. About five minutes after we'd reached the lake, our pager went off to let us know that our table was ready. We made our way back along the path.

For the most part, the girls I'd always been interested in up until now had always been interested in me as well and, for whatever reason, I'd always pretty much been able to get whatever girl I'd wanted – and been able to get whatever I'd wanted out of her.

But I was at an absolute loss as to what to do with Laci right now. I had no idea what I was supposed to do to move our relationship forward.

How exactly was I supposed to let her know what I was feeling? I wasn't even sure if *I* knew what I was feeling.

All I knew was that there was an odd mix of trepidation and exhilaration inside of me, creating a nervous excitement that made my heart feel as if it was going to explode at any moment.

I managed to make zero progress over dinner, until Laci jokingly quoted a line from the movie we'd seen a few nights earlier.

"That was a terrible movie," she noted after I'd laughed.

"Yeah," I agreed. "It really was."

"At least we got in cheap," she smiled with a shrug.

I smiled back.

"How come you two broke up, anyway?" Laci wanted to know.

I looked at her carefully before answering.

"Because I didn't care about her the way I should have," I finally said.

She laughed. "I didn't know that you cared about anybody you dated."

I looked at her earnestly for a moment.

"Am I really that bad?" I asked. I knew she hadn't meant anything by it, but what she said hit too close to home. She started to say something with a smile on her face, but the seriousness on my face must have stopped her.

"Of course not," she said apologetically. "I was only kidding."

"I care about *you*," I told her.

A look flashed across Laci's face and I knew that she wondered – if only for a second – exactly what I was saying. But then, just as quickly, I could see her talk herself out of thinking there was anything to it.

It's Tanner, *silly. He doesn't mean anything by it . . .*

But of course I meant *everything* by it. I cared about Laci in every way possible and I would have done anything for her. I just didn't have a clue how to let her know . . .

"I care about you, too," she said reassuringly. And then she smiled at me, and patted my hand in the most platonic of ways.

The next morning, Laci had to work, but she got off at four, so we decided to spend one last evening together on Cross Lake. We packed another picnic, this one for dinner, and once I had beached the boat on a small island, we set the basket and cooler down on the blanket that was spread on the sand. We ate in relative quiet. I don't know what Laci was thinking, but my mind was worried about the fact that this was my last night alone with Laci before all of our friends returned to Cavendish. If something was going to happen, it needed to happen tonight.

Now.

"Do you want to go for a walk?" I heard myself asking her.

"Sure," she agreed. We stood up and started down the beach.

After we had walked for several hundred yards, I heard the whine of a distant boat engine and instinctively hitched myself closer to Laci, grabbing her arm. I watched around the shore of the island until the boat came into sight, loosening my grip on her once it did.

She looked at me questioningly.

"Sorry," I said, shaking my head.

"What?"

"That boat," I hesitated, nodding toward it. "It sounded like the one that guy was driving the other day."

16

"Oh."

"And I just . . ." I let my voice trail off, unsure as to what to say. I let go of her arm.

"You just wanted to protect me?" she suggested with a gleam in her eye.

"Yeah," I nodded.

"You're very sweet," she said, giving me an appreciative smile.

I held her gaze, hoping that she would look at my face and be able to tell exactly how I was feeling about her.

She looked at my face, but I knew I was going to have to do something more than hope. She wasn't a mind reader.

"I meant what I said last night," I told her.

"About what?"

"That I care about you."

She looked at me intently for a long moment, and then laid her hand along the side of my face.

"I know you do," she replied with a smile. "I care about you, too."

It was a tender, sweet gesture, but it was easily just as platonic as the pats on my hand had been the night before.

I brought my hand up to hers, covering it, pressing it firmly against my cheek.

I held her gaze for another moment. Then I closed my eyes, savoring the warmth of her hand against my skin for as long as I dared.

When I finally opened my eyes again, I knew, without a doubt, that I had just taken us past platonic. Laci's smile was gone and her eyes wide.

"How is your hand, anyway?" I asked. I held it away from me and surveyed her healing gash.

"Good," she responded quietly.

"Good," I replied. I looked at her for another moment, and then asked, "Are you ready to go back?"

She nodded . . .

And I kept hold of her hand as we headed back to the blanket.

Laci and Natalie and Ashlyn might have all been touch-feely girls, but they didn't walk around holding hands with us guys. This was an activity strictly reserved for girlfriends and boyfriends.

Laci and I didn't say one word to each other as we walked along.

"I brought dessert," I finally told her as we reached the blanket.

She managed a nervous smile and I dropped her hand as we sat down.

I pulled a metal bowl with a plastic lid out of the basket and presented it to her. As she opened the lid, her eyes widened again, and she was able to give me a real smile.

"Salmonella?" she asked.

"I found a recipe with no eggs," I told her, and she smiled even more. I handed her a spoon and we both dug out a scoop of the dough.

"This is awesome," she said after a minute.

"Wait," I said, holding up a finger. "It gets even better."

I reached into the basket again and pulled out a towel. I unrolled it carefully, revealing two champagne glasses.

Her eyes widened for a third time.

"Tanner Clemmons . . . you'd better not have alcohol in there!"

I grinned at her and pulled out a carton of milk. She smiled back at me with a relieved look on her face as I filled the glasses and handed one of them to her.

"Should we make a toast?" I asked, holding up my glass.

"To what?"

I looked at her long enough to make her nervous again.

"To us?"

She hesitated, but only for a second, and then gave me a slow nod.

"To us," she agreed softly, clinking her glass against mine.

We ate the cookie dough quietly, finished off our milk, and then I took her empty champagne glass from her, setting it on the blanket. I looked back at her carefully.

"I really do care about you," I told her.

"I know," she said quietly. "I care about you, too."

"You're one of my best friends," I said, taking her hand again.

She nodded.

I leaned in closer, but I didn't kiss her. I raised my other hand and traced my finger along her throat, under her chin.

I felt her swallow nervously.

I looked into her eyes for a long time before I did anything else, giving her every chance in the world to let me know that this wasn't what she wanted.

She didn't let me know.

"Are you scared?" I finally asked quietly.

She nodded again.

"Don't be scared," I whispered. "I'd never do anything to hurt you."

18

"I know," she whispered back, nodding one more time.

I brought my finger up to her mouth, running it gently along her lower lip and then along her top one. At long last, I leaned even closer, and she closed her eyes.

When our lips met, it was so gentle that I could barely feel her mouth against mine. I brought my hand to the nape of her neck, pulling her closer to me and kissing her less gently, feeling her lips part beneath mine. It was a million times better than anything I could have imagined, and I drank in the feel of her soft skin against mine. When I finally pulled away, I squeezed her hand, looking at her expectantly.

She squeezed my hand back and slowly opened her eyes, staring at me with her lips still slightly parted. The look on her face didn't tell me anything about how she was feeling.

"Say something," I finally begged.

"I don't know what to say," she said quietly.

"How about, 'That was the best kiss of my entire life?'" I suggested.

"That was the *only* kiss of my entire life," she admitted softly.

I stared at her in utter amazement for a moment, then tightened my grasp on her neck, pulling her toward me for an even deeper, longer kiss. When I pulled away this time, she opened her eyes and I looked at her expectantly again.

She smiled at me.

"That was the best kiss of my entire life," she said.

As daylight faded, I lay down on the blanket and drew Laci to me, putting my arm around her. She nestled against me, resting her head on my chest. We didn't speak for a few minutes, and I marveled at the perfectness of having her so near.

"I can hear your heartbeat," she said, breaking the silence. She raised her head and looked at me. "I've never heard anybody's heartbeat before."

I felt myself smile as I tightened my arm around her and she lowered her head to my chest again.

"Everybody's coming back tomorrow," I said quietly after a moment.

"I know."

"Are you sure you have to work?" I asked.

She nodded against me and I sighed.

"What time?"

"Ten."

I sighed again.

She lifted her head once more.

"We could have breakfast together," she suggested.

"You want to go to Wilma's?"

"After you spoiled me with Dante's last night?"

"I know it's a dive," I said, "but they've got the best breakfast in town."

"I do love their waffles," she admitted.

"I can pick you up at eight."

~ ~ ~

I kissed her two more times . . . once when I held the truck door open for her in the parking lot of the marina, and again when I let her out back at her house. Each kiss was somehow better than the last, and as my lips lingered on hers as we said goodnight, I wondered how I was ever going to be able to go to sleep that night . . . how I was ever going to wait until eight o'clock the next morning.

At seven forty-five, however, Laci called me.

"Good morning," I answered my phone.

"I'm sorry," she said hurriedly.

"For what?"

"For . . . last night," she said. "It was a mistake."

"What?"

"It was a mistake," she said again. "It never should have happened."

"What are you talking about? Why was it a mistake?"

"We're just *friends*, Tanner," she explained. "You're on the rebound from Alden . . . both of us just got carried away."

"I'm not on the rebound from Alden–" I started to protest, but she cut me off.

"I just want to be friends," she said. "I shouldn't have let anything happen between us."

I didn't say anything.

"I'm sorry, Tanner," she said again, sounding on the verge of tears.

I took a deep breath. I had absolutely no idea what was going on, and I certainly didn't like it, but I knew enough to realize that if I pushed her, I was going to drive her away completely. That was not an option.

"It's okay," I said, "don't worry about it."

"It was a mistake. I . . . I just let myself get carried away."

"It's not a problem," I assured her. "It's fine."

"You're okay?"

"Of course I am," I said. "I'm great."

I heard her let out a slight sigh of relief.

"Are we still on for eight?" I asked.

"You still want to go?" She sounded surprised.

"We're still friends, aren't we?"

"Of course we are," she said quickly.

"Then I still wanna go."

"Okay," she agreed readily. "I'll see you in a few minutes."

"Right," I said. "See you then."

Ten minutes later, Laci opened the door after I'd knocked, and let me in.

"I'm just gonna run to the bathroom," she said, self-consciously avoiding my eyes. She set her phone and keys on the table in the foyer. "I'll be ready to go in a minute."

I nodded at her as she stepped into the half bath off the main hallway and closed the door behind her. She'd been in the bathroom for no more than ten seconds when her phone went off.

"Greg's calling," I yelled to her through the closed door.

"Tell him I'll call him in a minute," she yelled back.

"Hey," I answered her phone.

There was a very, *long* pause.

"Tanner?" he finally asked.

"Yep."

"Hi. How's it going?"

"Great."

"Good . . . good."

"How's Florida?" I asked

"Fine," he said. "Is, uhhhh, is Laci there?"

"She's in the bathroom," I said. "She says she'll call you back in a minute."

"Oh, okay," he said. "Well . . . thanks."

"Sure," I said. "No problem."

"Bye."

"Bye."

I closed her phone and stared at it for a moment.

Was it my imagination or was he *not* real happy that I had just answered Laci's phone?

I glanced at the closed bathroom door and then back at her phone. I thought about it for a moment, and finally opened her phone again, pulling up her recent calls.

Since I'd dropped Laci off last night, she had talked with Greg *five* different times. As soon as I'd dropped her off, she'd called him and they'd talked for thirty minutes. Then – not too long after that – he'd called her and they'd talked for almost an hour. They'd exchanged one more call last night for about twenty minutes and then another one this morning for five before she'd called me. Then she'd called him again – right after she'd talked to me and told me that yesterday had been a "mistake".

I heard water running in the bathroom and I quickly cleared the screen.

"Here," I said, handing the phone to her when she came out.

"Thanks," she said, still avoiding my eyes.

She called Greg back as we walked to my truck and climbed in. She talked to him briefly as we started on our way, but then told him she had to go, and hung up.

"They went out to eat last night at some Greek restaurant," she told me.

"Oh," I nodded. "That sounds good."

"Uh-huh," she said, nodding back.

We rode along in relative silence until finally Laci turned in her seat and looked at me.

"Tanner?"

I glanced at her.

"What?"

"I feel really bad," she said quietly.

"Don't," I insisted, shaking my head. "I already told you . . . it's fine."

"You're one of my *best* friends," she went on. "I don't want that to get messed up."

"It's not gonna get messed up," I promised.

"Things aren't going to be weird between us?"

"Come on, Lace," I said, glancing at her again and giving her my best smile. "Us? Weird?"

She smiled back at me and we drove on to Wilma's.

I had no idea exactly how weird things were going to be between us for the next forty years.

~ ~ ~

WHAT'S THAT OLD saying? Keep your friends close, and your enemies closer?

Greg may not have exactly been my enemy, but I was convinced that he was the only reason that Laci and I weren't together. So when I got a call from him a few weeks later, inviting me to go on a camping trip with the guys from their youth group, I agreed to go, even though I usually avoided church-related stuff like that.

"Great!" he said. "We're going do a lot of team building stuff and focus on self-esteem and healthy relationships, you know?"

"Uh-huh."

"Waiting until you're married," he went on. "Stuff like that."

Oh brother.

"Uh-huh," I said again.

"We're leaving from the church parking lot at eight, Saturday morning."

"Okay," I said. "I'll see you there."

There were a lot of reasons for me to *not* go on this campout – the first one being that it was already about two years too late for me to participate in a celibacy discussion. Another problem was that Greg, David, Mike, Laci, Natalie and Ashlyn all went to the same church . . . I was the only one who didn't go there. Although the six of them were my best friends and were fun to hang around with, deep down I think I always worried that it was only a matter of time before one of them wanted to put their hands on top of my head and pray for my soul, or ask me to hold a snake for them or something.

But if everybody was going to spend the weekend discussing "healthy relationships", there was a chance that I might be able to figure out exactly what was going on between Greg and Laci.

I was willing to put up with a lot if I could just figure that out.

It wound up being a pretty fun weekend. A very non-judgmental, non-people-touching-me and praying-over-me, non-snake-holding weekend. During the day we participated in a bunch of challenges and stuff and the conversations about sex (or lack thereof) took place in the evening, around the campfire.

Greg's dad, Mr. White, was the youth group leader, and he talked to us about how everything boiled down to respect: respect for women . . . respect for ourselves . . . respect for God.

I watched Mr. White as we talked around the campfire, thinking how different he was from my dad. When I'd started dating, my dad had given me a pack of condoms, saying, "Here. Don't make the same mistake I did," as he'd handed them to me.

"Gee, Dad," I'd said, taking them from him. "Nothing quite like being called a 'mistake.' Thanks."

He'd looked at me almost apologetically.

"That's not what I meant and you know it," he'd said.

Whatever.

I looked at Mr. White now and then I looked at Greg, his face illuminated by the glowing campfire. Greg was watching his dad as he talked, his face filled with something . . .

I tried to put my finger on what it was.

Admiration?

Reverence?

Whatever it was, I couldn't relate.

26

~ ~ ~

THAT CAMPING TRIP didn't really give me any insight into what, if anything, was going on between Greg and Laci. By the time school started back in the fall, I still didn't have a clue. Neither one of them acted as if they were anything more than great friends, but of course that's exactly how I acted toward her, too, and we all know how accurate *that* was.

After our last class of the first week, Mike and I were at our lockers, stuffing our book bags full for the weekend and getting ready to head to the gym. One of the varsity cheerleaders, Burtie, leaned up against the closed locker next to mine and gave me big smile.

"Hey, Burtie," I nodded at her, while Mike busied himself discreetly in his locker.

As far as dating went, Burtie was the female equivalent of . . . well, of *me*. Interestingly enough though, we had never gone out with each other – somehow we'd just never both been available at the same time. Apparently, however, that wasn't the case now.

"You got plans for after the game?" she asked.

"Uhhhhh–"

"Because," she went on, suggestively, "I was thinking . . ."

"What?"

She stood up on her tiptoes, pulled my head down toward hers and whispered exactly what she was thinking.

"As inviting as that sounds," I smiled, "I'm gonna have to pass."

"Are you sure?" she tempted.

"I'm sure," I nodded. "But I appreciate the thought."

"I figured you would," she smiled, raising an eyebrow at me.

"I'm sorry," I added.

"Your loss," she shrugged. "Maybe next time."

"Yeah," I agreed. "Maybe next time."

"What was that all about?" Mike asked after she'd left, closing his locker.

27

"She just wanted to get together later tonight," I replied nonchalantly.

"And what are you doing instead?"

"Nothing."

"So, you turned her down because . . ."

"She's not my type."

"Not your type," he repeated slowly.

"Yeah," I nodded.

"Since when are hot babes, 'Not your type'?"

"I dunno," I said, shrugging my shoulders. "I'm just not interested."

He looked at me for a moment and then put his hand on my forehead. "You don't feel feverish," he said.

"Oh, shut up," I said, knocking his hand away. "Not everything's about sex, you know."

"Oh, *I* know that," he nodded, closing his locker. "I just wasn't aware that *you* had any clue."

It was only a week later that Mike and I were eating lunch in the cafeteria like we always did. Laci, Greg and David surprised us by walking up to our table.

"What are you guys doing here?" Mike asked.

"We get to go to the middle school and talk to them about FCA," Greg told him, "so we have to eat early."

"Just like old times!" Laci smiled. They set their backpacks down and got in line.

I watched after them, absentmindedly twirling my fork in my fingers. After they'd disappeared into the serving area, I finally brought my attention back to my lunch. I was surprised to find Mike staring at me with his mouth open.

"What's your problem?" I asked him.

"You like Laci," he said slowly, clearly astonished.

"What?" I asked, alarmed. "I do not. That's stupid."

"No, it's not," he said, shaking his head. "This explains *everything* – why you haven't been going out with anyone . . . why you turned Burtie down the other day . . .

"Man, oh, man," he went on, looking down at his plate, still shaking his head in disbelief. "Unbelievable!"

28

"Shut-up, Mike," I said quickly. "You don't know what you're talking about."

"Uh-huh."

"You don't," I insisted. "I was just . . . I was just trying to figure out what's going on between her and Greg, that's all."

"Nothing's going on between her and Greg," he said matter-of-factly.

"How do you know?" I asked, taking a swig of milk and trying to act as if I couldn't care less.

"Because she likes David."

"David!?" I sputtered, choking on my milk.

Mike nodded.

"What makes you think that?" I asked, reaching for a napkin.

"Greg told me."

I looked back to where the three of them had disappeared and suddenly, I got it.

She didn't like Greg – he was her *confidant*. He hadn't talked her out of dating me because *he* wanted to go out with her. He'd done it because he knew that she liked David and he wanted *them* to be together . . .

I became aware once again that Mike was watching me.

"I don't like Laci," I reiterated, looking back at him. Even to my own ears it sounded entirely unconvincing.

"That's good," Mike said, "because it would never work between the two of you."

"What's that supposed to mean?"

"You know what Laci's like," he explained, shrugging. "She's not the right type for you."

"No," I said defensively, "what you mean is that I'm not the right type for her."

"Look," he said, "I didn't mean anything by it."

"People can change," I told him angrily

"Laci's not going to change."

"I'm not talking about *Laci* changing," I said, forgetting that I was supposed to be busy denying I was interested in her.

He looked at me for a moment.

"Forget I said anything," he said, holding his hands up in surrender and then looking back down at his tray. "I'm staying out of it."

"Yeah, that's a great idea," I nodded. "Why don't you do that?"

~ ~ ~

DAVID?

SHE LIKED *David*?

Until Greg had come along, David had been my absolute, best friend. We'd known each other ever since preschool, had been friends for just about as long, and we pretty much did everything together. Scouts, fishing, basketball, video games, baseball, laser tag, soccer, paint ball, snowmobiling, swimming, cards, hunting, biking, board games, canoeing . . .

What hadn't the two of us done together?

And it wasn't just that we did things together and had fun, it was that he was . . . he was a true friend. He had always been one of the few people in my life that I could count on . . . one of the few people that I could trust.

It had been David who had helped me when I'd decided to ice down our driveway for some extra good sledding one winter, making it impossible for my parents to get their cars into the garage after work. It had been David who had helped me "borrow" the next door neighbors' dog when I'd tried to turn an old wagon into my own special version of a horse drawn cart. It had been David who had helped me convince Chase that Mom and Dad really didn't need to find out that we had almost strangled him when we'd tried to lower him from the roof with a homemade winch.

In the sixth grade, I had decided that I wanted to compete in a triathlon. When David found out what I was doing, he had done everything that he could to help me. He looked up training schedules online and custom designed one that he thought I should follow. He spent hours counting laps for me at the pool and sticking his fingers under the water at the end of the lane to let me know how many more I had to go. He rode his bike alongside me while I'd jogged, supplying me with Gatorade from his backpack as I went. Whenever I got to the end of my bike loop, he was always there waiting for me, stopping the timer on his watch so that he

30

could record my progress in a notebook that he had bought just for my training.

Nerdy? Yes. But still, something that only a true friend would do. He had helped me like that – almost every day – for *six months*.

Three days before the competition, David and I had been sitting next to each other in social studies. We were working on our computers, learning about Andrew Jackson's Indian Removal Act, and David was complaining because one of the sites he wanted to go to was blocked.

"You're such a moron," I told him. "Don't you know how to get around the filter?"

He looked at me uncertainly and so I pulled up a *highly* inappropriate site . . . just to prove to him it could be done.

"Get that off of there, you idiot!" he cried when he saw the screen. He glanced up at the teacher in horror and smacked me on the arm. "You're gonna get in trouble and then you're not gonna get to compete this weekend. Is that what you want?"

"I'm not gonna get in trouble," I said, waving my hand at him casually.

"The tech lady can see what we're looking at all the time," he warned.

"You really think someone's sitting around, monitoring everything we look at?"

"No," he said, "but they probably monitor what *you* look at . . ."

Good point.

I switched sites.

Apparently not fast enough though, because within ten minutes, one of the assistant principals, Mrs. Donovan, opened the door to our room, took one look at me, and crooked her finger. I sighed inwardly, got up, and headed into the hall with her.

The two of us started walking toward the office, my mind busily trying to come up with a good story, when the classroom door quickly opened again. Both of us turned around and I was surprised to see David.

"Mrs. Donovan?" he asked.

"What?" she asked, appearing none too happy.

"Is this about . . ." he glanced at me and then back at her. "Is this about the computer in there?"

He pointed back toward the classroom.

She crossed her arms, obviously annoyed, raised an eyebrow, and asked, "What do *you* know about it?"

"It was me," David said hastily. "I told him I could get around the filters and he didn't believe me so I pulled it up just to show him that I could."

"On his computer?" she asked skeptically.

"Well I didn't want it on *my* history," he explained.

Mrs. Donovan turned her raised eyebrow to me. I stared at David, dumbfounded.

"Is that true?" she asked.

"I, ummm ..." I looked at her and hesitated, and – when I did – I heard something.

Beep.

David had started his stopwatch.

I glanced at him again. He was looking at me resolutely.

Don't do it. Don't ruin everything you've worked so hard for. I've never gotten in trouble for anything and they'll go a whole lot easier on me than they will on you ...

He managed to say all that to me with one little sound.

Beep.

I looked back at him for a long moment and then turned my eyes to Mrs. Donovan again.

"Yeah," I finally nodded. "It's true."

She looked at me doubtfully for a second, but then finally sent me back into the classroom. Before I stepped out of the hallway, I looked over my shoulder and watched as she marched off toward the office with David in tow ...

He didn't look back.

David got grounded and was upset that he missed seeing me win the triathlon for the fifteen and under age division, but (except for one little, "I *told* you you were going to get in trouble!" when I tried to apologize) he never said another word about it.

Like I said ... a true friend.

Of course not long after that Greg had moved in and replaced me faster than you can say, "Tanner, who?", but still.

And this was who Laci was hung up on?

I honestly wasn't sure what to do with that information.

~ ~ ~

IN REALITY, THERE wasn't a whole lot that I *could* do with that information . . . at least not until the Homecoming Dance.

It was the last slow dance of the evening, and Natalie and I had just started dancing together. Not too long into the song, she lifted her head from my shoulder and looked at me with one eyebrow raised.

"Well, well, well," she said, unable to keep a little smile off her face.

"What?"

"Take a look over there," she said, nodding her head to my right.

I turned, looked, and saw David, slow dancing with Samantha Massaro.

Samantha was the dark-haired beauty that David had been staring at, all goofy-eyed, for over four years now. He turned completely stupid every time she got within a hundred yards of him and his infatuation with her was obvious to everyone, except for maybe Samantha herself.

"Uh-huh," I responded.

"Oh," Natalie said, her smile growing bigger. "Don't act like you don't care."

"Why should I care?"

"I think a door of opportunity may be opening up," she said dramatically. "If David and Sam hook up, maybe that'll help Laci get over David and *then* . . ."

She shrugged.

"And how does this affect me?" I asked.

"She told me all about how you kissed her this summer," Natalie said with a glint in her eye. "And I see the way you look at her whenever you think no one's watching."

"She *told* you?"

Natalie nodded.

"What'd she say?" I asked, sounding a whole lot more desperate than I meant to.

"Nothing much," she said, shrugging again. "She thinks you're sweet."

"She does?"

"Yeah," Natalie nodded. "But she likes David."

I let out a sigh, despite myself.

"But now," Natalie went on, nodding toward David and Samantha once again, "if David gets out of the picture . . ."

I allowed myself another glance in their direction.

"You're all hung up on Laci," she said, shaking her head in mock dismay. "Laci's all hung up on David. David's all hung up on Sam . . ."

She looked at me knowingly and clucked her tongue.

"Unrequited love," she said, "sure is running rampant in our school."

I had to admit that Natalie had a point . . . a point that I took the opportunity to act upon later that evening, when I went to the locker room after the dance.

I'd seen Samantha and some of the other cheerleaders disappearing into the girls' locker room just ahead of me and I lingered in the hall after I'd quickly grabbed my stuff. I was pretending to be enthralled by a flyer about an upcoming blood drive when Samantha and a couple of her friends came out of the locker room. I fell into step with them as they passed.

"How's it going, Sam?" I asked as soon as I could without it seeming too forced.

"Good," she smiled. "How are you doing?"

"Great," I nodded.

She smiled again.

"Have a good time at the dance?" I asked, purposefully slowing down a bit so that her friends got comfortably ahead of us.

"Yeah," she grinned. "It was great."

"So," I said, "you and David, huh?"

"What?"

"Oh, nothing," I said, nonchalantly. "I just saw you and David dancing together, and . . . you know . . ."

"Oh," she said, shaking her head. "No."

"Why not?" I asked. "What's wrong with David?"

"I never said anything was wrong with him. It's just that there's nothing going on."

"So," I ventured, "if he were to ask you out or something, you'd probably go?"

"I don't know. I never really thought about it before."

"Maybe you should think about it," I said, matter-of-factly.

She stopped and stared at me.

"Are you saying he's going to ask me out?"

"Oh, no," I answered casually. "I don't think so. He's pretty shy."

"He asked me to dance . . ."

"Probably took him weeks to work up to it," I answered.

"Seriously?"

"Oh, yeah," I nodded. "He's super shy."

"Oh."

"So," I ventured, "if you're interested, you know, you should probably do something to let him know."

"I don't know if I am or not," she said hesitantly. "I hardly even know him."

"You should do something to get to know him better," I suggested. "Invite him to go do something with you and a bunch of your friends or something."

"I don't know," she mused, less hesitant now. "I guess he does seem kind of sweet."

"Oh, yeah," I nodded again. "He's definitely sweet."

The next week, Samantha asked David to go to the movies with her and some of her friends. By January, the two of them were dating.

I would have patted myself on the back for so efficiently getting David out of the picture, but Laci was far too miserable for me to enjoy my handiwork. Several times I caught her sorrowfully watching the two of them as they walked down the hall, hand in hand, and part of me actually wished I could undo it all.

I honestly wanted her happy.

One day in the early spring, I watched Laci as she watched David and Samantha. They were standing about ten yards away, in front of Sam's locker, talking animatedly with one another.

Laci looked about as depressed as I felt.

"Hey, Lace," I said, walking up to her.

"Oh," she said, startled. She turned away from the happy couple to look at me and then gave me a halfhearted smile. "Hi, Tanner."

"You doin' okay?" I asked.

"Sure," she nodded unconvincingly.

I studied her face for a moment.

"Laci?" I finally asked.

"What?"

"Why don't you go to the prom with me?"

She looked at me, surprised.

"You and me?" she asked.

I nodded.

"Seriously?" she asked.

"Of course, seriously."

"As friends?"

"I'll take whatever I can get," I said, giving her what I hoped was a kidding smile and holding my hands up in a helpless manner.

"It would have to be just as friends," she said earnestly. "I ... I like somebody else."

"Let me guess," I said, studying her for another moment. "David?"

She looked surprised again, and then asked miserably, "Is it that obvious?"

"No," I assured her, putting a hand on her shoulder, "only to the people who love you as deeply as I do."

I gave her another "I'm just joking," smile. because if she had any idea how serious I was, she'd probably never even talk to me in homeroom again, much less go with me to prom.

She gave me a little smile back.

"Come on," I encouraged. "Maybe seeing you out with somebody else will shake some sense into him."

"He's going with Samantha," she said unhappily. "I don't think he's going to be paying much attention to anything that I'm doing."

"He's an idiot," I told her.

She gave me another small smile.

"Go with me," I encouraged again.

"Are you sure there's not somebody else you want to take?"

36

"I'm positive," I said honestly. "There's no one else on earth I'd rather take than you."

I couldn't believe my eyes when I saw Laci on prom night. She was wearing a dress that could have been a wedding dress if it had been longer and didn't have a blue sash tied around the waist. It was a creamy, shimmery white, with white, lace flowers. It somehow managed to be elegant and simple and modest and sexy, all at the same time, and if I hadn't already been in love with her, this would have totally done the trick.

Of course I didn't delude myself into thinking that she'd gotten all gussied up just for me. I was fully aware that she was hoping to open up David's eyes, not mine. I was, after all, the one who had given her the idea in the first place. Still, I was not unpleased when I saw how beautiful she looked.

"Holy crap, you look good," I said, once she was standing before me.

"Tanner," she chided. "Don't say that!"

"I can't say 'Holy crap' now either?"

She thought about it for a moment . . . honestly *thought* about it.

"You can say 'crap'," she finally decided. "Just not 'holy'."

"Why not?"

"You know," she explained, shrugging her shoulders uncertainly. "Holy is . . ."

She hesitated, obviously unsure how to word what she wanted to say.

"Well, it's *holy*," she finally said.

I looked at her for a moment in mild disbelief. Somehow, "Crap, you look good," didn't quite have the same ring to it.

"You look *fantastic*," I told her honestly, and I leaned forward, taking her hand and giving her a kiss on the cheek.

"Are you sure you want to do this?" she asked apprehensively.

I just rolled my eyes at her.

I had picked her up early enough that we could have dinner at Dante's and still get back to Cavendish in plenty of time for the prom. She grew increasingly uneasy over dinner, and I knew she was worked up about seeing David and Sam. By the time we had driven back to Cavendish, she was a nervous mess.

After I parked and we went inside, we found a spot to sit near Mike and his date. We visited with the two of them, danced for a while, and then checked out the hors d'oeuvres and punch fountain. Then a slow song came on, and I led Laci out onto the dance floor again. She wrapped her arms around my neck and laid her head against my shoulder. I closed my eyes, enjoying every bit of having her so close.

Suddenly I felt Laci's entire body tense. I opened my eyes and saw David and Samantha dancing near us. David was looking at me, and at Laci.

I nodded at him over the top of Laci's head and he nodded back. Then he went back to dancing with Samantha.

Idiot.

"Hey, Lace?" I asked, pulling back to look at her.

"What?" She lifted her head from my shoulder and looked at me.

"You wanna get outta here?"

"I'm sorry," she said unhappily. "I'm being a terrible date."

"No, you're not," I laughed. "You're a great actress. I can almost believe that you want to be here."

"I'm not acting. I'm having a great time," she said, unconvincingly. "I'm really glad we came together. Thank you for bringing me."

"You wanna get outta here?" I offered again.

"No," she said, shaking her head. "I don't want to go home yet."

"I didn't say anything about going *home*," I said, raising my eyebrows suggestively.

"And where exactly would we be going?" she asked, smiling in spite of herself.

"Somewhere that I promise will take your mind off things."

"Lack of self-confidence has never been one of your weaknesses, has it?" she asked.

"Nope."

"Are you sure you wanna leave?"

"Oh, yeah," I nodded. "I've been ready to go ever since we got here."

She looked at me to see if I was serious, and then she nodded.

"Okay," she agreed. "Let's go."

"So where are we going?" she asked after we'd pulled out of the parking lot.

"It's a secret."

"Well, when am I gonna find out?"

"I reckon when we get there – unless you figure it out first."

"So if I guess it right you'll tell me?"

I nodded.

"Well you have to give me some clues!" she insisted.

"I ain't giving you nothin'."

"How long is it gonna take to get there?" she asked.

"I dunno," I shrugged.

"Oh, come on!" she pleaded. "How am I going to figure it out if you don't give me any hints?"

"I'll answer 'yes' or 'no' questions," I conceded.

"Okay," she nodded. "Is it more than ten minutes away?"

"Oh, yeah."

"More than an hour?"

"Yeah."

"More than two hours?"

I nodded. She stared at me.

"More than three hours?"

I shrugged.

"It's three hours away?" she cried, looking at the clock on the dash. "I won't be home until two in the morning!"

"Oh," I said, shaking my head. "You're not going to be home until after lunch tomorrow."

"Yeah, right," she scoffed. "Like my parents are going to let me stay out until then!"

I reached behind her seat and pulled out a canvas bag. I put it in her lap.

"This is mine!" she exclaimed, staring at it. "Where'd you get this?"

"Your mom packed it," I said. I glanced at her. She was looking at me with her mouth wide open. I turned back to the road and I heard her unzip the bag. Out of the corner of my eye, I could see her sifting through the contents.

"You're serious?" she finally asked after she'd examined the clothes that her mom had packed for her.

I just grinned at her.

"What could you *possibly* have told them that would've convinced them to let me stay out with you until tomorrow?"

I shrugged again.

She looked at the clothing once more – old jeans, an old t-shirt, old tennis shoes, a lightweight jacket.

"Three hours away," she muttered. She sat there for a minute, rubbing her thumb over the side of one of her shoes. All of a sudden she clapped her hand to her mouth and let out a muffled scream. She took her hand away from her mouth.

"The smelt are running!" she cried, and I gave her a big smile.

Smelt are small fish that live in the Great Lakes, and every spring they swim up the tributaries to spawn. At night – with headlamps and waders – you can wade up the streams with dip nets and scoop up loads of them. One weekend each spring, when we'd been little, our dads would take us to Carlton's Campground, which was situated along a wide river that fed Lake Michigan. Most of the people who stayed in the campground were there for the smelt dipping. We dipped for fish for a few hours before and after midnight, and then spent the next couple of hours cleaning, frying and eating them. Usually we'd topped it all off with some s'mores and then fall asleep inside our sleeping bags just as the sun was coming up – filthy, smelly, exhausted and happy.

"Are you SERIOUS?" she cried. "We're really going smelt dipping?!"

I nodded, still smiling. She actually undid her seatbelt and slid across the seat to give me a big hug and a kiss on the cheek.

"Thank you, Tanner," she said, still hugging me. "I love you."

Somehow I managed to keep the truck on the road.

"Are we going to Carlton's?" Laci asked after a moment. When I nodded she said, "So you brought two tents?"

"No," I smiled, raising an eyebrow at her. "Only one."

"My dad may trust you," she conceded, "but there's no way he trusts you *that* much!"

"No," I admitted. "You can either sleep in the back of the truck or you can have the tent – whichever you want. I'll take the other."

"Did you get my waders?"

"No," I said again. "Your waders were dry-rotted. I think you'll fit in Chase's though, so I brought those."

"Did you bring the fryer and everything?"

"Nope," I said, shaking my head. "We're just gonna have to make some fast friends when we get there."

We didn't have any trouble doing that. Some of the regulars from years earlier were still coming back to Carlton's and we recognized them immediately. Of course we had changed too much for them to recognize us, but once we reminded them who we were, there were vast exclamations of how unbelievable it was that we were all grown up and a lot of wondering about how our fathers were.

We were immediately swept up in the fun of the night, and by the time it was over we sat, exhausted, at a neighboring site's campfire.

Laci yawned, which made me yawn. I looked at my watch.

"What time is it?" she asked sleepily.

"Almost four."

"No wonder I'm so tired," she said.

"Come on," I suggested. "Let's go set the tent up."

"I'm too tired," she protested. "Let's just both sleep in the back of the truck."

"Yeah," I laughed. "Like I wanna deal with your dad tomorrow after he finds out about that."

"I won't tell if you won't," she said sleepily, and I realized that she was serious.

Twenty minutes later we were stretched out next to each other in our sleeping bags.

"Goodnight, Tanner," Laci said once I'd turned off the flashlight.

"'Night, Laci," I said. I lay in the darkness, listening to the sound of her breathing, inches away from me, and remembering every detail of our evening together.

I thought that she had fallen asleep, but after a moment she suddenly spoke.

"Tanner?"

"Hmm?"

She propped herself up on one elbow and looked at me in the faint light coming in from the surrounding campsites.

"You're wonderful," she said.

"Yeah," I said with a little laugh. "I'm wonderful."

"I mean it," she said. "I had an awesome time tonight. No one else could have ever made me have a good time tonight like you did."

With that, she leaned over and kissed me again on the same cheek she'd kissed earlier. I was going to have to bronze that cheek.

"There's nothing I wouldn't do for you," I told her carefully.

"I know," she said quietly. "Thank you."

And then she lay down, and went to sleep.

~ ~ ~

MY SUGGESTION TO Laci that she should go out with me because it might "shake some sense" into David, turned out to be a lot more farsighted than I ever could have imagined. Shortly after prom, David and Samantha broke up. Then, after a couple of months of cringe-worthy patheticness out of David, he and Laci finally started going out together.

It was when this happened that I realized exactly how much I loved Laci. Not just because of how envious I grew every time I saw her and David together, but because of how glad I was at the same time that she was no longer miserable.

That I wanted her to be happy – even if it meant that she was with someone else – proved to me that what I had said to her on prom night was the absolute truth: I really would do anything for her.

I watched after her daily with a twisted combination of contentment and longing, and I reminded myself often that the two of them were probably going to break up.

I mean, seriously, how many high school relationships actually last?

And who better than me, to help Laci pick up the pieces?

~ ~ ~

DAVID AND LACI did indeed break up, but what broke them up changed everything in our world as we knew it.

It was one of those things that I wish I could forget, but I never will.

It was early December, and Mike and I had just finished our weight-lifting class and were headed to the locker room. Outside, it had been spitting a mixture of rain and sleet and flakes for almost five hours – ever since we'd arrived at school that morning.

Coach James walked up to us with a Santa hat perched on the top of his head.

"We're on lockdown," he said.

"Oh, brother," I muttered.

"You know the drill," he said. "Get along that wall over there and have a seat."

"Can't I go ahead and get in the shower?" Mike asked. "I *promise* I'll be safe in there."

"Nope," Coach James said, pointing at the wall again. "Sit."

Mike and I rolled our eyes at each other and trudged over toward the wall, having enough foresight to grab our phones out of our lockers before sitting down.

We talked nonchalantly for a while (despite constant chastisements from the coach to be quiet), but, before too long, it became evident that something was going on.

Really going on.

Natalie was the first one to call me.

"Someone was shooting," she said.

"Where?" I asked doubtfully.

"Second floor."

"It was probably somebody setting off firecrackers or something," I said.

"Ashlyn and I both heard it," she insisted. "It was a gun."

My call waiting beeped and I told her I'd call her back later. I answered the other call. It was David.

"Where are you?" he asked.

"In the locker room."

"Ashlyn said she heard gunshots."

"Yeah. I know," I said.

"Do you know where anybody else is?"

"Mike's here with me," I said, "and I just talked with Nat. Where's Laci?"

"She's fine," he answered, and I breathed a sigh of relief. "She's in Mrs. Heath's room. Do you know where Greg is?"

"Wasn't he with you at lunch?"

"He left early," David said, his voice tight. "He had to go give his dad something."

That gave me pause. His dad's room was on the second floor – where Natalie and Ashlyn were so sure they'd heard gunshots . . .

David hung up and Mike and I sat for a long time before we were finally allowed to leave the school. The gym was one of the first areas cleared, but it was already dark by the time they let us out. Mike and I both called our moms before we even got to the parking lot, where it was spitting a harder version of the rain and sleet and flakes mixture we'd seen in the morning. Mike's mom, it turned out, was waiting in the parking lot with my parents, and we found them quickly, both of us being rushed to and hugged tightly as soon as they spotted us.

Jordan and Chase were there too.

"Are you okay?" Mom asked me frantically.

"I'm fine," I assured her.

"I'm hungry," Jordan complained.

"Shut up," Chase snapped at him.

"And I'm cold," Jordan added.

"Shut UP, Jordan!" Chase commanded.

"Let's go," Dad said to all of us. "Let's get out of here."

"No!" I said, instantly. "I can't leave yet."

Mom looked at me hesitatingly.

"Go ahead," I urged her. "Take them home. I'll be okay."

"I'll stay with him, Susan," Mike's mom promised, and I think that's the only reason my mom finally agreed. She and my dad hugged me tight one more time, and then they left with Jordan and Chase.

It wasn't too long after that that Natalie found us. She was sobbing . . . absolutely hysterical.

We got out of her what had happened and then her mom pulled her away, leaving me and Mike to stare at one another in disbelief. A few minutes later, someone came along and wrapped blankets around our shoulders because we were shivering. I guess they figured it was because we were wearing thin tank tops in the freezing rain, but I don't think that was the reason.

Then Laci found us.

"Oh!" she cried. "Tanner! Mike! I've been looking all over for you!"

She flung her arms around Mike and then me, squeezing hard.

"I'm so glad to see you! Have you seen Natalie or Greg?" she asked as she pulled away from me. "I haven't been able to get in touch with either one of them."

"Laci . . ." Mike said, his voice breaking. From the look on her face I think that was when she first noticed that we'd both been crying.

"What?" she asked, gripping my blanket. She looked at me.

"Natalie went home with her mom," I managed to say.

"You talked to her?" Laci asked.

I nodded.

"Oh," Laci sighed, nodding back. "Good."

"Laci . . ." Mike said again, reaching for her.

"What?"

"It's Greg . . ."

She stared at him for a long moment.

"What?" she finally asked again, this time in an unnatural, high-pitched voice.

Mike shook his head.

"What?!" she cried, looking back at me and pulling on my blanket. "What about Greg?"

I couldn't answer her.

"What? What about Greg?!"

Mike put his hands on her shoulders and turned her toward him again. She let go of my blanket and grabbed hold of Mike's instead.

"Greg's okay," she said, pleadingly to Mike. "Tell me that Greg's okay."

"I'm sorry, Laci," he said, shaking his head once more.

"What do you mean, 'You're sorry'?" she cried. "What's wrong with Greg? What happened?"

"He was shot," Mike said, his voice breaking again as he looked into her eyes. "He didn't make it."

She stared at him for a moment.

"No," she whispered, shaking her head. "No, that's not right."

"Laci," Mike said. "I'm sorry—"

"NO!" she yelled, shaking her head again. "Greg's fine! Do you hear me? Greg is FINE!"

"He was shot," Mike repeated gently. "He got killed."

"NO!" she screamed again. "No, he didn't! What are you talking about?"

She turned to me.

"Tanner . . ."

"I'm sorry," I said, choking on the words.

"Tanner," she begged desperately. "Please tell me he's okay."

"Laci," I said, shaking my head.

I reached for her, but she slipped away from me, sinking to the wet ground onto her knees. A scream escaped from her, the most primal, agonizing, heart-wrenching sound I'd ever heard. Mike dropped down next to her, wrapping his arms around her, and I knelt down on the other side of her, stroking her hair.

Mike told her gently that Mr. White had been killed too, and somehow Laci managed to cry even harder. She reached toward Mike blindly, grabbing the front of his shirt.

"Oh my God," she gasped, wrapping the thin cloth of his shirt around her hand. "Oh, my God!"

She looked up at Mike in disbelief.

"What are we going to do?" she whimpered. "What are we going to do!?"

He didn't answer her. She had one hand on the ground, supporting herself, and the other hand firmly gripping Mike's shirt. It was completely ruined by this point, almost ripped from his body.

"Oh, my God! Oh, my God! Oh, my God . . ." she repeated.

That is what I will always remember about that night. It was the absolute worst part of it all – hearing her say those words, over and over and over. Laci hated it whenever someone took the Lord's name in vain and I never did it in front of her because it bothered her so much.

And now, she wouldn't stop.

"Oh, my God . . . oh, my God . . . oh, my God . . ."

Nothing has ever disturbed me as much as that, and all I wanted was for her to stop.

"Oh, my God . . . oh, my God . . . oh, my God . . ."

But finally I realized that she wasn't taking His name in vain . . . she was calling out to Him.

Mike reached out to her, gently stroking her wet hair. He rested his forehead against hers.

"Mike," she finally cried softly, pulling even harder on his shirt. She lifted her face, looked at him, and whispered again, "What are we going to do?"

He started speaking softly into her ear. I couldn't hear what he was saying to her, but it quieted her down for a moment – until she suddenly turned away, and started vomiting.

I pulled her long hair back to keep it out of the way while she threw up.

"I'm sorry," she sobbed. "I'm sorry."

"It's okay, Laci," Mike assured her, rubbing her back as I continued to hold her hair, but I don't know if she heard him or not because she started retching again.

After a long time – when there was nothing left in her stomach – she finally stopped. She let go of Mike's shirt and sat back quietly on her knees, staring at her own vomit.

Mike took his shirt off and began trying to clean her up with it. She closed her eyes, drawing in ragged breaths, and allowed him to wipe her face as the sleet continued to pelt down on us.

Suddenly she grabbed Mike's hand, stopping him. She opened her eyes and looked at him.

"Where's David?" she asked.

"David's fine," he assured her.

"Where's David?" she said again, louder. She looked at me.

"I promise, David's fine," I said.

"Where's David? I want to see David! Where's David?"

She was starting to get hysterical again. Mike looked over the top of her head at me.

"I'll get him," I promised her, reaching for my phone.

"I want to see David . . . I want to see David . . ." she whimpered over and over as I heard his voice tell me that he couldn't take my call right now and that I should leave a message.

"Call me as soon as you get this," I told him, closing the phone.

"Where is he?" she cried. "I need to see David!"

I called his mom's number and she answered right away.

"Tanner . . ." she said.

"I need to know where David is," I told her.

"We're taking Charlotte and Mrs. White to our house," she explained. "We're almost there."

"Okay," I said, closing my phone.

"He's fine," I promised Laci. "He's on his way to his house."

"I need to go there right now," she said in a surprisingly calm voice. "I have to go see David, *right now.*"

"Okay," I said. "We'll take you."

I looked at Mike.

"Do you want to drive or do you want me to?" I asked as we helped Laci to her feet. I don't know why, but I felt a tremendous sense of urgency for the three of us to stay together.

He looked back at me and opened his mouth to speak, but his mother answered before he could.

"I'll drive you," she said.

I looked at her and nodded. Until then, I had completely forgotten that she was even there.

There were already a lot of people at David's house. When we went inside, Laci left me and Mike immediately and rushed to David's side. He put his arms around her and held her impassively, and then – after a few moments – he drifted away. Prayer broke out and I drifted away too, looking for David.

I opened the door to his bedroom and found him laying quietly on his bed, staring straight up at the ceiling in the dark.

"You okay?" I asked.

"Yeah," he nodded. "I'm just tired. I'm going to sleep for a little bit."

Sleep? I honestly didn't know if I was ever going to be able to sleep again in my entire life.

I studied him for a moment, but then nodded back and closed the door quietly, returning to the living room.

The praying was still going on and I hung back in the doorway, listening. They were praying for a peace that would surpass their understanding and they were praying that above all else, the name of Jesus Christ would be glorified because of what they were going through.

I stood there, watching in amazement . . .

And I wondered how God could do something like this to all these people who loved Him so much.

~ ~ ~

MY MOM TOLD me that Mrs. White wanted me to say something at Greg's funeral.

"You mean like a eulogy?" I asked and she nodded. "Why me?"

"You were his friend," she replied.

"Yeah, but . . . but why doesn't she ask David or something?"

"I think she is," Mom replied. "I think she's asking David and Mike, too."

"So I wouldn't be the only one?" I clarified.

"I don't think so," she said, shaking her head.

"Okay," I nodded. "Tell her I'll do it."

The first thing I did was look up "How to Give a Eulogy," (seriously – I typed it into the search engine and got all sorts of stuff). I read everything I could, and then I called David. He didn't answer his phone, so I called Mike.

"Are you giving a eulogy?" I asked him.

"Yeah."

"I'm supposed to give one too," I said. "I don't know what I'm supposed to say."

"Just talk about him," Mike said. "That's what I'm gonna do."

"Like . . . like say what a nice guy he was and everything?"

"Well, no," Mike said, "more like tell some stories about him and stuff."

"Stories?"

"Yeah, you know – tell about some time when you guys had a good time together or a time when he helped you out, or something like that."

"Really? That's what you're gonna do?"

"Yeah," Mike said. "When my dad died all sorts of people told me and my mom all sorts of stuff, but the things I remember – and the things I appreciated the most – were when people told us stuff about my dad that they said they'd never forget. It made me feel good that he was going to be remembered. You know what I mean?"

"Yeah," I said. "I get it."

"You'll do fine," he assured me. "Anything you say is going to be fine."

"Okay, thanks," I said, and I closed the phone.

As it turned out, David did not give a eulogy. By the time of the funerals, he was barely talking at all.

Mike gave one though. He talked about their mission trip to Mexico and about some of the things they'd done down there and how he knew that God was telling Greg now, "Well done, my good and faithful servant."

The eulogy I had decided on was shallow and superficial compared to all that. Mike had told me to tell about a good time that we'd had together or something, and that's what I'd prepared.

Not having anything else ready, I went ahead and told the story of the time that our mom's had dragged the two of us along with them to an antique mall. It had been one of those huge deals that was all divided up with a lot of different dealer's booths. Greg and I had gone off on our own, playing with an ancient croquet set and looking at old knives.

At one of the booths we'd found the head of a mannequin. It didn't seem like a particularly old mannequin head – certainly not an antique – and I had wondered aloud why it was there. I had held it up, joking to Greg that I'd found the perfect girl for him. I'd pretended to kiss it. He'd told me to get my hands off his girlfriend.

The incident would have been forgotten, except for the fact that, a few booths away, we found *another* mannequin head. This one wasn't kiss-worthy, it was just creepy. We had laughed about that one, too, and went on our way. By the time we'd gotten through the entire antique mall, we'd discovered about seven or eight of them, each one making us laugh more than the last. We were pretty much hysterical by the time our moms were ready to go.

A few nights later, I was awakened in the middle of the night by a strange scratching sound against the wall that divided my room from Chase's. I reached for the light on my bedside table, my hand brushing against something fuzzy as I did. When I finally got the light on and saw the mannequin head that my hand had touched, I actually screamed.

Loud.

And then I heard Greg and Chase on the other side of my wall, howling with fits of laughter.

As I told the story, I glanced tentatively at Mrs. White. She was smiling back at me and I knew that Mike had been right about talking about a memory, but somehow, what I was saying still felt so meaningless.

My mind searched around for another story I could tell, but the only one that came to mind was the time that Greg and Natalie had wound up over at my house, one lazy summer evening. We had just started a game of Yahtzee on the back deck, when Mom and Dad had gotten into a fight . . . a *big* fight.

They'd had some brawls before, but nothing like this one. Things were flying through the air . . . my mom's computer hit the floor. I got Chase and Jordan out of the house and Greg and Natalie took them for a walk down the street, while I had stayed behind and called the police.

Nothing had come of any of it, but the next day, Greg asked me how I was doing.

"Fine," I'd said, not wanting to talk about it.

"Good," he'd nodded, and I hoped that he was going to let it drop.

He did, but first he added, "I want you to know that I've been praying for you."

I looked at Mrs. White again now. She was still smiling up at me. Then I looked to where my parents were sitting, a few rows behind her.

"He was a lot of fun," I finally finished, "and I'll always remember all the good times we had together."

It was a dry and cold day. The sun came out as we made our way to the gravesite, but it did nothing to ward off the chill. The pallbearers for Mr. White's casket were my dad and David's dad, two teachers from the school, and two other men from their church.

Laci, Natalie, Ashlyn, Mike, David and I all carried Greg's, and as we made our way to the gravesite, it suddenly struck me . . .

It was the last time that the seven of us were ever going to be together.

~ ~ ~

A COUPLE OF weeks later, I was laying on my bed, staring up at the ceiling, listening to music. A movement caught my eye and I glanced toward the door, startled to see Laci standing there. She held up a hand, giving me a little wave, and I scrambled to sit up, pulling out my ear buds as I did.

"Hi," I said.

"Hi," she said back. "I hope it's okay that I'm here . . . Jordan let me in."

"Sure it's okay," I answered. "Come on in."

She stepped into the room and looked around.

"Wow," she said. "I can't believe how clean your room is. Greg and David's rooms are like pigsties compared to this."

Her voice faded off.

"Did you see the rest of the house when you came in?" I asked wryly. "This is my only sanctuary."

She gave me a little smile.

"Wanna sit down?" I offered, gesturing toward the foot of the bed.

"Thanks," she said. She took a seat and then pointed at my headphones. "What're you listening to?"

"Nothing you'd approve of," I admitted.

She shook her head and rolled her eyes. "I don't know why you listen to that crap," she said.

"I thought you weren't supposed to say 'crap'," I chided her. Then, before she could answer, I went on, "Oh, no . . . you can say 'Crap', you're just not supposed to say 'Holy crap'."

She gave me another small smile, but it was pretty obvious that she wasn't there for small talk.

"How are you doing?" I finally asked quietly.

She pursed her lips together and nodded, but then shook her head and closed her eyes. She covered her face with her hands, sobbing, and I scooted myself over so that I was next to her and put my arms around her. She buried her face into my chest and wept.

"I miss him so much," she cried, gasping for breath. I could feel hot tears soaking into my shirt. "I don't know what to do."

I pulled her tighter to me and put my cheek on top of her head.

"I mean, I know we're going to have hard times," she said, pulling away a bit to see if I understood what she was saying. I nodded at her and she went on. "I get that, but I never thought anything could hurt as bad as this."

I nodded again and she rested her head on my chest once more, crying for another minute. Finally she sat up and wiped her eyes.

"I'm sorry," she sniffed. "I didn't mean to come over here and unload on you."

"It's okay," I assured her. "Anytime you need to talk to somebody, I'm here."

"Actually I came over here for another reason," she said, still sniffling and wiping her face.

"What?" I asked, rubbing a hand across her back.

"It's David," she said, looking at me and swallowing hard. "I'm really worried about him."

I nodded one more time.

"He won't talk to me," she went on in a voice just above a whisper. "He won't answer the phone when I call, he won't see me if I go over there. His mom's tried to get him to go see somebody and he just acts like nothing's wrong . . ."

"I know," I admitted.

It was pretty obvious to anybody who knew David that he wasn't doing well. He was going straight to school every day – going through the motions – and then straight home again after it was over. He'd dropped off the swim team and hadn't even tried out for baseball. It was like watching the living dead.

She reached out and took my hand.

"I'm scared he's going to kill himself," she whispered, hoarsely, "and I don't know what to do."

I didn't have any comforting words for her – the same thought had already crossed my mind too. "I was wondering if you would go talk to him," she said, squeezing my hand.

"Me?" I asked in surprise. Every adult in David's life knew that he was in trouble – his teachers, his parents, the counselors at school. If they couldn't do anything about it, what was I supposed to do? I was seventeen years old . . .

She looked at me with fresh tears in her eyes, still clutching my hand.

"Please?" she said. "Please just try . . ."

I nodded at her, the girl I would do anything for, and wrapped my arm around her.

"I'll try," I promised, squeezing her tightly against me once again.

David's mom answered the door and let me in. She gave me a hug and told me she was glad to see me.

"Is David here?" I asked.

"Up in his room," she said. "Where he always is these days."

"Some of us are kind of worried about him," I explained. "I thought maybe I'd try to talk with him, but I don't know if it's a good idea or not."

Tears welled up in her eyes.

"Please do," she said. "He's just holding everything inside and won't talk to anybody – sooner or later something's gonna give."

"You wanna tell him I'm here?" I asked.

"No," she said, shaking her head. "Just go on up."

I headed up the stairs and knocked on his door. There was no answer, so I opened the door slowly, honestly afraid of what I might find. I was relieved to see that he was just sitting at his desk, punching away on a calculator with a pencil in one hand.

"Hi," I said.

The sound of my voice caused him to look toward the doorway.

"Oh, hey," he said, seemingly surprised to see me.

"Your mom said I could come on up," I explained. "I hope that's okay."

"Oh, sure," he nodded. "No problem." He turned away from me and wrote something down on a piece of paper before hitting a button on his calculator and finally turning to face me again.

"How you doing?" he asked.

"Great."

"Good," he nodded.

"How 'bout you?"

56

"Fine," he nodded again.

"Baseball starts next week," I said.

"I know."

"You shoulda come out for the team this year," I said. "Our catcher sucks."

"Who is it?" he asked. "McClure?"

"Yeah," I nodded.

"Aw, he'll do fine."

"Not as good as you. I bet Coach would still let you on," I said. "You should come talk to him."

"I can't," he said, gesturing toward the book on his desk. "AP Physics is about to kick my butt."

"David . . ."

"Our new teacher's an idiot," he said. "I'm pretty much having to teach myself."

"David," I said again.

"What?"

"You need to come out for baseball."

"I can't," he said again. "I've got too much to do."

"No, you don't," I said, shaking my head.

"Yes, I do," he argued. "I already told you–"

"David!" I interrupted. "Stop."

"What?" he asked again.

"Everybody's worried about you," I said. "It's not good for you to be shutting everybody out."

"I'm not shutting everybody out," he said. "I've just been really busy."

"You can't even answer the phone when Laci calls?"

He looked at me sharply, almost showing a thread of emotion.

"I've got a lot to do," he said carefully. Then he added, "You should go now."

"She's worried about you, David," I persisted. "The least you can do is talk to her and let her know that you're all right."

"I'm fine," he said. "You can tell her I said I was fine."

"Why don't you tell her yourself?" I asked.

"Go home, Tanner," he said, turning his back on me.

"David," I said, one more time. He ignored me and picked up his pencil. I stood and stared at his back for a minute, and then I left.

~ ~ ~

AS TIME WENT on, David improved slightly. He started talking to Laci again, and after that happened, we all quit worrying quite so much that he was going to kill himself.

He still basically shut everybody else out, and he still seemed to be pretty out of touch with everything most of the time, but at least he was going to school every day and seemed to be moving somewhat forward with his life.

"He's definitely going to State in the fall," Laci told me one day. She had seen me in the back yard, tossing the football with Chase, and had hopped the fence to watch. After Chase had lost interest and disappeared, she'd stayed around and we were sitting on the back steps now, talking.

"Maybe it'll be good for him," she went on. "You know? To get away from here?"

I nodded at her.

"Have you decided yet if you're going to go to Auburn," she asked, "or Notre Dame?" The deadline for me to sign my letter of intent – officially deciding which college I was going to play football for – was quickly approaching.

Before I could answer, Laci started crying. It still didn't take much to set her off these days, but it surprised me just the same because we hadn't been talking about Greg or Mr. White.

"You're going to be so far away," she sobbed, "and we're never going to see each other again."

"That's not true," I told her, wrapping an arm around her. "I'm not going to either one."

She stopped crying quite so hard, but not completely.

"Even if you go to Nebraska or Kansas State," she said through her tears, waving her hand in the air, "you're still going to be over three hundred miles away . . ."

58

"No," I said, shaking my head. "I'm not going there, either."

"Where are you going?" she asked in astonishment, looking at me through her tears.

"Central," I said, almost cringing as the word came out of my mouth. I could not believe I had just told her that.

"Are you serious?"

"Yeah," I nodded, squeezing her. "Absolutely. They've got a great football program."

This was an absolute lie, but of course I knew that Laci didn't follow football well enough to realize that. The truth was that Central, where Ashlyn happened to be going, *had* once had a great football program . . . but not anymore.

Ten years earlier, one of the assistant coaches had decided to treat about ten members of the conference championship team to a little celebratory party at his house – complete with a bunch of strippers and alcohol. This might not have been too bad if all but two of the players hadn't turned out to be underage and if the strippers hadn't also turned out to be prostitutes. The media jumped all over it and the NCAA decided to make an example out of them, imposing every sanction that they possibly could . . .

Their program still hadn't recovered.

I had almost laughed when their head coach suggested that I might want to strongly consider Central. "Close to home," was the only selling point he'd had going for him when he pitched his case to me. If I wanted to play in the NFL – which I did – both of us knew that I'd be shooting myself in the foot by deciding to go to Central. I guess he had figured that it wouldn't hurt to try though.

"We're only going to be an hour away from each other," Laci said now, looking at me in amazement. Her tears were completely gone.

"I know," I said, squeezing her shoulder again. "We're going to get to see each other all the time."

~ ~ ~

BUT WE DIDN'T see each other "all the time." As a matter of fact, after we went off to college in the fall, we didn't see each other *at all*.

Football kept me pretty busy right through Christmas, and except for a few brief phone conversations, I hardly ever talked to Laci. The rare times when we did talk seemed awkward, and I began resisting the urge to call her, instead keeping myself busy with football and schoolwork.

I said we didn't see each other at all, but that's not entirely true. I did see her one time . . . but she didn't see me.

I had returned to Cavendish during the only weekend that the football team didn't have a game and I went out of my way to drive by her house, late on the evening that I got home. I slowed my truck as I got closer to her yard, and that's when I saw her.

And David.

They were walking up her front sidewalk, and I drove even slower as they stopped at the bottom of the stairs and turned to face each other.

That's when I stepped on the accelerator and turned my face away, because I really hadn't wanted to see whatever was going to happen next.

At least back at college, Central was having its winningest season in recent history. We were invited to a bowl game and I was glad to have an excuse to not spend much time home for the holidays, trying to avoid seeing whatever David and Laci might be up to.

I had started in every game that fall, and the media was already picking up on the fact that I was a "player to watch." I was being credited with being a "huge factor in Central's unexpected turnaround," and suddenly? My NFL dreams were alive and well again . . . all was not lost.

Central happened to be located only a few minutes from Cross Lake, and my dad still kept a boat at the marina. By the time the first official weekend of the spring rolled around, when both football season and the ice were officially gone, I was making plans to spend the entire day on Saturday at the lake, fishing.

Like I said . . . all was not lost.

That Friday afternoon I played football on the quad with some of the guys from the dorm. We'd had a lot of cold rain for the first two weeks in March, but the ground was finally dry now and it was the first decent chance we'd had to do anything outside. We took full advantage and played for over three hours and – after we finally quit – I headed over to a low stone wall to grab the jacket that I'd had on when we'd first arrived.

"Somebody should give you a scholarship," I heard a voice say.

I looked to my right and, for the first time, noticed that someone was sitting on the stone wall on the opposite side from my jacket. My mouth dropped open. "Laci?"

"You look really good out there." She smiled at me.

"Laci!" I cried. "What are you doing here?"

She hopped down off the wall and stepped toward me, opening her arms for a hug.

"I'm kind of dirty . . ." I protested halfheartedly.

"I don't care," she answered, wrapping her arms around me. I hugged her back and she gripped me tightly for a long moment. When she pulled away, there were tears in her eyes.

"What's wrong?" I asked quietly.

"Nothing," she said, shaking her head. "It's just been a really hard year."

I nodded at her.

"And I'm really glad to see you," she went on.

"I'm really glad to see you, too," I agreed. "What are you doing here?"

"I came to see Ashlyn," she said, shrugging nonchalantly. "I'm staying with her 'til Sunday."

"That's great," I said.

"She's got a boyfriend," Laci went on.

"Yeah, I know," I said. "I've seen her with him. What's his name? Brad?"

"Brent."

"Right, Brent. He seems like a pretty nice guy."

"Yeah. I think she's happy."

"So where is she?"

"They went out," she said, shrugging again.

"*Without you?*" I asked, incredulous.

"I made them go on without me," she explained. "I was kind of feeling like a third wheel. I told her I wanted to look around the campus and everything by myself."

"Well, I'm glad I happened to be out here," I said.

"I might have kind of tracked you down," she admitted.

I looked at her questioningly.

"Ashlyn told me what dorm you were in," she said, shrugging one more time. "I went over there and someone told me you were probably here."

"Oh."

"But I don't want to keep you from anything," she said, gesturing toward my jacket.

"Oh, no," I assured her, shaking my head. "We should go get dinner."

"You don't have any plans?" she asked carefully.

"Nope," I assured her. "Let's get something to eat."

We went back to my dorm and I left her in the lobby while I showered and changed as fast as I could. I also took a moment to call David, but I didn't get an answer. I left him a message, and when I couldn't relax over dinner, Laci could tell.

"Are you sure you didn't have other plans?" she asked worriedly. "You seem distracted."

"No," I said. "Everything's fine."

An hour later – when we were in a darkened movie theater – David finally returned my call.

"I'll be right back," I told Laci quietly when I felt my phone vibrate.

She nodded at me and I quickly strode up the aisle, answering it as I hit the lobby.

"Hi," I said.

"Hey," he replied. "I got your message."

"Yeah."

"I was in the library when you called," he said. "Sorry."

"No big deal," I answered. "What's up?"

62

"Not much. What's up with you?"

"Oh, nothing," I said noncommittally. "I just wanted to tell you that I saw Mrs. White."

"You did?"

"Yeah," I said. "I've checked in on her a couple of times like you asked me to. Last weekend I went over there and put the ice melt away and made sure her lawn mower was ready to go for spring and stuff like that."

"Good," David said appreciatively. "How'd she seem?"

"Good," I said. "She seemed really good."

"Good."

There was a slight, awkward pause.

"You talk to Mike lately?" I asked.

"A little bit," he said, "but not much."

"Did you know his mom put their house up for sale?"

"Yeah," he said. "Mom told me."

"I guess she doesn't wanna be so far away from him once he goes off to school."

"Yeah."

There was another moment of silence until I worked up the nerve to get at what I really wanted to know.

"How's Laci doing?" I finally asked him, as casually as I could. This was actually a pretty risky question, since for all I knew he was going to say, *What do you mean, 'How's Laci doing?' I just talked to her a little bit ago and she said the two of you were having dinner.*

That's not what he said though.

"I don't know," he answered quietly.

"You don't know?"

"No."

"When's the last time you talked to her?" I asked, still going for casual.

"Ummm . . . Christmas I guess."

"Oh," I said. "You guys aren't seeing each other?"

"No."

I closed my eyes and quietly took a deep breath. Then I swallowed hard.

"Oh," I said again, opening my eyes. "I didn't know that."

I probably should have said, *I'm sorry to hear that*, but, *I didn't know that*, was a whole lot closer to the truth.

He didn't say anything.

I decided to change the subject.

"I see Ashlyn around sometimes," I said.

"Oh, yeah? How's she doing?"

"Good," I said. "She's dating some guy named Brent. They seem pretty serious."

"Oh. Well, that's good I guess."

"You ever hear from Natalie?"

"No. Do you?"

"I keep up with her a bit," I said. "I think she's doing pretty good."

"That's good."

I kept the small talk up long enough to ask him about his sister and his parents.

"Well," I finally said, "I'll let you go. I just wanted to let you know about Mrs. White."

"Thanks," he said. "I really appreciate it. I'm glad you went to see her."

"No problem," I said. "I'll talk to you later."

"Okay, bye."

"Bye."

I smiled at Laci as I lowered myself into the seat next to her.

"Who was that?" she whispered. Obviously she'd heard my phone go off before I'd left.

"Just a friend."

"Are you sure I'm not keeping you from something?" she asked quietly.

"I'm sure."

"I don't mind going back and waiting for Ashlyn—"

"No," I said. I put my hand on her arm and told her earnestly, "There's nowhere else I want to be."

She looked at me in the darkness for a long moment and then finally nodded and I ran my hand down her arm until I reached her hand. I took it in mine and gave it a reassuring squeeze and then she looked at me for another moment and gave me a small smile. I smiled back and then we both turned our eyes back to the screen.

Neither one of us pulled our hand away.

We were still holding hands by the time we reached Ashlyn's dorm, and we stopped and faced each other at the entrance.

"I had a good time," I told her.

"Me too," she nodded.

"I'm glad you tracked me down."

"Not too much like a stalker?" she asked, smiling.

"You can stalk me anytime you want," I assured her and she laughed.

I wrapped my arms around her and she hugged me back.

"Goodnight," I said, pulling slightly away.

"Goodnight," she replied quietly.

I looked at her for a moment, and then I leaned down and kissed her . . . on the forehead.

I stepped back and looked at her again. She gave me the slightest of smiles and a tight nod, then headed to the door, holding up her guest card to the reader and waiting for it to unlock to let her in. As soon as she was gone I covered my face with my hands and groaned. I stepped over to the lobby door and banged on it so that she stopped walking and turned around. She hadn't even made it to the elevator yet.

"Come back here," I called, motioning with my hands.

She returned to the door.

I looked into her eyes for a moment and then sighed.

"I'm sorry," I told her, taking her hand once again.

"You don't need to apologize," she said, shaking her head.

"Come over here," I urged, tugging her away from the entrance to the dorm with its bright lights. We walked to a spot where a stone wall ran along the sidewalk and a huge maple tree towered over our heads. I stopped and turned to face Laci, her hand still in mine.

"I'm sorry," I repeated.

"You don't have anything to be sorry for," she insisted, shaking her head again. "It's okay."

"It's *not* okay," I argued.

"Look, Tanner," she said. "I know I just showed up out of the blue and I don't expect you to—"

I stepped close to her and lowered my mouth to her ear, interrupting her.

"I want to kiss you," I whispered.

I felt her breathing quicken.

"You do?" she whispered back.

I nodded against her.

"Then why don't you?"

I pulled away from her slightly and brought my free hand to the side of her face, studying her for a moment before taking both hands, putting them on her waist, and lifting her up so that she was sitting on the wall, almost at eye level with me. I looked at her for another long moment.

"Because," I finally said, "I don't want to kiss you just tonight."

She gazed at me questioningly.

"I want to kiss you tomorrow, too," I explained.

A trace of a smile formed on her lips.

"You can kiss me tomorrow too," she promised quietly.

"How do you know that?" I asked seriously. "You were all gung-ho to kiss me last time, too, but then the next day you didn't want to have anything to do with me."

"You caught me off guard last time. I hadn't had any time to think about it."

"You haven't had any time to think about it this time either," I pointed out.

"Yes, I have," she said.

"How do you figure that?"

She bit her lip and dropped her eyes.

"Because I kind of lied to you earlier," she said, daring to look back up at me.

"About what?"

She looked into my eyes and hesitated for a long time before she finally admitted, "I didn't really come here to see Ashlyn."

I looked at her in wonder for a moment and felt my heart swell inside my chest. Then I pulled her toward me, covering her mouth with mine, and I marveled once again at the softness and warmth of her lips. I wrapped my fingers in her hair, lost in the nearness of her.

She reached her hand to the back of my neck and pulled me closer, and when our lips parted, she let out a soft gasp that made me want to kiss her all over again.

So I did.

Finally I pulled slightly away from her and whispered in her ear, "I'm going to be really upset if I don't get to do this again tomorrow, too."

"It's not going to be a problem," she whispered back.

We agreed that we would meet in the lobby the next morning at seven o'clock so that we could grab some breakfast and then go to the lake. I arrived at Ashlyn's dorm a few minutes before seven and only had to wait for about two minutes before someone came out and I was able to get in. I started getting worried by seven-ten when Laci hadn't appeared and by seven-twenty I had convinced myself that we were going to have a repeat of what had happened three years earlier.

I finally worked up the nerve to call her.

"Hi," I said tentatively when she answered.

"Hi."

"Is everything okay?"

"Yeah," she replied.

"Where are you?" I asked.

"In the lobby," she answered, "waiting for you."

"Where?"

"I'm on the couch in front of the TV," she said.

I was standing behind the couch in front of the TV – there was definitely no Laci on the couch.

"Ummmm," I said. "Exactly what dorm are you in?"

"Yours . . ."

"Oh," I said. "I think I'm beginning to see the problem."

I told Laci to stay put and I sprinted back to my dorm. She was waiting for me by the door when I got there and as soon as she saw me she gave me a big smile and my promised kiss.

A day fishing on the lake had never been so good.

~ ~ ~

I LOVED HAVING Laci as my girlfriend.

I loved kissing her and holding her hand and laughing with her and holding her body close to mine. I could talk to her about anything and we spent hours discussing whatever came to mind.

For the next two weekends, Laci drove to Central to "visit Ashlyn" and we spent every waking moment together, (and actually then some, since we fell asleep on the beach one day for a few hours). The third weekend was a long weekend for both of us since it was Easter, and both of us went home to Cavendish.

Laci had promised Natalie that she would spend Friday with her, and both of us had family commitments on Sunday, but we decided that we wanted to spend the entire day Saturday together and that there was still no place we'd rather be than in the boat on Cross Lake.

Unfortunately, it was pouring and windy when we woke up on Saturday morning and neither one of us felt like sloshing around in a boat on choppy water all day. Instead, Laci came over to my house in the morning. After a few hours of trying unsuccessfully to avoid my brothers, I turned to Laci and said, "Wanna get out of here?" She nodded and we ran through the rain to my truck.

I know I just said that Laci and I could talk about anything, but that actually wasn't true. There was always a white elephant in the room with us.

David.

Not once – in the entire year and a half that Laci and I dated – did we ever talk about David in a way of any consequence. We never mentioned the fact that the two of them had dated, that he had been my best friend, that it might not go over too well if he ever found out that the two of us were together now. David hardly ever came home, but Laci and I were still careful not to parade our relationship around whenever we were in Cavendish. We, ourselves, hardly ever went home either, but when we did, we stuck close to our houses, never going out together to eat or to go to the movies.

So, on that Saturday, after Laci and I had jumped into my truck, we went to a drive-thru and took our lunches back to Laci's house. After we'd finished eating, we snuck away from her mom's ever-watchful eye and wound up in the playroom of her basement, reminiscing about all the hours we'd spend there when we were little. Eventually we broke out a faded and well-used edition of Monopoly, set it up, and started playing – each passing Go about two times, before deciding that kissing was a much more fun and entertaining thing to do on a rainy Saturday.

That's when Laci's mom came clumping down the stairs with a load of laundry.

We pulled away from one another quickly and I sighed while Laci rolled the dice (even though it was completely not her turn).

"Don't let me interrupt," Mrs. Cline said cheerily, opening the lid to the washer.

"Mm-hmm," Laci said, scowling at her mom once her back was turned.

I leaned forward and put my mouth next to Laci's ear.

"We have *got* to find some place to go," I whispered.

"Mm-hmm," Laci said again.

An hour later we met in Laci's backyard in the tree house that her father had built for her tenth birthday. During that hour apart I had run to the grocery store while Laci had swept the tree house out and then dragged two bean bag chairs and an old quilt up to it.

"Sweet," I said, as I stuck my head through door and looked around. "It's like our own, private love shack!"

"Stop it," she said, swatting me. "It's not a 'love shack'. I had a hard enough time convincing my mom that nothing unseemly was gonna be going on out here. If she hears you talking like that she's going to drag me right back in the house."

"You're almost nineteen years old," I reminded her.

"Yeah," she scoffed. "Tell *her* that."

"Are you sure you got rid of all the spiders?" I asked, glancing around uneasily.

"It's hardly even been warm enough for spiders."

"'Hardly' is the key word there," I said.

"Get in here," she said, grabbing the straps of the back pack that I was wearing and dragging me all the way in.

We had both brought our school stuff along to work on, but neither one of us wanted any of that. I never even unzipped my back pack. I leaned back against one of the bean bag chairs, pulled Laci down into my arms, and pressed my cheek against the top of her head. She nestled against my chest and we lay there for a long time, listening to the sound of the relentless rain, hitting the roof of the tree house.

There was no way to express the way it felt to be there with Laci. The best I could do was to run my hand along her throat, cup her chin, and tilt her face toward mine. I bent my head toward hers and kissed her lips. She kissed me back . . . softly at first, but then with more urgency.

The intensity of our kisses grew, but things didn't get out of hand. (Trust me, I know when things are out of hand, and this wasn't it.) After a few moments of that, however, Laci suddenly pulled back with a frightened look on her face.

"I can't do this," she said breathlessly.

I smiled at her reassuringly and gazed into her eyes, letting my finger trace lightly across her cheek.

"I love you so much," I whispered.

Then she looked at me startled, and suddenly sat up, pushing herself away from me.

I sat up too, instinctively reaching for her, but she pulled further away and drew her knees to her chest, wrapping her arms around them.

"What's wrong?" I asked, not trying to touch her any more.

"You need to go home," she said quietly.

"What?"

"This was a mistake," she said, looking out the door of the tree house and into the steady rain that was still beating down on the back yard.

"What was a mistake?"

"This," she said, waving her hand and looking around the tree house. "Us. Everything."

"What do you mean?"

"I mean I'm not sleeping with you," she said crossly, staring out into the back yard once again.

"I know you're not sleeping with me!" I cried. "Where did *that* come from?"

She cast an angry glance my way.

"You think I told you 'I love you,' because I wanted to *sleep* with you?"

Her glare answered my question.

"Laci," I said, daring to put a hand on her shoulder. "I wouldn't let that happen. I know you want to wait until you're married . . ."

"How do you know that?"

"Because I know *you*!"

She looked at me uncertainly.

"Laci," I explained softly. "I know the kind of person you are and I'd never try to change that about you. I told you 'I love you,' because, I *love* you, not because I want to sleep with you."

She looked at me for another moment, and then stared back out into the yard. I didn't say anything.

"You've had a lot of girlfriends," she finally stated quietly.

"Nobody I ever cared about."

"But you slept with them." It was another statement.

I pursed my lips together.

"Some of them," I admitted, nodding reluctantly.

She closed her eyes.

"I'm sorry, Laci," I told her. "If I'd had any idea that you were going to come along . . ."

She took a deep breath and finally opened her eyes again.

"If I could change things," I continued, "I would, but–"

She interrupted me.

"How many?"

Oh, boy.

"I . . . I don't know," I answered, even more reluctantly.

"You don't KNOW?" she cried, looking at me in alarm. "How can you *not know*?"

"Does it really matter?"

"It matters to me!"

I sighed.

"I don't know," I said again. "I guess maybe five or so."

"Or so?"

"Yeah," I nodded. "Fivish."

"Fivish? Tanner, how can you *not know*?"

"Look," I said. "If I wanna sit here and think about it I could tell you for sure, but I really don't want to think about it. It was a long time ago."

"What do you mean?"

"I mean it was a *long* time ago."

"How long?"

"High school."

"You haven't been with anyone since high school?"

"No," I said. "I haven't been with anyone since that first time I kissed you."

"You haven't?" she asked in quiet disbelief.

"No," I said, shaking my head.

"Why not?"

"Because," I said. "That was the day I fell in love with you."

She still wanted me to go home, so I did.

I picked up my book bag and trudged through the rain, angry at myself for something that had happened almost two years earlier, and that night I lay on my bed in the dark, staring up at the ceiling, and praying.

I didn't usually pray, but I prayed that night.

I laid there on my bed thinking up all the things that I'd be willing to do if only He would bring Laci back to me:

Only listen to Christian music . . .
Read the Bible every day . . .
Go to church every Sunday . . .
Volunteer at the soup kitchen . . .

I was in the middle of my laundry list when the sound of something hitting my window interrupted my thoughts. The wind had picked up and I figured it was probably an acorn from the giant oak tree in our yard or possibly hail. I kept praying.

Please, God. Please. I'll never ask you for anything else. I just want Laci. Please don't take her away from me . . . And lying there, I was suddenly overcome with the overwhelming conviction that I was going to marry Laci one day.

Something else hit the window, but I ignored it again, amazed by this astonishing thought and feeling a remarkable sense of peace because of it.

Are You trying to tell me I'm going to marry her? I asked God hopefully.

I felt nothing but a continual sense of peace.

Would you give me some kind of a sign? I prayed. *Let me know that that's what You're telling me?*

And my phone went off to let me know that I had a text message.

I had never gotten a text from Laci before in my entire life . . . but I had one now.

Would you please come out here?

Out here?

I got out of bed and looked out my window. I could barely see anything through the darkness and the rain, but there she was, standing in the middle of the yard, looking up at my window. I realized that acorns hadn't been falling from the tree and hitting my window. She'd been standing out there *throwing* things at it . . . trying to get my attention.

I pulled on my clothes, slipped quietly down the stairs, and let myself out the back door. She was still standing in the middle of the yard in the pouring rain, wearing jeans and a sweatshirt. She didn't move when she saw me. I walked over to her and stopped a foot or so away from her. From the light of a distant streetlamp, I could just barely make out her face. She was soaking wet, water running from her hair in rivulets.

We stared at each other wordlessly and finally her lips parted and she spoke.

"I should have told you something."

"What?" I asked, looking at her expectantly.

She held my gaze for a long moment, took my hand, and then she told me.

"I love you, too."

~ ~ ~

THAT WAS THE beginning of the best year of my life.

That evening, we went back to the tree house to dry off on the quilt, and to make up, and to not let things get out of hand.

The following weekend, I drove up to Scottsdale and rented a camping spot not too far from her campus. I called Laci and told her where I was and she said she'd see me in a few minutes. When she pulled up in front of my campsite and got out of her car, I immediately noticed that she'd had her hair cut. Of course this wasn't at all unusual – Laci had been chopping her hair off and sending it to Locks of Love ever since she was little.

"Hey," I said, walking up to her and grinning as she got out of her car. I wrapped my arms tightly around her and nuzzled my face against her bare neck, kissing it.

She giggled and put her arms around me.

"Your hair looks fantastic," I murmured between kisses.

"Really?" she asked, uncertainly. "It doesn't look too boyish?"

"Are you *kidding*?" I asked, pulling back to look at her. "I've always thought you look super sexy when you get your hair cut."

"Really?" she asked again, sounding more pleased this time.

"Absolutely," I said, and I went back to her neck once more.

After a few minutes of kissing, hunger won out and we went to campus and ate dinner off her meal card in the cafeteria. Afterward, we picked up marshmallows and graham crackers and chocolate bars, and then we headed back to the campground.

We rolled down the windows of Laci's car and listened to music as we made s'mores over the open fire. It was Christian music, of course, because that was all we ever listened to (not because doing so was one of the many

74

things I'd promised God a few weeks earlier, but because half of "we" was Laci).

A song called *Kneeling Before You* began playing. We already considered it "our song", and I put down the marshmallow I was working on, asking Laci if she wanted to dance. She did, and I offered her my hand, helping her to her feet. We wrapped our arms around each other and moved slowly back and forth, Laci's head resting against my shoulder.

Kneeling Before You was the only song I'd ever heard, Christian or otherwise, that dealt with football. It started out talking about a little boy who was supposed to catch the punt return during a game, but it was his first time ever playing and he was scared that he was going to get mowed down by the other team. His coach told him to call for a fair catch by kneeling down after he'd caught the ball.

Of course it also had to talk about how he knelt down before God when he was older (because it was a Christian song and everything), but then it went on to tell about him kneeling down before his girlfriend and proposing to her. Even though it was Christian, it was pretty good, and I liked it a lot.

It was a popular song that year and it got played a lot on the radio and at weddings and stuff. As we danced to it now, I decided that we were going to play it at *our* wedding . . . when Laci and I got married to each other one day, like God had told me we were going to do.

After the song was over we sat back down in front of the fire and resumed our s'more making and I took a few more opportunities to remind her how sexy I thought her hair cut was.

"I have something to tell you," Laci said quietly a few minutes later as we sat watching the flames dance in the campfire. I was leaning against a log and she was leaning back against me. She looked up at me when she spoke.

"Something good?" I asked. "Or something bad?"

"I'm not sure what you'll think."

I looked at her, not too worried, still confident in my recent revelation from God.

"I decided that I'm going to take some classes this summer."

"Oh."

"So do you think that's good or bad?"

"I don't know," I said, shrugging. "If you go home you'll be about an hour away . . . if you stay here you'll be about an hour away. I guess it doesn't make much difference." (Either way, my scholarship pretty much dictated that *I* was going to be at Central for most of the summer.)

"I was thinking that I wasn't going to take them *here* . . ." she said tentatively.

"You're not going to Mexico or something, are you?" I asked, hearing concern in my own voice.

"No," she laughed.

"Where then?" I looked at her expectantly.

She hesitated.

"Central maybe?" she finally answered.

"Are you *serious?*"

I looked at her with my mouth hanging open.

"Unless you don't want me to . . ."

"Are you kidding? How could you possibly think that I wouldn't want you to spend the summer with me?"

"Well," she said hesitantly, "I didn't want to make any assumptions . . ."

I pulled her to me and wrapped my arms around her

"I want to spend every minute of every day with you," I told her. "I hate it when I'm not with you."

"I don't want you to think I'm trying to smother you . . ."

"I will *always* want to be with you," I said. "I can't believe you don't know that."

She looked up at me and smiled.

"And you can smother me any time you want," I added, smiling back. Then she giggled, and I pulled her close enough to make smothering a real possibility.

Like I said . . . best year of my life.

That summer, and the next, Laci took general education classes at Central that would transfer to Collins. In the fall, she drove to Central for every one of my home football games, spending the weekends with Ashlyn. Once football season was over, I did my fair share of driving to Collins, either camping, or getting a cheap hotel room, depending on the weather.

If I could have transferred to Collins, I would have and I tried more than once to convince Laci to transfer to Central. But Central didn't offer a major in missiology (which I hadn't even known was a *word*, much less a major) and ever since she had learned that living down in Mexico and ministering to the people there was a possibility, her entire life had revolved around making that happen.

I didn't want to change that or anything else about her, but by the end of our second summer together, I was really dreading the thought of spending another school year apart, only seeing her on weekends.

And that's why I came up with a plan so that the two of us wouldn't have to be away from each other anymore.

~ ~ ~

MIKE AND HIS mom had moved to Minnesota shortly after he'd graduated from high school and he hadn't been back to visit much since then. A week before the fall semester started up, however, Mike sent me a message and told me that he and his mom were going to be in Cavendish. They were planning on staying at Mrs. White's for a few days and he wanted to know if I wanted to get together.

Even though I hadn't seen Mike in a long time, I was reluctant to make plans with him. Summer classes had just ended and I was going to be home for a few days, but I had already decided exactly how I wanted to spend every minute of each of them. When Laci told me that Natalie was going to be home too though, and that she wanted to get together with her for a few hours on Friday, I told Mike that I would have lunch with him then.

We met at a diner in town.

"We should play disc golf this evening," Mike suggested after he stuffed a last bit of burger into his mouth. "I think it's gonna cool off later."

"I can't," I said. "Laci and I are going out."

"What are guys doing?"

"Having dinner."

"Oh," he said. "Well, maybe we could—"

"You're not invited," I clarified.

He looked at me carefully for a minute.

"You and Laci are *dating?*" he finally asked slowly.

"Yeah," I nodded.

He paused for a long moment.

"How long has that been going on?" he finally asked, picking up his napkin and wiping off his mouth.

"Since last summer," I said.

"Since *last summer?*" He was clearly shocked. "Is it serious?"

"Yeah."

"How serious?"

"It's serious," I said.

He paused again.

"What are we talking about here?" he wanted to know.

I hesitated before deciding to tell him.

"I'm going to ask her to marry me."

Tomorrow night . . .

A Christmas wedding . . .

An apartment between our two campuses so that we could both commute . . .

He stared at me in disbelief and then shook his head. "I had no idea."

I nodded.

"Does Dave know?" he asked.

"That we're getting married?" I shook my head. "No one knows. I haven't asked her yet."

"No," he said, shaking his own head. "I mean does David know you two are dating?"

"I don't know if he knows or not," I said, indifferently. "What difference does it make?"

"Because . . . because, I mean . . . David and Laci–"

"David and Laci WHAT?" I interrupted. "David and Laci haven't been together for two and a half *years* . . ."

"But . . . but Dave–"

"Dave nothing!" I said, angrily. "Dave turned his back on her a long time ago and hasn't been back since."

"He's been having a hard time," Mike stammered.

"*And Laci hasn't?*" I yelled, causing heads nearby to turn. "What about the rest of us? Don't give me any of this crap about David having a hard time. If David wanted to be with Laci he should have sucked it up and been there for her a long time ago!"

Mike shut up about it then, but I could tell he wasn't happy.

I made a special point not to care.

I was the happiest I had ever been in my entire life, and I was going out for dinner that night with the woman that I loved.

And the next day I was going to ask her to marry me.

Nothing was going to bring me down.

~ ~ ~

LACI AND I stayed out late that night and I slept in the next morning because of it. It was almost noon by the time I'd showered, dressed, and climbed into my truck to go pick her up. The picnic basket was packed in the back. I was ready to go.

I had just put the truck in reverse when Laci called.

"Hey!" I answered. "I'm just leaving now."

"Don't."

"What?"

"Don't pick me up," she said, and I realized that she was crying. "I can't go."

"You can't go? Why not? What's wrong?"

"I just . . . I need some time."

I froze.

"What's wrong, Laci?" I asked in a voice just above a whisper.

"I just need to think," she said, beginning to cry harder. "I just need to figure some stuff out."

"Figure *what* out?" I asked, putting the truck back in park.

"I don't know," she sobbed. "Things just aren't right and I gotta figure them out."

"What's not right?"

She just cried in response.

"What happened?" I asked, desperately. "What did I do?"

"You didn't do anything!" she wept. "This isn't about you."

"What's it about then?"

"It's about me," she wept. "I just . . . I just need some time."

"Tell me what's going on."

She just sobbed harder.

"Please talk to me, Laci."

"I can't see you anymore," she finally choked, crying again in earnest.

80

"Why, Laci?" I asked. "Why not? What happened?"

"I'm not supposed to be with you."

"What are you talking about?"

She stopped crying and was quiet for a long moment.

"I'm supposed to be with David," she finally said softly.

I gripped the phone.

"Mike did this," I said, the anger growing in my voice.

"This isn't Mike's fault," she said. "Don't be mad at him."

But it was already too late for that.

I put the truck back in reverse and drove over to Mrs. White's house and rang the bell. Mrs. White answered the door and smiled at me.

"Hi, Tanner! It's so good to see you! What a nice—"

"Is Mike here?" I interrupted.

"Yes," she said, still smiling. "Come on in and I'll—"

"Would you tell him I'm out here, please?" I asked, trying unsuccessfully to keep my voice even.

"Okay," she nodded, not bothering to try to smile anymore.

I turned around and walked back to my truck. I leaned against it and watched as Mike came out the door and walked toward me. He stopped when he was about two yards from me and just looked at me, not saying a word.

I didn't say a word to him, either. I just stepped forward and punched him in the face as hard as I could.

My fist connected with his jaw and he fell backward – sprawling onto the lawn. Mrs. White and Mike's mom, Mrs. Antonucci, both rushed out onto the porch.

"Tanner!" Mrs. White called out to me.

"Mike!" Mrs. Antonucci cried.

Mike got onto his hands and knees and looked toward the house. My fists were clenched.

"Go inside," he told them.

"Tanner!" Mrs. White called again, but I didn't look at her. I was still staring at Mike, who was struggling to his feet.

"Go inside," he shouted to them again, holding his jaw. "Go on!"

He didn't take his eyes off me and they didn't leave the porch. Mike squared his shoulders and stared at me defiantly. He wasn't going to back away, but he wasn't going to fight either. He was just going to stand there and take whatever I gave him.

"How could you do this to me?" I asked, my voice breaking.

"This isn't about you."

I shook my head at him.

"I hate you," I said, my voice trembling. I backed away toward the driveway. "If she breaks up with me, I will *never* forgive you for as long as I live."

And then I got back in my truck and I drove away.

I called Laci several times, but she didn't pick up. Finally, I sent her a text, telling her that I was in her tree house and that she needed to come out there and talk to me. She didn't answer that, either, and so I texted her again and asked her if she didn't think she owed me at least that much. A minute later I heard the back door open and then the sound of her slowly climbing the ladder. Her eyes were red and her face was puffy from crying. She couldn't even bring herself to look at me as she climbed inside.

As soon as she finally did look at me, I shook my head at her.

"Please don't do this," I said, my voice breaking.

That made her start crying again and then I did too. Not a few isolated tears, rolling down my face or anything like that, but full-blown, body wrenching sobs. She immediately put her arms around me and held me as I continued to cry uncontrollably.

"Please don't do this to me, Laci," I managed to beg, grabbing onto her desperately. "Please don't leave me."

"I have to, Tanner," she cried.

"Why?"

But she was sobbing just as hard as I was and she couldn't answer. That was when I realized exactly how difficult I was making this on her, and I somehow managed to pull myself together, just a bit.

"Look," I said. "I don't understand. Can you please try to explain to me what's going on?"

She took a deep, ragged breath and sat back, gripping my hand tightly.

And then she told me all about how, when she had been a little girl, that God had told her she was going to marry David one day. She explained how she had tried to be obedient to God's will for her, even when it wasn't what she necessarily wanted for herself.

82

"I wanted to go out with you in high school," she said, "that's why I kissed you back. But Greg knew what God had told me and he reminded me that I needed to be obedient to Him, and so . . ."

So she had called the whole thing off the next day.

When she and David had finally started dating, she'd thought that it was the fulfillment of what God had told her, but then Greg had died, and that's when everything had fallen apart.

"It was wrong of me to doubt God and to go against what He wanted for me," she said, "but I was so angry at Him that I started doing what I wanted to do instead of what *He* wanted me to do."

She looked up at me now.

"I have to be obedient to what God wants for my life," she said. "I can't see you anymore . . . David and I are supposed to be together."

"Do you love him?"

"I don't know," she admitted quietly.

"*You don't know?*"

She didn't answer me.

"Have you been seeing him?"

"No," she said adamantly, shaking her head.

I shook my own head too, my mind swimming. Wasn't I just as certain that God had told *me* I was going to marry *her*? I searched around frantically for something to say.

"Look," I finally said. "God told you this a long, long time ago, right?"

She thought about that for a moment, and then nodded.

"Well, maybe He changed His mind."

"I don't think God changes His mind."

"Yes, He does," I argued. "He told Abraham to go kill Isaac, but then at the last minute He told him not to."

Where I pulled that from, I have no idea.

"But He was just testing Abraham," she said carefully. "God just wanted to see if he would really do it. He never intended for him to actually do it."

"Maybe God was just testing *you*," I pointed out.

She looked at me uncertainly.

"Isn't it possible that God told you something, but now He doesn't want you to do it anymore?"

"I don't know," she said hesitantly. "I . . . I guess . . ."

I grabbed on to that like a life raft.

"If He still wanted you and David to be together," I reasoned, "don't you think He'd be doing something about it?"

"I think He *did* do something about it," she said slowly. "I think He sent Mike to talk to me . . ."

"No, no, no," I said, shaking my head. "I think Mike's kind of out of the loop here. I don't think you need to be listening to anything Mike has to say."

She studied my face.

"*I* think God wants *us* to be together," I told her. "I believe you that He might have told you that a long time ago, but now . . . now it's you and me."

She just shook her head at me.

"Has He told you *recently* that you're supposed to be with David?"

"No," she admitted.

"Well, then why don't you ask Him?" I suggested, still certain that what He'd convicted me of on that rainy night a year and a half ago clearly trumped any messages she may have received from Him when she was a little girl. "Don't you think you should talk to Him about it?"

She nodded slowly and I felt slightly mollified.

"But I can't think straight when I'm around you," she said. "I need some time alone so that I can really talk to Him and see what He wants me to do."

"You can have all the time you want."

She looked at me appreciatively.

"I love you," I whispered, reaching out to her one last time.

"I love you, too," she answered, blinking back a fresh set of tears.

"I'll be waiting for you," I told her, "no matter how long it takes. Until you tell me that it's over, I'm never going to believe that you and I aren't meant to be together."

She gave me a small, sad smile.

And that was how it ended.

~ ~ ~

THEY SAY THAT good things come in threes, but that wasn't true at all for me. It was the *worst* things that came in threes for me.

The day after I said goodbye to Laci, Chase came to me, sobbing and crying and telling me that our dad had killed himself in our basement a few weeks earlier. Mom had told me that Dad had left, and that made sense – I'd figured that the fighting between the two of them had finally just gotten to be too much. But now Chase was telling me that he'd been home the day it had happened. That he'd heard the gunshot.

Being young, stupid, and on probation, Chase had panicked and somehow arrived at the brilliant decision that hiding the body at the bottom of Cross Lake would be a much better move than simply calling the police. He knew now that he'd screwed up, but he was terrified that if he went to the cops at this point that they weren't going to believe him and that he was going to have a murder charge pinned on him.

It was definitely a possibility that the police might accuse Chase of killing Dad, but even if they believed him, other people would spend the rest of their lives suspicious of his story, wondering if he was really a murderer.

Was it really such a bad thing that Mom and Jordan thought Dad had run off and was finally living a happy life somewhere?

Chase and I both decided to keep our mouths shut.

I don't remember if I was thinking about that or if I was thinking about Laci when, during a scrimmage three days later, I hesitated for just a fraction of a second, instead of moving when I was handed the ball. George (the guy that I'd roomed with during my freshmen year and the guy who was one of our starting linebackers) naturally was expecting me to move as he dove for me with all his might, but I didn't.

I tore both my ACL *and* my MCL, and suddenly I was out for the entire season.

That fall I had two surgeries, followed by eight months' worth of rehabilitation. By the time football season started again in the fall of my senior year, I still hadn't heard a word from Laci. Fortunately I was in pretty good shape again (at least physically), and I was still hopeful that if I had a season as good as my first two had been, I'd be a fairly high pick for the NFL draft the following spring.

But I only made it to game one of that season before I took another hit.

Two more surgeries were to be followed by eight more months of rehabilitation, but this time I knew that my football career was over.

I had known it from the moment I'd taken that second hit.

~ ~ ~

WHEN LACI CALLED me in February, it had been over a year and a half since we'd said goodbye to each other that day in the tree house. She wanted to see me and she offered to come to Central. My leg was still in a brace from my fourth surgery and I wasn't in any shape to drive, so I named a restaurant where we could meet, choosing one close enough that I could hobble to. I arrived early, hoping to struggle into a seat without her watching me, knowing she was going to feel enough pity for me when she said what it was that she had to say.

I didn't want to make it any harder on her.

It had been snowing lightly when I'd arrived, but based on the large flakes that were covering Laci's hair and jacket when she came in, I figured it had picked up quite a bit. My breath caught in my throat like it always did when I saw her. She was as beautiful as ever.

She spotted me and headed for the booth I was in, trying unsuccessfully to give me a bright smile.

"I hope you don't mind if I don't get up," I said apologetically, pointing at my crutches.

"Oh!" she cried. "What happened?"

It didn't surprise me at all that she was completely unaware of the fact that I'd been out for the past two seasons. When she'd said that she'd needed time away from me, I knew that she was going to do everything possible to keep me out of her mind as well. No keeping up with me through television, social networks, or friends.

"Nothing much," I shrugged. "I had surgery last month."

"I'm so sorry," she said. "You should have told me – you didn't need to be getting out here in this weather."

"It's okay," I assured her as she carefully slid into the booth across from me, mindful of the leg that was propped up on the seat beside her.

"Are you going to be okay?"

"Sure."

"Well, at least football season's over with."

I nodded and our waitress showed up to see if Laci wanted something to drink. She ordered water.

"Came all this way for some water?" I asked.

"I need to talk to you about something."

"I know," I said, nodding again.

She looked at me for a moment.

"Did David call you?" she asked uncertainly.

I shook my head.

She paused again, looking at me anxiously.

"Just tell me, Laci."

"We're getting married," she finally said.

I nodded at her a final time.

"And he's *going* to call you," she went on.

"Why?"

"To ask you to be in the wedding."

From the moment I'd heard Laci's voice the day before, I'd known that she and David had gotten back together, so to hear her tell me that they were getting married didn't surprise me at all. But to hear that David wanted me to be in the wedding? For some reason, that caught me off guard.

I looked at her for a long moment. She bit her lip.

"You haven't told him about us yet, have you?"

She reluctantly shook her head.

"Why not?"

"I ... I was going to," she insisted, "and I *am* going to, but there's just been a lot going on. I haven't had the chance."

"Uh-huh."

"I'm going to," she said again.

"Tell him about us and I'll bet he won't even want me *at* the wedding, much less *in* it."

"No," she said, shaking her head. "That's not true. You're one of his best friends – nothing's going to change that."

I looked at her doubtfully, but decided not to argue with her.

We surveyed each other quietly for a moment.

"Are you happy?" I finally asked.

She nodded and I believed her.

"Good."

She gave me a small, thankful smile.

"What about you?" she asked.

"What about me?"

"Are *you* happy?"

"Yep," I nodded. "I'm doing great."

I could tell that she badly wanted to believe that.

"Have you ... have you been seeing anyone?" she asked hesitantly, taking a sip of water.

"No," I said, shaking my head.

"Why not?" She sounded disappointed.

"I told you I was going to wait for you, and you *know* I've been waiting for you. That's why you came here to tell me in person."

It was then that she finally dropped her eyes to her lap. When she looked back at me, they were full of tears.

"I'm so sorry, Tanner."

"Don't worry about it," I said, shaking my head. "It's okay. You got things worked out now, right? I'll start looking for someone else as soon as you're out the door."

She didn't smile.

I reached across the table and took her hand, giving it a squeeze. She nodded slightly, blinking back more tears.

"It's okay," I told her again.

"There's someone perfect out there for you, Tanner," she finally said. "I know there is."

"Sure there is," I agreed, nodding at her. "Don't worry about a thing."

Snow had covered the sidewalks by the time I finally got out of the restaurant, and every step I took was precarious. It took me a long time to get back to my dorm and – when I finally did – I lowered myself down into my desk chair and opened the top drawer, pulling out the latest bottle of prescription medication I'd been sent home with from the hospital. I gave it a shake, confirming what I already knew. It was almost full.

I'd always had a high tolerance for pain. Even when I was younger, the pain of workouts and tackles and injuries had rarely fazed me, and these past four surgeries and months of therapy hadn't been any exception. I had filled every prescription for pain medication that I'd been given, just in case I needed them, but I hadn't taken more than a couple out of any bottle.

Now I reached into my top desk drawer and pulled each of them out slowly, lining them up before me.

I opened the bottles and carefully poured them out until I had a tiny mountain of pills in front of me. Then I stared at them for a long, long time.

Until this very moment, I had always had the desire to go on.
I had always had some kind of *hope*.
But now I had no hope.
No future.
Football was gone . . .
Laci was gone . . .
I continued to stare at my mountain of pills.

I had always heard that people who are suicidal don't think about anything except how to make their pain stop: that they aren't able to think things through. But a year before he'd killed himself, my dad had bought two life insurance policies that would pay off even if the cause of death was suicide . . .

He had obviously thought things through.
And *I* was certainly thinking them through now . . .
Like father, like son, I guess.

I thought about Chase and Jordan and about how screwed up they were going to be if I killed myself like Dad had done. I thought about my mom, too.

But mostly I thought about Laci.
What would it do to her if I killed myself?

At the restaurant, she had been trying hard to downplay what had gone on between the two of us so that we could both move on with our lives, but she knew in her heart how much I loved her.

If I killed myself?
She'd know exactly why I had done it.
There would be no doubt in her mind.
And then what?

Then she'd spend the rest of her life, trying to live with that guilt. Even if she did manage to put on a brave face, she would still be weighed down with another deep sorrow inside of her.

And I could never do that to Laci.

Although I wanted to be with her and I wanted to love her and hold her and spend the rest of my life with her, I wanted her to be happy even more. I wanted Laci to have a lifetime of peace and joy and love – all of those things – even if it wasn't going to be me who was going to give them to her.

But how was I going to pull myself together enough to make that happen?

I slowly scooped up my mountain of pills and put them back into their bottles. All except for one. I took that one and held it between my fingers, rolling it back and forth, looking at it for a very long time.

Knee injuries and knee surgery can be very painful and the drugs they give you do a good job of taking the edge off.

That was what I needed right now . . . something to take the edge off.

After a long time, I popped the pill into my mouth, and swallowed it down without a drink.

And six hours later, I took the edge off again.

~ ~ ~

A YEAR AND a half earlier, in my junior year, right after my first surgery, a guy from the third floor had come knocking on my door. His name was William, but for some reason, everybody always called him "Bass", and it was common knowledge that he was a dealer. I hadn't known him very well back then, but I'd let him into my room just the same.

"What'd they send you home with?" he had asked, not beating around the bush about why he was there. I'd showed him the bottle.

"Doesn't look like you're taking too many," he'd noted, giving it a shake.

I had shrugged at him. "I'm doing alright," I'd said nonchalantly.

He'd nodded, trying to act as if he were impressed.

"Popular," he'd said, tapping the bottle. "You could supplement your scholarship nicely with these."

"Thanks," I'd said, reaching over and taking the bottle back from him, "but I'm good."

"Suit yourself," he had shrugged, and he'd shown himself out the door without another word.

Now, three weeks after Laci had told me that she and David were getting married, and I'd decided that I'd needed something to help take the edge off, I lay on my bed, thinking about that visit. Next to me, on the mini-fridge, was the only remaining bottle from my mountain of pills.

I picked it up and looked inside, knowing exactly what I would find.

Two.

I sighed, put the lid back on the bottle and finally sat up on the edge of the bed. I got to my feet, hobbled down the hall to the elevator and rode to the third floor. I hobbled down that hall too, and knocked on a door. It opened slowly.

92

"Finally need some money?" Bass asked with a casual smile. He didn't seem surprised to see me at all.

"No," I said, shaking my head.

"Oh," he said knowingly, looking at me for a moment. "You need *more.*"

This time I nodded at him, and he let me in.

~ ~ ~

ACTUALLY I DID need money, too. I needed it *bad* – especially once I started making weekly trips to the third floor to visit my new best friend.

Mom couldn't give me any because it was all she could do to keep the bills paid and food on the table. (The two big life insurance policies that Dad had bought weren't going to pay out anything as long as Chase and I were the only ones who knew that Dad was dead.)

I went down to Student Services and asked about their work study program, but the nice young lady there told me that there weren't any positions available this late in the year.

I thanked her and started to go, but then she hastily suggested that I try the bulletin board near the elevators.

"We let businesses post openings there," she explained. "They usually get scooped up pretty fast, but it wouldn't hurt to look."

I thanked her again and headed over to the elevators. I was walking with just my leg brace now . . . no crutches.

There were actually a couple of jobs posted. One of them in particular caught my eye.

It was for a local nursing home and they needed an orderly.

Cleaning out bedpans was not high on my list of things to do, but they said in the ad: *Must be able to lift 60 pounds, unassisted.*

I could lift sixty pounds with one hand . . .

I decided to give them a call.

My job at the nursing home mostly consisted of helping patients get into and out of their wheelchairs, onto and off of the toilet, into and out of bed . . . you get the idea. Of course I also did plenty of diaper changing and spoon feeding, along with a lot of cleaning up a variety of semi-solids, but I'd rather not get into that right now.

94

Surprisingly, I loved working there. I was dealing with patients all the time, and while I was helping them, I got to know them. It was fun to talk with them and try to imagine what they had been like when they were my age. Many of them were starved for company. All they wanted was for someone to listen to them and to pay a bit of attention to them, and I was happy to be the one to do it. Their eyes would light up when I came into their room, and the nurses said that some of them sat in the hallway looking for me on my days off.

My favorite resident was named Annabeth. She wasn't even eighty years old yet, but she had Alzheimer's disease and her husband had finally realized he couldn't take care of her anymore after she'd disappeared from their home and the police had found her, sixteen hours later, sleeping under a semi at a truck stop.

Annabeth didn't remember me from day to day or look for me on my days off, but she still loved to talk to me whenever I stopped in her room to see her. Every day, she would sweetly ask me to remove her ID bracelet from her wrist, and then curse like a sailor when I patiently explained to her that I couldn't. She had a baby doll with a car seat and high chair and she would insist on brushing its hair whenever I brushed hers.

Sometimes Annabeth would get agitated. She often complained that there was gum in her mouth and that she couldn't get it out. She would reach her fingers under her tongue and then pull them out again, asking for a trashcan in which to put the gum that only she could see. She would reach her fingers into her mouth again and again, trying to get rid of whatever it was that she was feeling and that was bothering her so much.

Other times, she would insist that her hands were tangled up in fishing line. She would relentlessly pull at the invisible line, winding it up into a ball, and then reach out, asking me to take it from her.

On days when she sat in the lobby that faced the parking lot, Annabeth worried constantly that someone was breaking into her car.

"You don't have a car here," I would tell her as she pointed at some unseen man and yelled at him to leave her property alone.

Sometimes she would tell me that he was sitting in her car, stealing quarters from the console.

"It's a hundred and five degrees out there!" I exclaimed. "Nobody's sitting in anybody's car!"

One day, Annabeth was worried about "her" red Honda, that happened to belong to Robin, the supervising nurse on duty. I left

Annabeth and found Robin, asking her for the keys to her car. After I took Annabeth out to the parking lot to show her that the car was empty, I had to unlock the door and open it up to prove to her that no one was inside.

"He's right there," she insisted, pointing at the empty driver's seat.

I sat down in the seat.

"Look," I said. "There's no one here."

"Yes, there is," she said adamantly.

"How can *I* be sitting here if *he's* sitting here?" I asked, exasperated.

"He's very, very small," she answered.

"How'd that go?" Robin asked with a smile when I brought her back her keys.

I rolled my eyes at her.

"You're not going to be able to convince her of anything," Robin told me. "You might as well quit trying."

"But she gets so upset," I complained. "I can't just let her sit there yelling at the parking lot."

"Reassure and redirect," Robin said.

"What?"

"Reassure her that everything's okay," Robin explained, "and then redirect her attention elsewhere."

"I've tried to take her somewhere else to get her mind off of it," I said, "but she doesn't want to leave."

"That's because you're not reassuring her first. You've got to convince her that everything's going to be okay, and *then* get her mind off of it."

Reassure and redirect.

That was all fine and well, but you couldn't just *tell* Annabeth that everything was okay, you had to *convince* her that everything was okay – like Robin had said.

The next time the imaginary car burglar was back in the parking lot, I went up to the window and put my face to it, looking in the same direction that Annabeth was pointing.

"I'll put a stop to that," I told her dramatically, turning around to face her. "Let's get you down the hall so you can get your teeth brushed, and while you're doing that, I'll come back here and take care of things!"

After I'd deposited her in front of her sink, left for a moment to let her rinse and spit, and then returned, Annabeth was still worried about it, so I again marched purposefully out of the room, picked up old man Berkman's breakfast tray from beside his bed, and walked down to the dining room to deposit it. When I was finished with that, I strode back in to Annabeth's room again, brushing my hand together as if I had just finished an important task.

"Everything is great now," I told her.

"It is?"

"Yep."

I don't think she had any idea what I was talking about.

I liked working at the nursing home so much, that at one point I even considered changing my major and becoming a geriatric nurse or something like that. But the middle of your last semester in college isn't a great time to change your major (especially when your school isn't about to pay for you to *not* play football anymore and your dad's life insurance policy is worthless since no one knows he's dead and what little money you *do* have is being spent on black market prescription pain medications), so I just stuck with my plans to graduate in the spring with a degree in athletic sciences and a teaching certificate.

One week that May, I was offered a job teaching PE at my old junior high school, starting the following fall. I made arrangements to live on campus for one final summer in exchange for helping out with high school football camps so that I could still visit Bass on a regular basis, and I told the nursing home that I wouldn't be leaving until August.

And then I went to David and Laci's wedding.

~ ~ ~

DAVID AND LACI got married a week before I graduated and, just as Laci had warned, David asked me to be one of his groomsmen.

It would make him and Laci very happy, he told me, so I told him that I'd love to. Then he told me that Mike was going to be a groomsman too . . .

It sure was a good thing I had something to take the edge off.

Getting through that weekend was one of the most difficult things I've ever had to do. By the time we got to the restaurant for the rehearsal dinner, I wanted to take enough pills to go catatonic. Instead, however, I settled for sneaking away to the bar while dessert was being served.

I had just finished my fourth shot of bourbon when Laci found me.

"I thought you'd left," she said, worriedly.

"No," I answered, shaking my head. "I'll be back in there in a little bit."

She looked at me and I glanced at the bartender, tapping my empty shot glass to let him know that I wanted another. He nodded and I looked back toward Laci.

"Tanner . . ." she said, even more worriedly.

"Don't start," I warned.

"I'm not," she said, shaking her head. She looked at me for another long moment. "I need to tell you something," she finally said.

"Oh boy," I said dryly as the bartender set a full shot glass down in front of me. "This outta be good."

She watched as I slugged down my drink and then she climbed up in the stool next to me. I stared at the empty glass while Laci waited for me to look her way . . . which I didn't.

"What?" I finally asked.

98

"It's stupid," she began. "You probably won't even remember what I'm talking about . . ."

"I remember everything," I told her.

Out of the corner of my eye, I could see her look down at her lap.

"What?" I asked again, a bit more kindly, finally looking at her.

"Remember that song we used to listen to?" she asked.

"Our song? *Kneeling Before You?*"

"Yeah," she nodded, and then she looked at her lap once more.

"What about it?"

"Well," she said, raising her eyes reluctantly, "we're playing it tomorrow at the wedding."

I looked at her for a moment.

"Oh," I finally said, turning away again.

"David wanted it," she explained hastily. "It turns out that he always liked it too and he wanted us to play it, and . . ."

I nodded dumbly at my empty glass.

"And I just thought I should tell you," she finished miserably.

I avoided looking at her for another very long moment.

"Thank you," I finally said, turning toward her. "I'm glad you let me know."

She nodded at me and then said, quietly, "I'm sorry."

"It's okay," I said, shaking my head. "Don't worry about it. It's fine."

She looked at me uncertainly.

"It's fine," I assured her again, and then I nodded toward the private dining room where her rehearsal dinner was going on without her. I said softly, "Go on."

She looked at me for another moment, gave me a little nod, and then got down off her stool.

"Laci?" I asked as she started to turn away.

She turned back to me.

"He still doesn't know, does he?"

She shook her head.

"No," she answered in a tiny voice. "Not yet."

"Why not?"

"I don't know," she said, shrugging uncomfortably. "I've hardly even seen him since we got engaged and I just haven't had the chance to tell him yet."

She looked at me.

"I should have," she finally sighed. "I should have told him that I didn't want that song played and I should have told him why. I'm sorry."

"No," I said, "that's not it . . . I can deal with the song, but . . ."

I looked at her meaningfully.

"I'm going to tell him," she insisted. "As soon as we get down to Mexico and get settled, I'll tell him. I just need to find the right time."

I nodded at her and then gave her the small, reassuring smile I knew she needed to see. She looked at me for a moment and gave me one back. Then she turned and walked away.

I watched after her as she went, and once she was gone, I turned back to the bartender, and signaled for him to bring me another drink.

~ ~ ~

I MADE IT through the wedding the next day somehow, and once the happy couple set off to start their new life together, I headed toward my truck. I was surprised when I reached it to find Mike leaning against it, since the two of us had managed to pretty much ignore each other for the past twenty-four hours.

I stopped short when I saw him, unsure what to say.

"How you doing, Tanner?" he asked.

I won't repeat what I said, but essentially I told him that I was absolutely fantastic.

"That's about what I figured," he said, managing a smile. Then he offered, "You wanna go get a drink?"

I eyed him suspiciously for a moment, but then decided to accept.

"I've been worried about you," Mike told me after we'd taken seats at a nearby bar. He was having iced tea. I was having more of what I'd had yesterday.

"Why's that?" I asked, although I really didn't care.

"I dunno," he shrugged. "I know this has to have been hard on you."

"What?" I asked. "Watching the only woman I've ever loved marry somebody else? Why would that be hard on me?"

He shot me a look that was somewhere between sympathetic and reproachful.

"You know," he said, "God has a plan for your life, too . . ."

"Oh, of course He does," I said. "It's just that the plan He has for my life happens to *suck*, that's all."

"It doesn't have to suck."

"Oh really?" I asked. "Let me guess. This is the part where you tell me that if I drop down on my knees and ask *Jesus* into my heart that everything's going to get all better."

"Not necessarily," he said, "but I think you'd be a lot happier . . ."

"You think I'm not happy?"

He looked at me doubtfully.

"Stick around," I said, tapping my empty glass on the bar to signal the bartender. "I can get to happy real fast."

"All I'm trying to tell you," Mike began, "is that God loves you and He wants to be a part of your life . . ."

"Ohhh," I said. "Is *that* what's going on? So He's been systematically taking away everything in my life that's ever meant anything to me because He *loves* me? Oh, I see now. Got it. Thanks."

"That's not how God works—" Mike began.

"You know what?" I said, cutting him off. "I really don't care how God works."

Mike pressed his lips together and looked at me unhappily. He stopped trying to talk to me about God, and in exchange, I decided to quit hating him quite so much for essentially ruining my life.

It wasn't entirely his fault, after all . . .

The God that Mike was so keen on had quite a bit to do with it too.

~ ~ ~

BY THE TIME I started my job at my old junior high school as a PE teacher, I had a problem.

Of course, actually I'd had a problem for a long time *before* I'd started my new job, but now it was an even bigger one because, basically, I couldn't get through the day without taking twice the amount of pills that any sane doctor would have ever prescribed for anyone. My dealer was over an hour away now and I drove back to Central once a month to get stocked up, but Bass was set to graduate in December, and he told me that he was moving out of state.

Like I said . . . I had a problem

I had attempted twice in the past to get clean, but both attempts had been equally unsuccessful, for different reasons.

One time I had tried to quit cold turkey and had only lasted for about ten hours before I'd caved.

The other time, when I'd tried to wean myself, I'd had slightly better success, actually getting to the point where I was only taking two pills a day.

But then I got word from the newlyweds that they were expecting their first child, and suddenly I had the need to take the edge off more than ever . . .

I needed help, and I knew it, but being that I was a brand new teacher, it wasn't as if I could check myself into a rehab place for a couple of weeks or anything like that. A doctor probably could have helped me, but I wasn't sure who to go see. If they knew that I was a teacher, would they be legally obligated to turn me in or were they bound by laws of confidentiality? I didn't know the answer to that one and I was scared to find out. I thought about calling Mike and asking him for help, but I was pretty sure that I wasn't ready to go there yet.

I already knew a lot of the teachers at the junior high school because they had been there when I'd been a student, but one of them, Kenneth, I knew because we had played football together in high school. He'd been a senior when I'd made the varsity team as a freshman, and now he was our School Resource Officer. He was always going on and on about how the kids could come and talk to him anytime they wanted and that anything they told him would remain completely confidential. I figured he could give me some advice on what to do, and I somehow felt that I could trust him.

When I went in to Kenneth's office and closed the door, he invited me to sit down and then he listened to me carefully. I started out by explaining about my surgeries and then glossed over the part about my dad, my career, and Laci by simply telling him, "I went through kind of a rough time."

He nodded understandingly as I told him how I'd started taking the pills just so I could get through each day and how, after my prescriptions had run out, I'd turned to Bass.

"But I can't keep driving up there every month," I explained. "Plus he's getting ready to graduate next month and then he's moving to Florida."

"I gotcha," he assured me. "I know why you're here."

Good.

"So can you help me?" I asked. "I really didn't know who else to talk to."

"Of course I can help you," Kenneth said. "I can get you whatever you want."

I surprised myself by how fast I jumped at his offer.

I guess I wasn't quite as ready to get help as I'd thought I was. What I was, however, was an expert at knowing exactly how many pills I could take while still remaining fully functional. During those times when I felt the need for more than what I knew I should take, alcohol was always there, waiting to help me out in any way it could. It didn't matter if it was a school day or not, there was never a time that I wasn't under the influence of something. And no one knew. No one could tell that the only way I was able to function was if I kept popping my little wonder pills. I kept things well under control . . . that is until David and Laci came home to have their baby.

Neither David nor Laci nor Mike noticed how desensitized I was on the night the four of us went out to eat. This, in and of itself, was pretty remarkable, considering that it had taken a *lot* – even for me – to be able to get me to the point where I could pretend that I was happy for them. But like I said, I was pretty much an expert.

I very much still wanted for Laci to feel joy and love and peace, and I actually wanted that for David too. I can honestly say that I truly wanted both of them to be happy. The thing was, however, that I couldn't bring myself to manage to *be* happy for them. I couldn't look at Laci's bulging stomach (indisputable proof that she'd finally had sex) with anything other than disdain. I couldn't feel anything toward that baby but bitterness.

I didn't want to feel that way, but I did.

So of course, the next day – when Laci's baby died – I couldn't feel anything but guilt.

~ ~ ~

YOU'RE PROBABLY FIGURING that at this point, I got so loaded that I almost died, hit rock bottom, and eventually sought the help that I so desperately needed.

If that's what you're thinking, you're right . . . on two accounts.

I *did* get so loaded that I almost died and I *did* hit rock bottom.

I did not, however, seek help.

And when help sought me, I ignored it.

The day before the baby's funeral, Mike came to my house. Maybe I hadn't been hiding my addiction as well as I thought I'd been, or maybe Mike just knew me well enough to know that I wasn't going to handle things well.

I'm not sure.

All I know is that when Mike didn't get an answer at my front door, he let himself in and found me nearly comatose. He gathered up all the pill bottles he could find, loaded me into his car, and drove me to the hospital, staying with me until they extracted what they could from my system and counteracted the rest. Then he drove me home and spent the night on my couch after dumping me on my bed so that I could sleep off what was left in my body.

Like I said, he had gathered up what he could find, but he hadn't found it all. The first thing I did when I pulled myself out of bed the next morning was to start getting some medicine back into my body so that I could function once again.

"You're going to kill yourself," Mike told me as I stood at the sink with a glass of water in my trembling hand.

"No, I'm not," I argued. "I would never do that."

"You almost did it yesterday!" he cried.

106

"Yesterday was an accident," I said, walking over to the couch. "I'm usually very careful."

"Do you know what it's going to do to Laci if you kill yourself?" he asked.

"Yes, I know what it would do to her!" I yelled. Didn't he know that that was the only reason I was still here at all? "I'm not going to let it happen again. I'll be fine."

"You need help," he said, shaking his head at me as he put on his coat. Then he went on, more to himself than to me. "But if there's one thing I've learned, it's that you can't help somebody if they don't want it."

With that, he turned to go. He stopped when he got to the door and looked back at me with sorrow in his eyes.

"I will help you," he said carefully, "any way I can. All you've gotta do is ask."

I looked up at him, but I didn't answer or even give him a nod.

Then he left.

I was at rock bottom when David and Laci went back to Mexico, and I stayed that way for almost two years. I knew that I needed to pull myself together, but *deciding* that you're going to pull yourself together and actually *pulling* yourself together are two entirely different things – particularly when you're as thoroughly addicted to something as I was by that point.

It didn't help matters any that Laci had three miscarriages over the next two years. Each time I found out about one of them it gave me one more excuse not to quit.

I managed to keep myself alive, but just barely. I couldn't go more than a few hours without taking something, even though I tried to quit almost daily. The need to feed my addiction or to deaden the pain was just too much.

One of those two things got me every time.

I hated that I couldn't get through a day without pills and I hated that my entire life revolved around getting my next fix.

Despite everything, though, I still managed to function amazingly well, and no one had any idea that my life had fallen apart.

I transferred to a position at the high school as the new head football coach and we had a winning season my very first year out. The next year, we went all the way to the State Championship Game, and when we won that, everyone was saying I had the Midas touch.

From the outside, everything looked just great.

On the inside, though, I was good as dead . . .

And it was going to take a miracle for me to ever start living again.

~ ~ ~

MY MIRACLE HAPPENED on the Monday following the State Championship game. I got up, showered and dressed, and spent the day teaching like I always did. With football season finally over, I was home by four-thirty in the afternoon for the first time since school had started back.

In addition to using pills to keep my mind off things, staying busy helped a lot too. Not being on my regular practice schedule and not having anything else lined up to do was probably why I was dreading my afternoon and evening a little more than usual, and that was probably why I *took* a little more than usual, too.

I loaded my dog into the truck and we went for a long walk in the park and then I came home and put a frozen pizza in the oven. I turned on the television, hoping to find something that would keep my mind occupied for at least another hour – the earliest I was going to allow myself to have another pill – and that was when my phone rang.

It was Mike.

We hadn't spoken since the baby's funeral. I couldn't imagine why he would be calling me now.

I turned off the television.

"Hello?"

"Are you sitting down?" he asked.

I had actually been *lying* down, but now I sat up to take in whatever he had to tell me.

"Yeah," I said. "What's wrong?"

"It's Laci," he answered quietly.

And then he told me.

Laci had cancer.

Cancer.

Mike had found out from his mom, who had gotten a phone call from Mrs. White.

He didn't know what kind of cancer, maybe uterine or ovarian, but he wasn't sure. He'd left a message for David to call him, but he hadn't heard anything back yet.

"I think they're coming home tomorrow," Mike told me.

"They're coming home?"

"Yeah," he said. "For her treatments."

Treatments.

"Are you okay?" he finally asked when I was silent for a moment.

"Yeah," I managed to answer.

"I'll call you as soon as I talk to Dave," he offered.

"Yeah," I said again. "Do that."

And I closed my phone.

Please don't do this . . .
Please don't take her . . .
Please save her . . .
I promise I'll never take another pill again . . .
I will do anything . . .
Please don't take her . . .

I had started out sitting on the couch, but before long I was on my knees, on the floor, crying out to God.

I don't know how long I kneeled there, begging Him to save her life, but when I finally finished, I was completely spent.

I sat on the floor, slumped against the couch, my mind as clear as it had been in months.

I looked at my phone and realized that it had been over an hour since Mike had called.

Time for another pill.

My phone rang again and I looked at the screen.

Mike.

I opened it as fast as I could.

"Mike," I breathed.

"Listen," he said, "I just talked to David."

"What did he say?" I asked quickly, getting back onto the couch. "How's Laci?"

110

"It's not anywhere near as bad as I was afraid," he said. "It's not uterine cancer *or* ovarian cancer."

"What is it?"

"Her last pregnancy was what they call a 'molar pregnancy'," he explained. "There was never really a baby there . . . it was a mass of cells that started developing abnormally."

"So . . . so she doesn't have cancer?"

"No, she *does* have cancer, but it's not uterine or ovarian cancer."

I didn't say anything.

"I looked it up," he went on. "It's treatable."

"How treatable?"

"Very treatable."

"What'll they do?" I asked.

"She's coming home for some chemo and I think that's about it. No surgery or radiation or anything."

I was quiet again.

"It's very treatable," he repeated, "and they caught it early. She's probably even going to be able to try to have another baby. I think she's going to be okay."

I closed my eyes.

"You there?" Mike asked.

"Yeah."

"You okay?"

"Yeah."

"Alright," he said. "Well . . . I just wanted to let you know."

"Thank you."

"She's going to be okay," he said quietly, one more time.

"Okay," I said, nodding and opening my eyes. And then we hung up.

The last time I had prayed to God like that had been on a rainy night, five years earlier. It had been that night that I'd made Him a million promises, begging Him to not let Laci break up with me. That had been the night He'd given me such a conviction that I was going to marry Laci one day . . .

We all knew how well that had turned out, but I hadn't exactly kept my end of the deal either. And that was when I realized exactly what I had just done . . . what kind of promise I had just made to God . . . what was going to happen when I broke it . . .

When I broke it, not if . . .

Because there was no way I was ever going to be able to keep this one.

I set the phone down next to me and looked toward the kitchen. I hesitated for a second, but then I stood up and walked out there, crossing over to the sink and picking up the bottle that was sitting on the counter. I went back into the living room, down the hall, and into the bathroom. I opened the bottle and dumped its contents into the toilet.

I opened the medicine cabinet and pulled out two more bottles and did the same with those.

I dumped all the empty containers into the trash.

I went to the truck and got another bottle out of the console and one out of the glove compartment and then I fished one out of my gym bag that was in the garage.

After I'd flushed all of those pills I got in my truck and drove to school. I took care of what was stashed in my desk drawer in the same way, and then I went back out to my truck and sat in the parking lot for a long time, thinking, trying to remember if I was forgetting to look any place else. When I finally decided that I wasn't, I drove back home, and sat back down on my couch.

And I waited.

I waited for my mind to convince myself that I needed to pick up the phone and call Kenneth.

I waited for my body to start screaming for more drugs.

I waited for myself to break.

But it didn't happen.

I sat there for the longest time, waiting and waiting and waiting for even the slightest craving to wash over me.

It never came.

After a while, I turned on the television.

And while after that, I went to bed.

To quit so suddenly with no help and to not suffer from a single withdrawal symptom is, quite frankly, impossible.

It doesn't happen. It *can't* happen.

But it did happen. It happened to me.

Every craving that I'd ever had – physical or otherwise – was suddenly gone . . . and I never again had another one after that.

At the time I didn't question it.

Maybe I was too busy thinking about Laci or maybe I was too stubborn to acknowledge what I know now is the truth . . .

That God didn't just save Laci that day . . .

He saved me, too.

~ ~ ~

LACI DID WIND up having surgery and – as it turned out – she never would be able to get pregnant again. But her treatments went well, her cancer was gone, and after that, she and David returned to Mexico again.

Once there, they adopted two kids from the orphanage where Laci worked. Whenever they came back to visit I could see in their eyes that they were both happy, and I was pleasantly surprised to find that that actually made *me* happy too.

Meanwhile, back in Cavendish, life went on. Following on the heels of our state championship, I was promoted to Assistant Athletic Director and, with that promotion, came a bunch of new responsibilities. Suddenly I had my hand in every sport that took place at the high school, and I often would spend fourteen straight hours on campus, sometimes six days a week.

This wasn't a bad thing. Something had to replace the pills, and staying busy was just the ticket. Sundays didn't keep me busy at all, so I started working through the rec league too, refereeing football and soccer, baseball and basketball ... whatever it took to keep my mind from settling down and realizing how lonely I was.

I managed to find time to date. I hadn't promised God anything about that, so I almost always had a girlfriend to help keep me busy when one of my jobs didn't. Each one of them, of course, was nothing more than a temporary distraction. I never tried to find someone who would be able to ward off the loneliness for me in a permanent way ... never entertained the idea that someday I might find someone who would be able to replace Laci.

I found that women, in general, were pretty much looking for husband material, and so, with each one that I dated, I made it clear – right from the start – that I was *not* the one.

A good time . . .

Some fun . . .

That's what I'm looking for. I'm not interested in getting married, making babies, or otherwise helping you in your never-ending battle against your biological clock. So, if that's not okay with you, I'll understand if you want to walk away right now.

Some women were just looking for the same thing I was – a temporary diversion against the loneliness.

Some hit the door immediately, thanking me for my honesty, thankful they hadn't wasted their time.

And some hung around for a while, secretly confident that they would be the one to get me to change my mind. Once it became clear to them that they weren't, however, then they would break up with me. *Gently . . . Apologetically . . .* How could they be mad, after all, that it hadn't worked out? I'd been nothing but honest with them, right from the start.

Megan wasn't like that, though.

Megan was different.

Megan lied.

Megan was a mistake.

I met her at the State Employee's Credit Union where she worked as a teller. Like always, I was straight up with her on our first date. She totally sympathized with me.

How unreasonable it would be, she said, *for someone to expect you to change.*

You don't have to worry, she said, *that I'd ever do that.*

All I want, too, she said, *is to have some fun.*

But it turned out that she wanted a lot more than that and once she realized that I really *wasn't* willing to give it to her, she started conniving.

I had some cardinal rules in place to protect myself – like the one about never spending the night.

Sleeping with someone is one thing, but spending the entire night with them is another. It takes things to a whole new level . . . one of more intimacy, one of more familiarity, one that screams: *Commitment!*

And so I never – never, ever – spent the night with anyone.

Until Megan.

She asked if she could stay. Said she was too tired to leave. Did it on a night when I was too tired to argue.

Once a rule has been broken the first time, it's a whole lot easier to break it a second time.

Before I knew it, we were spending almost every night together – either me at her place or her at mine.

It's so much more convenient, she said.

It's so much more practical, she said.

It doesn't mean anything, she said.

By the time I found out that David and Laci were moving home (not coming home, mind you, but *moving* home), Megan and I were living together.

116

~ ~ ~

I HAD BEEN afraid that David and Laci might not want me around their family once they found out that I was officially "living in sin", but they didn't seem too bothered by it. I was glad, because I absolutely *loved* David and Laci's kids. They were almost enough to make me want to have kids of my own . . . *almost*.

Dorito was getting ready to start kindergarten when they moved back to Cavendish and he talked constantly, sharing whatever it was that might be on his little mind at any given time. He was smart and funny and always ready for a good time and he gave me an excuse to be a little kid again myself. Lily was only about a year old. She was beautiful, and always stared at me with wide, dark eyes as if she didn't quite know what to make of me. I would stare right back at her and narrow my eyes menacingly, threatening her with tickling fingers. When a huge smile finally broke across her face, she'd bury her head against Laci's shoulder and peek up periodically to see if I was still there. I was.

I absolutely *loved* David and Laci's kids.

Oh, sorry. I already said that.

I got to keep Dorito for a couple of nights while David and Laci took Lily to Minnesota to have some tests done on her hearing. The first night, after we got back from Chuck E. Cheese's, I helped Dorito do his homework and then pulled out the futon in the office while he brushed his teeth and changed into his pajamas.

"Hop in, bud," I said, patting the bed when he came out of the bathroom.

"You have to read to me," he said as if he couldn't believe I was missing something so obvious.

"Read to you?"

"Yeah."

"Did you bring any books?"

"No," he said, shaking his head back and forth.

"Hmmm," I said, putting my finger to my lips while he looked at me expectantly. "Hang on."

I went into the living room and looked around. Megan had just gotten back from the gym and was in the kitchen, concocting some sort of disgusting-smelling tea.

"Okay," I said when I returned with an outdoor magazine. "I've got something."

I sat down on the futon with him and read an article about salmon fishing in Alaska.

"Doesn't that sound like fun?" I asked him when I'd finished.

"Yeah! Will you take me salmon fishing one day?"

"I'm a teacher, Dorito."

"Teachers can't go salmon fishing?"

"Teachers can't *afford* to go salmon fishing."

"What does 'afford' mean?"

"It means it costs money and I don't have any money."

"Oh," he said, disappointed.

"But, if I ever do go salmon fishing, you can come with me."

"Okay!"

"You ready for bed now?" I asked.

"Now you have to read me the Bible."

"I have to read you the Bible?"

He nodded.

"Did you bring a Bible?"

"No," he said, shaking his head.

"Well, then," I said, "you're outta luck."

"*You don't have a Bible?*" He sounded absolutely incredulous.

"I'm afraid not."

He stared at me with his mouth open.

"How come you don't have a Bible?" he asked in an awed whisper.

"I don't know, Dorito," I said. "I guess I just never ... Oh! Wait! I think I might have one. Hang on!"

I walked over to the closet and opened the door. Up on a shelf was a cardboard box. I heaved it down and set it on the floor.

"What's all this stuff?" Dorito asked as I started going through it.

118

"Just a bunch of junk I don't ever use," I said.

"And your Bible's in here?"

"I think so."

"You ... you keep it with *junk?*" he asked, looking up at me in disbelief.

"Well ... no," I lied. "I think maybe it got put in here by mistake."

"Oh."

"Here it is," I said, pulling it out.

"That's a Bible?"

"Yeah," I said, opening the silver box and taking it out for the first time since high school graduation. "See?"

"Yeah," he said, happily. "Holy Bible."

"Right."

He scrambled back over to the bed.

"What do you want me to read to you?" I asked, sitting down next to him.

"You can just pick one of your favorites," he said.

Right.

I let the Bible flop open and glanced at the top.

Kings.

I scanned down until I came to a passage entitled "The Wise Ruling".

That sounded good enough, so I started reading:

> *Now two prostitutes came to the king ...*

Oops. This probably wasn't exactly something a kindergartener needed to be hearing. I glanced at Dorito, expecting him to ask me what a prostitute was, but he didn't bat an eye, so I decided to keep going and hope for the best:

> *... and stood before him. One of them said, "My lord, this woman and I live in the same house. I had a baby while she was there with me. The third day after my child was born, this woman also had a baby. We were here alone; there was no one in the house but the two of us. During the night this woman's son died because she lay on him."*

Wow. It just kept getting better and better.

I glanced at Dorito again. He seemed to be listening intently so I went on:

> *"So she got up in the middle of the night and took my son from my side while I your servant was asleep. She put him by her breast and put her dead son by my breast. The next morning, I got up to nurse my son — and he was dead! But when I looked at him closely in the morning light, I saw that it wasn't the son I had borne." The other woman said, "No! The living one is my son; the dead one is yours." But the first one insisted, "No! The dead one is yours; the living one is mine."*

Laci and David were never going to let me keep Dorito again ...

> *And so they argued before the king. The king said, "This one says, 'My son is alive and your son is dead,' while that one says, 'No! Your son is dead and mine is alive.'" Then the king said, "Bring me a sword." So they brought a sword for the king. He gave an order: "Cut the living child in two and give half to one and half to the other." The woman whose son was alive was filled with compassion for her son and said to the king, "Please my lord, give her the living baby! Don't kill him!" But the other said, "Neither I nor you shall have him. Cut him in two!" Then the king gave his ruling: "Give the baby to the first woman. Do not kill him; she is his mother." When all Israel heard the verdict the king had given, they held the king in awe, because they saw that he had wisdom from God to administer justice.*

I looked down at Dorito and he looked up at me.

"That's one of my favorites, too," he smiled.

"Oh, really?" I chuckled.

"Yeah. My real mom was like that."

Like what? A prostitute?

"Oh, really?"

120

"Uh-huh," he nodded matter-of-factly. "She couldn't take care of me so she let my mommy and daddy have me."

I stared at him.

"If you really love somebody," he went on, "then you want what's best for them ... even if it means you have to let somebody else have them. Right?"

I looked at him for a moment, and then smiled, and wrapped my arm around his little body.

"Right," I said as he smiled back at me. "That's absolutely right."

When I came out of the office, Megan was watching TV. I sat down next to her on the couch and put my arm around her.

"Get him all tucked in?" she asked.

"Um-hmm," I nodded.

"You're really good with him," she observed.

"He's a good kid," I smiled.

"You'd make a really good father," she said.

I didn't answer, I just kept watching TV.

I'd make a really good father? Where had *that* come from?

I continue keeping my eyes glued to the television, but something about that statement – and the wistful way she'd made it – caught my attention. Something inside of me clicked.

And if you ask me, that was the moment that our relationship started going downhill.

Of course we weren't even supposed to be having a *relationship* ... we were supposed to be having a *good time*. But the more I thought about it, the more I realized that Megan was way more invested in our relationship than I was and that I was going to be hard pressed to get rid of her if I tried. All of her stuff was in my house and she'd actually gotten rid of her own apartment. If I wanted to start dating someone else, how exactly was that supposed to happen?

The more I thought about it, the more trapped I felt and the more trapped I felt, the more I started looking for ways to get out.

I was subtle at first, but as the months went by I became more and more desperate to get rid of Megan. And as I did, it seemed that she became more and more desperate to stay.

By early summer, I had finally decided that I was just going to have to man up and give her the boot. That's when she dropped a bombshell on me.

"I'm pregnant."

"You're *what*?"

"You heard me," she said. "I'm pregnant."

"How can you be pregnant?" I yelled. "You're on the pill!"

"It's not a hundred percent effective, you know!"

"Yeah, right," I scoffed. I had long ago worried that she might pull something like this – so much so that I'd started checking her pill dispenser every night. They'd always disappeared on a regular basis, but how hard is it to throw a pill down the toilet once a day?

"What's *that* supposed to mean?" she cried angrily.

I couldn't even answer her. I just glared at her, and then stormed out of the house.

I went to the high school, went into the batting cage, and fired up the pitching machine. I slugged away for an hour, taking it out on every ball that came my way. After I'd calmed down a bit (and broken two bats) I went back home.

"What do you want to do?" I asked her after we were sitting down together on the couch.

"I want to keep it," she said quietly.

"Okay," I nodded. "I'll do whatever needs to be done . . . I'll help you in any way that I can."

She gave me a little smile.

"Thank you," she said, reaching for my hand.

"But," I went on, pulling my hand away from hers, "I want you to move out. You need to find a place of your own."

"What?"

"This isn't working," I said, pointing my finger between the two of us. "It's over and you need to move out."

"You're breaking up with me NOW?" she cried "Now that I'm pregnant, you're going to kick me out?"

"I don't think we should stay together just because of the baby, do you?" I asked. "I don't think that's going to be good for anyone."

She glared at me.

"I'll do whatever I need to do to help you," I reminded her, "and I'll be there for the baby, too."

"Don't do me any favors," she said coldly, and she left the room.

Even though things were really bad between us, she did at least let me help her move out. Of course I didn't blame her for being upset with me, but if the two of us were going to raise a child together, we were going to have to figure out a way to work with each other, and so I tried to make peace with her as best I could. I called her every couple of days to see how she was doing. I had her rotors turned when she mentioned that her car was vibrating whenever she braked. I brought her Chinese take-out one night when she said she wasn't feeling well. I did the dishes for her one Saturday when I stopped by with a chair that I thought she could use in her new living room.

One evening, I took a bag of groceries over to her new apartment. She answered the door, red-eyed.

"What's wrong?" I asked.

"I lost the baby," she replied, taking the groceries from me.

"What do you mean?"

"I mean I had a miscarriage," she said angrily. "It's a pretty self-explanatory statement."

I stared at her, unsure what to say.

"What can I do?" I finally asked.

"You've done enough already," she said, and then she closed the door in my face.

One night, a couple of months after Megan had moved out, I suddenly had a crazy idea.

What if Megan hadn't really lost the baby?

I had, of course, already wondered if she'd gotten pregnant on purpose. I had also wondered if she'd lied to me about being pregnant in the first place – planning on claiming a miscarriage after a wedding band was securely around her finger.

Now I wondered if she'd just *told* me that she'd lost the baby so that she could go off and have it by herself without me being able to have any say in anything . . .

That thought stayed with me and bothered me long enough that I finally had to do something about it. One day I parked a block from her bank (which I had taken all of my money out of as soon as we'd broken up and hadn't been back to since) and then I went into the diner across the street. I waited until the bank closed and she finally came out to her car.

I looked closely. Very closely, and very carefully.

And I was surprised at the disappointment I felt when I saw how flat her stomach was.

~ ~ ~

JORDAN, MEANWHILE, WAS having baby troubles of his own in a way.

The previous spring, Jordan had started dating Greg's little sister, Charlotte White. Immediately I was worried for him.

Jordan was such a good kid – compassionate... kind... thoughtful... innocent. But Charlotte? Not so much.

Don't get me wrong, I could see why Jordan liked her and everything. She was pretty and smart and fun, but I was at the high school now and I saw what kind of a girl Charlotte was. And I knew that she wasn't his type

Every day Charlotte barely met the dress code, and most days I was surprised that the same person who had raised the chaste and upright Greg would let Charlotte out of the house wearing what she did (although probably what was happening was that she was dressing one way at home and then changing clothes as soon as she got to school). I knew for a fact that she was smoking and drinking, and – based on the way she acted – I figured she was sleeping around too...

Of course David didn't see any of this because Charlotte had always had David completely snowed and tightly wrapped around her little finger. She was Greg's sister and he refused to see anything in her other than that. Jordan, apparently, didn't see it either.

But I saw it. And I knew that Charlotte was the kind of girl *I* would have dated in high school... not the kind of girl that Jordan should date.

From the time he was a little kid, Jordan had always been different. He was quiet and introspective. He could be fun too and was usually up for anything that I suggested, but he wasn't always looking for trouble the way it seemed that Chase (and I) always were.

When Jordan was really little he would say his bedtime prayers out loud, and even then I couldn't believe how heartfelt and personal he was when he talked to God. That was when I'd realized that it wasn't just my friends who had some kind of a connection with God that I was clearly missing.

Even after Jordan stopped praying out loud, it was obvious that he still had something special with God and that that something was very important to him. Just like my friends, Jordan always played out his faith in ways that continually amazed me. Unlike the rest of my family, he *wanted* to go to church . . . and he was forever looking for ways to help other people. Every morning when he left the house to go catch the bus, he would walk across the street to the Parker's house first. They were an older couple in our neighborhood, whose kids were already grown, and Jordan would take the paper off their lawn and put it up on the porch for them so that they wouldn't have to go down the steps to get it in the morning.

He had missed baseball practice one day – something that was practically unheard of for him – because he had found a stray basset hound near the school. She'd clearly had puppies recently and Jordan called the number on her collar and left a message, telling them where he was and that he would wait there for them until they could come and pick her up. When he didn't show up for dinner, mom and I tracked him down and found him sitting in the dark, on the curb, still waiting. We loaded both him and the dog up and drove to the animal shelter, putting her into one of the after-hours cages that locked once you closed the door. We called the owner's number again and left them a new message, telling them where their dog was now, but he still cried for the rest of the night. And when a robin hit the dining room window and broke its neck, Jordan buried it in the back yard – and cried again then, too.

One time, in a rec league game, he'd tried to steal second base when there were two outs in the ninth inning. The umpire called him safe, but Jordan stood right up and looked him in the eye.

"I was out," he said.

The umpire shook his head. "Safe."

"No, I was out," he insisted. "I got tagged before I hit the base."

"Safe," the umpire said for a third time. I happened to be helping to coach Jordan's team that year, so I headed out to second base, arriving at the same time the head umpire did.

He assessed the situation and explained it to Jordan.

"It doesn't matter if you were safe or out," he told him patiently. "The umpire makes the call and that's what stands."

"But I was out," Jordan said, one more time.

I looked at Jordan and mouthed, "Shut up." He looked like he was about to cry (surprise).

"Safe," the umpire said one last time and they both left us standing there with the second baseman.

"I was out," Jordan whimpered to me.

"Look, Jordan," I said. I really felt like telling him to shut up again, but I also realized that if I wasn't careful he was going to redeem himself by intentionally getting out on the next play or doing something equally stupid like that. "Remember last year when that guy called you out, but you were really safe?"

He nodded.

"But you didn't argue then, right?"

He shook his head.

"It's the same thing here," I told him. "It's the rule of the game. Whatever the umpire calls, you can't argue with it – that's what you have to go by. It's the *rule*. You don't want to break the rules . . . do you?"

I had him and he knew it. He shook his head at me again, very unhappily. Then, a little bit later, he crossed home plate, also very unhappily.

And then we won.

Sheesh.

So, yeah. He drove me nuts sometimes, but deep down, I was really proud of him. You might think that I'm biased just because he's my little brother, but keep in mind that you don't hear me gushing on and on about how great Chase was.

Simply put, Jordan was one of the best people I'd ever known in my life, and Charlotte . . . well, Charlotte wasn't.

And so, when the two of them got together, I was pretty sure that Jordan was going to wind up getting hurt, and, of course, I was exactly right. It turned out that when they'd started dating, Charlotte was already pregnant with her old boyfriend's baby. When Jordan found out and the two of them split, he was really torn up about it. I felt sorry for him, but there wasn't anything I could do. I had a feeling that anything I might try to say to him was going to come out sounding a whole lot like "I told you so," (which I had), so I just left it alone.

The point is, though, that both of us were going through a lot when David and Laci announced that they were going to take Jordan's youth group on a mission trip down to Mexico. When Jordan told me that he was going to go, I decided that I would, too. I guess both of us needed something to help us get our mind off things.

~ ~ ~

WE WERE GONE over Christmas break, and almost everyone brought a lot of presents along to give to the little kids while we were down there.

I only brought one thing. I wasn't sure who to give it to, so I hung on to it until the day we went to the landfill. It was there – when Jordan and I were off by ourselves, taking food to some of the families – that I spotted a little girl standing all by herself, watching us intently as we handed things out. The way she stared at me with her large dark eyes reminded me of Lily so much that I was tempted to go after her with a tickling hand and narrowed eyes in an attempt to get her to smile at me, but I didn't. She was all alone, with no mother's shoulder to bury her face into for safety.

I glanced behind me and made sure that Jordan was busy. I knelt down in front of her and pulled a stuffed animal from the knapsack I was carrying.

"*Hola*," I said. "*¿Cómo estás?*"

She didn't answer me, but kept staring at me with those big, brown eyes. I'd had two years of Spanish, but "Hello. How are you?" was pretty much the extent of what I remembered. I switched to English.

"I have something for you," I said, holding the stuffed animal toward her. It was a little, yellow elephant with a shiny ribbon around its neck. "You can have it if you want it."

I know she didn't speak a word of English, but I could tell she understood exactly what I meant. She glanced at me uncertainly.

"It's okay," I went on. "Take it. I . . . I bought it for somebody a while ago, but they don't need it anymore. I want you to have it."

She took it out of my hands hesitantly.

Once it was in her hands I pointed to the silver key sticking out of its side.

"If you turn that," I said, "it'll make music."

She looked at me.

"Turn it," I said, miming with my hands what I wanted her to do.

She turned it and the elephant emitted one, lone note.

"More," I said, reaching out and showing her what I meant. When I took my hand off the key, the elephant's head started turning gently, and *Jesus Loves Me* began to play. It was the first time I'd turned that key since the day I'd bought it . . . the day Megan had closed the door in my face.

I finally got a smile.

I tried to give her a smile back and then I stood up and patted her on the head.

"*Adios*," I said. She looked up at me, concerned, and tentatively lifted the elephant in my direction.

"No," I said, shaking my head as the tune continued to play. "You can keep it."

She kept standing there, holding it out to me, unsure what I meant.

"I don't need it anymore," I told her, and I turned and walked away.

~ ~ ~

TWO WEEKS AFTER Jordan graduated from high school, our dad's body was found. Chase and I had to act all surprised, but Mom and Jordan didn't need to act at all – they were both legitimately shocked.

And once it was determined that Dad had died from a gunshot wound to the head, Jordan put two and two together and came up with three. He decided that *I* had killed Dad, and then he convinced David of the same thing.

I had never been as ticked as I was the moment I realized David thought I was actually capable of killing my own father and then covering it up for years . . .

I had been not speaking to him for two days when Laci showed up on my doorstep.

"David send you over here to make things right again?" I asked after I'd opened the door.

"He doesn't know I'm here," she said, shaking her head.

"Ahhh," I nodded with a satisfied smile. "Still keeping secrets from him. Nice."

She ignored me. "Can I come in?"

"Whatever." I stepped back so that she could get through the door. She helped herself to a seat on the couch and I took a chair. I noticed for the first time that she was holding a Bible on her lap.

"Here to preach the Word to me?" I asked. "Figure maybe if I'm saved I'll play pretty with your husband?"

"Look," she said, ignoring me again. "I don't have any idea what's going on between you and David, but–"

"He didn't tell you?" I asked, incredulous. She shook her head, and for some reason, I found it very interesting that he hadn't told her anything. I settled back in my chair to hear what she had to say.

"I don't have any idea what's going on," she said again, "but I know you're going through a really hard time right now."

This time it was me who ignored her. I looked away.

"I can't imagine what it's like to lose your dad like that . . ."

I ignored her some more and she sighed helplessly.

"I have something for you," she finally said. I could see her out of the corner of my eye, holding up the Bible. "This was Greg's."

That caught my attention and I looked back at her in spite of myself.

"Why do you have Greg's Bible?" I asked.

"Mrs. White gave it to me a long time ago," she said, "and now I want you to have it."

"I don't want it."

"If you'll read it every day," she pressed on, as if she hadn't heard me, "it'll help you get through this, Tanner."

"What part of 'I don't want it,' don't you understand?"

"I'm trying to help you!" she cried.

"I don't *want* your help."

"What do you want?" she asked.

"I want you to go home and leave me alone."

She pulled back and pressed her lips together and then she stood up – Bible in hand – and gave me a little nod. She headed toward the door, but stopped just before she reached it. She turned back around and looked at me intently.

"I care about you, Tanner," she said carefully. "I've always cared about you."

I didn't answer her.

"And I thought you cared about me, too," she said quietly, and then she turned to go.

It was the closest she had ever come to admitting what had been between us.

"Stop," I said.

She turned around again and looked at me hopefully.

"Give me the stupid thing," I finally said, holding my hand out. She crossed the room and extended the Bible to me. I narrowed my eyes and glared at her, but then – after a moment – took it from her.

132

"Promise me that you'll read it every day," she said quietly.

"Yeah, whatever," I said, waving her away with my hand. "Go on. Go home to your wonderful husband."

She looked at me for another long moment, but then she went to the door again, and this time I didn't stop her when she tried to leave.

~ ~ ~

THE FIRST THING I noticed when I started reading Greg's Bible was that there was writing all through it. It was obvious that Greg had read it a lot and apparently, whenever something stood out to him as important, he would underline it, or draw an arrow to notes that he had made in the margins, along the sides, at the tops, and the bottoms. Often he just wrote about the passage and what he thought it meant or how he felt it applied to something that was going on in his life. Sometimes he wrote about his family or his friends. Not surprisingly, I saw David and Laci's names quite a bit. I found that reading what he had written fascinated me. Often I would spend more time reading what Greg had written than actually reading the Bible.

I tried to start at the beginning, but I got pretty bored, pretty quick. I knew all about Adam and Eve and the genealogies didn't interest me at all. After only a day or two, I tried the first book of the New Testament, but got hit with genealogies right away then as well. I skipped to Mark and had better luck there, so I kept reading it every day, just like I'd promised Laci that I would.

The reading in Mark was more interesting, and Greg had written a lot more here than he had up front. Within only a few days, I realized that I was close to finishing the entire book of Mark.

One day I was surprised to actually find *my* name written in one of the margins. I felt a jolt when I saw it and I reached my hand out, running my finger along the letters that Greg had formed. I looked at the comment he had written. Then I followed the arrow and looked at the passage he had underlined.

And after that, I didn't read anything that Greg had written.

I started using a different Bible, the same one I'd gotten down when Dorito had spent the night months earlier. Once I finished Mark, I started on Luke, which seemed okay until I ran into genealogies again.

The day that our class was holding their ten-year reunion (which I was not going to attend because David was going to be there), I was flipping around again, trying to decide what to read next. I had felt a strange sense of accomplishment when I'd completed the entire book of Mark, and so I decided to find another book in the Bible that I would be able to finish off pretty quickly. A cursory glance of James told me that not only did it not have any genealogies, but that it was also really short. I decided to dive in.

As soon as I reached chapter four, I read the following passage:

What causes fights and quarrels among you? Don't they come from your desires that battle within you? You desire but do not have, so you kill. You covet but you cannot get what you want, so you quarrel and fight. You do not have because you do not ask God.

That really caught my attention, and I read it again.
I really *read* it:

You covet but you cannot get what you want, so you quarrel and fight.

David and Jordan *both* thought I was a killer, but I was only mad at David.
Why?

You covet but cannot get what you want, so you quarrel and fight.

I decided to go to the reunion, after all.

~ ~ ~

THAT EVENING, DAVID listened as we sat outside the convention center and I explained everything that had happened. When I was finished, he acted like there were no hard feelings about the inexcusable way I'd been treating him.

Laci had probably saved a spot for me at their table . . . did I want to go in with him and sit down?

I did.

Having David forgive me so readily and seeing everyone from high school put me in a very nostalgic mood, one in which I suddenly appreciated everyone who was in my life.

It was no coincidence that Natalie was sitting next to me, and I found myself appreciating her as well. When David and Laci went off onto the dance floor, I asked Natalie if she wanted to dance with me.

"It would make all of Laci's dreams finally come true if you and I would get together and live happily ever after," I told her.

"Oh, well then," she said sarcastically, holding out her hand. "By all means."

"We really could go out sometime," I suggested to her after I'd led her through the crowd.

"Yeah, right," she said, putting her arms around my neck.

"You could do a whole lot worse than me," I pointed out, putting my hands around her waist.

"Uh-huh," she said. "Somehow I don't think I'm your type."

"Why not?"

"Well," she mused, "for one thing, I still have my V card."

"Wow!" I said, feeling my eyes widen. "Still? Are you serious?"

"Not everything's about sex, Tanner."

"I happen to know that very well, thank you very much," I responded. "If you must know, I haven't had sex in over a year."

136

"A *year?*" she asked, looking shocked.

I shook my head.

"Isn't that, like, a new record?"

I shrugged.

"Your little scare with Megan really got to you, huh?" she asked sympathetically.

"Something like that," I said, "but my point is that there's no reason you and I couldn't go out."

"Sex isn't the only reason I don't want to go out with you."

"What do you mean?"

"I mean," she said, "that I have absolutely no desire to live in Laci's shadow."

"You wouldn't be in Laci's shadow!" I protested.

"Ha! What a joke," she laughed. "As if she's not the reason you're almost thirty years old and still haven't settled down."

"What's your excuse?"

"You'll always be in love with her, Tanner," she said, ignoring me, "and no one's ever going to be able to compare with her."

"I'm not in love with her."

"Uh-huh. Right."

"I'm not!" I insisted.

"Yeah," she said. "Keep telling yourself that."

"You don't know anything about it."

"I know a lot more than you think I do."

"Like what?" I asked, wondering if she and Laci had talked or something.

She hesitated for a very long moment before she answered me.

"I know what it's like," she said carefully, "to want somebody that you can never have."

I looked at her for a moment, struck by the solemnness of her voice.

"Oh," I finally said.

She glanced away.

"Who?" I asked.

"Oh, no," she said, looking back at me and shaking her head. "No way."

"Come on!" I prodded. "You can tell me."

She just shook her head some more.

"We could commiserate with one another," I coaxed and she gave me a little smile. "If I guess will you tell me?" and when she didn't say "No," I started guessing.

"Is it me?"

She rolled her eyes. "You're so full of yourself."

I grinned at her.

"How old is he?"

"I'm not telling you anything!"

"It is a *he*, right?" I asked.

"Yes, it's a he!" she cried, swatting me.

"Now we're getting somewhere," I said. "Come on. We'll play 'Twenty Questions'."

She laughed.

"Person, place or thing?" I asked.

"Person," she laughed again.

"Okay," I nodded. "Living or dead?"

The smile suddenly disappeared from her face and she pressed her lips together. I searched her eyes for a moment and then she laid her head against my chest.

Natalie and Greg had always been friends and they'd gone to the prom together, but . . .

"I didn't know," I said.

"I know," she said, nodding against me.

I hugged her tight and kissed the top of her head. She squeezed me back.

I wondered if they'd actually been going out or if it had been . . . *unrequited love*. Having experienced both first hand, I decided that it didn't really matter.

"I know it's stupid," she said.

"No, it's not," I assured her. "It's not any worse than me comparing everybody I try to go out with to Laci."

"Yes it is," she protested, pulling back and looking at me. "At least you're in love with someone who's still *alive*!"

"First of all," I told her, "I never said I was still in love with her, but anyway, the point is that she's just as unattainable for me as Greg is for you . . ."

She looked at me uncertainly.

"We're both going through the exact same thing," I explained. "It's like you said earlier, nobody else can compare with her, so nobody else seems good enough. Isn't that exactly what you're doing with Greg?"

She thought about it for a moment and then finally nodded.

"So it's okay," I said, quietly.

She gave me a little smile.

"And we should go out," I suggested again. "Especially now that it's a level playing field. I'm never going to be good enough for you . . . you're never going to be good enough for me . . . at least we'd both know where we stood."

She looked at me to see if I was serious, which I was.

"Why?" she finally asked quietly.

I thought about it for a moment.

"I guess I'm tired of being alone," I admitted. "Aren't you?"

She gave me a little nod.

"And maybe it'll work out between us," I shrugged. "You never know."

"I don't think so."

"Why not?"

"Because," she grinned. "You're not good enough for me and I'm not good enough for you."

I smiled back at her.

"But you never know," I said again. "It could work . . ."

"But if it doesn't?" she asked, worriedly.

"Then we'll still always be friends," I said and I pulled her against me again and gave her another kiss on the top of her head.

~ ~ ~

CHEMISTRY. THAT'S WHAT was missing between me and Natalie . . .

Chemistry.

Chemistry isn't something that you can *make* happen. It's either there or it's not. And – with me and Natalie – it was not.

But what *was* there with Natalie was a connection and a level of comfort and trust that I hadn't known in years . . . not since Laci and I had been dating. I could tell Natalie anything I wanted to and she wouldn't judge me. I could talk to her about Laci and she wouldn't judge me. She could talk to me about Greg and I wouldn't judge her. It was nice to have someone in my life once again that I could completely be myself with, and I think she felt the same way about me.

So, while the very few hugs and kisses that we did wind up sharing were pretty platonic, the brief period of time that I dated Natalie was one that I'll always remember fondly.

I told Natalie how Laci had guilted me into reading the Bible every day and I liked that I could ask her questions about that if I wanted. Of course I could have asked David, but he always started salivating whenever he thought I was finding my religion, so I stuck to Natalie instead. The fact that she'd been through seminary didn't hurt either.

One day I brought out Greg's Bible and I showed it to her. She took it from me almost reverently and held it in front of her with a look of awe on her face.

"If I could let you have it," I said apologetically, "I would. But I can't."

"Oh, I know," she agreed, opening it to the middle and turning a page. "I wouldn't expect you to give it to me, but . . ."

"You can come visit it any time you want."

She smiled at me and turned another page, running her finger along some of the words that Greg had written in it.

140

"I want to ask you about something," I said.

"Okay."

I took it gently from her and turned to the fourteenth chapter of Mark. I pointed at the verses:

> *"You will all fall away," Jesus told them, "for it is written: 'I will strike the shepherd, and the sheep will be scattered.' But after I have risen, I will go ahead of you into Galilee."*

The next verse was:

> *Peter declared, "Even if all fall away, I will not."*

That was the one that Greg had underlined. And next to it he had written, "Tanner is just like him!"

"Why did he say that?" I asked after she'd had a chance to look at it. "Am I really that bad?"

"That *bad?*" she asked, surprised. "Why do you think it's *bad* that he says you're just like Peter? Peter was great!"

"He denied Jesus three times!" I reminded her. "Right here! On the very next page!"

She looked at me, surprised.

"Yes," she agreed, "but that's not what Greg was talking about."

"It's not?"

"No," she said, shaking her head and smiling. "Not at all."

"What then?"

"You *act* like Peter."

I looked at her questioningly.

"Everything Peter did was larger than life," she explained, still smiling. "He could never do anything halfway . . ."

"What do you mean?"

"I mean, like at the transfiguration, Peter was all like, 'This is fantastic! Let's build shelters!' and God had to basically tell him to shut up and calm down and just listen. He was always saying stuff like, "Don't just wash my feet, wash all of me!" and "I wanna walk on the water too!"

I kept looking at her as she went on.

"When they saw Jesus standing on the shore after the resurrection, Peter jumped into the water and started swimming instead of just riding the boat back like everybody else," she said, tipping her head at me. "Everything he did had to be over the top."

She paused and looked at me.

"It's not because he thought I was a bad person?" I asked.

She looked at me gently and put her hand on the side of my face.

"Of course not," she said, leaning forward and kissing my cheek. "Not at all."

And after that, I went back to reading Greg's Bible, and all the little notes that he had written in it.

~ ~ ~

THERE WAS AN unspoken understanding between Natalie and me that it was going to be okay if one of us actually decided that we wanted to date somebody else. What surprised me, however, was how fast it happened, and the fact that it was Natalie who made that decision first.

"Remember that guy I told you about that interviewed me?" she asked me one evening over pizza. She was working now at a children's home as a part-time youth pastor.

"The social worker?"

"He's a counselor," she corrected. "Most of these kids have been sexually abused . . . they have a lot of problems."

"Oh."

"His name's Julian," she said.

"Oh," I said again, taking a drink.

"He asked me out today," she said.

Coke came out my nose.

"You've only been there a week!" I cried, reaching for a napkin.

She watched me as I wiped my face off. I looked back at her. Then I sighed.

"This isn't going anywhere," she said, waving her hand back and forth between us. "You know it isn't."

"I know," I admitted, "but I like having you around."

"I'll still be around," she insisted.

"It won't be the same," I said.

"No, but you know I'll always be here for you."

"I know," I nodded. "I'll always be here for you, too."

"And if things don't work out between me and Julian," she grinned, "the first thing I'm gonna do is come straight back here to you."

"Gee," I said. "Thanks."

Natalie and Julian actually wound up getting married a year and a half later, but what she and I had said to each other that day was true: the two of us would always be there for each other. She was there for me when we found out that Chase had Huntington's disease and that there was a fifty percent chance that Jordan or I had it too. She was there for me when I decided to get tested and she sat beside me in the doctor's office, holding my hand while we waited for him to tell me that I was fine. Throughout the years, I was there for her, too. I was there for her when Julian left her, pregnant with their third child. I was there for her when their oldest was diagnosed with diabetes. I was there for her when Parkinson's took its toll on her dad and she and her mom needed help until they were ready to take that final step of putting him into a nursing home.

I was there for her when she got remarried, and needed someone to walk her down the aisle.

144

~ ~ ~

OPENING DAY OF dove season was a big deal. It was always the first Saturday of each September and the official start of the hunting season. It was also the cause for a lot of preparation: shotgun shell-reloading, camo-buying, skeet shooting and dog training.

David and I had joined a paid hunt this year and drove about forty-miles south of Cavendish to a field that had been cut a couple of weeks earlier and promised to be loaded with doves. Dorito begged to sit next to me, and I said "Sure," since I figured that David could use a break from all that talking.

The two of us edged around the perimeter of the cornfield and finally plopped our dove stools down along a hedgerow. Dorito sat in his stool for all of about two minutes, and from that point on, he was playing on the ground.

Finally it got light enough to shoot and I convinced Dorito to help me watch the sky. I'd heard two shots from David's direction by the time I finally got one myself and I sent my dog, TD, after it, letting Dorito take it out of his mouth.

"Here," I said, reaching for the bird, intending to put it in the game pouch under my stool.

"No," Dorito said, shaking his head. "I made a nest for it."

"A nest, huh?" I smiled. Dorito nodded and I looked at his "nest".

"Uh-oh," I said.

"What?"

I scooped him up and walked over to where David was.

"I think we have a bit of a problem," I said when I reached David's stool.

"What?"

"Tell your dad what you did," I encouraged Dorito.

"What?" he asked.

"About the nest."

"Oh," he said proudly. "I made a nest."

David looked at me questioningly.

"Out of poison ivy," I elaborated, and David's face blanched.

"You have *got* to be kidding," he said.

"Nope. He's been sitting in a patch of it for about an hour."

"Whatdya put him in a patch of poison ivy for?"

"It was dark!" I defended myself. "I didn't know it was poison ivy!"

Defeated, David sighed heavily and shook his head.

It had been the previous spring when Dorito had gotten himself into some poison ivy at a soccer game, volunteering to go get a ball that had rolled off into some weeds. By the time David and Laci realized that Dorito had been exposed, it was way too late. For about four weeks, he had been one miserable little kid, looking as bad as he felt. They took him to the doctor for a shot and a dose pack of steroids, but those barely seemed to touch it. It would take another trip to the doctor, another dose pack, a couple tubes of creams and lots of bandages before he finally got over it.

Now we headed for my truck, and David broke into the first aid kit that was stored under the back seat as soon as we got there. While he wiped Dorito down with some disinfecting wipes, I drove to a little no-tell, motel that I'd seen a few miles down the road. We got a room, stripped Dorito out of his clothes, and plunked him into the tub as quick as we could.

"I'm going to Walmart to get him something to wear," David said, stuffing Dorito's fatigues into a plastic garbage bag.

"Okay," I agreed, filling up the ice bucket with warm water and dumping it over Dorito's arms.

"You'd better wash up too," David suggested. "There's no way you're not covered."

"You gonna buy *me* something to wear?"

"I'll see if they have any awnings," he said, and then he disappeared.

I decided that David was more than likely right – I probably at least had the oil on my arms from where I'd carried Dorito and it was almost certainly on my clothes as well. I stripped down to my boxers and then, remembering that dogs can get poison ivy on their fur and spread it around, I darted out to the parking lot – half-naked – just before David pulled away with my truck. I brought TD inside too.

146

Pretty soon all three of us were thoroughly soaped, rinsed and soaking wet, but hopefully poison ivy free.

Once TD got out of the tub, he went absolutely bonkers, tearing around the room in a crazy, infinite figure eight, stopping only periodically to bark at Dorito, who was beside himself with giggles. When a knock came on the door, I opened it without much thought, assuming that it was David . . .

It wasn't.

I'm not sure what bothered the two police officers I found at the door more: the fact that someone had called and reported "suspicious activity", the fact that Dorito and I were clearly not related (even though he kept calling me "Uncle Tanner", which I'm pretty sure didn't help), or the fact that Dorito was naked and I was only wearing one of those stupid little hotel towels that are nowhere near big enough. Of course Dorito sharing with them the fact that I had "a lot of guns" didn't help matters any and I was really glad when David showed up with a big bag of clothes, corroborating my story. I went in to the bathroom to get dressed, and by the time I emerged, David had pretty much convinced the officers that they could leave in good conscience.

Even though our actions hadn't been quick enough (Dorito and I both wound up breaking out the next day), the entire incident was something that the three of us would laugh and laugh about for years to come.

Don't get me wrong, though.

What happened to *us* was funny . . .

But I know that it's not funny that there are people out there who make it necessary for the police to respond to calls like that in the first place. I know it's not funny that – more often than not – when law enforcement arrives on a scene, they don't find situations that are humorous. I know that, every day, they are reminded that people exist who will do unspeakable things to innocent, little children . . .

I do know that.

But just in case I *didn't* know that, David was about to bring someone into my life, who would make sure that I did.

~ ~ ~

AMBER WAS DORITO'S best friend. She was a little girl in his second grade class, and apparently she had some problems – the main one being that she wouldn't talk. I guess that, in and of itself, was plenty to worry about.

David met Amber while he was volunteering at the school and immediately knew that something wasn't right. He also happened to fall head over heels for her, so when he found out that she was in foster care, he got it into his head that he was going to *prove* something wasn't right so that he and Laci could take her in.

Of course when *I* found out what he was doing, I couldn't wait to help him make that happen.

The only problem was that we had no idea how to go about "proving" that Amber's foster family wasn't fit to be taking care of her. David had already secretly followed her home from school and determined that she was letting herself in to an empty house every day, but that didn't warrant having her removed from her home. So, we decided to stake out Amber's house to see if we could come up with something that *would* warrant it.

The first thing we discovered, was that all the lower windows in their split-level house were covered up – either by curtains or by cardboard that was taped up tightly. We also discovered that a former student from the high school, Anthony Perry, was a foster child there too. A late-night snoop into his records at school told me that he had been sent to live with Amber's foster parents, Wayne and Rebecca Trent, after he had spent about a year at the Shawnee Home for Children, in the southern part of the county.

Remember the part-time job that Natalie got at a children's home? *Shawnee Home for Children.*

Remember what she told me about Julian, who also worked there?

148

He's a counselor. Most of these kids have been sexually abused . . . they have a lot of problems.

I wasn't an expert by any means, but I knew enough to know that kids who had been sexually abused were at serious risk for becoming abusers themselves . . .

So I went over to Natalie's, and told her that I needed a favor.

"I can't tell you anything about those kids!" Natalie cried. "All that information is confidential!"

"There is something seriously wrong with this little girl, Nat," I told her. "Just see if you see any red flags or anything in Anthony's record."

"Look, Tanner," she said, "even if I wanted to, I don't have access to anyone's files except for the kids I'm currently working with."

"Julian does," I said, even though I wasn't really sure if that was true. When she didn't argue with me, I knew that it was.

"I can't ask him to do that," she said. "He could lose his job . . . he could lose his license . . . he could go to jail. Both of us could!"

I looked at her for a long moment.

"Whatever has happened to this little girl is so bad," I told Natalie, "that she has shut down to the point that she can't even *talk*."

Natalie didn't answer me.

"Don't you think," I went on, "that we owe it to her to at least make sure that whatever caused that isn't something that's still happening?"

She stared at me for a long time.

"I can't," she finally said in a small voice.

I pursed my lips together and then blew out a long breath.

"Maybe you could look into it," I suggested, "and if there's nothing to be worried about, then you could just let me know that. You could let me know that I'm barking up the wrong tree and that I need to be concentrating my efforts somewhere else."

She hesitated for a minute before answering.

"I'm not promising you anything," she finally said, giving her head a slight shake.

I reached my hand up, cupped the side of her face, and gave her a little smile. She did not smile back.

"Thank you," I said, and I leaned toward her and pressed my lips to her forehead.

149

It wasn't long before Natalie called and asked me to meet her at the park. Being that it was the middle of December and drizzling, ours were the only two cars in the parking lot.

"Let's go for a walk," Natalie suggested. She had hopped out of her car as soon as I'd pulled in and was waiting for me as I opened my door.

"Ooohh," I said, rubbing my hands together excitedly. "Very 'cloak and daggery'. Probably a good idea . . . one of our vehicles might be bugged."

She glared at me as I hopped down out of my truck and closed my door.

"Wanna make sure I'm not wired?" I offered, holding my arms up. "It's okay . . . go ahead and frisk me."

"It's not funny, Tanner."

"Relax," I said, putting my arm around her.

"I can't relax," she said, shrugging my arm off. "If anyone ever finds out about this—"

"No one's going to find out," I promised seriously.

She walked along at a rapid pace for a little while before she spoke.

"You were right," she finally said.

"About what?"

"About everything. When he was seven years old he got removed from his home. His mom was doing drugs and her boyfriend was . . ."

She glanced at me. She didn't really need to finish her sentence, but she did.

"He was raping this little kid on a regular basis," she finally finished. "He got twelve to fifteen years."

I shook my head as we continued to walk along.

"Anthony got put in foster care," she went on, "bounced around to a bunch of different places. Eventually he landed with a family that had a little boy of their own and . . ."

She hesitated.

"Anthony went after him?" I guessed.

"Yeah," Natalie nodded reluctantly. "Then he got sent to Shawnee for a year and then he went back into the foster care system."

"How did he and Amber wind up in the same house?" I asked. "Why would the state put him in a foster home that had other kids? Especially younger kids? Isn't that kind of a no-brainer?"

"I don't know how it happened," Natalie admitted, shaking her head. "It was probably an oversight or something . . ."

Oversight.

We trudged along quietly for a moment.

"You can't tell anyone about this," Natalie said.

"You can't expect me to pretend that I don't know," I said.

She stopped and looked at me.

"Look. I told you that I'd let you know if you were wasting your time or not," she said, "and I did. But you can't use anything I've told you – Julian and I could both lose our jobs . . . we could go to *jail*. If Anthony's doing something to Amber, you're going to have to prove it on your own."

I stopped walking and looked at her.

"Do you think he's doing something to her?" I asked.

She looked back at me earnestly.

"Julian says you need to get her out of there," she finally said quietly.

I searched her eyes for a moment before I nodded, and then we turned around and headed back to the parking lot.

David and I tried to come up with evidence that Anthony didn't need to be in the same home with Amber by climbing a tree in their yard. We were hoping that we would be able to see into upper story windows and maybe take some pictures, but all that ended up happening was that David wound up in the hospital.

Lying there with a broken femur, David begged – *begged* – me to do something. I know they had him pretty drugged up, but there was a desperation in his voice that I'd never heard before, and, after what Natalie had told me? I was feeling pretty desperate myself.

I knew we needed to get Amber out of there . . . but how?

I needed help.

Years earlier, I'd coached a young man who'd gone on to become a cop with the Cavendish police force. Through the years I saw him around town from time to time and he was always friendly. He'd been a good kid, and instinctively I felt that I could tell him whatever I needed to without getting Natalie or Julian into trouble. His name was Jaron, and I was pretty sure that he would help me however he could, and then butt out.

I called him up and we met (I'm not kidding) for coffee and doughnuts.

"You need to get a PI," he told me immediately after he'd heard the entire story.

"Really?"

"Yeah," he nodded, tearing apart a bear claw and dunking it into his coffee. "Even if you guys had been able to get some kind of picture with incriminating evidence or something, you never would have been able to use it. You were trespassing in their back yard. It never would have held up in court."

"But what's a private eye gonna do for me?"

"They can get you information on everyone that lives in the house . . . they know how to get you evidence that will hold up in court . . ."

"How do I find a good one?"

"I know a guy," Jaron said.

The "guy" was named Grant Larson, and I had to admit that I was pretty impressed with him. Within a few hours of my original call, he called me back and already had a bunch of information.

"Rebecca and Wayne Trent took Anthony in about a year and a half ago," he said. "Rebecca'd been having some health problems and quit her job. I suspect money's one of the big reasons they decided to become foster parents."

"What kind of health problems?" I asked.

"Breast cancer, actually," he said. "On their foster care application they don't list anything like that – probably because they knew they wouldn't get a foster kid if she was that sick – but on her disability claims and stuff, she put that down."

"What else did you find out?"

"Well," he went on, "I don't think one foster kid combined with her disability insurance was doing enough to offset the fact that she wasn't working anymore. Wayne works first shift as a custodian at the mill downtown, and after Anthony came to live with them, he took a second, full-time job in the evenings and on weekends. They applied for a second foster child about eight months ago, and got Amber."

"Okay," I said.

"So, anyway," he said, "I'm monitoring things right now, but – like you said – the bottom windows are blocked. I can't see anything in the lower level at all."

"What do you mean, you're 'monitoring things right now?'"

"I mean I've got two cameras aimed at their house and I'm parked down the street, watching what's going on in a couple of the rooms upstairs."

"Seriously?"

"Yeah."

"What's going on?"

"Nothing much," he replied. "Wayne's at work, I haven't seen Anthony all day, Amber's been watching TV, and Rebecca's been lying in bed since I got here. She looks pretty sick."

"I don't understand how you can see anything," I said. "The windows are too high . . ."

"I've got one video camera up a light pole," he explained, "and then I made friends with the neighbor that lives behind them and put one up on his chimney. By the way, you're gonna owe me an extra hundred bucks."

"And this is legal?" I asked skeptically.

"I know what I'm doing," he assured me.

Grant said it was fine if I wanted to join him while he watched the house that evening.

"Keep me from falling asleep," he said. "This gets real boring, real fast."

He explained that everything was being taped and that if we saw anything, he'd have concrete evidence that he could use in court. Everything that the cameras picked up showed up on two computer monitors in the van that Grant had parked just down the street from Amber's house. Unlike the pictures that David and I had been trying to take, anything that Grant obtained would be admissible because he wasn't illegally trespassing on anyone's property to get it.

Grant said that Amber had made herself some instant macaroni and cheese, but other than that, there hadn't been too much excitement. Anthony appeared out of nowhere after I got there, and we decided that his bedroom was probably in the basement and that he'd likely been down there for most of the day, sleeping. He scrounged around in the kitchen for a while, poured himself a bowl of cereal, and then disappeared again. Our basement theory was confirmed when we saw lights come on beyond the cardboard and curtains that were blocking the windows.

And then . . . not too long after that . . . Amber disappeared, too.

"Where did she go?" I asked after she'd walked out of the room.

Grant shrugged.

"But . . . but what if she went downstairs with him?" I asked.

"There's nothing we can do about it," Grant said. "If that's where something's happening, we're not going to be able to see it."

"But of course that's where it's happening!" I cried. "Obviously that's his room down there and if he's doing something to her, *that's* where it's happening."

"There's nothing we can do about it," he said again.

I stared at him in disbelief for a minute.

"What if I sneak over there and can see through a crack or something?"

"Won't be admissible," Grant said, shaking his head. "You'd be trespassing on their property."

"So what you're saying," I asked, "is that this is all just a big waste of time."

"Look," Grant said, "I know it's frustrating to not be able to—"

"I'm gonna go see if I can see anything," I said, reaching for the door handle.

"You won't be able to use it," he warned.

"I don't care," I said, and I headed to the Trent house.

I'd already scoped the house out on that first night with David, but there hadn't been any lights on in the basement when I'd done that. Now, with light coming from inside, I was hoping that I would be able to find a crack big enough to actually see through.

I couldn't.

After a long time of trying, I finally gave up and went back to the van.

"What if some of the cardboard or whatever that was blocking those windows were to accidentally fall down?" I asked.

"I'm not doing anything to lose my license," he said, adamantly. "And even if I did, it wouldn't be admissible."

154

"I'm not asking you to do anything," I said. "I'm asking you if you were to come back here tomorrow and suddenly you could see into those windows from here on the street . . . would that be legal?"

He sighed and hesitated for a long time.

"I'm willing to come back tomorrow," he finally said. "But I don't want to know what you do with yourself between now and then."

And so, later that evening, I broke into the Trent's house.

I waited until a car pulled up in front of the house and Anthony came outside, lighting a cigarette as he climbed in. Before Grant had left, the two of us had seen Amber go upstairs and turn on a light. That light was off now. So was the one in Rebecca Trent's bedroom. The car pulled away from the curb and turned the corner at the end of the block . . .

It was now or never.

I crept into the back yard and tried the side basement door that I'd seen Anthony come out. It wasn't locked, so technically, I didn't "break" in.

It was quiet.

And dark.

I prayed that Amber was upstairs asleep and I prayed that Rebecca was upstairs dying, or whatever it was that she'd been doing all day. I know that sounds terrible, but she and her husband had been *using* Amber just to get money and I wasn't feeling sympathetic toward her one bit. All I cared about was that she didn't get up and decide to wander downstairs with a gun or something, while I was prowling around the basement of her house.

I felt near the door frame, found a light switch, and turned it on. To the right was a laundry room and to my left was obviously Anthony's bedroom. (I won't get into what it looked like, but if you're familiar with the word "squalor", you'll have some idea.)

I headed toward the windows that were facing the street, the ones that Grant and I would easily be able to see into without worrying about trespassing.

Trespassing . . .

Ha.

I went past Anthony's unmade bed with its crumpled sheets and convinced myself that nothing untoward had happened there only a few hours earlier. I convinced myself that nothing bad at all had been happening to Amber.

But of course, why was I here in the first place, if I was so sure that nothing was happening?

When Grant showed up the next night and turned his cameras on, I was dismayed to find that we wouldn't be able see into Anthony's bedroom from the street like I had hoped we'd be able to. I had tried to minimize what I'd done to the curtains and coverings so that Anthony wouldn't notice right off that people could suddenly see in from the street, but all the camera could see was his closet door, his dresser, and his TV. What the camera *needed* to see was Anthony's bed, and the peepholes I'd created the night before weren't allowing for that. Grant and I sat in the van anyway and watched, hoping that somehow, something would come of my efforts.

It was almost a complete repeat of the night before. Anthony came upstairs after apparently sleeping most of the day away, poured himself some cereal, and then disappeared back into the basement. This time there was no delay . . . Amber disappeared right away, at the same time Anthony did.

We caught a glimpse of both of them as they walked through the room, but then they moved off camera. After a minute of still not seeing them, and not seeing Amber reappear upstairs, I glanced at Grant. His eyes stayed focused on the computer screen.

"If we got the camera closer," I told him, "we could see the bed."

He shook his head.

"I'm gonna go see what's going on," I said, opening the car door.

"Don't," he said, reaching for my arm. "You're not going to be able to use anything if you do . . ."

"Yeah," I said bitterly, "like we've got so much we can use now."

I edged along the side yard and then dropped onto my belly, crawling like a commando toward one of the windows. I eased up to it quietly and peered through the opening I'd made on my visit the evening before.

When I put my face close enough to the glass, I could see.

I could see everything.

~ ~ ~

MY BLOOD RAN cold. Every instinct surfaced all at once, and I lay there frozen, with no idea what to do. *Punch the window out? Run back and tell Grant? Pull out my phone and call the police?*

It didn't take long for me to decide. I sprang to my feet and bolted around to the side of the house. I had my hand on the door when someone grabbed my arm from behind.

"You can't," Grant said, trying to pull me away from the house. I yanked away from him and flew through the door. I was glad that I already knew exactly where I was going.

Anthony didn't know what hit him . . . literally.

"Who the—"

He actually got a little more than that out before I pounded my fist into his nose. I'd never hit anybody or anything as hard as I hit Anthony at that moment. I could actually feel bones and cartilage breaking underneath his skin.

"Ohhhhh!" he cried in a muffled voice, bringing his hands up to his nose. Blood poured out onto his shirt and he staggered backward, but somehow managed to stay upright. I punched him in the stomach, which made him double over, and then I brought my knee up under his chin with every ounce of strength that I had in me.

Anthony crumpled into a moaning heap on the floor. I was about to start kicking him in the ribs too, but I suddenly remembered that Amber was there, quietly watching everything that I was doing. I turned and looked at her, sitting on the bed behind me, naked from the waist down.

Oh, God . . . please help me.

I squatted down next to Anthony and spoke quietly into his ear. "If you try to get up – if you so much as *move* – I will kill you. Do you understand?"

He made a little gurgling noise and I think he tried to nod, so I took that as a "Yes." I was pulling my phone out of my pocket when Grant stuck his head around the corner.

"What can I do?" he asked reticently.

"Nothing," I said, shaking my head. "I got it under control."

He looked at the mound that was Anthony, and then he glanced at Amber.

"I'll call the police," he offered.

"No," I said, holding up my phone. "I got it. Get out of here."

He looked at me uncertainly.

"Go," I insisted. "You were never here."

"Are you sure?"

"Yeah," I nodded. "There's no sense in both of us going down. Go on."

He looked around the room one more time, finally nodded, and headed back up the stairs. I called 911 and briefly told them that we needed an ambulance.

Then I turned to Amber.

She was still sitting on the edge of the bed, still half naked, still looking at me quietly.

"Hi, Amber," I said, pulling the corner of a sheet over her lap. "I bet you don't know who I am, do you?

She shook her head.

"You know Dorito?" I asked.

She nodded, her eyes brightening.

"You know Dorito's daddy, David?"

She nodded again and smiled.

"Well he's my *best* friend!" I told her, enthusiastically. She smiled some more.

"Did you know that David broke his leg?" I asked. She shook her head and I rolled my eyes dramatically. "He does the stupidest things, sometimes," I said, nodding. "And he was really upset because he wanted to come over and see you and see how you were doing, but then he broke his leg," I held up my hands in a helpless manner, "so he's stuck at home and couldn't come see you. So I told him I'd come over and check on you. Okay?"

She nodded again.

158

"So, listen," I went on, "I think we're gonna go to the doctor and have them make sure you're okay. Have you ever been to the doctor before?"

She nodded.

"What for?"

She pointed to her arm.

"Hurt your arm?" She nodded. "Anything else?"

She pointed to her throat.

"Sore throat?" I guessed.

She furrowed up her brow and I could tell that I was close. "Did you have your tonsils out?" I ventured. She nodded vigorously.

"I bet you went to the hospital for that."

Another nod.

"I think we might go to the hospital tonight, too," I told her. "Does that sound alright?"

She nodded indifferently.

"I'll go with you, okay?"

Anthony groaned and Amber leaned to one side to peer around me and look at him curiously.

"He's probably gonna go to the hospital, too," I told her. "But I'm gonna stay with you and keep him away from you, okay?"

She nodded again and gave me a little, noncommittal shrug.

"Listen," I said. "It's pretty cold outside. I think maybe you should get some clothes on. Do you know where your pants are?"

She pointed to the floor next to me.

"Right," I said, reaching over and grabbing her underwear. "Let's put these on first ..."

I guided her feet into the openings and then she hopped off the bed so that I could pull them up all the way.

Something trickled down the inside of Amber's thigh.

Evidence.

I had a fresh desire to return to Anthony and finish him off. Instead I grabbed Amber's jeans, turned them right side out, and then I helped her get into those, too.

After her jeans were around her waist and zipped up, I struggled with the button. Finally it caught, and – when it did – my mind flashed back to that summer day when I'd helped Laci with the button of her pants ... the day that guy had frightened her so badly on the island. I remembered that she had been so scared. The guy hadn't even *touched* her, but Laci had been shaking . . . trembling . . . crying.

I looked at Amber now.

No shaking . . . no trembling . . . no crying.

She just gazed up at me, calmly chewing her cuticle. She didn't appear to be even the tiniest bit upset about anything that had just happened to her.

Business as usual.

~ ~ ~

ANTHONY WASN'T MAKING any effort to get up, so when I heard sirens, I walked Amber up the stairs and onto the front lawn. I gave an officer a brief and discrete rundown of what had happened, since Amber was standing right beside me holding my hand, and he conferred with some other officers who had arrived. Two of them went into the house with their guns drawn, and another took Amber by the hand and tried to lead her away from me. To my surprise, she pulled away from him and wrapped her arms tightly around my leg.

I pulled Amber gently aside and squatted down, putting a hand on her shoulder.

"It's okay," I told her. "I'll be right here. He just wants to talk to you." But she shook her head and refused to let him take her away from me. I stood up and Amber grabbed my hand again, clutching it firmly.

The officer knelt down next to her.

"Honey," he said, "I'm Officer Blide. Can you tell me what happened?"

Amber just stared at him quietly.

"She doesn't talk," I explained.

"Excuse me?" he asked, glancing up.

"She's mute," I said. "She doesn't talk."

He muttered under his breath something that sounded like *Of course she doesn't*, sighed heavily, and stood up to face me.

"What's your name?" he asked.

"Tanner Clemmons."

"Address?" he asked, writing down my name.

"413 Liberty."

"And what were you doing in the area?"

"Taking a walk."

"Ten miles from your house?" he asked skeptically.

161

"I like walking in this neighborhood a lot better."

"Uh-huh," he said as another patrol car pulled up, followed by an ambulance.

"And so I suppose you were just walking by . . ."

"Yeah," I agreed. "I was walking by right out front here and all of a sudden I heard Amber screaming for help and–"

"I thought you said she doesn't talk," he interrupted.

"It was a Christmas miracle."

I think he was about ready to cuff me, but fortunately I heard someone say, "Coach?"

I looked toward the sound of the voice and was immensely relieved to find Jaron walking toward us.

"Donoho," Officer Blide said, jabbing his pencil in my direction. "You know this clown?"

"Yeah," Jaron nodded. "I know him. This is Coach Clemmons. From the high school?"

Officer Blide didn't seem impressed.

"Uh-huh. Well, I wonder if 'Coach Clemmons' here knows that it's against the law to knowingly make false or misleading statements to an officer?"

"It's only a misdemeanor," Jaron assured me and I bit back a smile. Officer Blide glowered at him.

"Pete," Jaron said, putting a hand on Officer Blide's shoulder. "I got it. Okay? Trust me."

Officer Blide shook his head and walked toward the house.

"I recognized the address when the call came out," Jaron explained, "so I headed over here."

"Thanks."

"What happened?"

"You want the real version or what I was going to tell him?"

"The real version," Jaron said.

"Okay," I agreed, "but she needs to go to the hospital. They need to do a rape kit on her."

"You sure?"

"Yeah," I said. "I'm sure."

"Okay," he agreed, nodding grimly. "Let's get her to the hospital. You can tell me on the way."

When we got to the hospital the nurse asked me and Jaron to step out of the room while they examined her, but Amber didn't want me to go.

"It's okay," I promised her. "I'll be right out there and I'll even call David and see if he can come see you, okay?" That made her agree and she let go of my shirt.

"I thought you didn't know her," Jaron said after we got into the hallway.

"I don't."

"She sure seems attached to you . . ." he said, surprised.

Honestly I was surprised, too. I would have thought that a little girl who was being raped on a regular basis would naturally fear men, not bond instantly with them the way she had with David, and now apparently me. But I guess fearing men wasn't how her brain was dealing with what she'd been going through – not talking to anyone was.

Just then a gurney came through the doors of the emergency room. Anthony was on it. An officer was walking along next to him and I was glad to see that he was handcuffed to the stretcher.

"Let me check in with them and I'll be right back," Jaron said. I nodded and stepped outside. It was after midnight, but I called David anyway and told him he needed to get down to the hospital. I headed back toward Amber's room, but Jaron caught me before I stepped in.

"We're gonna need you to sign a statement about what happened," he told me.

"Okay."

"I hate to tell you," he said, jabbing his thumb toward Amber's room, "but none of this is gonna stick."

"Whatdaya mean?"

"Any evidence they get off this rape kit – none of it's gonna be admissible."

"What?!" I cried. "That's ridiculous! How can it not be admissible?"

"It was all obtained under illegal circumstances," he explained. "You had no right to enter the house."

"But I–"

"Even if you'd really been 'taking a walk' and happened to hear her crying for help, you're only legal option was to call the police and let us handle it."

"It would've been too late by then" I argued.

"I know, Coach. I'm not saying you should have done anything different – as far as I'm concerned, you're a hero – but I'm just saying that the guy's gonna walk."

"That's not fair."

"No," he agreed. "It's not."

I slumped against the wall.

"We're still gonna go ahead and press charges," he went on.

"Why?" I asked, sullenly. "If it's not gonna do any good, what's the point?"

"So that she won't go back to that house," he explained, "and Social Services will never let him be placed in a home with children again."

"Can she go with David and Laci?" I asked.

"That's not up to me," he said. "But I can put in a good word with her social worker when she gets here."

"Thanks."

At that moment one of the nurses came out of Amber's room.

"You can go in if you'd like," she said to me.

"Thanks," I said again, and I walked in to wait with Amber, until David and Laci arrived.

~ ~ ~

ALTHOUGH JORDAN AND Charlotte had split up once they'd found out she was pregnant, the two of them had gotten back together before going off to college in the fall, and by January, they were planning a May wedding.

While this was definitely rushed, I think it was because they found out that Chase was dying and that Jordan might be too. I think they realized just how precious their time together was, and I think they decided they didn't want to waste any of it.

I wanted Jordan to get tested, but he didn't want to. He insisted that he had faith that God was going to take care of him no matter what, and that no test results were ever going to change that.

I was feeling a little bit better about God myself. (He had, after all, given *me* good test results and kept Laci cancer-free all these years.) But I definitely wasn't where Jordan was, or anybody else for that matter. Reading my Bible every day like Laci had wanted me to helped, just like the conversations I continued to have with Natalie did, but I was still a long way from where I needed to be.

David knew I was a long way from where I needed to be, but I didn't want to hear about it from him, and I shut him down whenever he tried to bring it up. It was interesting how receptive I was to anything *Natalie* tried to tell me, but the same exact words coming out of David's mouth would irritate me and have the completely opposite effect from what I knew he intended.

Although I would never have admitted it at the time, the main reason for this was because – even though David was my best friend and I loved him very much – deep down, I was resentful of everything that God had given to him. I just wasn't sure which one of them my resentment was aimed at . . . David, or God?

The truth of the matter is, it was probably both.

I imagine it was exactly because of that resentment that I finally "let it slip" to David, that Laci and I had dated in college.

It was spring, and he and Laci were officially Amber's foster parents by now – one more example of how everything always went David's way. We were out on the lake, fishing, and he was going on and on about buying a lake house, (because, you know, things weren't already great enough for him). Then he started talking about their upcoming anniversary, and how they were going to celebrate . . .

"I'm gonna take her to Danté's," David smiled. "It's her favorite restaurant."

That was when I snapped.

"I know," I said, before I could stop myself.

"How would *you* know?" David asked.

"Because," I shrugged casually. "I used to take her there all the time when we were dating."

"In high school?"

"No. In college."

He looked at me in shock and dismay and I felt a perverse sense of pleasure welling up inside of me.

"You . . . you *did* know that we dated in college?" I asked him innocently. "Didn't you?"

"Of course I did," he said, waving his hand at me dismissively. "Laci doesn't keep secrets from me," but he could hardly look at me for the rest of the day and when we got to my house, he said a hasty goodbye, jumped into his car, and drove away.

By then, of course, my perverse sense of pleasure was completely gone and had been replaced by a dreaded realization of what I'd done. I called Laci as soon as he left.

"*Please* tell me that David knew we dated in college."

The chance that he already knew was slim to none because it wasn't in David's nature not to obsess about something like that and bring it up repeatedly. But there was the *possibility* that he'd already known . . .

There was a very long pause.

166

"Don't worry about it," she finally said.

"*He didn't know?*" I asked. I actually sounded surprised.

"It's okay," she assured me.

"How come he didn't know?"

"I don't know," she said. "It just never really came up and I didn't really see the need to tell him about it . . . you know how he gets."

"I'm sorry," I said. At least that much was true.

"It'll be okay," she replied, and she hung up the phone.

I really was sorry.

I hated myself.

What was *wrong* with me?

I had been miserable before the reunion when David and I weren't speaking to each other, so why had I done something that I *knew* was probably going to tear our friendship apart again? And this was probably going to cause a rift in their marriage, too . . .

Deep down, was that exactly what I wanted?

Have I mentioned that I hated myself?

~ ~ ~

ALTHOUGH NOTHING COULD rankle me quite like David trying to talk to me about his faith, I had to admit that there must have been something to it, because as fixated as David usually got with things, it could only have been his faith that allowed him to immediately forgive Laci for keeping something like that from him and enabled him to move on with our friendship almost as if nothing had happened.

He came over the very next day with Amber, having her ask me if I would take her fishing, and then, just like at the reunion, he acted as if there were no hard feelings. Within a matter of minutes, all was forgiven if not forgotten, and a few weeks later, when David's company sent him to San Francisco, I wound up going to.

Amber wanted to go with David and she wasn't going to be able to unless someone (me) came along to watch her during the day while David was working.

Amber was a very hard little girl to say "No," to. One look into those earnest eyes that had seen more than any child her age should ever have to see and it was impossible not to let her have her way – especially after she managed to find the courage to whisper a request in your ear.

You want to go fishing this afternoon?
Sure, sweetie. No problem.
You want to go to the park to play disc golf?
We can do that.
You want to go to San Francisco?
Okay.

Not that I didn't want to go to San Francisco.

Amber and I spent every waking moment of our time there together. We went to Pier 39 and the Golden Gate Bridge, Chinatown, North Beach

168

and Candlestick Point. We rode the cable cars and walked through Nob Hill, Portsmouth Square, Union Square and Jackson Square. We learned about the Barbary Coast — not a coast at all, but San Francisco's former red-light district — a fact that I failed to mention to David. We took a ferry to Alcatraz, and one day we even rode out to Napa Valley, where I let Amber try her first sip of wine — another fact that I failed to mention to David.

You can't spend that much time with someone, especially when that someone is Amber, and not fall completely in love with them. I had already loved her because she was so vulnerable and so innocent and I'd felt an overwhelming need to protect her since the day I'd taken her from Anthony Perry's bedroom, but by the time I brought her back from San Francisco, I was over the top, just like David was.

Amber loved me, too, and she didn't hesitate to whisper this in my ear on an almost daily basis. I loved hearing it, but I didn't really get it. It still surprised me that she wasn't afraid of men in light of everything that had happened to her. I just didn't understand.

One day, while we were in a movie theater, sharing a bucket of popcorn with extra butter and waiting for the afternoon matinee to start, she got up on her knees and whispered it once again in my ear.

"I love you."

I usually I answered her with, "I love you, too," but this time, I didn't.

I looked at her for a moment, and then I asked.

"Why?"

She sat back for a moment as if she was thinking of an answer, and then she leaned forward again.

"Because you love me," she whispered, "and you treat me like I'm normal."

"You are normal," I smiled.

She shook her head at me.

"Yes, you are," I said, smiling bigger. "As a matter of fact, that's *why I* love you. Because you're so daggum normal."

She smiled back at me and settled down into her seat, waiting for the movie to start.

~ ~ ~

IT WAS BECAUSE we were all so in love with Amber that it was so hard for us when her mother regained custody a few months later. It was worse, of course, for David, and I watched helplessly as he sank into the same kind of depression he had when Greg had died.

He pulled himself out of this one a lot faster, but then – almost as fast – he moved his family back to Mexico City . . .

Dorito's biological mom had surfaced . . . she wanted to get to know her son.

Amber had left during the summer . . . David and Laci just after Christmas. Losing all of them like that was enough to sink *me* into a depression of my own, but it didn't. It was a good thing too, because Chase needed me.

By now, Chase had quit his job, quit driving, and over Easter break, I helped him move back in with Mom. He wasn't bad enough yet that he couldn't stay alone for periods of time . . . although it was obvious that that was coming soon. But he *was* bad enough that I soon found myself spending a lot of time over at Mom's.

Taking care of Chase wound up being a blessing to me, because staying busy was the best way I knew to cope with my loneliness. I looked for every opportunity I could to keep my mind occupied: applying for the job of athletic director at the high school, continuing to referee rec league sports, getting certified to teach conceal and carry classes at the community college.

Two months after Chase moved back to Cavendish, I went to a fundraiser at the junior high school. They were trying to raise money to get new bleachers in the gymnasium, and having taught there at the beginning

170

of my career and remembering how terrible they had been even then, I was all over that effort.

I bid on a few items in the silent auction and purchased a string of raffle tickets, dropping several into each of the buckets that sat in front of donated prizes and services. I didn't pay too much attention to what I was entering, until I wound up winning a "Free Financial Consultation" – from David's dad.

I'd always had enough money to pay my bills, buy what I wanted, and do what I wanted, so I had never given my financial status too much consideration. David's father set about to change that.

"Why exactly are you renting?" was one of the first things he asked.

"I dunno," I shrugged. "I like my house ... I like my neighborhood ... I don't have to worry if the hot water heater or something needs to be replaced ..."

"You're throwing your money away," he said, shaking his head. "The tax breaks alone make it worth your while to buy your own home."

"I don't know . . ." I hesitated.

"Have you thought about retirement?" he asked. "All you're doing right now is building up someone *else's* equity. Wouldn't it be nice to not have to pay anything for housing once you get ready to retire?"

"I guess."

"Are you itemizing deductions?" he asked.

"Uhhh . . ."

He held out his hand, asking for all the tax forms I'd brought with me. I handed him the folder and sat quietly while he looked at what I had.

"I didn't know you gave money to the orphanage," he said after a moment, looking up from the papers in surprise.

I had forgotten that was in there.

"No one knows," I said quickly. "And I don't *want* anyone to know . . ."

He looked at me carefully for a minute.

"Everything you share with me is confidential," he finally said. "You don't have to worry about me telling anyone."

I relaxed a bit and sat back.

"But," he said, "between you and me, I think it's very nice that you're doing that."

I nodded.

"And I appreciate that you're supporting my daughter-in-law."

I nodded again.

He continued to peruse my financial documents for a while and then sat back.

"You have a lot of money coming in, Tanner," he said, looking at me directly. "You were already pulling in extra from your coaching, and now you've got all these little side jobs bringing money in. When do you start as athletic director?"

"Not 'til July."

"I'm assuming there's a significant pay raise with that?"

"Yeah."

He sat back and sighed.

"You have a lot of money coming in," he said again, "but you're not being smart with it at all. I know that retirement seems like it's a long way off, but believe me, it'll be here before you know it."

"So you want me to buy a house?"

"Well," he said, "that, and a few other things. For one thing, I think you should sock away everything you make from Parks and Rec and your conceal and carry classes. Every penny that you make over and above your salary should be going into a 401k."

"And what exactly is a 401k?" I asked.

He sighed.

"You're really lucky you won that raffle," he said. "You know that?"

Since my base salary was getting ready to rise, we decided that I was going to "sock away" all that I made from my coaching positions throughout the year too. That meant my football stipend, my basketball stipend, and my baseball stipend.

I started working with Sierra, who I had dated for a few months before I met Megan, and who was now a real estate agent. Together, we found a house not too far from the one I was renting, with a huge back yard for TD and a basement that was just begging to be turned in to a man-cave.

Being a home-owner was a lot more fun than I expected. Suddenly I was interested in masonry and tiling and lawn care. Every home-improvement project that I took on helped the equity of my home rise as fast as my retirement account, and had the added benefit of keeping me even busier.

172

CHASE HAD A birthday coming up, and so in September, less than a year after David and Laci had returned to Mexico, I traveled to the town of Steep Ford, about two hours from Cavendish. My grandmother had lived in Steep Ford before she died, and we used to go there to visit her a lot when we were little. I had always liked visiting my grandmother. She'd understood that little boys didn't like sitting around in a stuffy old house full of doilies and cat litter and had always made sure that we did fun stuff whenever we went to visit her. Sometimes it was a trip to the zoo or to a ball game, or sometimes she just took us to the movies or the mall. But, no matter what we did, Grandma always finished off our adventures with a visit to Steep Ford Creamery.

The creamery had become a favorite tourist spot over the years, sporting mini-golf outside and lots of arcade games inside. As it grew in popularity, they had installed a bakery, and even added a gift shop.

Figuring out what to get for Chase these days wasn't easy since it was becoming increasingly difficult for him to do things as his disease progressed, but I finally decided that a sweatshirt, emblazoned with "Steep Ford Creamery" on it, and a gift certificate with the promise of a trip to relive childhood memories, would be just the ticket.

School had started back, so I had to go on a Saturday. I found the creamery to be fairly crowded, but pretty much the same as I had always remembered it. I stood in line for about five minutes, watching little kids get their picture made with the giant cast iron cow that stood by the front door, until I finally got to the counter and a guy in a red and white striped paper hat asked me if he could help me.

I paid for the sweatshirt and gift certificate, along with a double cheeseburger, fries and chocolate milkshake, and then slid on down the counter to wait for my food. It was while I was standing there, waiting, that I suddenly felt someone tug on my t-shirt.

I looked down . . . I couldn't believe my eyes.

"Amber!" I took a knee and looked her in the eye. She gave me a huge smile. "Hi, honey! How are you doing?!"

She smiled at me some more. I reached my arms out and she hugged me.

"Hi," she whispered into my ear as she wrapped her arms around my neck.

"It is *so* good to see you!" I said, engulfing her in a hug.

"Hello," I heard a voice above me say. I glanced up and saw a woman standing above Amber.

"Hi," I replied, standing up and shaking her hand. "I'm, um, I'm Tanner."

She looked at me curiously, but pleasant enough.

"I'm Karen," she said. "Do you work at Amber's school?"

"What? Oh . . . no," I answered, shaking my head.

Now she looked confused.

"How do you know Amber?"

"Amber – uhhhh – I know Amber from when she lived in Cavendish."

"You're from Cavendish?"

"Yeah," I nodded. "I just came in to town for something." I held up the bag containing the sweatshirt and gift certificate.

"I see," she nodded, her demeanor considerably cooler now. "Well, we need to be going now. Come on, Amber."

"No! Wait!" I said as she turned to walk away.

She looked back at me. Any trace of a smile was completely gone.

"I . . . I'd really like to talk with Amber for a minute–"

"Amber doesn't *talk*," Karen said, "not since she got back from *Cavendish*." She spit out the word and grabbed Amber roughly by the hand, pulling her toward a table.

But Amber dug her heels in and pulled her mother back. She tugged on her arm and Karen reluctantly leaned an ear toward Amber's mouth. Amber whispered in Karen's ear for a moment and when Karen straightened back up again, she looked at me carefully.

"Amber says you're her friend," she finally told me.

"I am," I nodded.

She looked at me for another minute.

"I would never hurt Amber," I added.

174

Karen finally nodded. "You want to sit down?" she asked, motioning to a nearby table that was littered with empty hamburger wrappers and milkshake containers. A baby was sitting in a high chair, picking Cheerios off the tray.

"Uhhhh, yeah," I agreed. "Thanks."

She nodded again and I followed her to the table. Amber took my hand and tugged me into a chair, plopping down next to me after I'd sat down.

"Who's this?" I asked Amber, pointing at the baby.

Amber crooked her finger for me to come closer and she whispered into my ear when I did. "Meredith."

"And who's Meredith?"

"My sister," she smiled.

"I didn't know you *had* a sister."

Amber smiled and nodded.

I turned to Karen. "How old is she?" I asked.

"Ten months," she answered.

I nodded and did some quick calculating, figuring out that Karen had probably already been about five months pregnant when she'd gotten Amber back.

"She's beautiful," I said, smiling. "Congratulations."

"Thank you," Karen said, smiling back for the first time.

"She's almost as pretty as her sister," I said, glancing at Amber, who rewarded me with another huge grin.

My food arrived.

"*How* exactly do you know Amber?" Karen asked as I started to eat.

"David's my best friend."

"David?"

"When Amber was in foster care?" I reminded her. "David and Laci?"

"I don't know names," she said bitterly. "All I know is that—"

She stopped herself and looked at Amber.

"Amber," Karen said, fishing around in her purse. "Do you still want to play skeeball?"

Amber nodded slowly.

"Here." Karen handed her some quarters. "Go play for a few minutes."

Amber looked at me and reached out and grabbed my sleeve. She tugged at it.

175

"I'll come play in a minute," I promised. "You go practice until I get there."

She nodded and left.

"David and Laci," Karen said. "Were they her *first* set of foster parents or her second?"

"Second," I said hurriedly.

She seemed to relax a little.

"I'm the one that gave her the ring," I told Karen. "You know? The pearl ring that was on that necklace with the cross?"

She gave me a small nod.

"Do you know what happened to Amber at her first foster home?" she asked.

"Yes," I answered quietly.

She looked at me for a long moment.

"She was *talking* when I went away," Karen said. "She was fine when I left."

"I'm sorry."

"I mean, I'm not saying that being in foster care was going to be a picnic or anything, but . . ."

"But she shouldn't have had to go through what she did," I finished for her. Karen nodded.

"They didn't even do anything to the guy," she said. "They said he was a minor. Nothing even happened to him!"

"I broke his nose."

She looked at me in disbelief and then asked quietly, "You did?"

"And I think his jaw."

"Really?" she asked, a smile tugging at her lips.

I nodded.

She stared at me for another moment and then glanced toward Amber who was collecting tickets from her skeeball game.

"I had to sell it," she said quietly, looking down at the table.

"Sell what?"

"The necklace," she explained, "with the ring and the cross."

"Oh."

"I'm sorry," she said. "I didn't want to, and Amber was so upset, but . . ."

"It's okay," I assured her.

176

"It's so hard," she went on. "DSS comes by whenever they want and everything has to be just right or they have a fit, and it . . . it takes money, you know? It's really expensive raising kids all by yourself."

I nodded in what I hoped was an understanding way.

"What about their dad?" I asked. "Does he help?"

"I don't really know anything about her dad," she said, nodding toward Amber. "And Meredith's dad . . . I haven't seen him in a while."

"How long's 'a while'?" I asked.

"Since I told him I was pregnant. Same thing happened with this one," she said, quietly, laying her hand on her belly.

"You're pregnant *again?*" I asked, unable to hide my disbelief. Three different babies, three different fathers – all of them apparently out of the picture. *Wow.*

"Ever thought about going on the Pill?" That kind of popped out of my mouth before I could stop myself.

"I've thought about it," she nodded, seemingly not offended. "I really like babies though." She gave me a slight smile and rubbed her hand gently over her stomach.

"Uh-huh," I said. "Well, congratulations."

"Thanks."

Amber came back to the table and tugged on my sleeve again.

"Okay, okay," I agreed. "Come on. Let me show you how a pro does it."

I made it a point to stay in touch with Karen over the next few months, driving to Steep Ford several times to see her and the girls. I was invited to Meredith's first birthday party and bought her a plush, stuffed dog with floppy ears. Meredith's eyes lit up when she pulled it from the bag.

"Uppy," she said with a smile.

"That's right," Karen told her, "Puppy dog," but it was known as "Uppy" from that point on.

Karen lived in a trailer park near the edge of town, and it wasn't a nice trailer park. I worried a lot about her, and especially the girls, and the more I worried, the more excuses I found to drive to Steep Ford to visit. Every trip, however, left me with new worries on top of the old ones.

In November, I arrived unannounced and discovered that Karen was wasted. The whole trailer smelled like pot.

"Are you crazy?" I cried after she let me in. "You're pregnant!"

"No, no, no," she said hurriedly. "It's not that bad if you don't do it that often."

I stared at her in disbelief.

"What if DSS drops by?" I asked. "You wanna to lose the kids?"

"But that's the whole point," she said. "They just came by. They won't be back for at least two weeks. I was just celebrating a little . . ."

"What if I call them right now?" I asked.

She looked at me, shocked.

"You wouldn't do that!"

"Don't bet on it," I answered, pulling out my phone.

"Please don't," she cried, grabbing my hand as tears welled up in her eyes. "Please don't! I don't want to lose my babies!"

"You have to promise me that you won't ever do drugs again while you're taking care of these girls."

"I promise," she nodded.

I had only been bluffing when I'd pulled out my phone. Although it was true that Karen could have been doing a better job, I couldn't stand the thought of Amber going back to foster care.

I looked at Karen carefully as she continued to nod her promise to me, and I decided to believe her.

I shouldn't have.

~ ~ ~

IN EARLY DECEMBER, my phone went off. It was three in the morning, and the screen said that it was Karen.

"Hello?"

"Tanner?" But it wasn't Karen, it was Amber . . . whispering my name. I sat up in bed.

"What's wrong?"

"Meredith won't stop crying."

"Where's your mom?"

"I don't know."

I put her on speaker phone and started getting dressed. I could hear Meredith crying in the background.

"Do you think maybe she's hungry?" I asked Amber.

"Maybe."

"Do you have any milk?"

Amber went and fixed a bottle of milk and gave it to Meredith as I climbed in my truck. She quieted down immediately.

"Amber," I said, "I'm going to hang up for a minute, but then I'm going to call you right back, okay?"

"Okay," she whispered, and I hung up the phone.

Then I called the police.

It was two days later that I called David.

"Hey," he answered the phone.

"Hey. Am I getting you at a bad time?" I asked.

"Not at bit. What's up?"

"Ummm, I've got a surprise for you," I said.

"A good surprise?"

"Are you sitting down?"

"I'm *always* sitting down," he answered.

"Okay," I said. "Well . . . I'm putting you on speaker phone."

"Ok-ay . . ." he said slowly.

I nodded at Amber.

"Hi," she whispered, hesitantly.

There was silence on the other end.

"Tell him who it is," I prodded. "He hasn't talked to you in a long time."

But she didn't need to.

"AMBER?!"

She giggled silently.

I could envision him leaning forward in his chair, gripping the phone.

"Amber!" he said again. "Where are you?"

"I'm at Tanner's house," she whispered, still smiling. She looked at me and I smiled back.

"Are you okay?" he asked.

"Yes."

"Why are you at Tanner's house?"

"I'll tell you all about it in a minute," I interjected. "I just thought that you'd want to say 'Hi,' to her."

"I do," he agreed. "Amber – it's so good to hear from you!"

She giggled again.

"How are you doing?"

"Good."

"Well, good!" he said. "I'm so glad you called me!"

"When do I get to see you?" she asked.

"Ummm, I'm not sure yet," he said. "Why don't you let me talk to Tanner for a minute and maybe he and I can figure something out, okay?"

"Okay," she said.

"Here," I said, handing her a remote and taking the phone back. "Just push this button and it'll start your movie back up."

She nodded and ran toward the living room.

"Are you there?" I asked him after she was out of earshot.

"Why is Amber at your house? What's going on?"

"I ran into her and her mom a couple of months ago over in Steep Ford," I explained. "I made friends with her mom then we kinda stayed in touch."

"You're dating Karen Patterson?"

"No. We're just friends."

"Well, how does Amber seem?" he asked. "She sounds great. Is she okay?"

"I've got a lot to tell you."

"Is she okay?"

"Yeah," I said. "She's really good."

"So her mom's doing okay?"

"Well," I hesitated. "Not so much."

"What's going on?"

"She got arrested again."

"Why?"

"Same as before," I explained.

"DUI?"

"Yeah," I said. "But this time she had an accident."

"But Amber's okay?"

"Amber's *fine*," I assured him again. "She wasn't in the car."

"Good," he said.

"But she killed somebody."

I heard him exhale.

"She's not gonna be getting out this time."

"What about Amber?" he asked frantically. "Why's she with you? Where's she gonna go? Is she in foster care again?"

"Relax," I said. "She's staying with me right now. Karen told Social Services she wanted Amber to stay with me and they approved it."

"She's staying with *you?*"

"Temporarily."

"For how long?"

"Until they can find a permanent home for the girls."

"Girls?"

"Well, that's the thing," I said, taking a deep breath. "Karen got pregnant right after she got out of prison."

"She had a baby?"

"Yeah. About three months after she got Amber back."

"A girl?"

"Yeah," I said. "She's a year old. Her name's Meredith."

"Where is she?"

"Actually," I said, "she's right here next to me. Sound asleep."

"She's with you too?"

"Yeah."

"I can't believe you're watching both of them," he said softly.

"There's more," I went on.

"More?"

"Yeah. More. She's pregnant again."

"Who's pregnant again?"

"Who do you *think*, you moron?"

"She's pregnant again?"

"Yeah. And she's having another little girl."

"When?"

"Any time in the next few weeks," I said. "I'm actually surprised the accident didn't send her into labor."

"She's going to have a baby while she's in prison?"

"Well, she's at the hospital right now," I explained. "She got kind of banged up. I don't know – they might keep her there until she has the baby."

"Is the baby okay?"

"I think so."

"What's going to happen to them?" he asked softly.

"That's kind of why I'm calling."

"Why?"

I hesitated for a moment.

"Do you want Amber?" I asked.

"You *know* I want her," he said, his voice catching. "But we can't move back! Dorito's mom is here and–"

"I know you can't move back. You don't *have* to move back," I assured him. "I talked with Karen. She's agreed to give you and Laci full custody."

There was a long pause.

"And let us stay in Mexico?" he clarified.

"Yes."

"I . . . I can't believe this. How'd you get her to do that?"

"There are some conditions."

"I'll do anything."

"One thing is that she wants to maintain contact and you'd have to promise to come for visitations four times a year."

"Okay," he agreed hurriedly. "No problem. When can I get her?"

"Basically anytime you want, but–"

"I'll be there tomorrow."

182

"No. Listen," I said. "There's more."

"What?"

I paused.

"She wants the girls to stay together. If you want Amber, you have to take Meredith and the baby, too."

There was silence.

"Are you still there?" I finally asked.

"Yeah," he said quietly. "I'm here."

"I'm sorry. It was the best I could do."

There was another long pause.

"I'm sorry," I said again.

"You did great," he finally managed, and then he said again, "I'll be there tomorrow."

~ ~ ~

TRYING TO HOLD hands with Amber at the airport the next day while we were walking down the concourse was pretty much impossible. She was hopping and skipping like a kangaroo that had swallowed a jack rabbit.

"Come *on*!" she whispered, tugging impatiently at my hand.

"Relax, kid," I said, tugging right back and hoisting Meredith up a bit higher on my hip with my other arm. "He's not gonna be here for ten more minutes."

She didn't stop hopping.

We went to the exit of the terminal where passengers were funneled into the airport. A steady stream of people came through the security gates and Amber hopped even higher, trying to see.

"Wanna sit on my shoulders?" I finally asked. She grinned and nodded.

I put Meredith down for a second and she stood in front of me, gripping Uppy tightly, while I lifted Amber high above my head and set her on my shoulders. Then I picked Meredith back up and tried to position her in a way so that Amber wouldn't accidentally kick her in the face. I was really glad that their little sister hadn't been born yet.

After a few minutes Amber started bouncing again.

"I see him!" she whispered. "I see him!!"

"Are you sure?" I asked, glancing up at her.

"Yes!" she nodded emphatically, and I set Meredith down again and lifted Amber to the ground.

She would have taken off running immediately if I hadn't kept hold of her hand, but I didn't release her until I saw David myself . . .

Then I let her go.

He was looking for her in the wrong direction . . . didn't see her until she was directly in front of him, but – when he did – he dropped his bag on the ground and fell right to his knees, burying his face against her neck and

184

wrapping his arms around her so tightly that it was a wonder either one of them could breath.

I watched the two of them – both completely oblivious to the throngs of annoyed people who were trying to get around them – and I felt myself smile.

"I've never seen him so happy," I heard a voice say, and I turned, surprised to see Laci standing next to me.

"I didn't know you were coming, too," I said.

"Right," she said, sardonically, reaching up to give me a hug. "Like he's bringing three little girls back to Mexico all by himself."

I returned her hug.

"Seriously, Tanner?" she asked when we parted. "*Three?*"

"Sorry."

She smiled at me and gave me another squeeze, and then we both turned our eyes back to the happy reunion that was still taking place in front of us.

It was two weeks later that Karen had her third daughter . . . David and Laci's fourth. By that time David and Laci, especially Laci, had spent a lot of time with Karen. I would say "talking", but I think the more appropriate term for it would be "witnessing". Through the conversations that Laci brought to dinner every evening after spending hours with her in the hospital every day, I learned that Karen was asking a lot of questions about God. I didn't press to find out more, but Laci seemed pretty happy with the way everything was going, and when she announced to me and David that Karen was going to name the baby Grace, she looked at both of us in a very meaningful way.

Two days after she'd given birth, Karen was taken out of the hospital and moved to the county jail, where she would be held until her trial.

And then, right after that, David and Laci took their three new daughters, and returned to Mexico City.

~ ~ ~

APPARENTLY SUDDENLY HAVING five kids didn't faze David and Laci too much, because they adopted *another* one only a few months after they returned to Mexico.

Marco had been sent to the orphanage straight from the hospital after he was born. He had a severe bilateral complete cleft and monodactylous symbrachydactyly. What that means in English is that he had a really bad cleft palate and no fingers . . . only a tiny, malformed thumb on one hand.

The way Laci told the story was that Marco had arrived at the orphanage on the same day that David came to pick up Grace, Meredith, and Lily, who often spent the day at the orphanage while Laci was working. He had already strapped all of the girls into their car seats and had started the car, when Meredith suddenly realized that Uppy wasn't with her. Knowing that there would be no peace until Uppy was retrieved, he unloaded all of the girls, trudged back into the building, and followed Lily to the nursery, where she was sure Meredith had left Uppy. He was there, Lily explained, because Meredith had let the new "broken baby" borrow him.

According to Laci, David had taken one look at that "broken baby" and instantly fallen in love. David was always quick to interject that after they'd returned from Cavendish with three new daughters, he'd had to promise Dorito that he'd keep his eyes open for a little boy to "balance things out a bit". At this point in the story, he would always glance at Laci and also add that he had known immediately that Marco would be the perfect little boy for their family, since he wouldn't be able to pick up Laci's annoying habit of counting on her fingers whenever she had to do math.

Laci would always smirk at David then, and he'd give her a big grin.

186

NOT TOO LONG after Marco began appearing regularly in the family photos that I received from David and Laci, I heard from my mom that Mrs. White was sick. She had been diagnosed with breast cancer, and that was something that I didn't want to hear.

Mrs. White had always been very special to me. After Greg had died, she had continued to come to the high school's home basketball and then baseball games. I couldn't imagine how painful it was for her to sit there and watch me and Mike play when Greg wasn't with us, but it seemed like she was always there, sitting in the stands and cheering the two of us on. In addition to helping her out with her yard and stuff, I had babysat for Charlotte from time to time when Laci hadn't been available. Throughout the years, it was not uncommon for her to invite me and my family over for dinner, and she came over for meals at our house too.

So I didn't want to hear that Mrs. White had breast cancer. I didn't want to think that she might die. I didn't want to see her lying sick in a hospital bed . . .

But I knew that it was something I had to do.

And so I went to visit her in the hospital, with a big bouquet of flowers, the day after she'd had her mastectomy.

I was scared before I walked into her room, worried about what I would find.

I shouldn't have been.

What I found was the same old Mrs. White I'd always known, sitting up in bed, grumbling to herself about her phone.

"This is the stupidest piece of–" She glanced toward the door and spotted me, breaking into a big smile. "Tanner!"

"Hi," I said, taking a step into the room. "How are you doing?"

"I'm ready to throw this piece of garbage into the trash," she said, holding her phone up, "but other than that, I'm doing good."

"What's wrong?" I asked, stepping toward her bed.

"Charlotte downloaded some stupid app for me and all the instructions for it are in Chinese," she complained, holding the screen out for me to see.

"I think that's Japanese," I said, looking at it.

"Really?" she asked, turning the screen back toward her own face.

"I have no idea," I smiled, and she smiled back.

I leaned over and gently gave her a hug, worried that I would hurt her. She reached up with one arm and hugged me back, being plenty careful herself.

I handed her the flowers and she thanked me for them.

"How are you doing?" I asked again after she'd gone on and on about how beautiful they were.

"I'm great," she said.

"Really?" I asked. "I mean . . . you look great . . ."

"Oh, I am," she said. Then, with a mischievous smile, she added, "Of course I'm only operating on one cylinder now . . ."

I laughed.

"What have you got there?" she asked, pointing at the other item I had brought with me.

I held up Greg's old Bible and showed it to her.

"Oh, wow," she said softly. "Did Laci give that to you?"

I nodded and Mrs. White shook her head slightly.

"I didn't know she gave it to you . . ."

"I was going through a really rough time," I said by way of explanation. "She thought it might help."

"That makes sense," she nodded. "I gave her that Bible when *she* was going through a really rough time."

"You did?" I asked.

I looked at her for a long moment, hoping she'd tell me about it, but she didn't.

"When?" I finally asked. "When Greg died?"

"Oh, no," she laughed, shaking her head again. "I wasn't ready to give it up then."

"When then?"

She studied me carefully for a moment before answering.

188

"When you two stopped seeing each other," she finally said.

"*Really?*" I asked, unable to hide the surprise in my voice.

She nodded.

"I . . . I didn't know it was that big of a deal for her," I shrugged.

"Oh, come on, Tanner," she said doubtfully. "Having to choose between doing what her *heart* was telling her to do and doing what *God* was telling her to do? You don't think that was a big deal for her?"

I didn't know how to answer that.

"Well, anyway," I said, "I thought that maybe you might want it back now."

I extended it toward her.

"You're worried about me," she stated, not taking it from me.

I nodded.

"I'm going to be fine," she said. "They caught it early. They think they got it all. I should be out of here in about two days."

"Good," I smiled. "I'm glad to hear it."

"Why don't you keep it," she suggested, nodding toward the Bible. "I know that it would mean a lot to Greg if he knew that you had it."

"No," I said, shaking my head. "I don't even read it."

"Well then start!"

"No," I said again, shaking my head even more. "What I mean is that I used to read it, but then I got a study Bible and that's pretty much the one I use all the time now."

She gave me a little smile and finally took it from me.

"Okay," she agreed. "I'll take it. Maybe I'll give it to Charlotte. I'm worried about her. I think something's going on."

"What do you mean?"

"I don't know," she said, shaking her head. "She insists that everything's fine, but . . ."

"But what?"

"I can always tell when she's lying to me."

I gave her a little smile.

"Jordan hasn't mentioned that anything's wrong?" she asked

"No," I said, shaking my own head. "Probably all that's wrong is that she's been worried to death about *you*."

"Yeah," Mrs. White agreed with a sigh. "That's probably all that it is."

The next week, Karen pleaded "no contest" to second degree vehicular manslaughter and was sentenced to seventeen years in prison. At four visits per year, I figured that she was going to get witnessed to at least sixty-eight more times.

Laci wasn't the only one who was witnessing. The worse that Chase got, the more often Jordan came home to visit, spending a lot of time with Chase, and talking to him in hushed, urgent tones.

If there had indeed been something for Mrs. White to worry about with Charlotte, I never did find out what it was, but I worried plenty myself about Jordan. Every time I saw him, I looked for evidence of Huntington's and peppered him with questions.

"You haven't noticed any problems with your balance?" I asked him one day while he was visiting.

"No, Tanner," he said wearily. "I wish you'd quit asking me about it every time I come home."

"Well," I said, "if you'd just get tested then I wouldn't have to ask you, would I?"

"Why don't you leave him alone?" Chase asked me, but his voice was being affected by the disease now, so it came out sounding a lot more like: *Whhhy dooon't yoooouuuu leeeeave hiiim aaaloooooneee?*

Jordan looked pained.

"Look," he said. "I know you're just worried, but you've got to stop bugging me about it. One of the reasons people decide *not* to get tested is because they don't want to be thinking about it all the time. You make it pretty much impossible for me to think about anything else."

"Sorry," I sighed.

He looked at me sympathetically.

"Look," he said, "I'll make a deal with you, okay?"

I eyed him questioningly.

"If I have any symptoms," he said, "anything at all, you have my word that I'll tell you right away."

"Okay," I said.

"But," he added quickly, "you've got to promise that you're not going to bring it up anymore or I'm going to quit talking to you altogether. Do you understand?"

I looked at him carefully.

"You'll tell me if you have *any* symptoms whatsoever?" I clarified.

"First sign of anything and I'll tell you," he nodded.

I studied him again and then nodded back.

"Okay," I agreed. "I'll stop asking."

"So just remember," Chase said. "No news is good news."

Noooo neeeewsss iiisss goooood neeewsss . . .

"That's right," Jordan answered. "No news is good news."

~ ~ ~

CHASE PASSED AWAY five years later with Jordan, Charlotte, Mom and me, all by his side. He had aspirated some milkshake into his lungs a few weeks earlier, but we hadn't realized it until it developed into pneumonia. That was what took his life. At least he lived long enough to meet his first nephew: Charlotte and Jordan had adopted their first child just a few weeks before Chase got sick.

I kept my end of our bargain and stopped asking Jordan if he had any symptoms, and I quit bugging him about getting tested. By the time Amber and Dorito graduated from high school, Jordan hadn't given me any news. Hopefully he was keeping his end of the bargain, too.

In Mexico, Amber did pretty well. All of David and Laci's kids had been enrolled in a small, private, Christian school where everybody knew everybody else. Once Amber warmed up to a teacher, she was likely to have him or her for another couple of years. She'd also known all of her classmates ever since she'd moved down there too, so she was pretty successful in school, all things considered.

David and Laci had started taking Amber to counselors, psychiatrists, and therapists as soon as they had gotten her, but as the years went by, it was obvious that she was never going to be completely healed from what had happened to her. Around her family and her friends she was fine and would even speak, but if the need ever arose for her to talk to a stranger, you could forget it – it wasn't going to happen.

Naturally this posed a problem when trying to determine how Amber was going to go to college.

How would Amber ever be able to function on a normal, college campus? By the time she finally got comfortable around one of her professors, it would be time for final exams, and then she'd have to start all over again the next semester. What if she was assigned to a group project and had to work with other people? Or what if she got called on during class? What if something in her dorm room needed to be fixed and she had to talk to the RA about it? What if her roommate didn't want to live with a mute?

To solve this problem, Amber went off to college with Dorito. I think it bothered David that Dorito wasn't following him into engineering, but at least he was going to State, and that made David happy to no end. Dorito, who had idolized Charlotte ever since he was a little boy, decided that he wanted to follow the same path she had taken and become an architect. Amber decided that she was going to major in communication.

Well, let me clarify that.

Amber was going to major in *written* communication.

State was about two hours from Cavendish and Amber and Dorito got an apartment near campus. I made the two of them promise me that they'd call me if they needed anything, and I promised David and Laci that I would look in on them from time to time, to make sure that they didn't get into any trouble.

For the first two and a half years, there was no trouble.

Dorito took good care of Amber while they roomed together. They both seemed happy and Amber appeared to be adjusting fairly well. During their freshmen year, they came to see me and their grandparents at least once a month and Dorito took Amber to see Karen about that often as well.

By the middle of their sophomore year, however, Amber knew everyone at the prison well enough that she could go through the visitation process all by herself, so she stopped making Dorito go with her quite so often. That worked out really well because, by that time, Dorito had gotten himself a girlfriend and suddenly had something better to do with himself on weekends than to drive Amber to a correctional facility for monthly visitations. Often, when Amber would go by herself, I would meet her there and visit with Karen too, and afterward, I would take Amber out to eat.

Dorito's girlfriend, Amanda, started coming along for their monthly visits to their grandparents and I could tell that Dorito was really serious about her. I was happy for him, but at the same time, it made me worry.

What was going to happen to Amber once Dorito decided to get married?

~ ~ ~

LATE ONE SATURDAY night, in the fall of Dorito and Amber's junior year, my phone went off. First I looked at the clock and discovered that it was one in the morning, and then I looked at the screen and saw that it was Amber. I knew instantly that something was wrong.

"Amber?"

She was crying.

"I'm sorry to call you so late," she sobbed.

"What's wrong?"

"I'm really scared," she cried. "I didn't know what to do."

"What's *wrong*, Amber?"

"It's Dorito," she said. "He's really sick."

"He's sick? Are you at the hospital?"

"No," she cried.

"What's wrong with him?"

"He got drunk," she sobbed. "He's so sick. I'm afraid he's going to die!"

I immediately felt myself relax.

"He's not going to *die*," I promised her. "He's going to be fine."

"What if he has alcohol poisoning?" she asked. "People can die from drinking too much."

True . . .

"If you're that worried about him," I said, "take him to the infirmary."

"But then he'll get in trouble for drinking," she bawled.

I rolled my eyes.

"Is he conscious?" I asked.

"Sort of," she replied, and – as if on cue – I heard Dorito groan in the background.

"Is he breathing okay?"

"I think so."

"Okay, listen," I told her. "I'm headed that way. Just relax. He's going to be fine."

About two hours later I pulled up to their apartment complex. Amber was watching out the window for me and opened the door quickly when I got to the landing, ushering me inside.

"I'm sorry," she said when I gave her a hug and surveyed Dorito, who was thoroughly passed out on the couch by this time.

I listened to his breathing, took his pulse, and then gave Amber my best annoyed look.

"He's not even *close* to dying," I told Amber, trying to sound disappointed. "What a complete and total waste of time."

"I'm sorry," she said again, tears welling up in her eyes.

"You're sorry he's not dying?"

"No," she said seriously. "I'm sorry I made you drive all the way up here."

I laughed and reached for her, tugging her hair.

"I love seeing you," I said, "and you never invite me to come visit. The only time I get to see you guys is when you want a free meal."

Amber somehow managed to look even more upset.

"Amber?" I asked.

"What?"

"You really need to learn how to take a joke."

She studied my face for a moment and then finally gave me a smile.

"Sorry," she said, one more time.

"Whatcha got to drink around here?" I asked.

"Ummm, regular milk, soy milk," she said, thinking, "orange juice, apple juice and Sprite."

"Soy milk?" I asked, grimacing.

"It's good for you," she insisted, heading for a cupboard to get a glass. "You should try some."

"Yeah, thanks," I said. "I'm good."

She looked disappointed and set the empty glass on the counter.

"How 'bout some of what he had?" I suggested, pointing at Dorito.

"I dumped it down the drain," Amber said, defiantly.

I looked at the empty liquor bottle she was pointing to that was sitting on the top of the trash and picked it up.

"What a waste," I said, shaking my head.

Amber glared at me and crossed her arms. I ignored her, threw the bottle back into the trash, and headed for the fridge.

"So what brought all this on?" I asked, jabbing my thumb toward the recumbent Dorito and pulling out the orange juice container. "I had no idea that Dorito drank."

"He doesn't," Amber said as I shook the carton. "He and Mandy broke up."

"Oh," I nodded, pouring some juice into the glass that Amber had pulled down earlier. "Why?"

Dorito picked that moment to start heaving. I dragged the trash can over to the couch and caught most of it before it hit the carpet. I pointed at what I'd missed and told Amber, "That's your job."

Dorito passed back out on the couch and Amber ran a dishrag under the water. First she gently wiped Dorito's face and then she went to work on the floor.

"He bought her a ring," Amber explained, heading to the sink to rinse out the rag. "He was going to propose."

"What happened?"

"He never got to ask her," she said, returning to the carpet to give it another going over. "He wanted to surprise her so he told her we were going to Cavendish this weekend."

"And?"

"She was supposed to be at work so he went over to her apartment with all these candles and flowers and stuff. He was going to be there waiting for her when she got home from work."

I already didn't like where this was going.

"He let himself in?" I guessed.

She nodded.

"And she wasn't at work?"

Amber pressed her lips together and shook her head.

I shook my head.

"Seriously?" I asked. "She was with somebody else?"

Amber nodded.

"I didn't think Amanda was like that," I said. "She seemed really nice."

"That's what Dorito thought too," Amber said quietly.

I glanced over at him as he slept and felt a wave of sympathy for him. I sighed and looked back at Amber and – for some reason – I felt sorry for her, too.

"Why don't you go to bed?" I asked, taking the rag from her. "I'll keep an eye on him."

"No," she said, shaking her head. "I'm fine."

"No," I insisted. "Aren't you going to church in the morning?"

"Well," she hedged.

"Go," I said. "Off to bed. I've got this covered."

"Are you sure?" she asked.

"Of course I'm sure," I said, kissing her on the forehead and pointing toward her room. "Get on in there."

Dorito awakened to throw up a few more times, but for the most part he slept for the rest of the night. Amber slipped quietly past us in the morning on her way to church and I waved silently to her from the recliner that I'd slept in. Dorito stirred a few minutes after she'd left and sat up on the couch, holding his head in his hands.

"I'm so thirsty," he moaned

"Wanna beer?" I offered.

He didn't even bother to give me a dirty look.

"You two are no fun anymore," I said. "You know that?"

He ignored that, too.

"Are you going to tell my dad?" he finally asked.

"I already did," I nodded. "He's catching a flight up here this morning so he can come and put you in a time out."

Dorito turned his head and peered at me, studying me for a moment. Then he buried his face in his hands again.

"Thank you," he said quietly.

"Mm-hmm," I said. "You owe me."

He nodded and looked back up at me. I gave him a smile that he didn't return.

"Mandy broke up with me," he said. This time I nodded at him.

"I heard about that," I said. "I'm sorry."

He shook his head and looked away, trying to hold back his tears. After a moment he quit trying and allowed himself to sob, burying his face in his hands.

198

I wasn't entirely convinced that he was finished throwing up, but I went over and sat next to him on the couch anyway, patting him on the back.

"It's gonna be okay," I assured him.

"No, it's not!" he cried, looking at me in shock. "I love her! I wanted to spend the rest of my life with her!"

"I know you thought she was the one—" I began, but he cut me off.

"I *know* she was the one," he said angrily, his tears suddenly gone.

"No," I said, gently. "She wasn't. If she loved you the way you love her then she wouldn't have done this to you and if she doesn't love you the way you love her, then she's not the one for you."

"What do *you* know about it?" he scoffed. "You're a great one to be handing out relationship advice."

I let that slide, chalking it up to how crappy he was feeling.

"I know more about it than you think," I said very quietly.

He stared at me for a long moment.

"I'm sorry," he finally said, shaking his head. "I shouldn't have said that."

"Don't worry about it," I assured him.

He wiped his face, looked away, and then sat silently for a minute until he said, "Tell me about her."

"About who?"

"Whoever it was that you were in love with."

Now it was my turn to look away. I took my hand off his shoulder and clasped my hands together in front of me, staring at them.

"You don't have to tell me," Dorito said when I didn't answer right away.

"No," I answered, shaking my head and glancing back at him. "It's okay. It's just that there's not much to tell."

"What happened?"

"I dunno," I shrugged, returning my gaze to my hands. "It just didn't work out."

"When was it?"

"College."

"How long did it take before you got over her?"

I turned back to him and looked into his eyes before I answered. "I never got over her."

Dorito gaped at me, clearly dismayed. "You're telling me I'm never gonna get over her?" he cried.

"Well, no," I said, shaking my head. "I don't think so. I think you're going to find somebody else and I think they're going to make you forget all about Amanda."

"*You* didn't find somebody else," he pointed out.

"That was different."

"Why?"

"Because there's never been anyone else that I've even come close to feeling the same way about."

"Well what makes you think it's going to be any different for me?"

"Because," I said, "she didn't hurt me like Amanda hurt you. Once you get over the pain that you're feeling right now, anger's going to start settling in in its place, and once you're mad enough? Every girl you meet's gonna seem better than Amanda."

"She didn't hurt you?" he asked.

I shook my head.

"Did you hurt her?"

I shook my head again.

"Then why'd you break up?"

"It's a long story," I answered.

He didn't press me on it further.

"You still love her?" he asked quietly. "Don't you?"

"In some ways," I nodded.

"Do you think you'll ever get back together with her?"

"No," I said, smiling and shaking my head. "Definitely not."

"You never know," he shrugged.

"No," I said. "I know. We're definitely not getting back together."

"Is she still alive?"

"Yes," I laughed.

"Well, then," he persisted. "You never know."

I didn't bother to argue with him anymore and he thought for a moment.

"You know, this isn't very encouraging," he finally decided. "Basically all I'm hearing here is that even if I *do* find the right person, there's no guarantee that things are gonna work out."

"No," I admitted, giving him another pat on the back, "there's no guarantee it's going to work out. All I'm saying is that I don't think Amanda was the one for you."

Dorito sighed and sat back on the couch.

We sat quietly for another moment.

"You know what?" he finally asked.

"What?"

"You're right."

"About what?"

"If she could do that to me," he said, "then she didn't love me like I loved her . . . because I never would have done something like that to her."

I nodded.

"You know that anger you were talking about?" he asked.

I nodded again.

"I think it's starting to settle in," he muttered.

I gave him a little smile.

"Amanda just wasn't the one," I assured him again. "You're going to meet somebody else who loves you just as much as you love her . . . and the two of you are gonna live happily ever after."

"I hope you're right," he sighed, resting his chin on his hand.

"I'm pretty sure I am," I said, and I gave him a final pat on the back.

~ ~ ~

AS IT TURNED out, I was exactly right. Within three months, I started hearing about a girl named "Maria" and before I knew it, *all* I was hearing about was this girl named "Maria". One weekend, when he and Amber brought her to visit, I made all of them watch *The Sound of Music* so that we could sing "How Do You Solve a Problem Like Maria?" to her. (Unlike Dorito and Amber, it turned out that Maria actually had a sense of humor.)

By the time they graduated, Dorito had asked Maria to marry him and when I asked with a smile how he was doing with getting over Amanda, he looked back at me and said, "Amanda who?"

After Dorito and Maria were married, they moved to Chicago so that Dorito could work on his master's degree. It turned out that there had been no need for me to have wasted my time earlier, worrying about what was going to happen to Amber after Dorito wasn't going to be able to be there for her anymore. Lily, who graduated from high school that same spring, decided to go to State, too. She moved right into the apartment into Dorito's old room after he moved out, and Amber started working on her master's degree.

Four years later, Lily got married, and her new husband found a job in Steep Ford, not too far from where Amber and Meredith had been living with Karen when I'd found them. The newlyweds rented an apartment in an old cereal mill that had been abandoned after a huge flood and then renovated at the turn of the century. Amber moved to Steep Ford too, and also leased an apartment, three floors below.

I probably should have just been happy that Amber was living almost completely independently, but because she was never required to converse with anyone in the outside world (Lily was there to take care of everything

202

for her if she needed something, and she even ordered groceries online), I worried that she was going to turn into a complete and total recluse.

I shouldn't have worried so much.

Lily, much like David and Laci had always done, gently forced Amber to interact with people whenever she could: pushing her to go to church programs with them, making her go out to eat with them and telling the waiter what she wanted, telling her that if she didn't let the repairman in when he rang the doorbell, she wasn't going to have any Internet access. As the years went by, she got better and better, instead of worse and worse.

After Dorito got his master's degree, he and Maria moved to Mexico City so that he could be near both of his families again. Meredith wound up also going to State, and after she got married, she and her husband settled not too far from Lily and Amber. She liked being near them and she liked that David and Laci came home frequently enough that she never had to go too long without seeing them . . . I happened to like that too.

Grace and Marco, who had graduated from high school together, finally broke the "I'm going to go to State," streak. Marco, who wanted to be a prosthetics engineer, decided to go to Princeton, and Grace (who had always been a horse of a different color – right down to her bright red hair) went to school in California, claiming that she wanted to get as far away from Marco as possible.

As the years went by, a lot of changes happened.
Jordan and Charlotte adopted another child . . .
Dorito, Lily and Meredith all made David and Laci grandparents . . .
My mom had a stroke and made a full recovery . . .
Laci's mom battled breast cancer and lost . . .
Her dad moved to Florida and remarried . . .
David's mom died unexpectedly . . .
His dad went into a nursing home . . .

Life marched on.

Amber made her living writing.

She started out as a freelance editor and picked up small writing jobs on the side. Initially she wrote blog posts and coupon articles for various businesses, anything that would pay her bills, but before long, she morphed into writing longer, full-length articles for newspapers and magazines and such. Eventually, she got herself an agent.

After she'd been out of school for about ten years, Amber finally had a piece published in a nationally acclaimed, weekly magazine. It accompanied an article on a major news story that had been making recent headlines about a seventeen year old girl who had just been found after having disappeared from a California shopping mall five years earlier. Authorities were saying that she had been held captive and sexually abused for almost five years, and that she'd given birth to a little boy during that time. They weren't releasing a lot of other details yet, but of course that didn't stop the public from *wanting* other details . . .

And that's where Amber's article came in.

It turned out that Amber's agent had encouraged her to start writing about some of her experiences, and the article was one of the pieces she had written, detailing some of the things she had gone through while she'd been living in that foster home with Anthony Perry. It was written under a pseudonym and the magazine had already been off the shelf for several months before any of us even knew that she'd had an article in it.

Eventually, Amber told us what she'd written, and by the time she did, she had even bigger news: a publisher had contacted her agent through the magazine and wanted Amber to write her *entire* story.

Once Amber was assured that she could continue using a pseudonym and that no one would ever have to find out who she really was, she finally agreed, and within two years, somebody not named Amber hit the New York Times' bestsellers list.

As the years went by, I continued to "sock away" enough money so that I could retire whenever I wanted, but I didn't have any plans to quit working any time soon because my *modus operandi* was still to keep as busy as possible. When I wasn't working, I was fixing up my home or landscaping the yard. By the time Grace and Marco finished their undergraduate degrees, my house looked like a showplace.

By now, I estimated that I had read through the entire Bible more than seven times. Every time I read it, I found something new that I had never seen before, and it seemed that I always had questions. Natalie never failed to be there for me, patiently trying to answer whatever I asked. She had told me a long time ago that all of us were created to hunger for God, and she was right . . . all of us are hungry. But so many of us try to fill that hunger with food or drugs or alcohol or sex or money or television or sports or friends or shopping or hobbies or jobs or home improvements or *something* . . . something besides the One thing that can truly keep us from being empty.

I was hungry, and I even knew what I was hungry for, but by the time I was fifty-four years old, I still wasn't satisfied.

That was when David came home to die.

~ ~ ~

I KNEW ALL about Alzheimer's, but I had a hard time believing that David had it. When he came home – when he told me – he seemed so . . . so *normal* . . .

He was certainly nothing like that kooky old Annabeth I'd worked with at the nursing home over thirty years earlier. David was on some kind of new medication called Coceptiva that was supposed to be very promising. Whether it was because of this new medicine or just because the disease hadn't progressed too far yet, I didn't know. I just knew that he seemed completely aware of everything that was going on around him and he was still kind and smart and witty and fun . . .

Like I said: *normal.*

David and Laci moved into his parents' old house, which was in complete disarray, and the two of them started to fix things up. Before very long at all, however, David made the decision that he wanted to spend the time that he had left, doing other things. It didn't make me unhappy, that those "other things" included spending more time with me.

Although Dorito and I had talked about going salmon fishing in Alaska ever since we'd read that article together when he was a little boy, we had never made any serious plans. But when Dorito called me up one day and suggested that we take David fishing in Alaska in July, and elk hunting in Montana in the fall, he didn't have to ask twice. Ever since David's diagnosis, each opportunity to spend time with the people that I loved seemed to take on a new urgency.

It was on our fishing trip, however, that I first saw evidence that David really was sick . . . that he wasn't so *normal* after all. Having to admit that there was something really wrong with David hit me hard.

A lot harder than I expected.

It happened on our last day in Alaska. Everything had been fine for our entire trip until our last night there, after we'd showered and changed and headed over to the dining hall to wait for dinner to be served.

Cora, our guide, met us there. She was younger than me, but not *too* much younger, and when the three of us sat down with her at the table, I immediately started flirting with her – something I'd been doing since the moment we'd arrived. While Cora and I talked about the day's events, David wandered over to the huge, stone fireplace that ran along one wall of the dining hall. I didn't pay too much attention because I had my mind on other things.

But then I heard Dorito say, "What is he *doing*?" and I turned to see David, taking off his boots. He set them on the hearth, turning them carefully so that their openings were facing the flames. Then he took off his socks and started spreading them out on the hearth as well. Cora, Dorito and I all exchanged curious glances with one another, and then Dorito stood up and walked toward him. Cora and I followed.

"What are you doing?" Dorito asked.

"My feet are wet," David said.

"How'd they get wet?" Dorito asked, perplexed.

"They're wet," he answered.

Dorito bent down, reaching out to feel David's boots.

"Don't!" David cried.

"Relax, Dad," Dorito said, sticking his hand in David's boot.

"Stop that!" David yelled. Heads in the dining room turned our way and Dorito looked at him with alarm.

I had heard a voice like that before – a voice laced with irrational hysteria.

Reassure and redirect . . .

"We'll let them dry," I told David firmly, reaching for his arm. "This will be a good place to let them dry. Let's go over there and eat our dinner while they're drying."

He looked at me carefully for a moment and then nodded slowly.

"But they're not wet," Dorito protested, and I shot him a dirty look. David and I walked over to our table, followed by Cora and Dorito. We all took our seats.

Our salads were waiting for us, but I could barely eat. I managed to change the topic to dressing and croutons, and after several inane minutes of that, I made a definitive announcement to David that his socks and boots were dry.

"They are?"

I nodded.

He looked uncertain.

"Go get them," I told Dorito. This time, he shot me a dirty look, but he went.

When he came back I reached out and took a sock.

"Oh, yeah," I exclaimed. "Wow. It's a good thing we didn't leave them there any longer. They're definitely dry."

I shoved it in David's direction. He reached out tentatively and felt it.

"Ready to put them back on?" I asked.

He nodded.

I bent over and helped him put them back on. Our main course arrived, and it was while we were eating our steaks, that David slowly came back to us.

He talked to us about the fish we'd caught that day and the bear we'd seen, and it was obvious that he had no memory of the "wet feet" incident that had just occurred. While we were eating dessert, David excused himself to go to the bathroom and I watched after him as he went. Then I turned to Dorito.

"Keep your eye on him," I said, nodding toward the bathroom door. Dorito nodded back and I pushed my chair away from the table.

There was a long deck stretching across the front of the lodge, overlooking the river, but it also wrapped around to the side of the building where it overlooked nothing but pines and hemlocks. That was the side of the building where the huge stone fireplace was and the only side where there were no windows

That was the side where I went.

I rested my elbows on the rail and laid my head in my hands. I stood there like that for a long time, trying to pull myself together.

And that's how I was when Cora found me.

I heard her coming, glanced her way, and then put my head back in my hands, hoping she'd just go away and leave me alone.

She didn't.

She walked up to me and stood quietly. Finally, she broke the silence.

"Alzheimer's?" she asked gently, and with that, something inside of me broke.

I started sobbing.

"I'm sorry," she said, putting her hand on my back.

I cried even harder at her touch and I couldn't believe I was standing there with a practical stranger, bawling like a little kid.

I hadn't cried like that since Laci had broken up with me in college. I hadn't done it when Greg had died or when my dad had died or when Chase had died . . . apparently I just did it over the thought of losing either Laci or David.

"My dad had Alzheimer's," Cora said quietly. "I know it's hard."

I managed to nod and wipe my face on my sleeve.

"Is he on anything?" she asked.

I nodded again and told her about the Coceptiva.

"That one's new," she said, her hand still on my back. "I've heard really good things about it."

I nodded one final time.

"I'm sorry," I said, embarrassed. I wiped my face again and tried to explain. "He got diagnosed a while back, but this is the first time I've actually seen anything."

"I'm sorry," she repeated.

We stood there quietly for a moment.

"How long have you two been friends?" she finally asked.

"Oh, only about fifty years or so," I replied, smiling in spite of myself.

"I thought so," she said, smiling back. "He recognized something in you."

"What do you mean?" I asked.

"He was upset with Dorito," she explained, "but when you talked to him, he calmed down. He trusted you."

"That's just because I didn't argue with him," I said. "I learned how to deal with people like that a long time ago when I worked at a nursing home."

"Maybe," she shrugged, "but I think there's something more to it. When my dad was sick, he didn't know who any of us were or anything. But

Uncle Ray – his brother – could always get through to him when no one else could.

"I don't think my dad knew who he was exactly, but there was something there ... something that clicked whenever my dad looked at him. My uncle could always deal with Dad even when no one else could. It was as if he had lost everything in his mind except for some part of his childhood, and I think there was something deep down in Uncle Ray that he recognized."

I looked at her uncertainly.

"I could be wrong," she said, shrugging again, "but I just have the feeling that he's really lucky to have you as a friend."

~ ~ ~

DAVID AND I went elk hunting in the fall, but he continued to worsen. The doctor upped David to the maximum dosage of Coceptiva and it helped enough that he and Laci and I were able to go to the Holy Land, but within just a few months of that, we were seeing very little benefit. The doctor added another medication as soon as we got back from Israel, but it didn't seem to even make a dent. He then added a new pill, telling Laci that it was in a different "family" of drugs from the first two and that if it was going to help, she would see some results within a week.

David had been taking it for only two days when I got a desperate phone call from her at about midnight. Apparently David was hallucinating and had come after her. I wasn't clear on exactly what all had happened, but I knew that things weren't good.

When I got to their house I could hear a lot of banging coming from inside. I ran in and raced to their bedroom, where the door was practically off its hinges, the frame, splintered. David was pounding on the door to their walk-in closet and Laci was obviously on the other side of it. I could hear her crying.

David backed up to kick the door, but I grabbed him from behind, just before his foot connected. I kept him in a bear hug as he struggled against me, and I yelled at Laci.

"Are you okay?"

"Tanner?" she shrieked.

"It's okay," I said, "I've got him."

She opened the door cautiously and peered out.

"Don't hurt him!" Laci cried when she saw us. "Don't hurt him!"

"I'm not hurting him."

"Please, Tanner!" she pleaded. "Don't!"

"Laci," I said as calmly as I could. "I'm NOT hurting him! I know what I'm doing."

"Tanner . . ." she sobbed.

"I know what I'm doing," I said again. "I promise. Look. Look how I'm holding him."

She looked at me carefully. David had almost completely stopped fighting, but I still had a firm grip around his body and had both of his legs pinned to the floor with one of mine.

"I'm not hurting him, okay?" I asked.

She slowly nodded and for the first time, I got a good look at her. The entire left side of her face was swelling up.

"David . . ." she said to him. He glanced at her wildly and started thrashing around again.

"Go call Dr. Hatcher and tell him what's going on," I told her. "Okay?"

She nodded again, but didn't move.

"Laci," I said. "Go on. I'm not going to hurt him. I'm going to take good care of him. Go on."

She finally left, hesitantly, and after she did, David stopped fighting again. I loosened my grip.

"Are you okay?" I asked him. He looked at me wild-eyed.

"They tried to kill me!" he said.

"They're gone now."

"How much gas is in the car?" he asked hoarsely.

"More than half a tank."

"We need to fill it up," he insisted.

"Okay," I agreed. "Why?"

"We've gotta get away from here."

"Where are we gonna go?"

"I get about forty miles to the gallon," he said, thinking hard. "We should . . . we should be able to drive for about seven hours without stopping . . ."

"Okay," I said.

He looked past me toward the door.

"We need to hurry," he whispered. "They're going to come back."

"We've got at least an hour," I assured him.

He looked at me uncertainly.

"You need to pack some stuff, okay?" I asked.

212

He thought for a moment.

"Okay," he finally agreed, "but let's hurry."

"No problem," I said. "I'll keep an eye on the door. You start getting out some socks."

He looked at me questioningly.

"I want you to put them right here," I said, patting the top of his dresser. It was against the far wall, so his back would be to the door while he was working. "You need two white and two black and three brown . . . and then we can go, okay?"

He finally nodded and opened his drawer, glancing toward the door one more time.

"I'm watching the door," I assured him. "You need to get to work."

I sent a text to Laci:

Stay out. We're good.

A few minutes later she peeked around the corner and I gestured for her to go away. She watched David sorting his socks for a moment and then looked at me.

Get out! I mouthed and pointed for her to go back downstairs. She looked at David one more time and left.

"How's it going?" I asked David when she was gone. He had a mound of socks on his dresser.

"I don't know," he said. "What do I need?"

"Two white, two black and three brown."

He looked at the pile and sighed.

"Can you help me?" he asked.

"Sure," I said. "You wanna lay down and rest for a minute while I do this?"

"I should help . . ."

"You can help me pack 'em up after I'm done, okay?"

"We've gotta watch the door," he reminded me.

"Right," I said, scooping all the socks back into the drawer and pulling the whole thing out of the dresser.

"I'll work right here," I said. I set it down on the floor in front of the door so I was facing the hall. "You need to take a rest before we leave, okay?"

"Okay," he finally agreed when he saw me sit down and start sorting, and then he laid down on the bed.

Once he was finally snoring gently, I got up quietly and found Laci. She was in the kitchen, holding an ice pack to the side of her face. I gently pulled her hand away.

"Oh, man, Laci," I said. I suspected that it wasn't even done swelling yet, but it looked horrible already and her eye was bloody. "We need to get you to the doctor."

"No," she said, putting the ice back.

"Yes," I argued. "We need to make sure–"

"Tanner," she interrupted, "It's fine . . . I can tell." She held my gaze with her one good eye until I finally nodded. "How's David?" she wanted to know.

"He's okay," I said. "He's sleeping. Did you call the doctor?"

She nodded.

"What did he say?"

"He said it's probably a side effect from the new medicine."

"No kidding."

She gave me a pained look. "He said it might get better or it might get worse. There's no way to tell right now."

"He's not taking any more of that," I said, shaking my head.

"But the Coceptiva isn't working anymore," Laci quarreled, pulling the ice pack away from her face. "We've gotta find something that works."

I looked at her for a long moment.

"Laci, there may not be anything that *works*," I finally said, carefully.

"No," she said, shaking her head. "When Dr. Hatcher put him on this he said, 'Let's try this one first'. That means there are other things out there that we can try – this is just the one that he started us out with."

"Put this back on," I said, reaching over and lifting her hand with the ice pack to her face. I looked at her again. "How would you feel about having Mike and Danica go with you when you talk to the doctor?"

"Why?"

"I think it would be really good if they went with you. Do you care if I call them and ask?"

"No," Laci said. "I guess not."

214

I spent the rest of the night lying on the bed next to David while Laci slept in the guest bedroom. He didn't wake up until morning and, when he did, he didn't seem agitated at all. I led him downstairs and got him some breakfast. He was eating a bowl of corn flakes when Laci tentatively stuck her head into the kitchen. Her eye and face looked terrible.

She looked at me questioningly and I nodded at her that she could come in. She cautiously came around the table and sat down opposite of David. He glanced at her once and then went right back to his cereal. All was well again.

I called Mike while Laci was in the shower.

"Did they take him off Coceptiva?" Mike wanted to know. "Or did they give him this new drug on top of it?"

"He's still on the Coceptiva, too," I said.

Mike was quiet for a minute.

"You know what I think?" I asked him.

"What?"

"I think that doctors – no offense – sometimes aren't really willing to tell somebody, 'There's nothing else we can do for you.' I think they feel like they've got to try something as long as people are coming to them, asking for help."

"I agree that there's some truth to that," Mike answered.

"And I'm worried that they're gonna keep sending Laci home with new drugs that are just going to raise her hopes and let her think it's going to bring David back to her, but all it's really gonna do is make things worse."

I heard Mike sigh.

"Isn't there a point," I asked, "where the best thing to do is to just leave somebody alone?"

"Yes," he agreed, "but I don't think we're there yet. I think there are some other combinations that are probably worth trying."

"And what's going to happen next time he attacks her? You should see her face, Mike."

He sighed again.

"We'll be down there this afternoon," he promised. "We'll figure something out."

David's appointment was for three o'clock, but of course we had to wait until almost five before the doctor was able to see us. It had been about twenty hours since he'd taken his last dosage of the new medicine, but already there were no more signs of the side effects ... except for Laci's eye. Mike gave her a good once-over and confirmed what she'd already insisted to me the night before – no broken bones ... no serious damage to her eye.

I think David's doctor was a bit surprised to find that David and Laci had three other people with them – two of them doctors. I shut up for most of the appointment, except for when he said that one of the things we could try was sticking with the new drug for a couple of weeks and seeing if things "stabilized".

"That's not an option," I said firmly, and Laci didn't argue with me.

We left the office with a new prescription for a new drug and – since David seemed to be doing pretty well – Mike and Danica hugged us all goodbye and headed home. The first thing I did after Laci and I picked the new medication up at the pharmacy was to look at the leaflet that accompanied it. I scanned my eyes across the paper until I found what I already knew was going to be there:

This medication may cause hallucinations, unusual restlessness, loss of coordination, unexplained fever or twitching muscles. This risk increases when used with certain other drugs ...

I slept on their couch that night.

~ ~ ~

THE NEXT DAY was Tuesday. I called Laci from work, mid-morning, and told her I would be bringing dinner over that night. Once we were seated around the kitchen table with Chinese takeout, I made an announcement.

"I resigned today."

"You what?" Laci asked. David ignored both of us and picked at his egg roll suspiciously with a fork.

"Well, I retired actually," I clarified.

"Why?"

"Are you kidding, Laci?" I asked, waving my hand in David's direction. "You can't do this alone anymore. I'm going to help you."

"That's ridiculous!" she cried, her voice rising. "I can't believe you did that! I want you to go back tomorrow and get your job back!"

"It's not ridiculous," I argued. I pointed at the side of her face. "Look at you! Look what happened!"

"No," she shook her head back and forth. "That was just a weird thing with his medicine. It's not gonna happen again."

"You don't know that."

"I'm sure the doctors can get it straightened out—"

"Don't kid yourself."

"No," she said. "It's not going to happen again."

"Laci, you don't understand . . ."

"Don't understand what?"

I looked at her and felt so much sympathy for her that I could barely stand to say what she needed to hear.

"Things are going to get *worse* with David," I told her gently, "not better. This thing may get worked out, but then there's going to be something else, and then something else and then—"

"I can deal with it, Tanner."

"Like you dealt with that?" I asked, pointing at her face again.

She didn't answer me.

"No," I said. "You aren't going to be able to do this by yourself. I know you want to take care of him, Laci, but you have no idea what it's going to be like as he gets worse."

"Then I'll hire someone," she said insistently. "I'll hire someone to come in and help me."

"Why can't it be me?" I asked quietly.

"I'm not going to let you quit your job and help me!"

"I already quit," I reminded her.

"Well you can just march right back in there tomorrow and tell them you made a mistake. It's not like they aren't going to take you back. I'm not going to let you do this!"

I was silent for a minute, trying to figure out a way to convince her.

"Why'd you spend half your life working in a landfill?" I finally asked.

"What?"

"You heard me."

"That doesn't have anything to do with this . . ."

"Answer me," I persisted. "Why would you spend half of your life in a place like that?"

She didn't say anything. I could almost see the wheels turning in her head as she realized that I was going to be able to use anything she said against her.

"This is different," she finally answered.

"Not really."

"Yes, it is, Tanner. That was what I was *meant* to do. Everything in my life led me to that point."

"And all I'm good for is being a PE teacher?"

"No. That's not what I meant and you know it."

"Why is it so hard for you to believe that maybe this is what God wants me to do?" I asked. "Why can't you believe that maybe this is what I was meant to do? That everything in *my* life has been leading *me* to *this* point?"

"Because it's not," she said, shaking her head.

"Have you forgotten that I took care of Chase for six years?"

"That was different—"

"And I helped Natalie with her dad for three years . . ."

"They had two completely different diseases," Laci protested.

"Yeah," I agreed. "Two completely different *neurological* diseases!"

She gave her head another slight shake.

"Did you know that I worked in a nursing home for six months when I was in college? Do you have any idea how many adult diapers I've changed? How many strawberry purees I've spoon fed to people?"

She was still staring at me. I reached over and gently put a hand on one of hers. She brought her free hand to her face, covering her eyes. She tried unsuccessfully to stifle a ragged breath.

"You guys are my *best friends*," I finished, and she started to sob quietly. "Don't tell me that this isn't what I'm supposed to be doing right now."

She took her hand down from her face and put it on top of mine. Tears were still running down her face as she looked at me for a long moment.

And then, finally, she nodded.

~ ~ ~

I MOVED IN to their guest room.

I rented out my house.

David continued to decline.

He was definitely himself from time to time and it was obvious when he recognized us because it was the only time that he would call us by name. But as the weeks and months went on, those moments – the ones that Laci lived for – became fewer and farther apart.

As David's moments of slipping away became more and more frequent, it became clear that he responded to me differently than he did to anyone else. What I had learned working with Annabeth very likely played a large part in how David reacted to me, but as time went on, I began to believe that perhaps there was more to it than that . . . that there had been some truth in what Cora had told me our last night in Alaska.

He would look into my eyes and agree to whatever it was that I asked him to do, and something about my touch would settle him when nothing else would. Sometimes David would reach out, grip my shirt, and just hang on like it was a security blanket. And if I touched his arm, he would cover my hand with his, as if to keep it there.

Further supporting the idea that David was trapped in some part of his childhood was the fact that he seemed to connect well on a certain level to some other people he had known all of his life too – like his sister Jessica, or like Mike. And even if he clearly was not himself, I could ask about his mom or his dad, and David would talk about them as if they were still going off to work on a daily basis. He would recall incidences from his childhood, easily remembering things that he and Mike and I had done together, or complaining about some infraction Jessica had committed against him over forty years ago, as if it had happened yesterday.

If I asked him about Greg, however, David would have no idea who I was talking about. It seemed that the childhood David was trapped in was the one from his elementary school years alone. He watched cartoons and game shows constantly and turned his nose up at whatever green vegetables Laci put on his plate just like a ten year old would.

"But why doesn't he recognize me?" Laci complained one day when we were talking about this theory. "I've known him just as long as you and Mike and Jessica have." David clearly didn't feel any kind of a connection with her when he wasn't himself. Usually he just ignored her, and sometimes it seemed to actually agitate him to have her around.

"I think it's because he didn't like you when you were little," I said. "He *liked* me. He *liked* Jessica. He *liked* Mike."

She smirked at me with a raised eyebrow.

"I can't help it if he didn't like you," I said, shrugging and trying to hide a smile. She regarded the whole idea skeptically, but the next time David was feeling talkative and willing to reminisce about the past, I tested it out.

"Do you know a girl named Laci?" I asked. We were out for a walk and I had my hand on his arm, guiding him lightly as we went along. Laci was trailing a few steps behind us, as she often did.

"Ugh," he said.

"Ugh?" I asked, glancing back at Laci and smiling. "Why do you say, 'Ugh'?"

"She's very . . ." he struggled to find the right word.

"Pretty?" I suggested.

"No," he said, shaking his head. "She looks like a boy."

"Oh. You mean when she cuts her hair?"

"Yeah," he nodded.

"What about when her hair's long?" I asked. "Is she pretty then?"

"Yeah," he admitted, and I smiled back at Laci for a second time. "But she keeps cutting it," he went on. "She's very annoying."

One day I bought adult undergarments at the grocery store and Laci had an absolute fit when I came home with them.

"I'm NOT putting him in those," she cried.

"Laci," I said, patiently. "We're having to clean up messes almost every day."

"I don't care," she replied. "Do you know what it's going to do to him when he's himself one day and he realizes that we've put him in a *diaper*?!"

"I think," I said slowly, "that he would be glad to know that you're doing whatever it takes to make things easier on yourself."

But she shook her head at me so adamantly that I put them under the vanity in the bathroom and didn't say another word about it. It was three weeks later when she reluctantly and tearfully told me that we could start using them.

"It's okay, Laci," I said quietly. "It's going to be okay."

"No, it's not," she said with tears in her eyes. "It's never going to be okay."

Not too long after David had attacked Laci, we tried two different rounds of experimental drugs. One did nothing for him and the other made things worse, and then we quit. Mike finally suggested that we try a "cleansing", during which we would take him off *all* of his medications, and then – after they'd been out of his system for a while – start him back on the Coceptiva again, since we'd initially had some success with that. When we tried this, we had more moments where David was clearly with us again and some of them actually lasted for quite a while, but – overall – it was obvious that we were losing him more and more, every day.

We lost David's dad, too. He developed a urinary tract infection that turned septic and he died in the nursing home with Jessica and Laci by his side. I was home with David when it happened, watching a game show on TV.

Not too long afterward, David asked about his father as he still did from time to time. Laci gently told him that he had passed away and David reacted by sobbing and crying. Naturally he didn't want Laci to comfort him, but after I talked to him for a little while, he stopped crying and then seemed to forget all about it. A week later, he asked again, and then grieved all over again, just as he had the first time.

"But I don't want to lie to him!" Laci worried later, when I suggested to her that she not put him through it a third time.

"You don't have to lie to him," I explained, and the next time it happened, I showed her what I meant.

222

"Where's my dad?" David asked after another few days.

"He went somewhere with your mom," I replied.

"When will he be back?"

"Oh, I don't think he's in too big of a hurry to come back," I said with a smile. "He's too happy where he is."

I glanced at Laci and she gave me a little smile back.

"When will I see him?"

"Soon enough," I answered. "You can have a freezer pop while you're waiting. Would you like that?"

"Do we have red?" he asked.

"Absolutely," I replied.

We didn't even bother to keep any other color in the house.

~ ~ ~

A FEW DAYS after the official arrival of spring, Laci set off in a cold rain to pick up some things she needed for David's birthday – he was going to be turning fifty-seven in just a few days. While she was gone and I was home alone with David, the doorbell rang. I answered it to find a man standing on the porch, looking at me intently.

"I . . . I'm looking for David Holland," he said tentatively.

"Why?" I asked. He looked pretty harmless, but still.

"I, umm, I was just hoping to talk to him about something."

I raised an eyebrow at him and leaned against the door frame.

"What would that be?" I asked.

"I, umm, is this the right address?" he asked, beginning to sound frustrated.

"You've got the right address," I said, "but you're not talking to anybody until you tell me why you're here."

"Is . . . is Laci here?" he tried.

"Why don't you tell *me* what you want?" I said. "And then we'll talk about who's here."

He sighed, resigned to the fact that he was going to have to talk to me first.

"My name's Carter Morris," he began. "I used to know David and Laci a long time ago."

"When?"

"When I was a kid," he said. "I went on a mission trip to Mexico with my church when I was in high school. David and Laci were working down there when I went."

I opened the door and let him in.

"I'm Tanner," I said, shaking his hand. "What'd you say your name is?"

"Carter," he replied, shaking it back.

224

"Laci's out right now," I said, "running some errands, but David's here."

He looked relieved to hear that David was home. I led him into the living room where David sat in his recliner, watching a game show on TV. Carter approached him with his hand stuck out, ready for another shake.

"David," I interceded, "this is Carter. He wants to talk to you about something."

David took his eyes off the television and looked at me, uncomprehendingly.

"Shake his hand," I encouraged, nodding toward Carter. David obediently reached his hand out and let Carter shake it.

"I know you probably don't remember me," he began. "I came down to Mexico when Laci was leading mission groups. We stayed at your house."

"Why don't you sit down," I suggested, pointing to the chair that was right next to David's.

Carter took a seat and looked at David, who still hadn't said a word.

"David has Alzheimer's," I told him frankly. "He's probably not going to remember you, even if he remembered you."

"Oh," Carter said, sounding both surprised and sad at the same time. "I didn't know that. I'm sorry."

I nodded.

He looked at me.

"I . . . I wanted to tell him something," he said, looking at me.

"You can tell him anything you want," I agreed. "I just don't know if any of it's going to sink in."

Carter nodded and looked at David again.

"I can leave if you want," I offered.

"No," he said, shaking his head and glancing at me. "You can hear this too."

He turned his eyes back to David.

"I just . . . I just wanted to let you know that I really appreciate what you and Laci did for me," he said, "and I wanted to let you know that it didn't go to waste."

David had clearly turned his attention back to the television.

"Seven!" he said. "Number seven!"

The contestant listened to the studio audience instead and went with number four. Carter glanced at me and I shrugged my shoulders in a helpless manner.

"Sorry," I said.

"It's okay," he replied. "I just wanted to thank him. He talked to me and I know that he and Laci prayed for me and . . . I just wanted to let him know that it wasn't all in vain, you know?"

I nodded.

"And I guess I wanted to apologize, too," he said. "I was kind of a pain in the butt."

I smiled.

"Four!" David yelled. "Four!!"

"I wish I'd come earlier," Carter said wistfully. "I wish I could have let him know."

"Laci's going to be home in a little while," I said. "Maybe you could let her know instead."

Laci was thrilled to meet Carter and invited him to stay for dinner. While we boiled pasta and prepared salad, he regaled us by going on and on about all the trouble he'd gotten into on the mission trip and we spent the entire meal listening to how he'd spent most of his life since then, running from God.

About two years earlier, he told us, he had finally dedicated his life to Christ and now he was sort of on a "mission of redemption", trying to track down people who had helped him, so he could thank them, or people he had hurt, so he could apologize. Apparently David and Laci fell into both categories.

"I'm sorry about the way I acted," he told Laci. "I wish I could do something to make it up to you."

"I really barely even remember it," she assured him again.

"I bet he would," Carter said, nodding toward David. "I bet he'd remember it. I wish I could make it up to him somehow."

I looked at Laci and then I looked at Carter.

"Do you really mean that?" I asked, and then, when he nodded, I said, "Do you like to play cards?"

David *loved* to play cards. We had to keep our decks hidden from him at all times because – if they were out where David could see them – he would be reminded that they existed, and then he would beg to play until you finally gave in and settled down at the kitchen table with him.

For *hours*.

226

I liked to play cards too, but not the way David played (at least not the way he played anymore). Before Alzheimer's, when you played cards with David, it was a challenge. He was very competitive and very smart and it took a lot of skill and concentration to beat him, unless you were playing something that was a complete game of chance, like War or something. Now, however, playing cards with David was both a boring and frustrating experience. He would slowly, methodically deal out random piles of cards and get agitated if you picked up your hand before he felt it was time. After much deliberation, he'd finally "play" a card. Then, it would at last be your turn.

The fact that there was no rhyme or reason to what we were doing made no difference to David. If he didn't like the card you put down for some reason, he would pick it up and give it back to you, insisting that you put it back in your hand and play another. There was just as great of a chance that he wouldn't like the next card you laid down either, or the next one or the next, so sometimes you spent a lot of time just laying down random cards, hoping that one of them would please him enough so that you could finally move on. Oftentimes the card that was ultimately approved was one of the same cards you'd already tried to play earlier, but now – for no apparent reason – it was suddenly deemed acceptable.

Like I said, it was very frustrating to play cards with David.

It wasn't all bad, though. When David was playing cards, he wasn't asking a million questions. He wasn't hiding margarine in the linen closet or taking all the shirts from his hangers and dumping them on the floor. He wasn't sneaking out the front door when your back was turned for one, teeny, tiny second.

And when David was playing cards, he was happy.

"Cards?" Carter asked.

"Yeah," I nodded, standing up to retrieve a hidden deck. "You want a chance to redeem yourself? I've got just the ticket."

~ ~ ~

A FEW WEEKS after our visit from Carter, Amber stopped by unexpectedly. She was still living a couple of hours away – still living near Lily and Meredith and their families – so it wasn't unusual for her to visit. But it *was* unusual for her to stop by unannounced . . . all by herself.

Of course we were thrilled to see her. We ushered her in and had her sit down, but when she chose the chair right next to David's and avoided our eyes, we knew that something was definitely up. Laci and I sat down on the couch and waited patiently . . . interrogating Amber wasn't going to get us anywhere.

David was watching television and, aside from a brief glance her way when she first sat down next to him, he hadn't seemed to notice that Amber was even there. She took his hand and sat, holding it, for a long time. She pretended to be engrossed in the game show that was on.

"Daddy?" she finally said.

He didn't take his eyes off the television.

"Daddy?" she said again. "I have something to show you."

She held her left hand up in front of his face. There was something on her ring finger. Laci and I glanced at each other and Laci's face showed the same shock that I was feeling. David finally acknowledged that Amber was sitting next to him.

"Do you have any freezer pops?" he asked her.

She looked momentarily dismayed, but then glanced at us, questioningly. I nodded at her.

"Sure," she said, and she stood up and headed for the kitchen. I think she was glad for an excuse to get out of the room.

As soon as she was gone, Laci turned her head and looked at me.

"Please tell me that was *not* a diamond ring," she whispered.

I took in a deep breath and shrugged, holding my hands up helplessly.

"What's going on?" Laci whispered.

228

"I don't know," I admitted, "but I'm sure everything's fine."

Laci shot me a doubtful look and then Amber returned with a red freezer pop. She had cut the top off the plastic wrap, and David smiled as she handed it to him.

She managed to smile back at him before finally casting a nervous glance toward Laci, and then toward me.

"I'm getting married," she said feebly, holding her ring up again.

"To *who*?" Laci asked.

"His . . . his name is Paul," she said in an even quieter tone.

"Paul?" I asked. "Who's *Paul*?"

"I haven't even heard you *talk* about anyone named Paul!" Laci cried.

"Well, it all happened kind of fast," Amber said. Her voice was threatening to fade away into nothing.

Laci and I glanced at each other again. Her face was white now.

"Come here," I said, patting the seat between us on the couch. Amber reluctantly left David and sat down next to us, already looking defeated.

I took her hand and studied her ring.

"Don't you think we have the right to be a little surprised?" I asked, looking into her eyes.

She nodded miserably. David continued with his freezer pop and the game show.

Which river flows through Rome?

"Mississippi."

Amber took a deep breath and looked across the room.

"I met him online," she finally said.

I looked over her head at Laci, who rolled her eyes in despair. I gave her an imperceptible shake of my head back.

"Online?" I asked, turning back to Amber.

"In a support group," she nodded.

"A support group."

She nodded again.

"A support group for what?" Laci asked gently.

"For people like me."

I looked at Laci again and then back to Amber.

"So," I said carefully. "He, uhhh . . ."

"Yes," she said, looking at me angrily. "He was abused. When he was a kid. Just like me."

"Okay," I said slowly.

"Why haven't–" Laci began, but Amber cut her off.

"I know *exactly* what you're thinking!" Amber cried, turning to her. "You think there's something wrong with him. You think he must be just as screwed up as I am!"

"That is not what I'm thinking!" Laci protested.

"And you're not screwed up," I added.

"Yes, I am," Amber said, leaning back against the couch and letting out a deep breath. "I'm screwed up, and everybody knows it." Then she looked at me. "But he's not," she said. "He's *normal*."

"Okay," I again said slowly.

"He *is*, Tanner," she insisted. "He's completely normal and . . . and for some reason . . . he loves me."

I sighed.

"How long have you known him?" I wanted to know.

"A month," she said.

"A month!?" Laci cried. "You've only known him for a *month* and you're already planning on getting married?"

"Well, I've *known* him for almost a year," Amber quickly amended. "But we just met face to face for the first time a month ago."

"And when are you planning on getting married?"

"This summer."

"This summer?!" I asked. "Why are you in such a rush?"

"I'm thirty-seven years old, Tanner," she said, turning her eyes toward me with an anguished look on her face. "I want to have kids!"

"Just because you want to have kids is no reason to rush into getting married!" Laci said.

"I'm not," Amber insisted. "I *love* him."

I felt myself sigh again.

"We're just . . . we're *worried* about you, Amber," I finally said.

"I know you are," she nodded, "but if you'd just meet him, you wouldn't be worried. You'd love him too . . ."

Laci and I exchanged one more glance over Amber's head.

"Well then let's meet him," I agreed, and Amber finally gave me a smile. She looked over at David, who was still watching television and finishing his red freezer pop, completely unaware of the conversation that had just taken place between the three of us.

What country holds the most World Cup titles?

"Fort Worth," David answered, without missing a beat.

Paul lived in Virginia, and it turned out that he and Amber had only been face to face two times – the first time when they'd met, and the second time when he'd proposed. This made me even more leery of the whole situation, but it made Laci practically frantic.

Paul flew back to Cavendish for a third time and Amber brought him to dinner.

"Hi," he said, as he grasped my hand firmly in the living room. "You must be Tanner. Amber's told me a lot about you."

"Hi," I said back. "She's pretty much told me *nothing* about you."

He looked briefly startled, but then smiled and glanced back at Amber, who was shooting me a very unhappy look.

"Why does this not surprise me?" he asked her, and then he turned to face me again. "Don't worry. I'll tell you anything you want to know."

What I want to know is if you fully understand the fact that I will track you down and kill *you if you ever do anything to hurt Amber . . .*

"Hi," Laci said, sticking her hand forward.

"This is my mom," Amber said.

"Call me Laci."

"Hi, Laci," he said.

"Where's Daddy?" Amber asked her.

"Out on the back deck."

"Come on," she said to Paul, taking him by the hand and leading him outside. Laci and I followed.

I was really hoping that David would have a good moment or two while Amber was there – be himself, know what was going on – but he didn't. He shook Paul's hand when Amber introduced them, but then immediately looked away.

Then there was an awkward silence.

"Do you like to play cards?" I asked Paul.

"Cards?"

"I want to play cards!" David said, suddenly interested in our presence.

"Sure," Paul said carefully, "I like to play cards."

"I'll go get some," I offered quickly.

Laci followed me into the house.

"That was mean!" she scolded, swatting me when we got back inside.

"Don't you want to see what he's made of?" I asked with a grin. She smiled back in spite of herself.

"You don't have to do this," Laci told Paul when we got back outside. David was already sitting at the patio table, anxiously waiting. I handed him the deck.

"I don't mind," Paul assured her, sitting down in a chair. He looked at David pleasantly. "What do you wanna play?"

I smiled at Amber and she glared at me.

If looks could kill, I would have been a dead man.

It was nice to have David so thoroughly occupied while the grill was going so that we didn't have to worry about keeping him away from it. Paul, incidentally, did great with David . . . he was kind, and he was patient.

He definitely passed the first test.

After a long game of cards, we finally convinced David that it was time for dinner.

"Did Amber tell you how we met?" Paul asked after we had all started eating.

"She said you met online," Laci answered, cutting into her steak.

He glanced at Amber questioningly.

"You didn't meet online?" Laci asked.

"No, we did," he said, "but I have a feeling she didn't tell you the whole story."

He looked at Amber again, who put down her fork, rolled her eyes and crossed her arms.

"She probably didn't want you to think I was a stalker," he went on, and Amber gave a loud sigh of defeat as she slumped back in her chair.

"A stalker?" Laci asked.

Paul laughed.

"I kind of tracked her down," he explained. "After I read her book."

He looked at Amber.

"You told them about what happened to me, didn't you?" he asked.

"Sort of."

"I was abused, too," he said honestly, turning back to Laci. She nodded at him. "And when I read her book and I was just like, 'Wow! I've gotta talk to whoever wrote this.'"

Then he turned to me.

"I found her in a support group and we talked for like six months before she even told me what her real name was. I didn't know how old she was, or if she was single or married or anything. I just knew that I'd never been able to talk with anybody like I could talk with her . . . you know?"

I nodded.

"I mean," he went on, "I've never had anybody in my life who understood everything that I've been through."

He looked at Amber and smiled and she looked back at him, tenderly.

Laci and I looked at each other and I knew that she was thinking exactly what I was thinking – that Paul had better turn out to be every bit as great as Amber apparently thought he was, because she was way too head over heels in love for us to ever get her away from him if he wasn't.

After dinner, Laci and Amber started in on the dishes. Paul surprised me by asking, "You wanna go for a walk?"

I did, and after helping David put a jacket on, all three of us headed outside.

"Amber says that you and Laci are fine with this," Paul said after we'd headed down the driveway.

"With what?"

"With me and her," he said, gesturing with his hand. "With us getting married and everything."

"Oh."

"But," he went on without pausing, "I find that hard to believe."

"You think she's lying to you?"

"I don't think she's lying," he said, hesitantly, "but I don't think she's telling me the whole truth, either. Amber tends to avoid conflict whenever she can."

He did seem to know her well, I had to give him that.

He looked at me and stopped walking. I had my hand lightly on David's arm and I tugged on him gently so that we stopped walking too.

"Look," he said, "I don't want to press her about it because I don't want to upset her, but I just find it hard to believe that you guys are okay with all this."

"Why?"

"Because if it was *my* daughter–"

"She's not my daughter," I interrupted.

"But you know she thinks of you as a father."

I didn't say anything.

"And if my daughter was planning on marrying someone that she'd met online, and who she'd only seen in person a couple of times, well . . . I'd have a real problem with it."

I still didn't say anything.

"Especially considering what's happened to both of us," he finished quietly.

We looked at each other for a moment before Paul turned and all three of us started walking again.

"What did she tell you about me?" he asked, looking straight ahead and avoiding my eyes.

"She said you were 'normal'."

He looked at me and then chuckled.

"Like I said," he laughed, "she tries to avoid conflict."

We walked along for another moment and then he stopped again and turned to face me once more.

"Look," he said. "I'm just as screwed up as she is." He pursed his lips together and then glanced away. "Maybe more. I mean, I might *talk* just fine, but . . ."

He shook his head and looked back at me.

"You can't go through what I did and come out of it *normal*. I've got plenty of problems."

I nodded at him.

"But nothing that's going to hurt Amber," he insisted. "She already knows everything that there is to know about me. I want you to know that she's not going into this blindly."

"But why the rush?" I asked. "Why can't you guys date for a while and take it slow?"

"I offered to get a job and move out here," he said. "I told her we should date for a while and get to know each other's families and everything, but . . ."

"But what?"

"She wants to have kids," he said. "And she's worried that it might take a while."

He looked at me meaningfully.

"There's a good chance," he explained, "that one or both of us are going to have some . . . issues."

234

I didn't ask him to elaborate.

"You can always adopt," I told him.

"I know," he agreed, "but that can take a while too."

He paused for a moment before going on.

"This is what she wants," he finally said, "and I love her. I want to spend the rest of my life giving her what she wants.

"I mean, if I thought it would be better for her for me to walk away, then that's what I'd do . . . even though there's nothing I want more in the world than to be with her. If it was best for her for me to leave and never see her again, then that's what I'd do. Do you understand what I'm saying? I would do *anything* for her. I love her enough that I would give her up if that's what I needed to do."

He searched my eyes for a moment.

"But I don't think that's what's best for her," he finished. "I think I'm good for her. And I think the two of us are supposed to be together."

I looked back at him for a long moment, and then nodded to let him know that I knew exactly what he meant.

I could tell by the look on his face that he knew he had my approval. He smiled at me gratefully and we turned around.

"There's something I'm worried about though," he said as we started walking back toward the house.

"What's that?"

"Well, of course she doesn't want a big wedding or anything like that, but she really wants him," he nodded toward David, "to walk her down the aisle."

"Oh."

"When she was a little girl," he explained, "he promised her that he would walk her down the aisle when she got married."

"Oh," I said again.

"And I'm kind of worried that we're going to have a hard time making that happen."

"Don't worry," I said, giving Paul a smile. "We can definitely make that happen."

On Amber and Paul's wedding day, David stood quietly in the narthex, dressed in a tux, while Amber's sisters kissed her and marched down the aisle ahead of her. David didn't have a problem with Amber looping her arm through his, but once she tried to tug him down the aisle, he balked.

Of course that's why *I* was there . . . also dressed in a tuxedo.

I gently took David's other arm and looked him right in the eye.

"I'll go with you," I told him, patting his arm and pointing to the front of the church. "We're going to walk up there, and I'll go with you, okay?"

He looked at me uncertainly for a moment, but then nodded and the doors opened up and the three of us started walking forward: me and Amber with David in between, both of us with an arm looped through one of his. I leaned in front of David just as we entered the sanctuary and whispered to Amber, "I have never felt so *gay* in my entire life!"

She burst out laughing and giggled the entire rest of the way down the aisle.

We finally got to the front, and led David over to where Laci was sitting. He let Amber kiss him on the cheek, and before I sat down on the other side of him, she kissed me too.

"Thank you," she said, still smiling. "I love you."

"I love you, too," I smiled back, and then I nodded to where Paul was standing, patiently waiting for her. "Now go get married."

At the reception, Jordan grinned as we ate wedding cake together.

"I'm paying the photographer for the digital rights of the processional," Jordan said, and Charlotte laughed.

"Shut up," I said. "I can still pound you into the ground any time I want to."

"I don't think so," he said, shaking his head. "I think the fact that you're nine years older than me is no longer working to your advantage."

"Don't bet on it," I growled.

"Now, now, boys," Charlotte scolded.

She stood up and headed toward her mother, who was standing with David and Laci. I watched David for a moment to make sure he wasn't getting agitated, and then I turned my attention back to Jordan.

"You look like you're doing good," I said seriously.

"I am," he nodded.

"Still no symptoms, right?" I asked.

"You're not supposed to ask," he sighed.

"There's no way you have it," I muttered, ignoring him. "You're almost *fifty*. If you had it, you'd be showing symptoms by now."

"Sometimes people don't start getting sick until they're in their sixties or seventies," he said, shrugging nonchalantly.

"I know," I agreed. "That's why I wish you would just get tested."

"Why?"

"So you can quit worrying about it."

"Do I act like I'm worried?"

"No," I admitted. "I just wish you'd get tested so *I* can quit worrying about it."

"Are you worried?" he asked gently.

I nodded.

"Don't be," he said, shaking his head and putting his hand on my arm.

"You should get tested," I pressed again, "so that if you *do* have it, you and Charlotte can get prepared . . ."

"Charlotte and I *are* prepared," he assured me, looking over at her for a long moment. As if she sensed the he was looking at her, Charlotte turned away from her mother and looked back at him, their eyes locking on one another. They smiled at each other and then he turned his gaze back to me.

"No matter what happens," Jordan said, still smiling, "Charlotte and I are ready."

~ ~ ~

IT WAS A year later that Amber and Paul came to visit and share their big news. Amber waited until we were all gathered around the dinner table and Laci was trying to convince David to eat a piece of broccoli before Amber announced, "We're going to adopt embryos."

"Huh?" (That was me.)

"What?" (That was Laci.)

"I don't want any." (That was David.)

"We aren't going to be able to get pregnant," Amber said, shaking her head, "but they think I can carry a baby okay."

"We thought about doing invitro," Paul went on, "but there're all these frozen embryos out there that are left over from *other* people's invitros, so we just figured . . ."

"That we should adopt some of them," Amber said.

"SOME of them?" (That was me again.)

"Well, three to start with," she said. "They're going to put me on some hormones and implant them in a couple of months."

"THREE?" (Laci again.)

"They probably won't all take," Paul said. "Actually we'll be lucky if *one* takes.

"Do you have any freezer pops?" (David.)

"They like to actually try about five or six at a time," Paul went on, as Laci distractedly stood up and got a freezer pop for David without even trying to make him eat something healthy first, "but you have to sign this agreement that if you get pregnant with four or more then you'll let them go in and abort anything over three . . ."

"And obviously we weren't going to do that," Amber said as Laci reached into a drawer for the scissors. "I mean one of the whole reasons we're going this route it to *save* those little babies . . . not to let somebody kill them."

238

"Are you sure you don't want to go the *regular* adoption route?" Laci asked, handing the freezer pop to David. "As you may remember, your dad and I did that and we happened to think it worked out pretty good."

Amber smiled.

"We might do that too, one day," Paul said, "but right now this is what we're starting out with."

Laci and I looked at each other.

"It's red," David said happily, and he took a bite.

~ ~ ~

BY THE FOLLOWING Christmas, David and Laci's house was still pretty much in disarray. I had tried to fix some things up along the way since I'd moved in, but it had turned out that power tools and Alzheimer's patients don't always mix real well, so I hadn't actually gotten a lot done. My renters had moved out of my old place just before Thanksgiving, and I purposefully didn't replace them right away, knowing that everyone was going to be coming into town for the holidays, and that we were going to need all the room we could get.

I stayed close to David for most of Christmas day because it was so crowded and there was so much going on that I worried how he might react, but he didn't seem too fazed by it.

One time, when I did leave him briefly, I came back to find him wearing a Santa Claus hat that had been getting passed around. Dorito was standing next to him.

"He was here," Dorito said.

"What?"

"He just called me Dorito," he explained. "He totally knew who I was."

I smiled at him.

"But he's gone again, now," he said wistfully.

"He doesn't usually stay around much," I acknowledged.

"What is that smell?" Dorito asked, wrinkling up his nose.

I took a whiff.

"Oh," I said, nodding at David. "I think someone needs to make a trip to the bathroom."

I started to lead David away when Dorito grabbed my arm.

"I want to help," he said.

"No, you don't," I laughed.

"Yes, I do," he said, seriously.

240

I looked at him.

"Do you know how many times he changed my diaper?" Dorito asked quietly, holding my gaze. He hesitated and then said, "I *want* to help. After everything that he's done for me, it's the least I can do."

I looked at him for another moment.

"Well, then," I finally nodded. "Let's go change a diaper."

In the bathroom, Dorito helped me take down his dad's pants and then we took off the diaper.

"Oh, no," Dorito said. "He's got diarrhea."

"Oh," I said, shaking my head. "It's always like that."

"What do you mean?" he asked as I reached for some toilet paper.

"I mean," I said, shrugging my shoulders, "that it's *always* like that."

"But that's not *normal*," Dorito said in a dismayed voice, and as the words were coming out of his mouth, I realized the awful truth in them.

I looked at Dorito and he looked back at me.

"How long?" he asked.

"I ... I don't know," I stammered, trying to think. "Like since his birthday maybe?"

"That's *nine months*, Tanner!" He was clearly horrified.

"I know," I agreed quietly.

"We've gotta tell mom," he said, turning to leave the bathroom.

"No!" I said quickly.

He turned and looked at me, waiting.

"It's Christmas," I explained. "We can't do anything today. Let her enjoy today. We'll tell her tomorrow and we'll take him to a doctor ... tomorrow."

I looked at him pleadingly and he looked back, finally nodding.

"Okay," he agreed. "We'll tell her tomorrow."

~ ~ ~

"TOMORROW" TURNED OUT to be a crappy day. Even the preliminary tests didn't look good.

One day later, a colonoscopy with a biopsy revealed that David definitely had colon cancer.

Three days later, surgery let us know that it was already at stage four.

Twenty days later, we called in Hospice.

~ ~ ~

HOSPICE IS A great organization and all the nurses were wonderful. One of them in particular, however, wound up being our favorite during the last two months of David's life.

She and Laci hit it off right away as soon as Laci learned that her name was Lilly.

"That's my daughter's name!" Laci exclaimed. "How do you spell it?"

"L-i-l-l-y."

"Oh. My Lily only has one *l*," Laci told her somewhat disappointedly, but the two of them were fast friends after that.

David had no discernible pain that we could tell. Lilly and the other nurses were always ready to give him medicine at the first sign of any discomfort because Laci had made it *beyond* clear that she did not want him to experience even the tiniest amount of suffering, but as it turned out, they rarely had to administer anything.

Toward the end, when David stopped eating, he still wanted liquids and he still sat propped up in bed with his eyes fastened on the television set that we'd moved into their bedroom.

And at the very end, we didn't know that it was the very end.

One of us was by his side all the time. David didn't really *need* one of us there all the time, but Laci refused to leave his side unless one of us agreed to sit there instead, so Amber and Meredith and Lily all started taking turns coming to spend the day.

Before Meredith left one evening, she reported that he had slept for most of the day. After she left, I took her place next to David's bed and Laci agreed that she would try to get some sleep after she finished the dishes.

Like Meredith had said, David seemed unusually sleepy, but at about ten o'clock, he woke up and looked around the room.

"How are you feeling?" I asked.

"Good."

"You're not having any pain?"

He shook his head.

"Do you want to watch TV?" I asked, picking up the remote.

He shook his head again.

I put the remote down.

"Guess what?" I asked.

"What?"

"Tomorrow's your birthday."

"It is?"

"Uh-huh."

"How old am I going to be?" he wanted to know.

"Fifty-nine."

"Really?"

"Uh-huh."

"That's a good number," he said, pausing for a moment. "Fifty-nine is a prime number I think. Isn't fifty-nine prime? I can't remember for sure . . ."

I looked at him questioningly.

"Hi, Tanner."

"Hi, David," I smiled.

"How's Laci?" he asked.

"She's fine," I said. "I'll go get her—"

"No, no," he insisted. "I really want to know how . . . how's she doing?"

I looked at him for a long moment.

"It's hard," I finally admitted. "But I think she's doing pretty good . . ."

"She's going to be all right?"

244

"Yes," I assured him. "She's going to be all right."

He nodded slightly and looked away. After a moment he looked back at me.

"This has been hard on you, too," he stated.

"No," I said. "I'm okay."

"Thank you . . . for everything you've done."

"I'm glad to help," I managed to say with a short nod.

"Tanner?"

"What?"

"I know it hasn't been easy for you to be my friend."

"What?"

"I mean . . . what I mean is that I know ever since you and Laci broke up . . . I know it hasn't been easy for you to be my friend."

"No–" I said, shaking my head.

"It's okay," he interrupted. "I'm just trying to say that I'm glad you decided to stay my friend."

I shook my head at him and looked away, trying to blink back tears.

"You've been a *great* friend," he went on.

There was no stopping the tears after he said that and I brought my hands up to my face and sobbed into them.

"It's okay," he said again quietly and I felt his hand on my arm. "We'll see each other again . . . you know?"

I just cried harder.

"Don't you know, Tanner?"

"No," I choked.

"How can you not know?" he asked. "What's wrong with you? God loves you *so* much and all He wants is for you to love Him back. How do you *not* know that?"

And there it was.

God loves you so *much and all He wants is for you to love Him back.*

That was what I'd been missing all along.

God loved me . . . He always had.

All my life He had loved me, even though I had done nothing about it.

He loved me so much that He had brought David back to me – one last time – just to let me know.

And suddenly, I could feel God running toward me . . . wrapping His arms around me tight. It was something He had been trying to do for years, but this time, I let Him.

I didn't ignore Him . . .
I didn't push Him away . . .
I didn't pretend any longer that I wasn't missing something.

I just let Him hold on to me.
And for the first time in my life, I held on to Him right back.

~ ~ ~

I'M NOT SURE how long I sat there like that with my hands covering my face. I don't think it was more than a few seconds, but I don't know.

It could have been hours.

Engulfed in a peace I'd never known before, I finally looked back at David in amazement.

How can you not know?

"I know," I told him, my tears suddenly gone. "I know now."

"Do we have any freezer pops?" he asked.

I looked at him for a moment and then pressed my lips together and nodded. I gave him a little smile.

"I'll go get you one," I said, patting his hand gently. "I'll be right back."

"I'll get it," I heard Laci say.

I looked up, startled to find her leaning against the doorway with tears streaming down her face.

"I'll get it," she said again. "You stay there."

I nodded at her slowly. She looked at me for a long moment and then turned around and disappeared.

"Who was that?" David asked, almost whispering.

"That's Laci," I replied. "She's going to get you a freezer pop."

"Really?"

"Yep."

"Okay." he said. "I like red."

"I know. She's going to bring you one in just a second."

"I like freezer pops."

"I know."

A minute later, Laci was back. She came over to the same side of the bed that I was on and leaned down, kissing David's forehead.

"Here," she told him, holding it in front of him. "Would you like this?"

"It's red," he noted.

She nodded.

"I like red."

"I know you do," she said, smiling back at him. She sat down in the empty chair next to me and watched him for a moment as he started in on it. Finally she turned to me, her eyes brimming with tears.

"Tanner," she said in a whisper, reaching for my hand. She closed her eyes and the tears slid down her cheeks. She lifted my hand to her cheek, and then – still gripping my hand – leaned forward, putting her head down on David's bed. She didn't say anything, but she sat like that, bowed down, holding my hand against her wet face, for a long time. Finally she sat back up.

"You were praying for me, weren't you?" I asked.

She nodded.

"I can tell," I told her, breathlessly. "I feel so different."

"You don't feel different because I was praying for you," she said.

"I don't?"

"Tanner," she said, patiently. "I've been praying for you *every* day for forty years."

"You have?"

"Of course I have. So has David, and Natalie, and Jordan and Mike . . ." She cocked her head to one side and looked at me. "How can you not know that?"

"I'm just a big, dumb jock."

She smiled and squeezed my hand.

"Why don't you go get some sleep?" she suggested. "I'm up now."

"I don't mind sitting with him."

"No, it's all right," she said. "I want to be alone with him for a little while."

"Okay," I agreed, standing up. I walked to the door, stopping before I left the room.

I turned around and looked back at Laci. She looked at me and smiled again, and then she reached for David's hand.

248

I went into my bedroom and I prayed. It wasn't as if I had never prayed before, but the prayer I prayed that night was very different from any of the other prayers I had ever offered up before.

That night it was the prayer of someone who finally understood that they were loved by God ... and the prayer of someone who finally loved Him back.

~ ~ ~

IT WAS A few hours later that Laci roused me from my sleep by gently shaking my shoulder. I opened my eyes and looked at her.

"He's gone," she said quietly.

I sat up.

"What?"

"He's gone," she said again.

I searched her eyes, trying to understand.

"Are you sure?" I finally asked. It was a stupid question, but it seemed unreal that what she was telling me could possibly be true.

She nodded. "Lilly's in there with him now. She said we can go in in a few minutes."

I nodded at her, but I still don't think I completely comprehended what she was telling me. I looked at Laci closely and wondered why she wasn't crying. Maybe it didn't seem real to her yet, either.

"He was breathing faster," she said quietly. "Lilly said he seemed to be working harder to hold on . . ."

She glanced at me.

"She said that sometimes people are waiting for . . ." she went on in a hesitant voice, "for permission to leave."

I nodded at her and she looked away.

"And she told me that maybe I needed to tell him that it was okay for him to go . . ."

I reached out and took her hand.

"So I told him to go see Greg," Laci said, almost as if she were talking to herself. "I told him to go see Jesus."

She looked back at me and I nodded again, squeezing her hand.

"And . . . and then he said that he saw him," she went on, her voice filling with awe.

"Saw who?" I asked. "Greg or Jesus?"

250

"I don't know," she admitted. "I asked him, but he just ... he just smiled ... and then he went."

We stared at each other for a long moment, the significance of what she was saying settling over both of us.

After a minute, I finally said, "If he saw Greg, you know what I bet they're doing right now?"

"What?"

I gave her a little smile.

"Calculating the probability of dying on your own birthday."

She looked at me for a moment and then smiled back ... and then she actually laughed ... and then we both laughed.

And then both we cried.

~ ~ ~

BY EIGHT O'CLOCK the next evening, Laci and I were both completely spent. It had been decided that Dorito, Maria, and their five girls would sleep in the basement of David and Laci's house – which, I guess, was technically just Laci's house now – where there were two bedrooms downstairs and a separate living area, even though it was pretty much still a big mess. Marco and Grace and their families, meanwhile, could stay over at my old house, and Lily, Meredith, Amber and their families – who all still lived relatively close – would drive back and forth every day.

Lily, Meredith and Amber, along with Paul, came down as soon as they found out that David was gone. The six of us spent the day getting things ready for everyone's arrival the next day: cleaning, changing sheets, and crying.

We also went to the funeral home to finalize plans, and Paul and I disassembled the hospital bed that we'd gotten after David had had his surgery. Once it was taken down, we got it out of the house and put the bedroom back in order as best we could, trying to make things seem as normal as possible.

By the time everyone left after dinner, Laci and I were beyond ready for bed. We hadn't really had much sleep at all the night before, and it was barely dark outside when I hugged her goodnight and she headed up the steps to her bedroom and I went to mine.

It was less than an hour later, however, that I heard a noise in the living room and went out to investigate. Laci had taken the throw pillows off the couch, put them on the floor, and replaced them with her bed pillow. She was busy now, spreading a blanket out on the cushions.

She saw me standing in the doorway, watching her.

"I can't sleep in there," she explained quietly, gesturing toward the stairs that led up to her bedroom.

I nodded at her, understanding.

252

"Is there anything I can help you do?" I asked.

"No," she said, shaking her head. She climbed into her newly made bed and pulled the blanket up around her. "If you want to get the light, that would be good."

"Okay," I said nodding again.

But half of an hour later, I saw the living room light back on again, streaming under the door of my bedroom. When it stayed on, I got up and went back out. Laci was half-sitting, half-lying on the couch.

"I can't sleep," she said when she saw me. Tears started streaming down her face. Her voice rose as she went on. "I'm so tired and I can't sleep and everyone's going to be here tomorrow and I've got so much to do and–"

"You don't have anything to do," I said, crossing the room and sitting down on the couch near her feet. I put my hand on her ankle and gave it a reassuring squeeze. "Everything important has already been taken care of and everybody will understand if you need to take a nap or something. There's nothing that you need to worry about."

"I'm so tired," she said again.

"I know," I said, giving her ankle another squeeze. After a minute, I suggested, "What if I make us some hot cocoa? Milk's supposed to help you go to sleep."

She nodded at me, bleary-eyed, and I got up and went into the kitchen.

When I returned she was still propped up a bit, but she had definitely sagged down onto the couch some. I handed her a steaming mug and sat down on the floor, near her head.

"You can sit back down," she said, starting to draw her feet up again.

"No," I said quickly. "I'm fine right here. I want you to lie down and go to sleep if you can."

She looked as if she wanted to argue with me but was too tired. Instead, she took a sip of cocoa.

Before she'd even finished half of it, her eyes closed and I took the mug from her as she settled herself all the way down onto the couch. I set both of the mugs on the end table and sat quietly in a nearby chair, watching until her breathing became steady and I was sure she was finally asleep.

Deciding that it was safe to head back to my room, I stood up, but as soon as I did, her eyelids fluttered back open.

"Please don't leave," she whispered.

"I'm not," I said. "I was just going to turn out the light."

"No," she said. "I want it on."

I looked at her for a moment and then nodded, reaching toward her and pulling the blanket up around her to tuck her in. She reached out and caught my wrist.

"Don't leave," she said again, still gripping my wrist tightly.

I looked at her for another moment, and then sat down on the floor, leaning back against the couch. Once she was finally convinced that I wasn't going anywhere, she let go of my wrist and I stretched out on the floor beside her, tucking one of the throw pillows under my head. I was so exhausted that I fell asleep almost immediately, but then Laci whispered my name and I opened my eyes again.

"Tanner?"

"What?"

"Thank you."

"No problem," I said. "Try to go to sleep."

"Okay," she said, and then she did.

By the next evening, everyone from out of town had arrived and Laci suggested to Dorito and Maria's daughters that all of them sleep in the living room – with her.

"It'll be like a sleepover," she enthused and they all jumped on the idea. Dorito and Maria slept in the basement, alone, and I went back to my bedroom. And that's how the sleeping arrangements were until the seven of them flew back to Mexico, four days later.

Meanwhile, we made final arrangements for David's funeral, which was to be held the next day. Years earlier – when he had found out that he had Alzheimer's – David had planned exactly how he wanted everything to go. He worked with Lily and Meredith to make a video montage of pictures of their family over the years and he said that he wanted it shown at his funeral. He wanted to be cremated and he wanted his ashes spread over Cross Lake. He wanted us to play "Revelation Song" by Phillips, Craig and Dean. He wanted me to give a eulogy.

I had desperately not wanted to give the eulogy and I had immediately told him so.

"It doesn't have to be some big thing," he'd promised.

"I don't have any idea what I'd say," I'd argued.

254

"You've got plenty of time to think something up."

"I'm not good at stuff like that," I'd said.

"You don't have to be good at it," he'd persisted. "Just say something."

"Why me?" I'd complained.

"Because you're my best friend," he'd answered simply.

"That's dirty pool," I'd muttered.

"I learned from the best," he'd smiled.

Now, however, I wasn't hesitant at all about giving the eulogy . . . as a matter of fact, I was completely ready to go.

"If I had to pick one word to describe David," I began, "I would choose 'faithful'. He was a lot of things: he was funny and fun and he was the smartest person I ever knew, but – above all – he was faithful."

I looked at Laci.

"He was faithful to his wife," I said. "I don't think she needs to be assured of that, but I want to state for the record that it never even occurred to him to be anything but faithful to her. Not just faithful in that he never had an affair, but faithful in that he didn't even *look* at other women. I've never known a man before who would look the other way when a commercial or something would come on TV, but David was like that. He only had eyes for his wife, and I want to make sure that she knows how much he loved her."

A little smile crossed Laci's face and tears came to her eyes, and then I went on.

"And he was faithful to his children," I said. "He loved each of you more than anything in this world. Anytime he spoke about any one of you, his eyes would light up and you could see the pride, shining on his face. He would have done *anything* for each one of you . . . and there is no way that anyone could have ever loved any of you more than he did."

I scanned the pews and found each of them: Dorito, Amber, Lily, Meredith, Grace and Marco. I made sure that I looked at each one before I went on.

"The only thing that made him happier than his children were his grandchildren. Nine wonderful little girls – so far – and I doubt that we're done yet. He always teased about how much he wanted a grandson, but I want you girls to know that he wouldn't have traded a single one of you for all the little boys in the world."

The older girls all looked up at me with teary smiles before I continued.

"And he was faithful as a friend," I said, my eyes this time looking for Mike and Natalie, Jordan and Charlotte. I didn't know if I was going to be able to say this next part or not, but I decided to try. "He told me one time that no one shows a greater love than when he lays his life down for his friends, and David was like that. I know – and I think you do too – that he would have given his life for any one of us, at any time."

I had to move on.

"And finally," I said, "David was faithful to his God. Nothing was more important to him than trying to do what God wanted him to do. One of the things that God wanted him to do was to let others know about Him and about His love for us, so David spent his entire life doing just that. And I want you all to know that he never stopped, even after he got sick. The very night he died, David told somebody about how much God loved them and led that person to Christ. He was faithful, right to the very end."

I finished up without mentioning who that "somebody" was. I wanted the focus of what I was saying to be on David, not me.

It must have been pretty obvious who I was talking about, however, because as soon as the service was over, Natalie came bounding up to me with her bright eyes shining and asked, "You?" and when I nodded, she threw her arms around me and gave me a big hug. I think Mike and Jordan must have figured it out, too, because both of them seemed pretty happy, considering that we were at a funeral and everything.

The first night after Dorito, Maria, and the girls flew back to Mexico, Laci managed to sleep by herself through the night: in the dark, but still on the couch. Marco and Grace had left Cavendish too, and I slowly started packing up my things, preparing to move back to my house. I worried about Laci and how she was going to do once she was there in that house, all by herself.

Apparently she had been worried about the same thing.

"I'm going to sell the house," she said over breakfast.

"What?" I asked, not able to hide the alarm in my voice.

"I can't stay here by myself," she said, her voice rising as she waved her hand around. I started to open my mouth to say something, but she stopped me before I could. "And you're not going to keep staying here with me," she insisted. "You've done enough and you have your own life to get back to."

256

"I don't mind," I said. "I'm glad to be here."

It was true . . . I was. Plus, I didn't have any idea what my "own life" was that I had to get back to. For the past five years, my life had been nothing but David and Laci.

"I know," she said gently, "but we can't live here together by ourselves and besides that, I can't keep sleeping on that couch. My back is killing me."

"You could sleep in the basement," I suggested.

"I probably will," she nodded, "until I figure something else out, but I don't want to be here anymore. I need to get out."

I didn't ask her where she was going to go because I already knew. She was going to move back to Mexico with Dorito and Maria and I was never going to see her again. I had just lost David, and now I was going to lose her, too.

"Move in to my place," I said quickly.

"What?"

"My place," I repeated. "You stay there and I'll stay here and we can get things fixed up before you try to put it on the market."

"I couldn't ask you to do that," Laci said, shaking her head.

"You're not asking me to," I pointed out. "I'm offering. We can do the countertops and the floor in the kitchen and finish the molding in the basement and paint and fix the siding. We could finish insulating that room over the garage and put some paneling up so it could be used as a library or something . . ."

She looked at me hesitantly.

"If you try to sell this house right now," I said, "the way it is, you're probably not even going to get half of what it could be worth."

"I don't know . . ." she said, still hesitant.

"And it would give me something to do," I told her honestly. "It's not like I have a job anymore . . ."

She looked at me sympathetically for a moment, and I could tell that she was carefully considering what I was saying.

"Are you sure that's what you want to do?" she finally asked.

It was probably going to take a year before we could have it anywhere near ready to sell . . .

"I've never been more sure of anything in my life," I told her.

~ ~ ~

FOUR DAYS LATER, Meredith's husband, Amber, Lily, and *their* husbands, all helped me move Laci into my old house. Meredith had stayed in Steep Ford to look after all the girls, so everybody except for Paul and Amber returned home as soon as most of the moving had been taken care of. The remaining four of us ordered a pizza that night, sitting around the kitchen table, and talking about all that we had accomplished, and all that still needed to be done.

During a lull in the conversation, Amber cleared her throat, almost imperceptibly. She glanced nervously at Paul and when he gave her a reassuring smile, I knew that something was up.

Amber had come a long way, but she still did a whole lot better talking when there wasn't a crowd around. Even though the "crowd" that had been here earlier had been all family, the way she was acting now made me suspect that she had something to say and that she had waited until everybody else was gone to do so.

I also had a hunch that I knew exactly what it was that she wanted to announce . . .

I hoped that I was right.

After a final, reluctant glance toward Paul, who nodded his head, silently urging her to go on and tell us, she did.

"I'm pregnant," she finally said.

Yeah, I smiled to myself. *That's what I thought.*

~ ~ ~

AMBER HAD TAKEN a pregnancy test just the day before David's funeral and she hadn't even had a chance to go to the doctor yet. Her first appointment confirmed that she was indeed pregnant and her next trip – four weeks later – told us some even bigger news.

Twins.

~ ~ ~

HAVING AMBER EXPECTING and having so much work to do on the house helped me and Laci both to get our mind off the sadness of David being gone. There were still a lot of tears and we still missed him terribly, but we also experienced a real sense of peace in the days that followed.

I know that a huge part of the peace that I was feeling had a lot to do with my newfound relationship with God, but I think it also had a lot to do with the fact that I knew where David was, and I knew that I was going to see him again one day. Somehow that made everything easier to deal with.

When God becomes a priority in your life, you start to think about things differently than you did before . . .

At least, that's how it worked for me.

Not only did I find myself trying to act the way I knew God wanted me to act, but I also found myself thinking about things in the past . . . times when I knew I had acted in a way that God wouldn't have wanted me to act. I found myself remembering how Carter had shown up at the front door a few years earlier to apologize to David and Laci, and now I finally understood why he had stopped by to visit – why he had felt the need to make amends. The more I thought about it, and the more I prayed about it, the more I felt that God was leading me toward doing something similar.

There were a lot of people I had known in my life that I could have apologized to, but God only convicted me to go and see two of them – neither of whom I really had any desire to ever see again. But I thought about David and I thought about how hard he had worked to do whatever God wanted him to do, even when it wasn't what *he* wanted to do, and I found that I wanted to do the same thing.

260

I wanted what David had had with God and I knew that I was going to have to be obedient if I ever expected that to happen.

And so I made up my mind to track down both of the people that God convicted me to go see, even though it was the last thing I felt like doing.

The first person was Megan, and she wasn't hard to find at all. Thirty minutes of social networking and one friend request later, and suddenly I was telling her that I needed to talk to her about something and asking her if she'd meet me somewhere.

To my surprise, she said, "Yes."

Four days later I drove to Omaha and met her at a restaurant she'd suggested. As we approached each other, I was taken aback by how much she had changed. I wondered fleetingly if Laci and Natalie and Mike and I had all changed that much too but maybe I just hadn't noticed because it had snuck up on us so gradually. When I looked at each one of them, I still saw the exact same people I had known all my life.

Megan and I gave each other an awkward cross between a handshake and a hug, briefly touching our lips to each others' cheeks. Once that was over, we sat down and looked at one another.

"Thanks for meeting me," I said.

"I was surprised to hear from you."

"I bet," I smiled.

She looked at me expectantly.

"Tell me about yourself," I said. "Are you married? Do you have kids?"

She hesitated for a moment and then told me, "I've been married and divorced twice. I have two sons – one from each marriage. Three grandkids . . ." She shrugged as she finished. "I sell insurance now."

I nodded.

"What about you?" she asked.

"I retired from the high school a few years ago," I said. "No marriage. No kids."

"Held on tight to that dream, didn't you?" she asked under her breath.

I nodded again.

We made small talk for a little while longer and then she asked, "Why are we here, Tanner? What's going on?"

"I came here to apologize."

"For what?" she asked, surprised.

"When ..." I hesitated, "when you told me you were pregnant," I finally said, "I . . . I should have asked you to marry me."

"You didn't love me," she stated matter-of-factly.

"Then I shouldn't have been sleeping with you," I said.

She gave me another little shrug. "It was a two-way street."

"But, I . . . I feel really bad about everything," I said. "I always have."

"So you're trying to ease your guilty conscience?" she asked.

"Something like that," I admitted.

She looked at me questioningly.

"I'm a different person then I was then," I tried to explain.

"What happened?" she asked jokingly. "You find Jesus or something?"

"Actually," I said, "I think it's more like He found me, but yeah."

She looked even more surprised, but recovered quickly.

"Sorry," she said reticently.

"Don't worry about it," I said.

"Look, Tanner," she said, "I get it and it was really nice of you to find me and everything, but . . ."

She stopped and looked at me for a very long time.

"It wasn't only your fault," she finished.

I looked back at her.

"I didn't *accidentally* get pregnant," she explained quietly.

I looked at her and gave her a little nod.

"I knew you wanted out," she went on, "and it was the only thing I could think of to keep you . . ."

"But you *were* pregnant?" I asked.

She nodded and held my gaze.

"Yes." I nodded at her and there was silence until she finally added quietly, "But I didn't have a miscarriage."

"Yes, you did," I argued.

She looked at me, startled.

"I saw you a few months later," I explained. "You definitely weren't pregnant."

"No," she agreed. "I wasn't pregnant anymore."

She looked at me again – this time in a very meaningful way.

"But I didn't have a miscarriage either," she said softly.

I looked back at her for a long moment.

"Oh," I finally said.

She dropped her eyes to the table.

"I really thought you'd marry me if I got pregnant," she explained softly. "And when you didn't . . . well, I knew I wasn't ready to be a mom all by myself."

"Oh," I said again.

"It was a huge mistake," she said, looking back up at me. "It's something I've regretted every day of my life."

"I'm sorry," I managed to barely whisper.

"It wasn't your fault."

"It was just as much my fault as it was yours."

"I should have talked to you about it first," she said, "I'm sorry."

I shook my head. I put my hand up to my face and rubbed my eyes. I felt her reach out and touch my arm.

I pulled my hand away from my eyes and looked at her. She looked back at me for another long moment, and then she made me cry.

"You really would have been a great father," she said.

Anthony Perry wasn't hard to track down either – he was serving a life term at a correctional institute just outside of Springfield, Missouri.

I wasn't sure if he would agree to see me or not, but he did, and a week after I'd sat down with Megan, I found myself seated at a small table with him in a large visitation room.

"Who are you?" he asked.

"Tanner Clemmons."

"I know *that*," he said. "I mean, 'Who are you?' Why are you here?"

"I'm a friend of Amber's," I said.

"Who's Amber?"

"Amber's the little girl you raped," I said.

"You're going to have to be more specific."

I closed my eyes and took a deep breath, trying to compose myself.

"I'm the one who broke your nose and possibly your jaw," I finally said when I opened my eyes.

"Oh, yeah," he said, narrowing his own eyes at me. "I remember you. You taught at the high school."

I nodded and he reached his hand up to his jaw.

"You definitely broke it," he said absentmindedly, rubbing it with his hand. "I can always tell when a front's coming through."

"Well, I'm sorry about that," I said. "That's why I came here ... to apologize."

He looked at me suspiciously for a moment.

"That's why you're here?" he asked. "To apologize?"

I nodded.

"Why?"

I was a little more prepared to answer that question than I'd been when Megan had asked.

"I have a relationship with Jesus now," I said forthrightly, "but I didn't back then. I felt like He wanted me to come here and talk to you."

"I don't believe in all that 'Jesus' crap," he said. "Don't waste your time talking to me about it."

"I'm not," I said, shaking my head. "I just came here to apologize."

He surveyed me for a moment and then gave me a reluctant nod.

I wasn't sure what else I was supposed to say. It seemed like I had driven an awfully long way just to make one little apology, but that was all God had convicted me to do, so I waited to see if Anthony had anything else to say.

He did.

"You know," he said, "the same thing happened to me when I was little."

"I know," I admitted.

"That shouldn't happen to a little kid," he said.

"No," I agreed.

"You tell that little girl that I said that I was sorry."

"She's not a little girl anymore."

"Oh, right," he nodded. "Well, anyway. You tell her I said I was sorry."

Reluctantly, very reluctantly, I gave him a nod back. And then I drove home.

~ ~ ~

I DID NOT want to tell Amber that Anthony Perry had said he was sorry. I didn't even want Amber to know that I'd gone to see Anthony Perry. Of course Laci knew that I'd gone to see him because we spent time together every single day and it wasn't as if I could just drive to Omaha and Springfield without her finding out what was up. She had found the idea that God was leading me to go see Megan and Anthony wonderful, and now she was certain that Amber was going to be just fine with the message I had to deliver to her.

I, however, wasn't so sure.

"Who knows what's going to happen if the past gets all dredged up again?" I said anxiously.

"She'll be fine," Laci assured me. "Don't worry about it."

But I did worry about it. I worried about it all week until Friday, when Laci and I finally drove up to spend the weekend with Amber and Paul.

Amber's belly had grown a lot since the last time we'd seen them. She was doing so good . . . she looked so happy . . .

I really didn't want to ruin all that.

After dinner, however, I suggested to Amber that we take a walk.

"Let me get these dishes done first," she said.

"Paul and I'll do it," Laci told her. "You go ahead."

"Okay," she agreed sounding suspicious for the first time. As soon as we were in the driveway, she turned to me.

"What's wrong?" she asked.

"Nothing's wrong . . ."

"Something's wrong," she said. "You weren't yourself all through dinner and now we're suddenly taking a walk by ourselves. What's wrong?"

"Nothing's wrong," I insisted, taking her hand. "I just want to talk to you about something."

"What?"

I didn't answer for a moment and we walked along quietly, gently swinging our hands between us.

"Anthony Perry," I finally said.

She faltered only slightly in her step and kept going. I squeezed her hand.

"What about him?" she asked quietly.

"I saw him last week," I explained.

"*Where?*"

"In prison," I said. "He's in prison."

She stopped walking.

"Why is he in prison?" she asked.

"Same thing," I said, shrugging slightly. "Someone else."

She looked at me for a moment and then started walking again.

"Why did you go there?" she finally asked.

"To see him."

"Why?"

"Do you remember the day I met you?" I asked.

She nodded.

"Well," I said, "I don't know if you remember this or not, but I beat him up pretty bad that day."

"I remember," she said, nodding again.

"Oh. Well, the only reason I didn't *kill* him that day is because you were watching . . ."

I glanced at her.

"But I did hurt him pretty bad," I finished.

She nodded one more time.

"And I really felt like I needed to apologize to him."

"You *apologized* to him?" she exclaimed. She stopped walking again and stared at me.

I nodded and stared back at her. "I felt like God wanted me to," I explained. Then I asked, "Do you hate me?"

She thought for a moment and shook her head. This time she squeezed my hand. I smiled at her and we started walking along.

"Why are you telling me all this?" she asked quietly.

"Because he wanted me to tell you something," I said.

She didn't ask me what, so I just went ahead and told her.

"He wanted me to tell you that he's sorry."

"Oh." After a moment, she asked, "What else?"

266

"That's it," I said.

"Oh."

We continued walking along again.

"That's why you were so weird at dinner?" she asked.

I nodded.

"What's the matter?" she asked with a playful smile. "Did you think I was going to stop talking again or something if you mentioned the name 'Anthony Perry' to me?"

"The thought crossed my mind," I confessed.

She pretended to try to talk, choking on words that wouldn't come out. Then she gave me a mischievous grin and laughed.

"Tanner," she said, dropping my hand so she could hold both of hers out, palms up, to her side. "Look at me!"

I looked at her. At her pregnant belly and her bright eyes and her glowing face.

"I'm doing great!" she said, shaking her hands for emphasis. "I'm a best-selling author and I'm married to the greatest guy in the world and I'm getting ready to have the two most perfect babies in the world . . ."

I smiled at her.

"What more could you want?" she asked.

"Nothing," I admitted. "Absolutely nothing."

She smiled back at me, took my hand again, and we started walking back to the house.

"Want to hear a secret?" she asked before we got back to their yard.

"What?"

"Baby 'B' finally turned so that we could get a good look."

"Really?"

She nodded.

"*And?*" I asked.

"And I really wish Daddy was here," she said, "so I could tell him that he's finally going to have a grandson."

~ ~ ~

LACI AND I worked diligently on her house, and by Christmas time, it was in those final stages of unbelievable clutter that only come right before everything wraps up all neat and tidy. Marco and Grace and their families weren't going to come to Cavendish until the day after Christmas, and while this was sad in one way, it was fortunate in another because we would have been hard-pressed to accommodate so many people at one time. Only Dorito and his family were coming in from out of town before Christmas, and they planned to stay with Laci, at my old house.

Shortly after David had been diagnosed, he had given me access to a small bank account that he'd set up, and he had left me very explicit instructions on how to use it. Every Valentine's Day, Christmas, and birthday, I was supposed to buy Laci a present and give it to her, from him. I had started buying her gifts with this money as soon as he was no longer able to do it himself, and – now that he was gone – I continued to do it.

Fortunately, David had given me a good idea on what to buy for her, and the task at hand was relatively easy. There was a Christian organization that Laci liked that would purchase items – in her name – to give to families in third world countries. People could buy livestock or pay to have a well dug, or whatever, and David had told me that unless something else came up that I was sure she would want, I should get her something from there.

On Christmas Eve, we gathered together at my old house and exchanged presents. By now, everyone knew that Laci was going to receive a gift from David, so it wasn't too big of a surprise when she opened an envelope from him. The only surprise was what had been purchased . . . in this case, a camel.

Camels were actually kind of expensive. I know I said that David had given me access to a "small" bank account, but that was relatively speaking. There was actually enough money in that account to keep things going until Laci was approximately a hundred and fifteen years old, so I didn't worry a

268

whole lot about how much a camel cost. Plus, you've got to admit that a camel is a pretty cool gift.

Anyway, Laci opened the card, got a little teary-eyed, and then passed it around for everyone to look at. She mouthed "thank you" to me and gave me a little smile. I smiled back, and then she opened the card that was from me.

"Oh, Tanner," she said, looking fondly at the card. "You got me a goat!"

And then we exchanged smiles, one more time.

When it came time for me to leave, I said goodbye to everyone and headed out to my truck, grabbing the handle and opening the door wide. I was about to hoist myself in, when – suddenly – Dorito appeared out of the darkness.

"Oh!" I said, startled. He was standing right next to the door, almost in front of me . . . almost blocking me from climbing into the truck.

In the dim glow of the dome light, I could tell that something was wrong.

"What?" I asked.

He narrowed his eyes, surveying me carefully before he spoke.

"It was her," he finally said quietly.

"What was her?"

"My mom."

I looked at him, confused.

"That girl you dated," he replied. "The one you said you couldn't be with, but that you'd never get over. The one you said you'd always love . . ."

His voice trailed off.

"It was my mom."

I stared at him, dumbstruck.

"All this time," he said, "you've been in love with my mom."

"It's not what you think," I insisted, shaking my head.

"You pushed yourself into their lives," he went on, ignoring me. "You . . . you were *living* with them!"

"You don't understand—"

"And he was sick," Dorito cried, looking at me in dismay. "He had diarrhea for *nine months* and you didn't do one single thing about it!"

"It's not what you're thinking," I said again, still shaking my head.

269

"You don't have any idea what I'm thinking," Dorito said coldly, and then he stormed away from me and went into the house.

I called Mike late that night.

"That's stupid," Mike said when I told him what had happened. "You didn't do anything wrong."

"But he's right," I protested. "Nine months of diarrhea? That's not normal . . . I knew that. Why didn't I do something about it?"

"It's very common," Mike explained patiently, "to not notice something like that when it comes on so gradually."

"Nine months?" I asked.

"I know this one couple," Mike said, "whose kid was losing weight even though they were feeding her constantly. She was thirsty all the time, hungry, getting up to urinate about seven times in the middle of the night . . ."

"Diabetes . . ." I said quietly.

"Yeah," Mike agreed. "So this goes on and on and she's getting more and more lethargic as time goes by. By the time they finally brought her in, she was unconscious.

"They were kicking themselves after they found out what was wrong," Mike went on. "It was so obvious to them once they started looking back at things, but – at the time – they were too close to it. It had come on so gradually that they couldn't see it. It's the same thing that happened with David."

I didn't say anything for a moment, but then I told him what was really on my mind.

"What if, deep down, I knew?" I asked. "What if – in my subconscious – I wanted him gone?"

"Do you think Laci felt that way?" he asked.

"What?"

"Do you think," he said, "that deep down, Laci knew something was wrong and she didn't do anything about it because she wanted him gone?"

"No," I said, practically laughing. "Absolutely not. That's ridiculous."

"Didn't she change just as many diapers as you did?"

I didn't answer.

"How come it's okay," he asked, "for Laci to miss something like that, but it's not okay for you to miss it?"

I still didn't answer.

"You're not any more to blame for what happened than she is," he explained patiently. "Both of you did everything that you could for him . . . you don't have anything to feel guilty about."

"But," I began. "Dorito—"

"Dorito's just upset right now," Mike assured me. "He'll come around."

I was quiet for a minute.

"Okay," I finally said. "Thanks."

"No problem," Mike said. "Now go back to sleep."

"I wasn't asleep," I told him.

"I was."

Dorito did indeed come around.

He knocked on my door the very next morning and when I opened it he looked at me for a moment with such anguish in his eyes that I immediately wanted to put my arms around him.

I didn't though. I just stood there and watched as he blinked back a few tears before he finally managed to speak.

"I miss him so much," he choked before letting out a sob.

"I know," I said quietly, and this time I did put my arms around him, pulling him to me.

We both stood there in the doorway for a minute, crying, and then we finally retreated into the living room and sat down.

"I'm really sorry," Dorito said, wiping his eyes and looking at me earnestly. "I didn't mean what I said."

"I know you didn't."

"I know that you'd never do anything to hurt him," he said.

I gave him a little smile, hoping that what he was saying was true.

We looked at each other for a moment.

"I never thanked you," he went on, "for everything that you did . . . for helping her take care of him."

This time I gave him a bigger smile.

"No problem," I said. "I'm glad I could do it."

I knew for sure that that was true.

~ ~ ~

BEFORE HE LEFT, Dorito told me something.

"I want you to know," he said, looking at me seriously, "that if anything were to ever happen between you and my mom . . ."

"There's nothing going on between us," I said quickly.

"I know," he nodded, "but I'm just saying that if anything were to ever happen . . ."

He held my gaze for a minute and I waited to see what he would say.

"Well," he finished, "I just want you to know that you'd have my blessing."

I smiled at him.

"Thanks," I said. "That means a lot to me, but the two of us are just friends."

"I know," he said. "I'm just saying . . ." and I nodded.

We didn't talk anymore about it, but that conversation really got me thinking about things . . . just in case I hadn't been thinking about them already.

Laci and I were spending nearly all day together, every day. Part of that was under the pretense of fixing up her house: picking out wall paper and paint, installing countertops, lighting and flooring. But even on the days when we didn't work on her house, we almost always spent time together. I would go over to my old house where she would make me dinner, or she would come over to her old house so I could cook for her. If neither one of us felt like cooking, we would go out. We went to Steep Ford a lot for day trips to see the girls. Sometimes we went out with Jessica and Chris to the movies.

I wasn't sure where – if anywhere – things were headed between the two of us. She was definitely my best friend, and I was hers, but it wasn't unrealistic to think that things might progress. Of course it was also entirely possible that nothing was ever going to happen between the two of us, and that was fine.

I didn't care.

Okay, that was a lie.

I cared.

But I also knew that the two of us might just remain friends, nothing more, and if that's what happened, I really was totally fine with it.

As always, the most important thing was that Laci simply be around.

But if something *did* happen between the two of us?

I happened to be totally fine with that, too.

~ ~ ~

BY THE END of January, Amber had gone full term with the twins. Paul and Amber hadn't told anybody what they were planning to name the babies, but they hardly needed to. I was pretty sure that the boy was going to be named after David and/or Paul, and that the little girl would be named after Laci's mom Lynn, who had died about ten years earlier.

Turns out I had things figured right . . . for the most part.

When the big day arrived, Laci and I made the two hour trip and reached the hospital just before the twins were delivered. We joined Meredith and Lily and their families in the waiting area until we were finally ushered in to Amber's room to see the babies for the first time. Paul, who had come out to get us, reached into a bassinet and handed a little bundle to Laci, telling her, "This is David Paul."

I knew it.

Laci didn't say anything (I think because she was trying really hard not to cry). But she looked down at her first grandson, and gently ran her finger across his tiny, little face.

Amber was sitting up in her hospital bed, watching as Laci held the baby. She glanced at me and smiled, and I smiled back, and then Paul reached into the bassinet and lifted out the second baby.

"And this," he said, looking at me, "is Tanner Lynn."

"I thought you were having a boy and a girl," I said as he placed the baby in my arms.

"We did."

I looked at the baby Laci was holding (in his blue knit cap) and then at the baby in my own arms (with her decidedly pink one). Then I looked at Amber and Paul with growing alarm.

"You can't name a girl TANNER!" I cried.

"Why not?" Amber asked.

"Because it's a *boy's* name!"

274

"No, it's not," she said, waving her hand at me, dismissively. "Tanner is a gender-neutral name."

"It is NOT!" I cried. "Tanner is a very *masculine* name!"

Everyone was laughing at me, but I knew that it was no joke: they really had named their little girl after me.

I thought about that for a minute and I looked down again at the little bundle resting in my arms. I looked over at Laci and at baby David and I thought about it some more.

David and Tanner . . .

I decided that I liked it.

AMBER WAS UNDERSTANDABLY tired, and after a while, Paul encouraged all of us to go down to the cafeteria to get something to eat so that she could get some sleep. I don't think she got too much of a nap in, however, because when we got back to the room, the hospital's pediatrician was there, talking with them about what he had found when he'd examined the babies.

All of us stood there, listening to him explain how both of the babies seemed very healthy and how it would be normal for a bit of jaundice to appear within the next few days.

"It shouldn't be any cause for alarm," he promised them.

Laci, who had been intently eying the doctor ever since we'd entered the room, spoke when there was a break in the conversation.

"Is your first name Darion?" she asked hesitantly.

He turned to her and nodded, looking at her carefully for the first time since we'd entered the room. His name tag said Dr. Casteen.

"It's me," she said in an awed voice, putting her hand against her chest. "Laci. Laci Cline."

His eyes widened with recognition.

"Oh, my goodness!" he exclaimed, smiling and closing the few steps between them to give her a hug.

"Darion was on that trip I took to the Dominican Republic my junior year!" Laci explained excitedly to the rest of us. There were introductions all around and then everyone went back to fussing over the babies as the two of them caught each other up on what had been happening over the past forty years. Eventually Laci told him about David dying, telling Darion, "It's been almost eight months."

"My wife died almost two years ago," he said, and the two of them looked at each other sympathetically. When he finally left the room to finish his rounds, it was with a promise to Laci that the two of them would get together soon and catch up further.

Laci looked at him and gave him a smile.

~ ~ ~

WHEN THE BABIES were almost three weeks old, Laci traveled back to Steep Ford to spend a few days helping Amber out. I was supposed to go too, but I wasn't feeling great on the day that we were supposed to leave. Mostly I was just tired and rundown, but I worried that I was coming down with something and finally decided that I'd better not take a chance on exposing Amber and the twins just in case I was.

"Are you sure you'll be okay driving up there without me?" I asked Laci over the phone after I'd told her.

"I know how to drive," she reminded me.

"I know," I said. "I just . . ."

"I'll be fine," she said assuredly. "Don't worry about me."

I was actually starting to feel so bad that I decided I would do just that . . . not worry about it.

By the next morning I was so sick that I dragged myself to the doctor. I barely made it there and he promptly diagnosed me with the flu, scolding me for not getting my flu shot the previous fall. He gave me a prescription for some medicine that "may or may not help," and sent me home to go to sleep. He didn't have to tell me twice. Somehow I managed to drive myself back and make it up the stairs before I collapsed onto the bed. I had never felt so terrible in my entire life.

When I woke up later that day, it was almost dark. I took some ibuprofen and forced myself to drink something so that I'd stay hydrated. Then I called Laci.

"Hello?"

"Laci?" It didn't sound like her, but I figured maybe I was hallucinating or something.

"Hi, Tanner. No . . . it's Amber. She left her phone here."

"Where'd she go?"

"Remember Darion?" Amber asked, as crying started up in the background. "The pediatrician at the hospital?"

"Yeah . . ."

"Hang on a second," she said.

I heard a clunk and then the sounds of Amber quieting one of her babies. After a moment Amber returned to the phone.

"Are you still there?" she asked.

"Yeah."

"Do you want me to have her call you when she gets in?"

"No," I said. "That's alright. Just . . . just tell her that I'm really sick."

"Are you okay?" Amber asked in alarm.

"Oh, yeah," I assured her. "I mean it's just the flu . . . I'm fine. But what I meant was that I'm contagious. Tell Laci not to come over here when she gets back tomorrow. I don't want her to get sick too."

"Are you sure you're okay?" Amber asked worriedly.

"Yeah, I'm fine," I said. "Don't worry about me."

Of course I should have realized that nothing would bring Laci to my side faster than telling her that I was really sick and that she should stay away. It was early the next morning when I awoke to find her worriedly wiping my forehead with a cool, wet washcloth.

"You shouldn't be here," I managed to say. "You're going to get sick."

"No," she said, shaking her head. "I'll be fine."

I knew that there was no convincing her to go home, plus what she was doing felt really good, so I didn't argue with her anymore.

"I made you some chicken broth," she said, pointing to a bowl on the nightstand. "You need to get some fluids down you."

I nodded and managed to sit up long enough for her to spoon feed me almost half of the bowl. That effort wore me out like I couldn't believe and when I was done, I flopped back down and immediately fell asleep again.

As unsettling dreams of Laci and Darion intruded upon my rest, I thought I heard Laci say, very quietly, "I don't know what I would do without you."

I don't know if I was dreaming or not and I was too lethargic to find out.

"That's funny," I managed to utter before I fell back asleep. "I was just thinking the same thing about you."

~ ~ ~

SHE MAY NOT have known what she'd do without me and she may have stayed by my side until I was feeling better, but – after that – things were different between me and Laci.

And by "different", I don't mean different in a good way.

She distanced herself from me.

She came up with one excuse after another as to why she wasn't coming over to help me with one of our ongoing projects.

We went from eating together once or twice a day to almost never.

She often didn't answer the phone when I called and she could barely bring herself to make eye contact with me on the few occasions that we did get together.

And she kept going to visit Amber, without me.

I *knew* she was seeing Darion . . . I didn't even need to ask, but – in the interest of not jumping to conclusions – I did ask. I called Amber one evening and wanted to know flat out if Laci was seeing Darion.

"They go out to eat every time she comes up here," Amber said, matter-of-factly. "I think they have a lot in common."

Unseen, I covered my eyes with one hand and slowly shook my head.

"Don't tell her that I asked," I finally told Amber.

"Okay," she agreed. I knew that she was confused, but I also knew that I could trust her.

She wasn't going to say anything to Laci.

Over the past year, God had spent a lot of time showing me that it was okay for me to be honest with Him.

I learned that He was okay with me telling Him exactly what was in my heart – especially since He already knew, anyway – and I learned that if I prayed for Him to change my heart, He would do it.

And He did change my heart. I know this because – as it became more and more clear to me that I might be losing Laci again – I realized that if that *did* happen, it was only going to be because He had something better in mind.

Not necessarily some*one* better, but some*thing* better. Something that would glorify His name . . . something that would work to the good of those who loved Him. That didn't stop me from praying to Him and telling Him exactly what I wanted to have happen, but I always managed to end each prayer with, *Nevertheless, not my will, but Yours.*

I was glad that I was putting God first, and pleased with myself to discover that I actually meant what I was telling Him.

The previous summer, Laci had borrowed my boat so that she could fulfill David's wishes by spreading his ashes over Cross Lake. It had surprised everyone when she'd decided it was something that she wanted to do all by herself.

Now, two days before the anniversary of David's death, Laci talked to me long enough to ask if she could borrow my boat again. I drove up to Cross Lake the next day and got it out of dry dock for her, taking a quick loop around the lake to make sure it was in good, running order. The next day I stopped by her house with the key.

"Here," I said, handing it to her. "It's good to go."

"Thank you," she said, taking it from me.

"Are you sure you don't want me to go with you?" I asked, but she shook her head just like I knew she would.

I nodded and turned to go, praying to God to help me to not be angry if I found out later that she wasn't going alone this time.

I spent David's birthday over at Laci's house – my old house – replacing a basement window that had cracked somehow over the winter. It

282

took me several hours, and when I was finished, I went home to clean up. I was surprised to find Laci waiting for me on the front step when I arrived.

"Thank you for letting me use your boat," she said, holding the key out to me.

"No problem," I said. "You want to come in?"

She surprised me again by looking me right in the eye and nodding. She stood up and followed me through the door.

"You want something to drink?" I asked.

"Some water would be great," she nodded again.

I went into the kitchen and filled up a glass for her. When I returned to the living room, she was sitting on the couch.

"It's David's birthday," she said quietly, taking the glass from me.

"I know," I nodded, sitting down in a nearby chair.

"I just kind of wanted to be near him today."

I nodded again and she dropped her gaze, staring at her glass of water.

She hesitated for a long time before looking back up at me.

"I actually wanted to talk to him about something," she finally said. I looked at her. "I know that probably sounds stupid," she added hastily when I didn't answer.

"No, it doesn't," I assured her, shaking my head.

There was a long moment of silence. Finally she spoke.

"I told him . . ." She hesitated again.

"What?" I asked.

She pursed her lips and looked back down at her glass.

"What?" I asked again.

She brought her eyes to meet mine once more.

"I told him that I wanted to start dating someone," she said.

I stared at her for a moment, but then stood up and walked to the window.

"Tanner?"

I couldn't even answer her.

"Tanner?" she asked again.

"What?" I finally managed.

"I just . . . I just wondered what you thought about that."

"I think it's great," I said.

"You do?"

"Yeah."

"You don't sound very happy about it," she said.

"Happy?"

I turned to look at her. She nodded slightly.

I didn't stop to pray . . . I just let myself be angry.

"Do you really expect me to be *happy* about it?" I blurted. "Do you honestly have no idea how I feel about you?"

She stared at me for a long moment, narrowed her eyes, and then finally said, "You know that I'm talking about *you*, right?"

"Huh?"

She closed her eyes, shook her head, and then opened them again.

"*You*, you idiot!" she said. "I want to start dating *you*!"

"Oh . . ."

"Who in the world did you *think* I was talking about?"

"Ummmm . . ." I hesitated before finally answering. "Dr. Darion?"

She looked at me quizzically.

"Darion Casteen?"

"Yeah," I nodded.

"Why in the *world* would you think that I wanted to start dating him?"

"Because you two 'have a lot in common!'" I exclaimed. "And because you keep going up there to see him and . . ." My voice trailed off. "And because you haven't wanted anything to do with me ever since you started going up there," I finally finished.

She smiled at me sympathetically.

"Come here," she said, patting the couch next to her. "Sit down."

I walked over to the couch and sat down, facing her.

"What Darion and I have in common," she explained, "is that both of us lost our spouses and we're both having a hard time. We've been trying to help each other move on."

"Move on?"

"I've been talking him into trying one of those online dating services," she explained.

I looked at her.

"You have?"

She nodded. "Two weeks ago he went out with someone named Belinda. She brought her pet rabbit with her to the restaurant."

"A rabbit?"

"In her purse," Laci explained. "She kept asking Darion for stuff out of his salad to feed it."

I covered my mouth with my hand.

"He's supposed to go out with someone named Dixie tomorrow night," she went on. "It was all I could do to convince him to give it another try."

She looked at me for a moment.

"And he finally managed to convince me that I needed to tell you how I've been feeling."

I looked back at her.

"But you've barely been able to bring yourself to look me in the eye since that first time you went up there," I said.

"I know," she sighed. "When you got so sick and I came home and found you lying there in bed like that . . ."

She shook her head at the memory of it and glanced away. She finally looked back at me.

"It reminded me so much of when I was losing David," she went on. "I mean, I *knew* you were going to be okay – I knew it was just the flu and that you were going to be fine – but I let my thoughts get the better of me. That was when I realized exactly how I felt about you, but I started having a really hard time with it."

She sighed again.

"I mean, I was married to David for almost *thirty-seven* years," she said, "and I felt so *guilty* whenever I thought about going out with you."

I nodded at her, understanding.

"It was Darion's idea for me to go to the lake today," she finished. "He said that talking to David about it would help me convince myself that he'd be okay with it."

"And did it?"

She gave me a little smile, and then she nodded.

~ ~ ~

OUR FIRST OFFICIAL date in over forty years took place the next night.

It was an absolute disaster.

I took her to Dante's, but it wouldn't have mattered where we'd gone . . . things just were *not* going to turn out well.

I was nervous and I think Laci was too, because she was back to not being able to make eye contact with me again as soon as I picked her up. We hardly spoke on the ride there and at the restaurant Laci looked up long enough to order her drink when our waiter came, but then stuck her nose right back into her menu after he left.

Once our drinks arrived and we ordered our meals, the waiter took our menus and then Laci didn't have that to stare at anymore. She concentrated, instead, on the embroidery along the edge of her napkin.

I tried to make small talk, but all I got out of her were brief nods and one word answers. After a while, I decided to try and lighten things up a bit.

"I gotta tell ya, Lace," I finally said, "this is the worst date I've ever been on in my entire life."

Laci looked up at me in dismay and then burst into tears, bringing that napkin up to her eyes.

So much for lightening things up . . .

"I'm sorry," she cried as her shoulders shook up and down.

"Come on, Laci," I said, standing up and walking to the other side of the table. I sat down next to her and wrapped an arm around her shoulder. "Come on. I was just kidding. You know I was just *kidding*."

"I know," she sniffed, "but it's true. This was a terrible idea. I don't know how I ever thought I was going to be able to do this."

"Here," I said, standing up and pulling her toward me. "Let's go take a little walk."

"But our salads are coming . . ."

"We'll come right back," I assured her. "Let's just get out of here for a minute."

Our waiter met us as were leaving and I told him that we'd be back in soon. We walked out onto the back patio where they had built a new little pond since we'd last visited, complete with goldfish and padded benches and sat down. I put an arm around her and she rested her head against me.

"I want to go out with you," she said, miserably. "I *want* to do this."

"I know."

"But I can't stop thinking about David."

"I know. Me too."

She lifted her head off my shoulder and looked at me, surprised.

"Really?"

"Of course, really. He was your husband," I explained. "He was my best friend. How could I *not* be thinking about him?"

She thought about this for a minute.

"What are we going to do?" she finally asked.

"I don't think we're going to do anything," I shrugged.

"But . . . but I want to go out with you," she said again.

"I know," I agreed, "and I want to go out with you, too. But obviously we're not ready for this right now."

"So we're not going to go out?"

"Not right now."

"But," she said, "but we're going to keep trying, right?"

"I don't think so," I said, shaking my head. "I don't think we should really have to *try*. I think if it's supposed to happen . . . it will."

She looked at me.

"But what if it doesn't?" she asked quietly.

I reached out and took her hand.

"If it doesn't," I said, squeezing her hand, "You're still my best friend – no matter what."

She held my gaze for a moment and I could tell that that was going to be enough for her too, if it had to be.

She nodded at me and I gave her a little smile, and then we went back into the restaurant and sat down, just as our salads were being served.

Deciding not to go out had been a good move. Now that our "date" was officially over, Laci acted almost like her old self. We talked and laughed throughout the meal and I felt myself smiling a lot. I had Laci back, and I couldn't remember when I'd ever been happier.

After the bill arrived and Laci and I fought over it for a minute, she smiled and said, "I remember when the kids were little. Whenever we went out, David used to–"

She stopped herself short and looked at me.

"I'm sorry," she said quietly.

"Why?" I asked. "For mentioning David?"

She nodded.

"Not talking about him isn't the answer here," I told her. "We can't *not* talk about him."

She looked at me uncertainly.

"What did he do?" I asked. "Tell me."

She continued her story.

"Amber always wanted gum," she said. "You know, from those machines at the front of the restaurant?"

I nodded.

"And so since he was always trying to get her to talk to people and stuff, he'd give her his card and he'd make her take it up to the cashier. He told her if she didn't pay the bill, she couldn't have any."

"Did she do it?" I asked, smiling as I imagined it.

"Oh yeah," Laci nodded, laughing. "She really wanted gum."

After dinner we went back out onto the deck and sat in front of the fishpond for a while. The weather was mild for the end of March, and the moon was full.

"You know how you said that we shouldn't *not* talk about David?" Laci asked quietly.

"Yeah," I nodded.

"Do you . . ." she hesitated. "Do you want to see where I put his ashes?"

I looked at her, surprised.

"Yeah," I said now, nodding my head earnestly. "I really would."

We went to the marina and pushed the boat out of its slip, turning on the running lights because the sun had already slipped down over the horizon.

"Which way?" I asked Laci before I turned the motor on.

288

"That way," she said, pointing to the northern end of the lake. This surprised me because there was nothing significant there – no popular fishing spot . . . no sandy beach . . . no great memories – at least not as far as I knew.

Laci continued to direct me until finally we came to a small cove filled with driftwood. I cut the motor, tilted it up, and put down the trolling motor, guiding us further toward the shore until Laci finally told me to stop.

We drifted quietly for a moment until Laci spoke.

"Right here," she said, indicating a broad area with her hand. "I put them right here."

I didn't say anything. I looked down into the water, the lights from the boat reflecting off its darkening surface.

We both sat there quietly for a moment, each looking down into the water. After another minute, Laci broke the silence.

"Do you know why I picked here?" she asked.

"Ummm . . . it's quiet?" I asked.

"No," she said, shaking her head. In the dim glow of the running lights, I could see the tiniest of smiles playing across her lips.

"Why?" I asked.

"Because," she explained, breaking into a full smile. "This was as far away from Mexico as I could possibly get him."

~ ~ ~

IT WAS SO nice to have Laci back.

After that night, our friendship was firmly intact once again, and I honestly don't know when I had ever experienced such a total feeling of complete contentment.

Of course it would have been even better if things were to go beyond just friendship, but, as always, having Laci in my life in *any* capacity was definitely better than not having her in my life at all.

We continued to spend most of our time together every day and we fell into such comfortable habits with one another that we often didn't even need to communicate about what we were going to do . . . we just already knew.

If we were planning on grilling, we would do that at her old house if the weather was nice, but at my old house if it was bad, because I had covered the deck years ago. If we agreed to go to the hardware store the next day for supplies, I would drive to her house in the morning and join her for breakfast before we took my truck to pick up whatever it was that we needed. On the days that we forgot about home improvements and decided to hit the lake for a day of fishing, Laci would always bring the salad and bread, and I would provide the main dish and drinks. We prayed together before every meal and we held hands while we were doing it. Everything about our relationship was definitely platonic, but that didn't make it any less nice, and I enjoyed every minute of being with her.

I also didn't worry very much anymore that Laci was going to go back to Mexico. I was pretty sure that she felt the same way about me that I did about her, and she kept making comments like, "Next year we should cover the chimney in the spring so the birds don't get down in there again," and "I think in the fall I'm going to dig up all those bulbs and put them in the basement for the winter."

I'll admit that I did worry from time to time that she might want to go visit Dorito at some point, and I could easily see how she might get all caught up in the orphanage again and not want to come home, but for the most part, I did a pretty good job of convincing myself that she was here to stay.

The day before Laci's sixtieth birthday, I was working on the molding around the recessed lighting over the sink. I dropped a finishing nail and it fell, naturally, into the garbage disposal.

I knelt down on the counter and was feeling around for it when Laci came into the room.

"Please don't turn on any switches," I begged. She smiled slightly and watched as I fished around in the garbage disposal, finally came up with the nail. I rinsed it off, dried it on my shirt and then placed it once again between my teeth.

I climbed back up onto the counter and worked for a moment before I realized that Laci was still standing there, looking up at me.

"What are you doing?" I asked, except that, because I still had the nail in my mouth, and it wound up sounding more like "Vht err ou oing?"

She looked up at me for another moment and then she said, "I'm ready."

I almost swallowed the nail.

I spit it out and looked at her in disbelief.

"Right *now*?"

She nodded.

I got off the counter and stood before her, looking down carefully at her, making sure that she really was ready. I didn't say anything, but after a moment I moved closer and put my hands on her waist, pushing her gently back toward the counter and then lifting her up and setting her on it so that her beautiful face was almost level with mine.

I stepped even closer and brought my hand up to her face, running a finger over her cheek, down her throat, and finally up under her chin, drawing her face toward mine.

She closed her eyes.

It was a perfect kiss – slow and gentle and warm. I had been waiting forty years for that kiss.

291

When we parted, a soft moan escaped from her lips and then she whispered my name and I had to lean even closer and kiss her all over again.

"I love you so much," I whispered when we'd pulled apart from that kiss too, resting my forehead against hers.

"Still?" she whispered back, looking into my eyes, "or again?"

I thought about that for a long moment.

"I guess both," I said, answering as honestly as I possibly could.

"Oh," she said, and then she gave me a little smile. "I love you again."

~ ~ ~

WE SPENT LACI'S birthday the next day on the lake, beaching the boat on the deserted shore of a small island, and spreading a blanket out on the sand. When we weren't swimming or fishing or holding hands while walking along the shore, we were laying on that blanket, making up for lost time. I lay on my back with my hands under my head, soaking up the warmth of the sun and Laci as she nestled against my chest.

"It's supposed to rain tomorrow and the next day," Laci said. She propped herself up on one elbow and looked down at me. She gently traced a finger along my lips.

"I know," I said, putting my hand to the back of her neck, and pulling her down toward me for a kiss.

"So," she said with a smile when I finally let her go. "I wondered what we're going to do for *your* birthday."

"I can think of plenty of indoor activities."

She smirked at me.

"No, seriously," I said. "All you've gotta do is make me a dinner as awesome as what I'm going to make for you tonight, and I'll be fine."

"Wonderful," she said. "No pressure there."

"Oh, please. My favorites are *way* easier to make than yours are. All you've gotta do for me is throw a couple of baked potatoes in the oven and some ribeyes on the grill."

"And sour dough bread," she pointed out.

"Well, yeah," I admitted, "but still, it's a whole lot easier than broccoli salad and Cornish game hens are going to be."

"And grilled Portobello mushrooms?"

"Yes," I sighed.

"And focaccia?" she asked meekly.

I sighed again and looked at my watch. "We'd better get going," I said. "There's no way I'm going to have everything done before midnight."

293

"No, no, no," she said. "You can forget the bread. I'd rather stay here longer."

I smiled at her and pulled her down to me for another kiss.

The next day was indeed rainy, and we spent it indoors: staining . . . painting . . . kissing. It was also dreary on my birthday and I spent lunch and the early afternoon with my mom. At seventy-eight, mom was completely independent and totally on top of things. She insisted on making me a big lunch for my birthday, and then we continued with our yearly tradition of watching *Friday Night Lights*, (because somewhere along the way, she had become convinced that it was my favorite movie ever and I'd never had the heart to tell her otherwise).

Once the credits started rolling, I thanked her for everything and told her I needed to get going.

As I drove over to Laci's, I reflected on the fact that I was sixty. There'd been a time when sixty had seemed so old, but right now I felt as if I had my whole life ahead of me . . . a life with Laci.

When I arrived, I knocked and let myself in.

"Laci?" I called. She didn't answer, but I could see her in the kitchen with her back to me, looking out onto the deck. She didn't turn around when I came in.

"Hi," I said, walking up behind her and wrapping my arms around her. I kissed the top of her head, but she didn't make any effort to turn around and give me a proper kiss. That's when I noticed that there were no steaks grilling on the deck, no baked potatoes in the oven, no sourdough bread on the counter . . .

"What's wrong?"

She didn't say anything right away, but continued staring off into the distance before answering.

"I decided I was going to make strawberry parfaits," she finally began in a far off voice.

"Okay," I said, slowly.

"And I needed the blender." She turned and looked at me. "I remembered seeing one up in the cupboard above the fridge."

"Okay," I said again.

"So I pulled a chair over there," she said quietly, "so that I could reach."

"Did you fall?" I asked, alarmed.

"No," she said, shaking her head.

"Then what's wrong?" I asked again.

She quietly lifted her hand.

"I found this," she said quietly, showing me the diamond ring that she was holding between her fingers.

I stared at it in disbelief.

"Laci–" I began.

"Our champagne glasses are up there," she interrupted. "It was in one of them."

Our champagne glasses . . .

"I'd completely forgotten about all that stuff," I told her honestly.

"Why was it even there in the first place?" she demanded. "Why do you even *have* it?"

I looked at her quietly for a long moment.

"What do you want me to say?" I finally asked.

"I want you to tell me why you have this," she said again, shaking the ring for emphasis.

I was quiet again, and my silence confirmed what she already knew.

"When did you get it?" she asked quietly.

"Right before," I said. "Right before we broke up."

She pressed her lips together and shook her head in dismay.

"Why is this such a big deal?" I asked.

"Don't you understand?" she cried. "Don't you get it?"

"No," I said. "You're talking about something that happened forty years ago . . . I have absolutely no idea why you're so upset."

She walked past me and pulled a chair out from the kitchen table, sitting down. I did the same and looked at her expectantly. She held the ring between her fingers, staring at it, and I reached out and laid one of my hands on top of hers.

"Why don't you tell me what's going on?" I asked.

She sighed resignedly and I rubbed my thumb across the back of her hand.

"You were going to ask me to marry you?" she asked, glancing at me.

I nodded.

"But I broke up with you before you had a chance?"

I nodded again.

She looked at me for a long time.

"I would have said 'Yes'," she finally told me.

"I know," I said, squeezing her hand and nodding one more time.

"Even though that wasn't what God wanted for me."

Suddenly I knew where she was going with this.

"I loved you so much," she went on, glancing away before bringing her eyes back to me, "that I didn't really care what God wanted."

She paused.

"And I love you even more than that, now," she said, tears welling up in her eyes again.

"You don't think He wants us to be together?"

"I don't know," she cried. "That's the whole point. I haven't asked Him what He thinks, I haven't talked to Him about it or anything. I just . . . I've just been doing whatever I wanted. Just like last time."

"Then why don't you talk to Him about it?" I asked quietly. But I worried that she already had. I worried that maybe that's what she'd been doing all afternoon instead of cooking my birthday dinner. That maybe she'd already gotten an answer from Him and it wasn't something that I was going to want to hear.

"I've been trying," she said, "but I can't think straight when it comes to you. I've never been able to think straight when it comes to you."

I stared at her for a moment and then bowed my head toward the table, resting my forehead against our hands.

Please God, I said. *Don't let this happen again. Please don't take her from me . . .*

But then I stopped myself and I remembered how much He loved me and I remembered how He would never let anything happen to me unless it was what was best . . .

This is not what I want, God, I tried again. *You know that. But mostly I want what You want . . . I really do. Please show me what You want me to do . . . show us what You want us to do . . . and then please help us to do it . . .*

And almost instantly, He did.

I sat back up and looked at Laci.

"You should go to Mexico," I told her.

She looked at me in shock.

"Go visit Dorito and Maria," I went on. "Stay with them for a while. Figure out what He wants you to do."

She stared at me, incredulous.

"You . . . you want me to go to Mexico?" she finally asked, slowly.

I studied her carefully before answering.

"Is there any place else in the world," I asked, squeezing her hand, "where you've ever felt closer to God?"

She looked back at me for a moment and then she shook her head, and I nodded at her as if that answered everything.

"But Tanner," she finally said. "Aren't you afraid that if I go to Mexico, I won't ever come back?"

I squeezed her hand again, and I nodded again, too.

"Yeah," I said. "I'm scared to death."

Two days later, I drove Laci to the airport. We checked her bags and then – when we saw that the line through security wasn't going to be too long – we sat down for a few, final minutes together.

I wrapped my arms around her and she buried her head against my chest. I held on to her tighter than I ever had, trying to sear every second of it into my brain. I pulled back, looked into her eyes, and then I kissed her, trying to sear that into my brain, too.

"I'll be waiting every day to find out what God tells you," I whispered to her.

"It might be a while," she warned.

"I'll give you twenty years."

"*Twenty years?*"

"Yeah," I nodded. "It's always been a goal of mine to be settled down by the time I'm eighty."

She looked at me and smiled, but then her face turned serious.

"I love you so much," she said.

"I love you, too."

"But I'm not going to call you," she said, shaking her head at me.

"I know."

"I mean, that would defeat the purpose," she went on as if she were trying to convince herself. "I need time *away* from you."

"I know."

"So I can think."

"I know."

She looked at me and then kissed me again.

"But I love you so much," she said again.

"I love you, too."

"We have a very weird relationship," she said. "Don't we?"

"Yes," I nodded. "We always have."

I sat at the airport for a long time after she'd disappeared through security, wanting to be as close to her as I could for as long as possible.

After I'd been there for about half of an hour, I got a text from Laci. The second one I'd ever gotten from her in my life. She said:

No one has ever loved me the way you love me.

She didn't say: *No one has ever loved me* as much *as you've loved me*.
She didn't say: *No one has ever loved me* more *than you've loved me*.

She said: *No one has ever loved me* the way *you love me*.

And I texted her back.

I know.

~ ~ ~

AFTER LACI LEFT I moved back in to my old house and set about trying to ward off the loneliness and boredom that immediately threatened to settle in. I might have had God in my life now, but that didn't stop me from needing something to fill my days . . . something to keep my mind off the fact that once again I was all alone in Cavendish. Keeping busy had always worked well for me in the past, so now I once again set about actively finding things to do to occupy my time.

Of course there were always little, small odd-jobs at either Laci's house or mine, but for the most part, things were looking pretty good in both places. I wasn't interested in teaching at the high school again, but I filled out an application to start doing some substitute teaching there in the fall. That was almost three long months away, however, and the summer was still looming large in front of me. I talked with the guy who had replaced me as head football coach and started attending summer practices, skating a thin line between "helping" and "taking over". I went back to teaching conceal and carry classes once a month through the local community college. I refereed rec league games again for the town.

Two months passed, and – as promised – I barely heard from Laci after she left. Dorito and I touched base periodically, and I heard through him that she was doing well, apparently spending almost every day at the orphanage, and loving every minute of it. I kept praying, but as time went on, I became more and more accepting of the idea that Laci very well might not ever be coming back to me.

~ ~ ~

I MET ADDIE on the second Saturday in August. She showed up to one of my conceal and carry classes on a rainy morning, looking uneasy, out of place, and twirling her long, blonde hair.

I noticed her right away. She was pretty, but I don't think that's why I noticed her. I think I noticed her because she was obviously nervous, and – the longer the class went on – the more distressed she seemed to grow. After the first two hours, I let everybody go for a fifteen minute break, and when I looked up from my computer, she was standing there in front of me, still tugging at a strand of long, blonde hair.

"I'm sorry to bother you," she said meekly.

"You're not bothering me," I answered, looking at her carefully. She was younger than me, but not by too much. She had blue eyes that darted back and forth from my face to the floor.

"I think I've screwed up," she said. Then she added quietly, "Again."

"Screwed up how?" I asked.

She held up one of the fliers that was used to advertise the class.

"I want to carry a gun," she said. "I thought that's what this class was going to be about . . . how to carry a gun."

"It's *conceal* and carry," I explained. "It lets you get permission to carry a gun in your purse or whatever . . . where people can't see it."

"So you're not going to be teaching us *how* to use one?" she clarified.

"No," I said. "You need to already know how."

I had a feeling by the look on her face that she'd never even held a gun before.

"Do they offer classes about that?" she asked.

"Not here at the college," I said.

"Oh," she replied, appearing even more downcast.

"Don't you have anyone who can teach you?"

She shook her head.

"Why do you want to know how to use a gun?" I asked her.

She seemed reluctant to answer, but finally said, "My ex-husband."

"Self-defense?" I clarified.

She nodded.

"Look," I said, "for the most part, this class is pretty much about pistols . . . revolvers and stuff. If you really want a good, home self-defense weapon, what you need to get is a shotgun. You don't need a permit for that."

"Do they have classes in how to use those?"

"No," I said, laughing lightly as I shook my head.

"Oh."

Her eyes dropped to the floor once again.

"But I can teach you," I said quickly, "if you want."

"Really?" she asked, lifting her head and looking at me, her blue eyes hopeful for the first time since she'd entered the room.

"Sure."

"I don't want to put you out . . ." she hedged.

"No problem," I said. "It's not like I've got anything else to do."

I had been right: Addie had never even held a gun before in her life. I didn't take lightly the fact that her safety and the safety of others was riding on the instruction that I was going to give her. I met her at the gun range the following week with a small arsenal, and started with basic safety lessons before we moved on to actual shooting. She was scared the first time she had to pull the trigger, but once she finally did it, there was no stopping her.

"I want one of these," she said with a grin, looking up from the Glock she had just fired.

"Uh, yeah," I said. "I'm not sure if you need to be walking around with a semi-automatic weapon just yet. I think you need to wait until you're more comfortable with the idea of handling a gun."

"I am comfortable with it."

"Let me rephrase that," I said. "I think you need to wait until *I'm* more comfortable with the idea of you handling a gun."

"Am I doing that bad?" she asked, sounding dismayed.

"No," I assured her, shaking my head. "You're not doing bad at all. I just don't think you need to rush into buying anything right away."

She didn't seem too happy with my response.

"Are you in some kind of hurry?" I asked.

"He gets out of jail in two and a half weeks," she said quietly.

I studied her for a moment and then nodded.

"Okay," I said. "We can have you ready by then."

We met at the range the next Saturday, too, and when she proved to me that she'd remembered everything I'd taught her the week before, we went gun shopping.

She bought a shotgun like I'd recommended, but she also decided that she really wanted something she could carry with her at all times, too. She was already signed up for my next conceal and carry class and I had no doubt that she was going to pass, so I helped her pick out a pistol as well. Addie still liked my Glock a lot (because who doesn't like a Glock?), but had trouble chambering the first round sometimes, so she wound up getting a .357 instead.

Naturally she wanted to try out her new purchases, so we met at the range the following afternoon. After we'd been there for a few hours, she followed me home so that I could show her how to clean both of them.

I liked spending time with Addie. She was fun to be around and had a good sense of humor. She told me all about her ex-husband and why she was worried about him getting out of jail. I told her that she should call me if she ever needed me, and then I made her promise me that she would.

Once we were finished with our gun-cleaning lesson, we walked out to her car. I carried her new shotgun for her and laid it in the back seat, while she leaned in through the driver's side and put the revolver on the passenger seat up front. She turned and looked at me as I closed the back door.

"Ear plugs," she reminded me. "You said you had some extra ones that I could have."

"Right," I nodded, and I went back into the house.

It took me a few minutes to find them, and by the time I returned, Addie had gotten into her car. She had also apparently gotten her new toy out and had been playing with it while I'd been gone.

I opened up her door to hand her the ear plugs, but when I did, she looked at me desperately.

"Help," she said.

I looked closely and saw that her long, blonde hair was tangled around the cylinder.

"What in the *world* have you done?" I exclaimed.

"Help," she said again.

302

I couldn't get a good look at the situation from where I was, so I walked around to the other side and climbed in.

"Were you dry firing it?" I scolded.

"No," she insisted. "I just swung the chamber out and then popped it back in again."

"Uh-huh," I said, trying to swing the chamber out again, but with no luck. It was firmly tangled up in her hair.

"I did!" she cried.

"At least it's not loaded," I sighed, shaking my head.

"Rule number one," she replied sheepishly. "Ow!"

"Well, hold still!" I chided. I reached into my pocket and pulled out my knife.

"What are you doing?" Addie shrieked when she saw what I had.

"We're gonna have to cut it out," I said.

"NO!"

"It's just a few little strands," I promised. "You'll never be able to tell."

She wasn't too happy about that, but finally agreed, and held still while I sliced her free.

"Here," I said, handing her gun to her when I was finished. "I think we'd better put in a few extra hours next week."

"I think I just need to wear a ponytail holder," she argued.

I rolled my eyes at her and smiled before I climbed out of her car and headed back into the house.

I took a couple of trips upstairs to put my guns away in the safe and then I returned one final time to get my gun cleaning kit off the kitchen table. I had just gotten to the bottom of the stairs when the doorbell rang, and I turned to answer it, figuring that it was Addie and that she needed something else.

It wasn't.

"*Laci?*" I cried when I opened the door.

I looked at her in disbelief.

She looked back at me coolly, didn't answer, and we stood there, staring at each other for a minute. I wanted to hug her, but something was obviously wrong, so I held back.

"What are you doing here?" I finally asked.

"I came back to get some things."

"You . . . you're not staying?"

"No," she answered, a definite edge to her voice. "I'm not staying. I'm going back to Mexico."

I looked at her again.

"What's wrong?" I asked quietly.

"Nothing's wrong," she said, completely unconvincingly.

I looked at her for another minute and then asked, "Do you want to come in?"

I held the door open for her. She hesitated at first, but finally stepped inside.

I closed the door and turned to her. She crossed her arms in front of her body and an uneasy silence hung in the air.

"What's wrong?" I asked again.

"Nothing's *wrong!*" she insisted.

"Don't tell me nothing's wrong," I said. "I know you well enough to know when something's wrong, and something's wrong."

She looked at me angrily, arms still crossed in front of her body. Then, suddenly, she unleashed on me.

"I *saw* you!" she cried.

"Saw me what?"

"Saw you *kissing* her!"

"Kissing who?"

"I don't know *who!*" she yelled, gesturing toward the front door. "Whoever that was out in your driveway!"

"Huh?" But then I suddenly remembered. "You mean *Addie?*"

"*I don't know her NAME!*" Laci spat.

I actually laughed out loud.

"I wasn't kissing her," I said, still laughing.

Laci glared at me, obviously not amused.

"She got her hair all tangled up in her gun," I explained quickly, "and I was cutting it out for her."

"What?"

"I'm teaching her how to shoot," I explained, pointing to the dining room table where my gun cleaning kit was still laying. "She wants to get her conceal and carry permit."

Laci looked at the table and then back at me carefully.

"Even you couldn't make something like that up," she said slowly. Then she asked, "You weren't kissing her?"

I stepped closer.

"Of course I wasn't kissing her," I said softly. "Why would I kiss anybody besides you?"

I tipped my head and looked into her eyes.

"Don't you know me better than that?" I asked, quietly. "Don't you know that I've been waiting *every day* for you to come back here to me?"

She lowered her eyes guiltily to the floor.

I reached over and cupped her chin in my hand, lifting it until her eyes looked into mine.

"I'm sorry," she said, meeting my gaze.

"It's okay," I smiled. "I guess it's not really any worse than when I thought you were dating Dr. Darion."

She managed a small smile back and then we looked at each other for another moment.

"You're so beautiful," I said, stroking her cheek with my thumb. "I missed you so much."

"I missed you, too."

I looked at her a little bit longer, hardly able to believe that she was standing in front of me.

"I love you," I whispered.

"I love you, too," she whispered back, and I leaned down until our lips met. We kissed tenderly at first, but then more fervently, and I brought my other hand up to her face, too, pulling her even closer.

After I finally pulled my lips away from hers, I kept my hands on either side of her face, looking at her in amazement.

"I can't believe you're here," I said.

She smiled at me, bigger this time, and I felt myself break out into a huge grin. I wrapped my arms around her and buried my face in her hair and she hugged me back.

"And you're not really going back to Mexico, are you?" I whispered into her ear.

I leaned back and tugged at a strand of her hair, playfully.

She stopped smiling and looked at me seriously.

"Actually, I am," she said.

I felt the smile drop off my face.

"I *belong* there, Tanner," she explained quietly when she saw my reaction. "It's where I'm supposed to be."

I stared at her, trying not to look dismayed. I managed to give her a nod.

Wasn't this what I'd been praying for? For God's will? For His direction? Hadn't I been praying for Laci to know what God wanted her to do and for Him to give both of us the strength to do it? Whatever it might be?

"Look," she said, shaking her head. "None of this is going the way I planned. Why don't we start over?"

"Start over?"

"Yeah," she nodded. "I have a present for you out in the car anyway. I'll go out and get it and come back and ring the doorbell and we'll just pretend none of this ever happened, okay?"

"You weren't going to give me my present when you thought I was kissing Addie?"

"No," she said, raising an eyebrow at me. "As a matter of fact, I wasn't."

"Okay," I agreed, holding the door open for her and motioning outdoors. "Go get it. We'll start over."

She smiled back and went out the door. I closed it behind her and prayed hard while she was gone for God to help me do what He wanted me to do.

Less than a minute later, the doorbell rang.

"Who is it?" I called.

She knocked loudly on the door and I knew she was rolling her eyes at me on the other side. I opened it.

"Hi!" she said brightly, a brown paper bag in her hand.

"Laci!" I exclaimed in mock astonishment. "What a surprise!"

She smiled.

"Do I get another kiss?" I asked hopefully. She nodded and we kissed again. When we separated, I asked, "And are you still going back to Mexico?"

She nodded for a second time.

"This conversation isn't going any better than the last one," I pointed out.

"Why don't you invite me in?" she suggested.

I stepped aside. "Would you like to come in?"

"I'd love to!" she replied. She walked over to the couch and sat down, patting the cushion next to her. "Come sit here."

I sat down next to her and she looked at me, her eyes still bright. Then she reached out and took my hand in one of hers, the other still holding the brown paper bag.

306

"I know it wasn't easy for you to send me to Mexico," she began earnestly, "but going down there was the best thing I ever could have done."

I nodded at her.

"It's where I belong," she said softly. "It's where I've *always* belonged."

I nodded again.

"And all my life," she went on, squeezing my hand, "you've always wanted what was best for me."

I nodded a third time and squeezed her hand back.

"Even if it wasn't what you wanted," she said softly, "and even when it wasn't what I wanted . . ."

I swallowed hard and closed my eyes. When I opened them, she was looking at me intently.

"You've always wanted what was best for me," she said softly.

She let go of the bag and reached her other hand out to touch my face. I closed my eyes once again at her touch.

"What's even more important," she said when I finally opened them again, "is that you want what God wants. You've always been willing to sacrifice for *me*, but now you're willing to sacrifice for God, too. You don't have any idea what that means to me . . . how important it is that both of us are putting God first."

I nodded again, one final time. She took a short breath and continued.

"As soon as I got down there," she said, "as soon as I stepped off of the plane . . . I knew that it was where God wanted me to be. It's where He's *always* wanted me to be. You know?"

"Yeah," I said. "I know."

"When I'm down there," she went on, "I feel a peace inside of me that I don't feel anywhere else in the world."

I gave her a small smile.

"But that doesn't mean that I don't love you," she said.

"I know."

"You're my best friend," she said, "and nothing's ever going to change that."

"I know," I said again, managing another smile.

"I wanted to make sure you know that, and I wanted to make sure you know how much I appreciate everything you've done. And I want to make sure," she paused, "that you know how much I love you."

"I do know," I said.

"Well, I wanted to make sure," she said again. "So I got you this."

Her hand had still been on my face, but now she took it off so that she could reach for the paper bag again and hand it to me.

"What is it?" I asked, looking down as I took it from her.

"Open it."

Reluctantly I let go of her hand so that I could open the bag. I pulled out a cold, plastic tub of cookie dough and stared at it.

After a moment I finally dared to look at her again.

She was smiling at me.

"I thought maybe we could share it," she said. "You know? With some milk?"

I didn't say anything. I just kept looking at her with my mouth hanging slightly open.

She watched me, expectantly.

"You want milk?" I finally managed to ask.

She nodded.

I didn't say anything again.

"So why don't you go get us some?" she finally suggested, nodding toward the kitchen.

I stared at her, trying to read her face.

"You want milk?" I clarified.

She nodded.

"I'm very confused," I finally said. "Are we really talking about milk?"

"Well, *I'm* not . . ."

"But . . . but you said you're going back to Mexico . . ."

"I am," she agreed.

It took a moment for that to register.

"You want me to move down there with you?" I asked, my mouth hanging open further now.

For the first time, she looked worried.

"Would you?" she asked.

I glanced around my living room. "And give up all this?"

Her face broke out into a smile and I reached for her, grabbing her up in my arms and holding her close against me.

"I love you," I breathed, my eyes closed and my face buried in her hair. "I love you so much."

"I love you, too," she whispered back, her arms wrapped tightly around me.

308

We sat there like that, holding each other for a long moment.

"Being in Mexico made me so happy," she finally said, sitting back and looking into my eyes, "but the whole time I was there . . ."

"What?" I asked when she hesitated.

"I kept looking for you," she explained, taking my hand. "I kept waiting for you to show up, you know? Like to surprise me?"

"I was supposed to surprise you?"

"Well," she shrugged, "I kept hoping."

"I . . . I had no idea I was supposed to surprise you," I said. "I thought I was supposed to be giving you time."

"Yeah," she agreed. "I finally figured out that that's what you were doing and that I was going to have to come up here to get you."

I smiled at her.

"I'm really glad you did."

"Me too," she nodded. "But Tanner?"

"What?"

"I still really want some milk."

"Oh, yeah," I said sheepishly. "About that . . ."

"What?" she asked in dismay.

"Well, you see," I began, "I had this really big yard sale while you were gone and—"

"That's not even funny," she interrupted.

I grinned and pulled her toward me for another long hug and an even longer kiss. Then I buried my face in her hair again and held her tight once more, reveling in the fact that she was actually there in my arms.

"I'm so glad you're here," I finally whispered after a moment, still holding her tight.

"Me too," she whispered back, "but Tanner?"

"What?" I asked.

She pulled back far enough so that I could see her face again, and then through gritted teeth she said, "*Go get my ring!*"

After I proposed (yes . . . kneeling before her), we sat together again on the couch. Laci leaned back against me, holding her hand out in front of us, as we both admired her diamond.

"It's beautiful," she told me, not for the first time.

"I've always had good taste," I said, kissing the side of her head.

She laughed lightly and nestled her head back against my chest.

"When do you want to get married?" she asked.

"Right now."

She laughed again.

"I'm serious," I murmured into her ear. "I cannot *wait* to be married to you."

I reached out for her hand and rubbed the back of it with my thumb. We sat quietly for a long moment, until she broke the silence.

"What do you think David would say?" she asked, sitting forward and turning her head to look at me.

"About us getting married?"

She nodded.

"You mean after his initial meltdown?" I asked.

She smiled at me.

"I don't know," I said, giving her a little shrug. "I think eventually he'd be okay with it."

She thought about it seriously for moment.

"You're right," she finally agreed. "After he'd had a chance to think about it, he would have come around."

I gave her a smile and she reached her hand up, laying it against the side of my face.

"He loved you," she said quietly, "and he loved me."

She ran her thumb lightly across my cheek, looking at me intently before she went on.

"And I don't think he would have wanted either one of us," she finished softly, "to ever be alone."

~THE END~
(sort of)

Thank you SO much for reading the *Chop, Chop* series. I hope you have enjoyed following the faith journeys of David, Jordan and Tanner as much as I have enjoyed sharing them with you.

Although this eighth book is officially the last in the series, there are at least four companion novels planned and I hope you will look for them in the future. (For those of you who don't know, companion novels contain characters from other novels, but – unlike sequels – stand completely alone and are not dependent upon other books.)

The next novel to be released will be told by David and Laci's son, Marco, and is entitled *What I Want* (the next few pages of which are included just ahead!) Paul's story will be revealed in *Taken*, and I am also tentatively planning at least two additional novels: one told from Mike's point of view about his life with Danica, and one about the son that Charlotte put up for adoption when she was in high school. These last two novels are not yet titled.

If you have not already left a review for *Chop, Chop*, would you please consider taking a moment to do so now by <u>clicking here</u>? I appreciate reviews left for all of the novels, but if you only have the time to leave one, please make it for *Chop, Chop* as that is the best way to let others know about the series.

If you are interested in reading the lyrics to the original song: "Kneeling Before You," please be sure to visit and "like" <u>http://www.facebook.com/ReadChopChop</u>. If the song is not yet available in the "Notes" section of the *Chop, Chop* page, keep checking back . . . it should be soon. I would also love to hear from you while you're there.

Many blessings to each of you. Thanks again for letting me share these books with you.

And now, please enjoy a sneak peak at the first companion novel to the series: *What I Want*. I hope you will choose to read the entire novel when it is released.

L.N. Cronk

What I Want
A Companion Novel to the Chop, Chop Series
By L.N. Cronk

~ ~ ~

Feisímo.

My entire life, people have called me this.

Most often, my sister, Grace, hissing it into my ear whenever she could get away with it. Other times it was my classmates, counting on their words to be drowned out by the noise of other children on the playground during recess. Sometimes it would be a little kid in a restaurant, blurting out the truth before a mortified parent shushed them into silence. Occasionally it might be a stranger on the street, not actually saying anything, but glancing away in embarrassment for me, and telling me the same thing without using any words.

Throughout the years, many different people have told me in many different ways, and despite my parents' constant attempts to convince me otherwise, I know exactly what I am . . . what I've always been.

I have always known.

Feisímo . . .

Ugly as sin.

~ ~ ~

FIRST OF ALL, let me make it perfectly clear that it wasn't just because she's blind that Bizzy and I got together.

I'll admit that that helped . . . I never would have gotten up the nerve to even talk to Bizzy on my own if she'd been able to see what I looked like right off.

I'd seen a movie one time with a blind person feeling somebody's face so they could "see" what that person looked like with their sense of touch, so the first time I laid eyes on Bizzy, I immediately reached my hand to my upper lip and felt my scars, trying to determine what they would feel like to her if I ever let her touch my face.

I decided that it didn't feel as bad as it looked.

I was born with a cleft palate. Not just a hare lip or something, mind you, but a *severe* cleft palate. Go right now to your nearest search engine and type in "complete bilateral cleft." Pick out the worst picture you see. That was me.

I'm nothing like that anymore of course. I've had reconstructive surgeries and if you saw me you might not notice the scar and the asymmetry of my nose and lip right off . . .

What you'd notice right off is my hands.

Now type into your search engine "symbrachydactyly." Find a picture of a pair of hands that look pretty normal, but with no fingers – just little nubs.

There isn't any reconstructive surgery for that.

By the way, I absolutely *hate* that word.

Nubs.

I wouldn't use it if I didn't have to, but sometimes I don't have any choice.

314

Anyway, I do actually have one finger . . . a thumb really. It's not a great thumb, but it's all I've got.

If it sounds like I feel really sorry for myself, I want you to know that I don't. Not at all.

I don't wish anything was any different about any part of my life. Everything that has ever happened to me has made me who I am today, and I wouldn't have it any other way. And by the way, I really like my thumb. It comes in very handy.

So, anyhow, after I felt my scars, I thought about my hands. I thought about how Bizzy was bound to find out about them eventually, but that since she was blind she might actually get to know me a little bit *first* – before she found out.

That intrigued me.

And so, as soon as I saw Bizzy that very first day and thought about all this, I decided that I was going to go for it.

Despite the way I look, I had never really doubted that there was someone out there for me. I had always known that the person I was going to end up with one day would probably have something wrong with them, but it had never occurred to me that the "something" that was wrong with them might be that they were blind.

Deformed is what I had always imagined actually . . . another person, like myself, who would be better suited for the Island of Misfit Toys.

But Bizzy wasn't deformed at all. She was pretty. Her hair was black and shiny and her skin smooth and clear and her smile was the prettiest one that I'd ever seen. The only thing wrong with her was that her pupils were milky white instead of black . . . and someone like me had no right to complain about something like that.

The day I first met Bizzy, Grace and I had walked from school to the orphanage. Our mom worked there and it was where we had practically grown up, spending hours of our free time, helping out with things, or playing with the orphans.

My least favorite job at the orphanage was doing the dishes. The plates and cups and silverware just had to be rinsed off and run through this automated thing, but the pots and pans had to be washed in a sink with disgusting bits of food floating around in it.

Volunteering to take Grace's place at the sink probably wasn't the smartest move I'd ever made since it immediately made her suspicious, but I did it anyway because I needed a good excuse not to have to shake hands with Bizzy if she wanted to. Grace went off with a perplexed look on her face while I started scrubbing on a bread pan.

"Hi," I told Bizzy as I worked. "My name's Marco."

"Hi, Marco," she smiled. "I'm Isabelita, but everybody calls me Bizzy."

"They didn't waste any time putting you to work," I noted as I set the pan into the rinse sink and she began to spray it off.

"No," she agreed, as she rinsed. "I guess it's better just to jump right in to everything."

"Where are you from?" I asked.

"*Villa de Paz*."

Villa de Paz was another orphanage on the other side of Mexico City, and sometimes, when their funding was running low, they would send kids to our orphanage.

"How long have you lived here?" she asked, setting the pan on the drain board.

"I don't," I said. "My mom works here."

"Oh . . . are you Grace's brother?"

"Um-hmm," I admitted, hoping I didn't sound too sour about it.

"Yeah," Bizzy said. "I just met her. She seems really nice."

I rolled my eyes. Yeah. I'm sure she *seemed* really nice . . .

We chatted through the rest of the pots and pans and I told her all about how I was the youngest of six children and how all of us had been adopted – three of us from this very orphanage. She told me that her parents had given her up as soon as they'd discovered that she was blind, and that she'd lived in one orphanage or another for her entire life.

In my opinion, it's hard to turn out normal when you're not only handicapped, but you've been abandoned, too. I was turning out pretty good (if I do say so myself), but that was only because my parents were exceptional people. If it weren't for them, I can't even imagine where I'd be.

I think that was one of the things that always amazed me the most about Bizzy, was how normal she was, despite her circumstances. She was brilliant and friendly and happy and full of life and self-confidence, and I was always really glad that I'd decided to do the dishes that day.

It was possible that Grace saw the same things in Bizzy that I did and simply wanted her for a friend, but it's also entirely possible that Grace just realized that I liked Bizzy and she just couldn't stand the thought of me having something she didn't have for even one teeny, tiny second. Whatever the reason, Grace's friendship with Bizzy grew as fast as mine did, and if Grace hadn't had gymnastics two days a week, I never would have had any time alone with Bizzy at all.

It was on one of my "alone" days with Bizzy that I decided I'd better tell her what I looked like, because on TV shows and stuff, people always keep secrets over some little thing and then it winds up turning into a big, huge deal, full of problems that could have been avoided if only someone had been honest right from the get-go. Bizzy and I had been spending time together every day for two weeks, and her first impressions of me were long gone. Either she liked me or she didn't, and I was kind of thinking that maybe she did. No matter what though, I knew her well enough already to know that she wasn't the kind of person who was going to be put off by what was wrong with me, but that she might be really hurt if she found out that I'd been being dishonest with her. Two weeks was pretty much the borderline between, "Oh, it just hasn't come up yet," and "Oh, I've been pretty much been keeping a secret from you."

And so, on gymnastics day, I asked Bizzy if she wanted to go out front and sit on the steps.

"The sun feels good," Bizzy said, turning her face toward it once we got outside.

"Yeah," I agreed.

We sat quietly for a moment until I got up the nerve to break the silence.

"I want to tell you something," I finally said.

"What's that?" she asked, turning her face from the sun toward me instead.

"I . . . I want you to know something about me," I said.

"Okay."

"There . . . there were some things wrong with me when I was born," I began. "I don't look like everyone else."

"You mean your hands?" she asked.

"How did you know that?" I asked, dumbfounded.

"Grace told me," she said, shrugging. "She told me about your cleft palate, too."

"She did," I said flatly.

"Yes," Bizzy nodded.

I *hated* Grace.

"Why didn't you tell me?" I asked.

"I didn't want to make you self-conscious about it or anything," she explained, shrugging again. "I figured you'd tell me when you wanted to."

"Oh."

And that was when I suddenly realized that Bizzy had been purposely avoiding my hands for two weeks whenever I'd offered her my arm to guide her someplace. Until then, I'd just thought that I'd gotten really lucky.

"Are you mad at me because I knew and didn't say anything?" she asked.

"No," I said. "Are you mad at me because I didn't tell you before now?"

"No," she said with a smile.

"Do you want to feel my face?" I asked her.

"What?"

"You know," I said. "So you can see what I look like?"

"That's not going to help me know what you look like," she laughed.

"It's not?"

"No," she said. "Where'd you get that from? Some movie?"

I bit my lip.

"Blind people don't go around feeling other people's faces," she explained with a laugh. "Just tell me what you look like."

"Apparently Grace already told you."

318

"Not really," Bizzy said. "I want you to tell me."

"Well," I said. "I've got really bad scars where they closed up the gap between my nose and my mouth and my hands don't really have any finger, just these little . . ."

I sighed inwardly.

"These little *nubs* that are kind of webbed together."

I paused and waited for her reaction.

"No," she said, giving me a big smile, "I mean tell me what you look like. What color is your hair and everything?"

"Oh," I said. "Well, my hair is dark and wavy and I keep trying to grow it longer and my dad keeps making me get it cut. I have really dark brown eyes and I'm fairly tall for my age. I'm skinny . . . too skinny. My mom says I should quit complaining about that."

She smiled at me.

"What about your skin?" she asked.

"Well," I said. "I'm Latino like you. My skin's a lot like yours."

"I don't really know what I look like," she reminded me.

"Oh," I said. "Right."

"Will you tell me?"

"What?"

"Tell me what I look like."

"Oh," I said again. "Well, umm, you're Latino . . ."

She laughed.

"And your skin is fairly light. It's like butterscotch and it looks really smooth and soft.

She smiled at me.

"And you have the prettiest smile I've ever seen," I told her.

"What about my eyes?" she asked.

"They're dark brown," I said. "Like mine."

"Do they look like everyone else's?" she asked.

I hesitated for a moment. In thirteen years, had no one ever told her what her eyes looked like?

"No," I said. "Most people have black pupils. Yours are white."

She seemed to be taking that in as she sat quietly for a moment.

"You're very pretty," I told her. She smiled again, but it didn't seem like her heart was in it that time.

"Do you want to go in and play rummy?" she asked.

Bizzy had a braille card deck and killer instincts. She was a lot of fun to play cards with.

"Sure," I agreed. "But I'm gonna beat you this time."

The next day, when Grace and I arrived at the orphanage after school, Bizzy was wearing sunglasses.

"Cool shades," Grace told her, but as soon as I had the chance, I pulled Bizzy aside and asked her why she had them on.

"I wear them sometimes," she said, shrugging.

"No, you don't," I argued. "You've been here for over two weeks and you haven't worn them once. The only reason you have them on is because of what I said yesterday."

"I just want to look pretty," she said quietly.

"You *do* look pretty," I said. "I already told you that you're pretty."

"Well, then," she said, shrugging again slightly, "I want to look even prettier."

"These don't make you look prettier," I told her, reaching for her face and gently taking them off.

She didn't answer.

"When you smile," I said, "it lights up your whole face. All these do is cover half of that up."

She still didn't say anything.

"Don't wear these," I said. "If you want to be prettier, just smile even more."

"Okay," she said, and then she did.

She didn't wear her sunglasses anymore after that, but I always felt really guilty that she had ever put them on in the first place. The very last thing that I had ever wanted to do, was to make Bizzy feel for even one tiny second, the way I had been feeling for my entire life.

A few weeks later, Mom let me and Grace have Bizzy come over for dinner one evening. Of course Grace monopolized her like

320

always, but during the meal, Dad asked us about our homework and found out that Grace still had algebra to do. After that, I got Bizzy all to myself for a bit, while Grace and Dad fought about math.

I took her around the house, describing everything to her that she couldn't see, and finally we ended up in my bedroom.

"What's that noise?" she asked.

"What noise?"

"It sounds like water," she said. "And a motor."

"Oh," I said, nodding even though she couldn't see me. "That's my fish tank."

"You have fish?"

"Yeah," I said. "Guppies."

"Guppies," she repeated.

"Yeah," I said again. "They're live breeders. One of them had a bunch of babies yesterday."

"Really?" Her entire face lit up.

"Uh-huh."

"What do they look like?" she asked.

"They're really little," I answered. "They're basically see-through bodies with eyes."

"Oh," she said, wistfully. "I wish I could see them."

"You can hold one if you want," I offered.

"Really?"

"Yeah."

"It won't hurt it?"

"I don't think so," I answered. Actually I was worried that this might not be such a great idea. I didn't want anything to happen to any of my guppies, but I decided that I wanted to see Bizzy smile even more.

"Okay," she said, excitement growing in her voice.

I got out my net and ran it through the water, catching several babies. I pulled it out of the water and held it over the tank, turning it inside out and carefully getting one of the babies onto my hand. I reached for one of Bizzy's hands and gently put the baby guppy onto the end of her finger.

"Can you feel it?" I asked.

"That's a *fish*?" she asked in awe.

"Yeah."

"I can't believe how small it is!"

"I told you they were little."

Carefully, Bizzy brought her thumb to her finger so that the guppy was lightly caught between them. She held it for a moment, her face glowing.

"I want to put him back now," she said after a minute. "I don't want to hurt him."

"Okay," I agreed, and I guided her hand to the tank, dipping her finger into the water.

"Is he okay?" she asked, worriedly.

I looked at him. He floated on his side for a moment and then righted himself. He sat motionless for another second, but then darted off toward the heater.

"He's fine," I told her, and she broke into a big grin.

I looked at her smile. I loved that smile.

I still had hold of Bizzy's hand. I kept holding it and continued looking at her, and slowly her smile started to fade. Not as if she wasn't happy anymore, but as if she knew that I was looking at her, and as if she knew exactly why.

I didn't say anything, but I moved closer, knowing she could tell. I watched her face to see her reaction.

And her reaction was, that she closed her eyes.

I hesitated, but only for a second longer. I leaned closer still and kissed her lightly, hoping desperately that my lip wasn't so messed up that she could tell and hoping desperately that I was doing it right and . . .

What I *should* have been hoping was that Grace wouldn't pick that moment to come traipsing down the hall.

I heard her gasp and Bizzy and I quickly pulled apart from each other. I turned toward the door, horrified.

Grace gaped at me with her mouth open for a second, but then she quickly pulled herself together, and a nasty little grin spread across her face. She turned on her heel and started back down the hall. Immediately, I took off after her.

"Don't," I said after I'd caught up with her and grabbed her by the arm.

"Don't what?" she asked innocently.

"Don't screw this up for me," I pleaded quietly. "Please don't."

"You don't need me to screw it up for you," she said, the grin returning to her face. "I'm sure you'll take care of that all by yourself." And then she yanked herself free from my grasp and continued down the hall.

I watched after her as she disappeared around the corner.

Getting inside my head was one of Grace's specialties, but I wasn't going to let her do that to me this time . . . I was *not* going to screw this up.

I headed back to my room.

"I'm sorry," I said as soon as I was in front of Bizzy again.

"For what?"

"Umm," I hesitated. "For anything you might possibly be upset about right now?"

She laughed. "I'm not upset about anything."

"You're not?"

"No," she said, shaking her head and smiling at me again.

"Good," I said, and I hoped that she could hear in my voice, that I was smiling too.

Grace and I both rode along when my mom took Bizzy back to the orphanage that evening, and Bizzy told Mom that I'd let her hold a baby guppy. She didn't mention anything about kissing.

"I would love to have a pet," Bizzy said longingly.

"Have you ever thought about getting a Seeing Eye dog?" my mother asked her.

"Yes," she said, "but there's a lot to it."

"Like what?" Grace asked.

"Paperwork and travel and training . . . it's . . . it's just not real easy."

She didn't say it, but I knew that what she meant was that it wasn't real easy when you're an orphan. Not real easy when you don't have a mom and a dad to help you.

It made me sad to think that Bizzy was never going to have what I had. No family to take her on vacations. No one to tell her stories about all the cute and funny things she'd done when she was a little kid. No house to live in so that she could own a pet. I found myself wishing that there was a way I could help Bizzy to have everything that she was missing. Everything that I already had.

When we arrived at the orphanage, we walked Bizzy in to the building and Mom went to talk to the director while Grace and Bizzy and I hung around in the commons area. Grace and Bizzy were carrying most of the conversation, but whenever Grace wasn't talking, she was pursing her lips at me, closing her eyes, and making exaggerated, but silent kissing motions into the air.

Once Mom was finally ready to go, we all said goodbye to Bizzy and headed out to the car. We had barely made it out the door though, when Mom suddenly remembered that she had one more thing to take care of. She turned and went back into the building, promising to be right back out. Grace and I continued on to the car.

I got there before she did and took the front seat, and as soon as Grace climbed into the back, I turned around and started pounding her as hard as I could. She pounded right back until she saw Mom coming, and then both of us sat down and I faced forward, crossing my arms.

Neither of us said a word.

"What's going on?" Mom finally asked after we'd ridden along for a while in silence. It wasn't unusual for Grace and me to not talk to each other, but usually we talked to her.

"Nothing," I said.

But at that same exact moment, Grace blurted out, "Marco and Bizzy were *kissing*!"

"Shut-up!" I yelled, undoing my seatbelt. I turned around and climbed halfway over the seat, starting to pound on her again.

Mom caught me and forced me back down, ordering me to do my seatbelt back up while Grace continued on.

"They were in his bedroom," she said. "And they were all like 'oohhh . . . mmhhhmm.'" She started kissing at the air like she'd done earlier, but this time not so silently.

"Shut-UP!" I yelled at her again.

"Grace," my mom said wearily. "I want you to leave your brother alone."

Having six kids, Mom knew exactly how to handle kissing teenagers, but none of our other siblings had ever fought like Grace and I did. Mom still didn't have a clue how to deal with the two of us.

324

I crossed my arms in front of me again while Grace ignored her, calling out in a sing-song voice, "Mar-co's got a *girl*-friend."

"Grace," Mom said, now using her warning voice. "Apologize to your brother."

"Sorry," Grace said. I didn't look back at her, but I could tell from the way she said it that she had a big grin on her face.

"Marco," Mom said. "Tell your sister you forgive her."

"Whatever," I muttered.

Mom sighed again and didn't push it.

I kept my eyes straight ahead, keeping my arms crossed and trying to act upset. In reality, however, I could barely suppress the happiness that was welling up inside of me.

I thought about what Grace had just said.

I wondered about it, and the more I thought about it, the happier I felt.

Then I crossed my arms even tighter, trying to hold everything inside that I was thinking about so that I could savor it forever.

Had Grace actually meant what she'd just said? And, if so, was it true?

Did I really have a girlfriend?

Made in the USA
Coppell, TX
26 February 2023

13443747R00194